THE WORKHOUSE GIRL

THE
WORKHOUSE
GIRL

Jessica Stirling

Hodder & Stoughton

First published in Great Britain in 1996
by Hodder and Stoughton
A division of Hodder Headline PLC

10 9 8 7 6 5 4 3 2 1

British Library Cataloguing in Publication Data

Stirling, Jessica, 1935–
The Workhouse Girl
1. English fiction - 20th century - Scottish authors
2. Scottish fiction - 20th century
I. Title
823.9'14 [F]

ISBN 0 340 60784 X

Typeset by Avon Dataset Ltd, Bidford-on-Avon, Warks

Printed and bound in England by
Clays Ltd., St. Ives PLC

Hodder and Stoughton
A division of Hodder Headline PLC
338 Euston Road
London NW1 3BH

The actions of human beings are not invariably governed by the laws of pure reason. We are by no means always in the habit of bestowing our love on the objects which are most deserving of it.

Wilkie Collins: *The Law and the Lady*

CONTENTS

BOOK ONE

The Courtship

One

From the moment Cassie clapped eyes on Robert
Montague she sensed that there was something different
about him. It was not just that he had power and authority,
though that was certainly true, or that he had the most
commanding voice she had ever heard. What she found
unsettling was that at certain moments during the course
of the sermon his eyes would flick towards and hold upon
her, not long enough to seem to be a stare, certainly not
long enough to be considered ill-mannered, but with just
that degree of concentration which an inexperienced girl
of seventeen might construe as more than casual interest.

At first Cassie responded as any well-brought-up young
lady would under the circumstances. She lowered her
head, picked at the stitching of her glove and showed the
preacher the brim of her best bonnet as if his exposition
on the nature of original sin and the corruption of the
flesh had touched a nerve in her and brought a flush of
remorse to her pale cheeks – which, of course, was quite
ridiculous. Cassie Armitage had no more notion of what
the Reverend Montague meant by original sin than had the
pigeons in the belfry or the gulls that shrieked on the
church roof.

Every minister who occupied the pulpit of Ravenshill

church suffered competition from the gulls. Robert Montague was no exception. Unlike some preachers, however, he did not *tut* and raise his eyes impatiently to heaven or introduce into his sermon witty references to 'our feathered friends'. Reverend Montague seemed willing to shout the creatures down or even, so Cassie thought, to let their demonic cries augment his remarks as if he and the herring-gulls were equally intransigent.

It was an airy day in June in the year of 1858. Sunlight outlined the pulpit, lightened the oppressive gloom of the kirk and released in Cassie a strange feeling of expectation, as if air and sunlight were her natural habitat and flirtation not anathema to a well-bred young lady raised south of the River Clyde. For that reason she neglected to lower her eyes when next Mr Montague glanced in her direction. She cocked her head, tilted her chin and stared straight back at him, bold – Cassie thought – as brass. She had never flirted with a grown man before, let alone a minister, and she was intimidated by her own temerity and, to say the least of it, alarmed by its effect.

Sullen and stolid in a black Geneva gown, Reverend Montague – who had rowed for an Oxford college, fought in several wars, travelled far and wide and published four or five books on learned subjects – was completely caught off guard. To Cassie Armitage's astonishment, he lost the thread of his dissertation, stammered and almost stopped, while she sat rigid in the family pew and waited for retribution to descend from on high. With an effort of will the minister finally tore his attention away from her, shuffled papers on the lectern, cleared his throat and recommenced his harangue with no less commitment than before, except that he was smiling now, his thin upper lip curved and a tiny curlicue of flesh puckering his smooth cheek like a scar.

Cassie's little sister Pippa whispered, 'Well, did you ever see the like of that?'

Cassie bowed her head. Blood rushed upward from her bosom and coloured her throat, neck and ears. Tingling

4

with embarrassment, she had the dreadful feeling that everyone in church had noticed the exchange, that everyone was staring at her, from house-servants in the gallery down to Mr Grimmond, the elderly pew-opener. Possibly even Sir Andrew Flail himself, though how that could be when Sir Andrew and his wife had their backs to her was beyond rational explanation.

Pippa's sharp little elbow nudged Cassie again. The upright pew protected the sisters from observation. Only their bonnets were visible above the sides of the seats where the noble folk of the parish displayed themselves like pheasants in a basket.

'Did you, Cass?' Pippa whispered. 'Did you see how he looked at me?'

'You?' Cassie exploded. 'He wasn't looking at you.'

Papa's hand appeared over the pew back and tapped her shoulder.

'*Sssshhh*,' Cuthbert Armitage hissed.

Cassie sank down, her summer-weight mantle slithering against the polished oak. Only the dusty cushion under her thighs kept her from sliding into an unladylike crouch. To hide her trembling, she tucked her hands into her bell sleeves and sat very still in the hope that Reverend Montague would forget that she had dared to meet his eye. When she risked raising her eyes to the pulpit again she was, however, disappointed to discover that her wish had been granted and that the handsome preacher had apparently lost all interest in her and had transferred his attention to the labourers who occupied the unprotected benches. Indeed he was giving them such mighty licks that even burly ironworkers clung to their seats as if the minister's voice had the force of a westerly gale and they were in danger of being whirled up and blown away by it.

'And the seas shall open and consume the lands round about,' Robert Montague thundered. 'And the dead and the living will be mingled one with the other. And the God of Abraham and of Isaac will pluck you up like little fishes to see if He finds your flesh sweet or corrupt. Those who

5

are sweet and clean in the flesh He will admit to His presence to rejoice there with the saints and angels. But those whom He finds wanting He will cast down to rot, days without number, in the sediment and slime of the great heaving sea of sinfulness.'

Cassie watched in fascination but listened with only half an ear. The minister's voice was so sensuous that it hardly mattered what message it delivered. She watched him weave and sway, arm erect, fist closed, the sunlight shrinking from him. He was dark-browed, dark-eyed, hawkish and handsome and she longed for him to let his glance linger on her just once more.

Under cover of the pew lid Pippa's hand brushed Cassie's knee. Pippa's forefinger pointed upward in the minister's direction then turned and tapped her, Pippa's, breast.

'Me,' Pippa mouthed. 'He smiled at me.'

Primly, Cassie compressed her lips and said nothing. She mustn't rise to the bait. She must set a decorous example to her diminutive sister who had somehow – goodness knows how – acquired a knowingness far beyond her fifteen years; yet the temptation to point out that ministers of the Gospel were far too serious and sober to make sheep's eyes at mere children was almost overwhelming.

'Me, me, me,' Pippa mouthed again, digging away with her elbow.

'Oh, be quiet,' Cassie snapped, rather too loudly. 'Not you – me.'

In the sudden silence her declaration seemed to echo round the kirk, accompanied only by the jeering of the herring-gulls and by Robert Montague quietly pronouncing, 'Amen.'

There was, of course, an afternoon preaching and another at six o'clock. Cubby Armitage's daughters were not expected to attend the additional services. In fact, they were discouraged from doing so. The presentation of the living of Ravenshill parish was about to be settled that fine

June day and that was hardly a matter that concerned young women.

Although Cassie knew little about the procedures of the Church of Scotland she appreciated the gravity of the affair and identified a certain smugness in Papa that the best man had won out in the end. The fact that Reverend Montague had had no competitor in the 'race' for the vacancy did not detract from her father's satisfaction. Montague had been put up by Sir Andrew Flail and any involvement the congregation thought it had had in making a decision stemmed only from Sir Andrew's skill in bending lesser mortals to his will.

Creed and dogma were less important to the heritor of Ravenshill than class and style which, by Sir Andrew's lights, meant finding a clergyman who was willing to keep the lower orders firmly in place and who was able to intimidate neighbouring gentry with a knowledge of Greek and Latin. Robert Montague filled the bill on both counts. It was virtually assured that Montague would gain the pulpit of Ravenshill kirk and that any upstart who tried to exercise the power of veto would have to answer to a body much more fearsome than the local Presbytery, for here on the long alluvial plains that bordered the south bank of the Clyde the Flails' word was law.

The Flails had owned the lands of Ravenshill for going on three centuries. Sir Andrew's grandfather had paid for the building of the church, had established the first ironworks and had laid down the first wagon ways. Sir Andrew's father had commissioned the building of a quay, had brought the railway to the parish and had erected the first tenements. Sir Andrew had done better than any of his forefathers, however, for he had acquired property across the river in the city of Glasgow and cut quite a famous figure in the Merchant House for his wealth, swagger and ambition.

Robert Montague might be Flail's choice for Ravenshill but he was not, and never would be, Flail's man. He had an obdurate streak which, it seemed, would not yield to

7

flattery. Nor had he need of the living. Apparently Reverend Montague was well enough heeled to dismiss as irrelevant the meagre stipend which the post offered and what had prompted him to apply for the ministerial commission of the sprawling riverside parish was a mystery which even his sponsors had so far failed to unravel.

Perhaps the manse appealed to him, a huge, remote old house which stood on a hill a quarter of a mile above the rural hamlet of Bramwell. Farmlands undulated away to the south and west, ground upon which masons and contractors had not yet laid hands. To the north was the Clyde and the funnels of steamers moving over the level of the intervening fields and, morning and evening, a distant glimpse of the 'black squad' trudging to and from work at the shipbuilding yards further down river.

The manse was decently removed from the reek of the ironworks and the bustle of the quays that marred the bulk of Ravenshill and only Flail House, a massive red-stone edifice, half home farm, half baronial manor, had a better situation. For a gentleman with an adventurous past and an urge to settle down, the gaunt three-storey building might represent a haven of peace and tranquillity. On the other hand, there was vigour in the nearby town and a rich intellectual community centred around the Glasgow colleges only four or five miles away. Sir Andrew could not be sure which aspect of Ravenshill most appealed to Robert Montague, for, although he had been thorough in examining Montague's credentials, he had not enquired too deeply into the minister's motives for returning to Scotland.

Mr Cuthbert Armitage was even more inclined to accept Robert Montague at face value. Like almost everyone in Ravenshill, Cubby was dazzled by Montague's reputation. He welcomed him with all the obsequiousness he could muster when he was chosen to provide Sabbath afternoon hospitality and the Reverend Montague, still sweating from his *post meridian* exertions, invited himself to tea at

8

the Armitage residence in Normandy Road between afternoon and evening services.

Cubby Armitage might believe in the sanctity of the home and the purity of women but he was pompous enough to make sure that everyone who was anyone in Ravenshill saw him walking arm-in-arm down Main Street with the parish's next incumbent. Cubby would have loitered to point out the sights, to sing the praises of the ironworks, extol the convenience of the railway and brag about the depth of the new dock. But Robert Montague, hot and thirsty, was in sore need of a dish of tea and a buttered scone, and, with another session in the pulpit still to come, lacked the inclination to play the sightseeing game. Instead, he studied Cuthbert Armitage as if the little Scottish stockbroker were wonder enough to be going on with.

'Tell me, sir,' Robert Montague said, 'how long have you lived here?'

'All of my life, sir,' Cubby answered. 'Forty years, and more.'

'In which time you must have witnessed many changes?'

'Indeed, indeed I have.'

Cubby raised his arm to point towards the gigantic crane that towered over the stacks of Flail's 'Blazes'. But Robert Montague gave him no opportunity to expand on the theme of progress.

'Have you always been employed by Sir Andrew?'

'Indeed not,' Cubby answered. 'I'm not, strictly speaking, employed by him at all.'

'I was under the impression that you brokered for the Flails.'

'I do, of course. That's why I have my office in Glasgow close to the Exchange,' Cubby explained. 'But I'm also a broker in my own right.'

'You must then be a man of the world; by which I mean you must travel extensively in connection with your correspondents?'

'Not at all, sir. I travel as little as possible. I have no taste for it. I leave all the foreign travel to my partner, Charles Smalls. My business is here in Glasgow which is the centre of the iron trade, at least for those who require pig.'

'Pig?'

'Pig-iron, the product of the furnace.'

'Is there money to be made from trading in pig?'

'Indeed there is, much money. And in all iron products.'

Reverend Montague's frown was one of concentration, not disapproval.

'What of the rest of it?' he said. 'Your business, I mean. Share dealing, perhaps?'

'Oh, share dealing, yes.'

'On whose account, may I ask?'

'On account of anyone who requests the service.'

'And on your own account?' said the minister, lightly.

'Certainly, certainly. I'm not without – what shall we say – substance.'

'I trust you do not think me excessively curious, Mr Armitage?'

'Not at all, sir, not at all,' said Cubby. 'Perhaps you will have some wee pieces of business to put my way when the time comes.'

'Perhaps I shall,' the minister said. 'Is this your house?'

'It is, sir, it is.'

'A very handsome house, if I may say so.'

'My father, rest his soul, purchased the lease from Sir Andrew's grandfather many years ago.' Cubby opened the iron gate and ushered the minister before him on to the garden path. 'You are most welcome to enter it, sir.'

'How kind of you, Mr Armitage.' The minister nodded in the direction of a figure that stood in the wrought-iron pergola that occupied the side lawn. 'Is that your wife, by any chance?'

'No, my daughter, sir. One of them, one of a pair.'

'Which one is she, Mr Armitage?'

'Her name is Cassandra.'

'After the Greek, no doubt?'

'Oh, aye,' Cubby Armitage agreed. 'After the Greek.'

10

* * *

When Papa ushered Robert Montague into the garden Cassie's first impulse was to gather up her skirts and run for cover. It was not that she wanted to avoid meeting the great man – on the contrary – but she knew that she had transgressed one of the rules of conduct which her father had laid down for the household. This, after all, was the Lord's Day when, according to her father, respectable ladies didn't flaunt themselves upon the lawns or luxuriate under the wisteria that draped the iron pergola.

Cassie's mother was already ensconced in the drawing-room. A silver teapot would be warming on the candle-stand and butter cooling in the water-dish. Pippa was also hidden within the house, most likely sulking in the back parlour.

The sisters had quarrelled throughout luncheon and had bickered away the afternoon until, with more jibes in her than Saint Sebastian had arrows, Cassie had flounced out to hide her suffering in the forbidden sanctuary of the garden.

Why Pippa's sarcasm had affected her so adversely, why she felt so weak and vulnerable were questions without answers, until, that is, her father appeared at the garden gate with the Reverend Montague. The moment Cassie set eyes on the minister the source of her restlessness became plain. She could not define it precisely, could not give it a proper name. Nevertheless as soon as she saw Robert Montague again her irritation vanished. She had no doubt at all that the minister had come to call upon her and that whatever excuse he offered for the visit he too had felt a magnetism between them.

'Cassandra?'

'Yes, Papa.'

'Do not run away, girl. Reverend Montague wishes to meet you.'

She waited, motionless, under trailing fronds of honeysuckle, her gloved hand upon the iron rail.

11

He approached across the grass, his eyes fastened upon her.

It was as it had been in church only now there was less need for pretence. She felt his gaze penetrate her, thin, sharp and painless, like a steel pin through the body of a butterfly.

'Miss Armitage?'

'Reverend Montague.'

'How pleasant it is to see you again so soon.'

'Thank you, sir,' Cassie said. 'Have – have you come to take tea with us?'

'I have.'

'Then Papa will show you to the drawing-room.'

'Do you not take tea in the garden?' the minister said.

'Not on the Sabbath, sir,' her father chipped in.

'Why not?'

Cassie heard herself say, 'Because a Christian home is the tabernacle of the Lord and bread must be broken only under its roof.'

'Ah!' the minister said. 'Obviously I've much to learn about observance.' She had expected him to be more severe. The vitality he had displayed in the pulpit was manifest now as a suave, almost sinister intimacy.

'Aye, this, sir, is a very devout household, though I say so myself,' Cassie's father declared, and, laying a hand on the minister's elbow, made to steer him towards the front door of the house.

The movement was too slight to be offensive. It might even have been accidental. Robert Montague lifted his arm and adjusted the cuff of his morning coat. When he lowered his arm again, the elbow was slanted towards Cassie.

'With your permission, Mr Armitage,' he said, 'perhaps your charming daughter would be good enough to show me the way.'

Cassie did not wait for sanction. She stepped from the ledge of the pergola and took Robert Montague's arm. To her surprise she could smell sweat from him, an odour like

12

that of warm fur, dry and musky, mingled with a touch of lavender and the faint, dusty undertow of oakwood from the kirk. She leaned into him, skirts brushing against his thigh, slippers sliding on the soft, warm grass. He felt solid beside her, solid and vibrant.

Suddenly everything in and around her was vibrant, from dappled sunlight on the house walls to the scut of white cloud that floated overhead.

Best of all, though, was the satisfaction that trickled through her when she noticed Pippa outlined in the window that overlooked the garden; Pippa, who thought that Robert Montague was far too grand to pay court to a girl from the backwaters of Ravenshill; Pippa who, without logic or reason, wanted the new minister for herself.

Two

In August the wealthy burghers of Glasgow abandoned the Merchant House and the floor of the Exchange and headed off by rail and steamer to holiday in their houses by the sea. The exodus was particular, not general, for only a very special few could afford the upkeep of an out-of-town residence.

The Armitages did not holiday by the sea. The Armitages did not holiday at all. Cubby was old-fashioned enough to believe that if God had wanted man to vacate his native environment from time to time then God would have designed man with iron wheels instead of feet. The extent of Cubby Armitage's voyaging was to travel the four miles to his office in the city each and every day and the little stockbroker was, in fact, somewhat irked that so many of his acquaintances were absent in the August month and that he was considered a stick-in-the-mud for not rushing off to join them on holiday.

Naturally this view was shared by Cubby Armitage's daughters. Every July the girls embarked on a wheedling campaign to persuade Papa to take them out of Ravenshill and spare them the suffocating tedium of another summer stuck at home. However much Mr Armitage valued education, though, he was not about to yield to the female

15

argument that travel broadened the mind or to the suggestion that the only way his daughters were going to find husbands was to net one on a beach somewhere, as if husband-hunting were as simple a sport as shrimping.

That summer neither Cassie nor her sister set up their customary cry to be transported to a fashionable seaside resort and the silence worried Cubby a whole lot more than their whining had ever done.

'What's wrong with them, Norah?' he enquired of his wife one evening when the girls had gone early upstairs. 'Are they sulking?'

At the best of times Norah Armitage was a woman of remarkably few words. She answered, 'Not sulking.'

'What is it then? An ailment?'

'No ailment.'

Norah Armitage cupped the buns of grey hair that protruded from the sides of her lace bonnet and gave them a little shake as if they were directly connected to a source of inspiration.

At length, she said, 'Love.'

'Love?' Cubby shouted.

'Infatuation.'

'What? With whom?'

'Reverend Montague.'

'What's Montague been up to?' said Cubby in alarm. 'I mean, what's the fellow done to turn their silly heads?'

'Montague doesn't know,' Norah said.

Norah Armitage was angular and tall, so much taller than her rotund little mate that Cubby had developed a habit of looking up at her even when they were both sitting down. The transformation that marriage had wrought on the lively young governess whom he had met at Bible Assembly in the late Mr Calderon's house almost twenty years ago had taken place so gradually that Cubby was unaware of it. He sincerely believed that Norah had always been as stiff and reticent as she was now.

'Doesn't know?' said Cubby. 'Doesn't know what?'

'How much he has affected them.'

16

'Of course he does. He must.'

Norah said nothing. Not for the first time Cubby Armitage was tempted to grasp those solid buns of hair and shake them to expedite communication.

'Has he not encouraged them, Norah? Is that what you're telling me?'

'He doesn't have to encourage them.'

'They're young, so young. Pippa, at least,' Cubby said.

'You married me at seventeen.'

'That was different. You had – em – no one else to look out for you.'

Norah Armitage did not contradict him.

She sat, as she always did, absolutely upright, straight and stiff as a ramrod. The old-fashioned day-dress with its draped bodice and plump sleeves hung from her shoulders like leathers on a drying-rack. She had become so desiccated, so bony that Cubby wondered if she were harbouring a wasting disease; yet she'd never had a day's illness in her life apart from a few unfortunate months all too soon after their wedding.

Cubby cleared his throat. 'Are they ready for marriage?'

'They're ready.'

'But they're so young, Norah.' Cubby sat up and planted an elbow on the table's edge. 'Montague, you say?'

'Infatuation,' his wife repeated, adding, 'it may come to nothing.'

'Well, it's a beginning, I suppose,' Cubby said. 'But Montague must have some inkling how they feel about him. I assume that a man of his calibre attracts female admirers by the score. How may we discover if he's – what? – aware of our daughters?'

'Ask him.'

'What do I ask him?'

'If he's in search of a wife.'

'Oh, come now, Norah, that isn't a topic I can raise without embarrassment. After all, he's a clergyman. And he's – what? – twenty years older than the girls. Then there's the matter of a dowry. He's bound to require portion to go with a wife. I'm not sure I can scrape up the sort of sum he'll expect.'

'One thousand pounds.'

'What?'

'The sum your father invested in trust for each of the girls.'

'It was nothing like a thousand.'

'Seventeen years of accrued interest, Cuthbert,' Norah stated. 'If it isn't a thousand pounds by now then you haven't been doing your job.'

'It's – em – all tied up in stock,' Cubby mumbled.

'Then untie it,' Norah said. 'With Scotch pig selling at seventy-two shillings per ton you would be obliged to shed a mere three hundred tons at most.'

'That isn't how it's done, Norah.'

Cubby opened his mouth to embark on an explanation of the intricacies of market trading then he thought better of it. He had always made a point of keeping his professional and domestic lives separate and distinct.

He hemmed and hawed for a moment then said, 'Even if Cassie does come generously endowed surely Robert Montague is well out of our reach?'

'He'll take her if he wants her badly enough.'

'But they hardly know each other.'

'Throw them together.'

'How?'

'Invite him to dinner.'

The frown vanished from Cubby Armitage's brow.

'Are you – I mean, *do* the girls like him?' he said.

'Yes.'

'Very well. In that case I will extend an invitation to the gentleman just as soon as he's settled,' Cubby said, then, frowning again, asked, 'By the way, which one do you think is right for him?'

'Cassie,' Norah Armitage replied and, to her husband's surprise, added on an emphatic little nod and the whisper of a smile.

* * *

18

In Cubby's opinion the problem with the doing of good works was that it inevitably involved contact with undesirable characters.

However much he browsed through texts on the meaning of charity, however much he sympathised in principle with the poor and needy, Cuthbert Armitage could not quite shake the feeling that the poor and needy were essentially responsible for their own condition and should be encouraged to develop fortitude and self-reliance and not be given food, coals, clothing and an allocation of that most valuable commodity, consideration.

He was emphatically in favour of mission work in the town's mean back streets and applauded the efforts of lay preachers, such as Albert Lassiter, to provide succour for the town's down-and-outs. But he was not moved to visit the Lassiters' mission and felt no compulsion to involve himself in 'that sort of thing'. So shy was he of association with those who were down on their luck that he had forbidden Norah and the girls from visiting the poorhouse orphans, even on Christmas Day and would have no truck with the beggars who occasionally came knocking at the kitchen door.

As a result of Papa's prejudice, the Armitage girls grew up in an environment that was not only sheltered but seemed almost detached from reality. After the boys and girls with whom they had attended dame-school went off to college, their lives became increasingly narrow. This situation had been bearable when Ravenshill had been a village but as the girls grew older and the town expanded the house in Normandy Road became less like a home than a prison and even Cubby's friends considered his children oppressed beyond anything that social grace demanded.

Cubby had his work in Glasgow and his kirk meetings to keep him occupied. His wife and daughters had nothing with which to divert themselves except what Cubby chose to allow them.

Norah's domestic burdens were lightened by an elderly cook, Mrs McFarlane, and a succession of young girls hired from the workhouse to act as maids until marriage broke the chains of one sort of servitude and carried them off into servitude of another kind.

For entertainment the Armitage ladies were permitted to call upon old Mrs Pitt, an eighty-year-old widow, Mrs Calderon, widow of the previous minister, old Miss Penrose, Miss McClean and the spinster sisters Isa and Bella Coulter; a visiting list so hoary that Norah and her daughters felt as if they had been condemned to haunt these frowzy parlours as a punishment for unspecified sins.

Even before the advent of Robert Montague there had been a few diversions to add lustre to the girls' conversations and lead them to speculate on just what they were missing. Most diverting of all had been the employment of Nancy Winfield, a lively young scullery maid whom Cubby had been persuaded to bring in from the workhouse. From Nancy the girls had learned of drunken brawls between ironworkers and navvies, of unwanted babies and clandestine marriages between unsuitable partners and Nancy, an outspoken girl, might have carried into the Armitage house even more instructive gossip if she had not been suddenly dismissed for reasons that Cubby had refused to explain.

The Armitage girls still missed Nancy's cheerful company. Now and then they asked Cook for news of her but Mrs McFarlane professed to know nothing of the girl's whereabouts.

By the summer of 1858, however, Nancy Winfield's fate was the last thing on their minds, for conversations between Cassie and Pippa were devoted exclusively to the Reverend Robert Montague's impending arrival at their dinner table.

Robert – yes, he was Robert to them now – was all they talked about, indulging in speculation and mad little fancies which, like infants with a box of shells, they tumbled out and rearranged endlessly.

'What did it feel like?' Pippa would ask. 'His arm, I mean.'

'Wonderful. Like a piece of wrought iron.'

'Do you think he'll take your arm again?'

'I do hope so.'

'Perhaps he'll take mine too?'

'No, you're too young for him.'

'I am not. In my blue dress, with my hair up a little, I look as old as you do.'

'Nonsense,' Cassie would say. 'You've no figure at all.'

'I have.' Pippa would look down at her bosom with a frown. 'I'm just naturally petite. Perhaps Robert prefers petite ladies.'

'It was *my* arm he took.'

'I gave him sugar, remember? He asked *me* for sugar.'

'Only because you were nearest the dish.'

'No, I was not.'

'Yes, you were.'

Indoors and out, upstairs and down, as soon as the sisters were out of earshot of Mama and Papa on they would go, mulching the memory of that June afternoon as if there were no other topics in the wide world to engage them.

However she might behave in Pippa's company, though, Cassie was intelligent enough to realise that behind their wistful longings was a man who had a character and a history about which they knew nothing.

She could not forget the way his eyes had alighted on her, not just in church but later too, in the garden and at the tea-table, how he had held her glance as he took his farewells that Sabbath afternoon. She had also remarked Robert's indulgent attitude towards Pippa. It was as if he considered her eagerness entertaining but essentially frivolous, like that of a persistent little kitten; not at all like his manner towards her, Cassie thought, which was altogether more serious and mature and, because of that, more disturbing.

She kept these observations to herself, however.

If she antagonised Pippa and sent her into a sulk then she would have no one with whom to share the excitement of a summer in which everything had to be reviewed in the light shed by Robert Montague's arrival in Ravenshill.

The induction of the Reverend Montague took place on the last Thursday in August. The occasion was marked by much celebration, for the congregation of Ravenshill church had been without a minister since the death of Mr Calderon in May and the lack of a proper pastor was sorely felt in the parish.

Robert Montague was introduced to the flock by no less a personage than Professor Matthew Salmond who held the chair of Old Testament Theology at the University of Glasgow and was reputed to be a friend and colleague of Mr Montague's father who nursed a rural pulpit in the Highlands.

Cassie and Pippa were crammed into a pew to the left of the pulpit. Papa was on one side, Mama on the other and a brace of Sir Andrew's out-of-town cousins were breathing down their necks. The odour of serge and flannel and damp fustian was overpowering, for the evening was marred by a miserable drizzle which dampened everything except the congregation's enthusiasm in welcoming its new minister.

When the service was over night was well down and the rain had increased. Cassie and Pippa hurried outside in the hope of catching a glimpse of their hero but Robert was lost to view among the glossy horseflesh and black-lacquered hoods, the top hats and three-tiered skirts.

Sunday was more rewarding. The weather was fine for one thing and even in a crowded kirk Robert managed to catch Cassie's eye and accept the prim little smile which she had rehearsed into her hand mirror in the privacy of the first-landing water-closet. Even Pippa recovered her optimism on Sunday and with restless gestures attracted Robert's attention long enough to beam and dimple and despatch some sort of message with her brows.

If Sunday was rewarding, the minister's first Bible Assembly on Thursday was truly fulfilling. At its conclusion Robert managed to disengage himself from a gaggle of admiring females, come to the Armitage ladies, bow and make himself pleasant, so pleasant, in fact, that it was all Cassie could do not to call him 'Robert' to his face.

On the following evening, prompt at half past six o'clock, Robert Montague arrived at the front door of the villa on Normandy Street to dine *en famille* with the Armitages.

New-fangled gas cooking-stoves were not for Mrs McFarlane. She had perfected a dozen dishes over the years and served them in strict rotation. Mrs McFarlane had learned the value of adding alcohol to gravies and sauces, not to mention soups, puddings and pies. Unfortunately she had learned how to apply alcohol in a more conventional way and would often prepare dinner in a state of unnatural merriment, a slap-dash enthusiasm that somehow found its way into the pot and, like an extra ingredient, resulted in an entrée or dessert that could only be described as *par excellence*.

Those, in fact, were the very words used by Robert Montague in respect of the oxtail soup, liberally flavoured with sherry, with which Friday night's dinner began. He used the same phrase again, embellished with several appreciative *ummms*, as he dug half a lamb's kidney out of an ocean of red wine gravy and bit into it with relish.

Cassie was used to Papa shifting vast quantities of meat but he ate neatly and without haste, in a manner that suggested asceticism. Mama, on the other hand, professed no fondness for any particular dish except pickled red cabbage which, it seemed, she could not resist.

Apparently Robert liked red cabbage too and consumed it mouthful by mouthful in competition with his hostess so that even before the rum and raisin pudding made an appearance he was sufficiently relaxed to lift a corner of the veil that obscured his past and, like Salome, waft it about a bit.

'Women,' he said, without warning, 'women in Ottoman

23

countries won't touch cabbage, you know. It is just the opposite in Russia and, as one may imagine, in Syria.'

Silence around the table. Cubby Armitage stopped chewing. With a crumb of pastry clinging to the fringe of his moustache, he cleared his throat and opened his mouth but couldn't seem to find anything intelligent to say in response to Mr Montague's information.

Pippa was quick into the gap. 'Why, sir, must we imagine that it is the opposite in Russia?'

'And Syria?' Norah Armitage added.

'Because it is the case. Syrian women will eat absolutely anything.'

'Have you been to Syria, then?' Cubby finally managed to get out.

'Oh, yes.'

'And to Russia?' Cassie asked.

'I haven't travelled in that country, no,' Robert Montague admitted, 'but I have had some connection with its inhabitants.'

'Soldiers?' said Cassie.

'Soldiers, and travellers.'

'And women?' said Pippa.

Before Cubby could reprimand the girl for impropriety Robert Montague's answer was upon them. 'Contrary to popular perception,' he said, 'the Russian wife is a very cleanly animal, at least in my experience.'

'What,' said Norah, 'does this have to do with McFarlane's cabbage?'

Robert Montague laughed. 'Not much, I confess. Regrettably I appear to have reached a stage in my life when the smallest sensations in the present unite me with larger recollections of the past.'

'Just like the Coulter sisters,' Pippa put in.

For a moment Robert's expression was flinty, as if he disliked being teased, then he shook his head. 'I've met the Coulter sisters, you know.'

Pippa was undaunted. 'All they talk about is how it used to be in Bramwell when the cows came down to drink at the water's edge and they flirted with the salmon-fishers at the ford by the whinfield.'

'Obviously they did not flirt successfully,' said Robert.

'Or they were too ugly for even salmon-fishers to bother with,' said Pippa.

'Pippa!'

'Yes, I'm sorry,' Pippa apologised instantly. 'I should not be uncharitable. It's just that the Coulter sisters are so frightfully boring.'

Cassie swallowed a piece of mutton and, in the hope of protecting her sister from further gaffes, said, 'How long did you serve in the army, Mr Montague?'

'I was not strictly speaking in the army at all.' Robert turned towards her and placed his fork upon his plate with a little click. 'I take it that you have not read the printed account of my travels?'

'I regret that I have not,' said Cassie.

Cubby wiped his moustache with his fingertip and said, 'Hardly suitable reading matter for a girl of tender years, Mr Montague.'

'Certainly not,' Robert agreed. 'But you, sir, have read it, have you not?'

'In part, yes. I found it – em – rather distressing.'

'Which part affected you most? My account of the massacre at Kabul?'

'Certainly, certainly. Quite horrible.'

'The attack on the Residency?'

'Very distressing. Very distressing, indeed.'

'Inkerman? The siege of Sebastopol?'

'Yes. Yes.'

'You fought in the Crimea?' Pippa put in, no longer inclined to tease.

'I was a chaplain, not a conscripted officer,' Robert said. 'I tended to be embroiled with the civilian staff rather than the military, especially in the embassy at Constantinople. I did, however, act as agent to Sir Henry Curran in several active campaigns.'

'Agent?' said Pippa. 'What's an agent?'

'Rather like a secretary,' Robert explained.

'Or a spy,' said Norah.

Robert hesitated. Again Cassie detected that hard, flinty look in his eyes.

'Ah, madam,' he said. 'I see you have my measure. Secretary, spy, spiritual comforter? I confess to having been a little of each in my time.'

Until that moment Cassie had been under the impression that Robert Montague had served his country as a harum-scarum youth. Clearly this was not the case. It startled her to realise that Robert had been a participant in the Crimean campaign, news of which had managed to penetrate even the sheltered villa in Normandy Road.

She said, 'Why did you come back to Scotland?'

'I had had enough of foreign places and foreign parts.'

'Why here, to Ravenshill?'

'Cassie, don't be impertinent,' Papa told her.

'The young lady has every right to ask, Mr Armitage, though I fear my answer may not be entirely satisfactory.' Robert inclined himself towards Cassie once more. 'I came home to Scotland to find a charge, to marry and settle down.'

'The call, sir, you received the call to serve the Lord,' Cubby suggested.

'I did, Mr Armitage,' Robert replied. 'Loud and very clear.'

'How dramatic,' said Pippa.

'Not at all,' Robert said. 'There was nothing sudden or glorious about it. It did not come upon me abruptly as it did to Saint Paul. It arose, rather, out of weariness and disappointment.'

'Is this your first charge then?' Norah enquired.

'I was attached for a brief period to the Scottish Mission in Jerusalem.'

'Jerusalem,' Cubby Armitage sighed. 'Ah, Jerusalem.'

'And now,' Pippa said, 'you've come home to marry?'

'If I can find anyone who'll have me,' Robert said.

Pippa opened her mouth but Mama was there before her.

'I'm sure that will not be difficult,' Norah said and, before her youngest could rush headlong into another indiscretion, rang the handbell to summon up the maid.

The Beast of Bengal Street appeared early that night. She thanked her lucky stars she had come out early too or she might have missed him and gone home not only hungry but penniless.

She crouched beneath the cellar steps and listened to him beat upon the door and roar threats at the man who protected the women sprawled within the cellar. If the Beast was drunk this early, she thought, she would have no trouble taking him. She had taken him once before, when she was desperate. She had been too sick to couple with him that night but fortunately he had been too drunk to realise he had had his pocket picked.

Afterwards, so frightened was she by what she had done that it had taken her all her time to scuttle back through the lanes and across the waste ground to her bed below the embankment. At that, she had been too late to secure her bed space for the others knew she was sick and refused to let her in. They were afraid of the cholera coming back, though there had been no sign of it in Ravenshill for seven or eight years.

She had tried to persuade Mr Sinclair to let her sleep in the taproom but, even although he liked her well enough, he would have none of it, not at that late hour, not with her being sick. In the end she had been forced to crawl under the tarpaulins that covered the stones by the wall of the new harbour in the hope that she would survive the cold of the night and not die with the money in her purse to pay the bill for Daisy.

Since then she had returned to the neighbourhood of Bengal Street a dozen times or more to couple with the big, brown-skinned man who never seemed to remember her one time to the next and had never even asked her for her name. She could have rifled his pockets near every time and got away with it but she was ashamed of what she

27

had done that one time and had vowed she would never stoop to thieving again.

She still believed that if the Beast ever caught her with her hand in his pocket he would kill her. If she turned up dead in the river there would be few to grieve. There would be nobody to put a name to her white face, except Mr Sinclair or Madame Daltry. Even they might never know what had happened to her since they were hardly likely to frequent the morgue, and the police constables would not waste much time asking questions just to put a name to another dead puss. What would happen to Daisy, though, if she was not there to see to her welfare was the thing that really worried her and it was for Daisy's sake more than anything that she struggled to keep herself alive.

Nobody in the back end of Ravenshill knew who she was, for she did not commune with the street whores or the men who protected the street whores. She did not think of herself as a puss and she certainly wanted no protector who would force her to lay out for him time and time again and take most of her money for himself. She went with men only when there was no other paying work to be found, which was why she took on the man they called the Beast, because he paid her price, no questions asked.

She had a notion that the Beast's name was Brownlee. She preferred to think of him by the handle that the women had given him. They called him the Beast because of his brown skin and shaggy hair, because of his huge size and his reputation for violent temper. Also, perhaps, because he had worked the middens and cesspits for years without ever falling sick and only a beast, they reckoned, would be so ignorant as to stick with that job when there was work to be had in the ironworks just for the asking.

Some things they said about him were true, some not. His hands and arms were scarred with rat bites. His bristling beard was matted. Sometimes, though not always, he smelled bad. It was to her advantage that everyone was afraid of him. None of the publicans or dramshop owners, none of the keepers of women would have anything to do with him. They refused to let him drink at their tables, sit on their benches or sprawl on their damp earth floors. They sold him whisky through door-ways or brought a jar out to the close-mouth, though, for they were not the sort of men to turn down ready cash. But they would not let their women go with him under any circumstances for fear that in his passion he might kill one of them and bring the constables nosing into the lanes and alleyways where the law, as a rule, never came.

Now she had grown used to him she did not mind being with the Beast. She was not as afraid of him as she had been at first, for at least one of the things the women had said about him was a lie. He was dependable. He never refused her. He was honest. He paid before they began. He had his own room too, a foothold in an old tenement in the neighbourhood where Ravenshill spilled into the Barony of Gorbals and the towns and villages, old and new, met and mingled all higgledy-piggledy among the warehouses where sugar was once kept and where stocks of pig-iron were kept now ready for shipping away on the boats. And she still reckoned that being alone with a man in a room was better than writhing on a mattress in a cellar while other men and women watched.

She crouched under the arch, waiting for the Beast to emerge from the close that led down into the dramshop.

She was relieved that she had come early that Friday, for she was short on the week and he was her best hope of earning what she needed. If she had missed him she did not know what she would have to do, for navvies or sailors off the bum boats paid her next to nothing since she'd next to nothing to offer them, her figure being slight.

Rain poured from the eaves and splashed against her knees. She could feel wetness against her thighs through her skirts. It had started as she came round the back of the embankment and by the time she had reached the tenements the gutters were running wet and the brick walls were slick and the lantern that hung over the Bengal Street lane shone fuzzy and yellow in the heavy drizzle. She could hear the rain hissing over the rooftops and splattering on the cobbles and she cowered deeper in under the worn stone steps to keep herself dry while the Beast roared at the dramshop keeper because the man would not let him shelter inside where it was dry and warm.

Seconds later he came lurching out of the close with a black bottle held in one hand, mumbling to himself, still angry. He wore a heavy canvas jacket and a wrinkled canvas vest, moleskin breeks and big, iron-capped boots, and a battered brown felt hat clung to his greying hair. He paused, glowering, held up the bottle, pulled the cork with his teeth and drank from the neck. No matter how brutal he seemed, at times like this she knew that he was a slave too, a slave to rum and rotten whisky, to work and weather like so many of them.

Pressed against the wall she waited until he had taken a long suck from the bottle and had pulled it from his mouth. Then she called out to him, 'Mister, mister,' in a voice as soft as she could make it and still be heard.

Bewildered, he turned this way and that.

She tucked her rat-tails away under the brim of the old straw bonnet that was all that was left of her servant days and pinched her cheekbones hard to give them colour, and showed herself. She could smell the drink clean, the body dirty, the dampness over all. She was wary because he had not had as much to drink as was usual for a Friday night. She wondered if he might even remember her from the time before. Because it was early he would also have money in his pocket, money he had not yet had time to spend.

She tried not to think about that.

'Don't you remember me?' she asked.

He shook his head.

'Have you got a bed?' she said.

'Aye.'

'Do you want t' take me t' your bed?'

'Aye.'

'It'll cost you a shillin'.'

'Aye.'

Shocked, she realised that he was hardly drunk at all. She had never seen him so sober before and felt fear in case he recognised her for a thief. She leaned meekly on the step and waited for him to strike her.

'You're no' much t' look at, are you?' he said.

She knew how bad she looked, slight and pale and flat-chested.

'Good enough for the likes o' you,' she said.

'Aye, that wouldna be hard, would it?'

He put the cork in the bottle, slipped the bottle into his pocket, put both hands about her waist and lifted her up and set her down on the step above him as easily as he might have a doll.

'I've a doss in Bengal Street,' he said.

She bit her lip and said nothing.

Sober, he seemed threatening again, his massive chest and shoulders thrust out and his bear-paw hands around her waist. She remembered how he seemed to fill the narrow room on the top floor of the tenement, how the floorboards groaned and the iron bedstead flexed under his weight. She was frightened that next time he picked her up he might remember her. She did not want him to remember her in case he suddenly realised what she had done to him.

He nudged her up the steps ahead of him. 'Ga'n then.'

She pulled herself up into the lane. He came after her.

By the corner of the lane, near the old pump, three street women loitered. Further on, where the warehouses sloped towards the river, four or five men lounged by the door of the wine vaults. Beyond that again, in neuks and crannies a tribe of street urchins played some vicious game. She felt tiny beside him as they walked towards the women.

If the women recognised her they gave no sign. He was

31

recognised, though, and when he came abreast of them the women shrieked and cried out things she had never heard put into words before. The Beast walked on as if he were deaf and dumb, holding her by the waist, his head up and chest thrust out.

Then he said, 'Have I seen you before?'

'I've been with you before,' she told him.

The men were too cowardly to jeer but they smirked and eyed her up in the blue light of the wine vault door. Loungers and cadgers, men who had never done an honest day's labour in their lives. She resented their ridicule and slid closer to the Beast and slipped her thin arm about his waist.

'D' you know what they call me?' he said.

'No.'

'Todd Brownlee's my name. What do they cry you?'

On impulse she told him the truth.

'Nancy. Nancy Winfield,' she said.

The stimulation of entertaining Mr Montague had made sleep impossible for the Armitage girls. Clad in night-gowns, their hair down, the sisters lay side by side across Pippa's bed, kicking their legs and rolling about like foals in a meadow.

Pippa's gestures were sudden and theatrical. She was a dramatic sort of person, for ever posing and pirouetting and tossing back her ash-blonde hair with such force that it seemed as if her slender neck would snap.

One disadvantage of leading a sheltered life was that Cassie's moods were constantly being imposed upon by those of her sister and every change in the Armitage girls' circumstances had been paced to accord with Pippa's needs.

She was, she knew, more intelligent than her sister. She had taken more learning than Pippa ever had from the various God-fearing instructors whom Papa had employed to round out his daughters' education. Even so, Cassie remained enslaved by her sister's vivacity, by that childish

32

energy which had no consistency to it but gushed and bubbled like an unchannelled spring.

She lay on the bed tummy down and listened with mounting bewilderment while Pippa sang the minister's praises and engaged in speculations so wild that Cassie could hardly follow them, particularly as neither she nor Pippa could do much to make themselves attractive to a man who had lived as Robert had done and who, at thirty-eight, was so much older than they were.

'What would you do,' Pippa whispered, 'if he came to us now? I mean, if he climbed up the ivy, knocked upon the window and implored us to let him in?'

'Don't be ridiculous. It's raining.'

Cassie glanced at the lead-paned window. The half-length floral curtains had not been closed. Pippa liked the view of the riding lights of cargo vessels out there on the river. The glow of the oil lamp was reflected in the window glass and the image of bedsheets and plump pillows seemed to hang in darkness beyond the ribbons of rain that weaved over Normandy Road. She and Pippa were out there too, robed in white cambric, hovering in space like wingless angels.

'If he did, though,' Pippa whispered, 'what *would* you do?'

'I – I don't know.'

'You'd let him in, wouldn't you?' said Pippa, slyly. 'I know I would. I'd fling open the window and invite him to join us.'

'Mr Montague would never do such a thing.'

'He might,' Pippa said, 'if he were driven by passion.'

The meaningless word chimed in Cassie's head. She could not imagine Robert Montague clinging to wet ivy below their window, not for any reason. Instead she conjured up a vague image of Robert kneeling on the ground, like Jesus, hands clasped and face raised to heaven, mimicking the passion that the preachers talked about.

'I'd give him – what did Nancy call it? – a proper eyeful.'

'Oh, stop it,' Cassie snapped.

She had been listening to Pippa's prattle for so long that it had become not merely monotonous but offensive.

'I really think it's time we went to bed,' Cassie said. 'I'm beginning to find this conversation very tiresome.'

'You sound just like Papa when you put on that voice,' Pippa said. 'What's *wrong* with you? Don't you think Robert's interested in how we look?' She knelt upright and stretched her arms high above her head. 'I wonder how many Russian ladies he saw in their nightclothes.'

Cassie rolled away and flung herself to her feet. Pippa's teasing bothered her more than she cared to admit. She preferred to think of Robert as he was now, not as he had been in time past.

'Oh, she *is* in love,' Pippa chanted softly. 'Our Cassie's in *looove.*'

'What if I am?' Cassie snapped. 'It's got nothing to do with you.'

Pippa giggled again and let herself topple on to the quilt. She lay on her back, exposing her legs.

'If you wait too long,' Pippa said, 'it will have.'

'I beg your pardon?'

'Robert would be a good catch for any girl,' Pippa said. 'I'm not sure I'd want to live in the manse, though. It seems such a gloomy place.'

'That's only because the Calderons did nothing to it.'

'I wonder what Robert will do to it?'

'Brighten it up, I expect,' said Cassie, relieved that Pippa had turned away from teasing. 'He's waiting for furniture arriving from England.'

'Is he really? When did he tell you that?'

'When you were out of the room.'

Pippa digested the information. She was calmer now. The lace around the collar of her nightgown rose evenly in rhythm with her breathing.

She said, 'If you did marry Robert, he'd be my brother-in-law.'

'Of course he would.'

'That might be rather nice,' said Pippa.

'On the other hand,' Cassie said, 'Mr Montague may have someone else in mind altogether.'

'For instance?' said Pippa.

Cassie hesitated and then said, 'Bella Coulter, perhaps.'

'Oh, Lord, yes. Bella Coulter. How absolutely awful and how absolutely perfect.' She laughed and Cassie laughed too. 'You wouldn't wish that fate on poor Robert, surely?'

'No,' Cassie said. 'I most certainly would not.'

Pippa turned on to her elbow and seriously and solemnly said, 'I think it must be one of us, dear, don't you?'

And Cassie, equally seriously, answered, 'I do.'

Three

The shipping agents who unloaded Reverend Montague's possessions from the lighters at Ravenshill's quay were unable to determine from whence the consignments had originated, for everything was packed in wooden crates so stoutly secured with nails and rope even the most determined carrier was unable to prise up the boards to nose about inside.

The cost of packing, let alone shipping, indicated that Robert Montague was no pauper and that whatever plans he had for refurbishing the manse would surely enhance its appearance and bring credit to the parish. A fact less reassuring to the conventional members of the minister's flock was that he chose to live alone. He imported no manservant, hired no cook or housekeeper and, apart from retaining the Calderons' gardener, seemed unwilling to staff the house at all.

The subject of the minister's 'domestic arrangements' was tactfully raised at the first Session meeting of the new term and Mr Montague indicated that he was perfectly able to look after himself, at least for the time being. Having been a soldier of sorts for many years he declared that he was not lacking in the skills of bed-making, cooking, and washing his own shirts; a radical announcement that brought sniffs of disapproval from those elders who were shocked by the very idea of doing anything that smacked of woman's work. The majority, however, professed themselves admiring of the minister's self-reliance and put it down as idiosyncratic but not reprehensible.

Cubby Armitage had more information than most as to what was going on at the manse. He made a point of visiting the house one quiet afternoon on the pretext of calling upon the minister.

'Painters,' he told Norah, later. 'Painters and varnishers. Carpenters and joiners. Cabinet-makers and paper-hangers due to arrive from Glasgow any day now, at Montague's expense, I gather.'

'Settling in,' Norah stated.

'And I have never seen so much foreign furniture,' said Cubby.

'German?'

'Worse.'

'Not French?'

'I don't know what fashion it is, my dear,' Cubby said. 'Oh, I recognise bookcases when I see them, and andirons and rugs, but, grand though it appears, it isn't a house I would want to live in.'

'No servants yet?'

'None that I could see.'

'Servants first,' said Norah, sagely, 'then a wife.'

'Do you think so?'

'In that order,' Norah Armitage said.

What Robert Montague did with his leisure time was less of a mystery. He was here and there and everywhere, sampling the pleasures of tables and cellars in and around the parish. Sir Andrew had him to dine at Flail House. Ewan Flail took him riding in the parks and shooting by the loch. But there were no young Flails currently on the marriage market to catch the minister's eye and the aristocratic gap was rapidly filled by members of the local bourgeoisie who considered Mr Montague quite the best catch ever to enter the Ravenshill pond.

All this information came to Cassie and Pippa via their visits to the old women who were prime sources of parish gossip and could tell you who had bought a new gown, who had hired a hairdresser and which past-her-prime spinster had suddenly taken to using face enamel and hair dye. It was said – by old Mrs Calderon, of all people – that you could hardly breathe in the kirk these days for the pong of *Rose en tasse.*

The Armitage girls were undaunted by such acerbic observations and by the time that the big moons of the harvest month had waned and the leaves came falling thick and fast, it was obvious to everyone, not least Cassie herself, that her dream of marrying the new minister was in danger of becoming a reality. While the Reverend Montague might sup with other parishioners, the Reverend Montague was no longer surveying the field.

Cubby was anxious to impress the minister with his worth and to discover by exchange of confidences just how well off Robert Montague might be and what he, Montague, might expect to take Cubby's elder daughter off his hands. On such delicate matters Robert Montague would not be drawn, though. He was too much the sponge, too much the clam. He sucked in all the information that Cubby chose to impart and gave out nothing that Cubby could confidently carry back to his wife.

The other side of Robert's courtship of Miss Cassie Armitage was more easily accomplished. Now that she had accepted she was not for him, Pippa had become a little zealot in the cause of love and would carry secret notes from Robert to Cassie and ask no reward but a share in the reading of them. They were, disappointingly, hardly love letters at all and began with Scriptural quotations and ended with blessings. Between the professional niceties Robert did manage to insert a tender line or two, expressing not love but fondness and giving no hint as to the true tenor of his desire.

For Cassie and Pippa it was enough to pore over the sentiments which, they both agreed, were devout and devoted and much more sincere than the gushings of some young fool with more heart than head.

What Cassie did not share with her sister were the unsatisfactory feelings that came over her whenever Robert laid his hand upon her shoulder or stroked the side of her neck. His attentions were never insistent, the contact never prolonged but the effect of his touch was mesmerising and not entirely pleasant. Cassie did not dare mention her doubts to Mama, for Mama would have been angered to learn that Robert had abused the trust that had been placed in him by touching her at all.

Cassie, therefore, kept her apprehension to herself and consoled herself with the thought that after marriage, when she had become Robert's wife, he would somehow make everything right.

On the twenty-third day of October, after dinner with the family, Robert requested that Cassie be allowed to walk with him as far as the garden gate.

Lights from the parlour window and the open door outlined the gravel and the row of painted stones that marked the border of the lawn. There was a piece of moon among scudding cloud and a strong wind blowing off the north and the garden rustled with fallen leaves and the boughs of the oaks creaked.

Cassie, with a shawl about her shoulders, clung to Robert's arm with one hand and kept her bonnet in place with the other. Robert wore a long, loose overcoat and a silk half-topper with the bands tied under his chin; minister's sober garb, but with the wind flapping his coat skirts somehow dashing and distinctive. His hair, longer than was fashionable, whipped about his brow and he slipped a hand discreetly around Cassie's waist to protect her from the buffeting.

Mama would be watching from the window, Papa lurking in the hall, as if she were a valuable possession, like an Old Testament wife; something that did not seem to trouble Robert at all.

One moment she was walking on the path, the next she was standing on the grass as if she had been carried there by the wind. The evergreens swayed all about her and she could hear the massy sighs of the dense little trees.

Robert put both hands about her waist and kissed her urgently on the mouth. His ardour needed no interpretation. Even so, when he kissed her once more Cassie did not understand the significance of what was taking place between them or what Robert intended by it. Fear of disappointing him prevented her from pushing him away and when he slipped a hand beneath her shawl and caressed her throat, she instinctively cocked her head as if to offer the length of her neck to his fingers.

'Oh, yes, Cassie,' he said. 'Yes, you will make me a good wife.'

She felt a shrinking within her, a kind of revulsion.

'I'd dearly like to marry you,' Robert murmured. 'Would you like that, my darling? Would you enjoy being my wife?'

'My father, my papa . . .'

'In two weeks, or three, when the manse is ready,' Robert told her, 'I will ask him for your hand. Meanwhile, between you and me, all other things being equal, would you agree to become my wife?'

'Is this – are you . . . ?'

'I am.'

He had made no mention of love. She wondered if a touch, a rapacious kiss were what men substituted for soft words, if men preferred to demonstrate rather than explain what they found desirable.

She said, 'Do you wish me to answer you now?'

'Most certainly. I need to know where I stand.'

'Do you not require me to love you?'

'Love me?' he said, taken aback. 'What do you mean?'

'To cherish you with all my heart.'

'Ah!' he said. 'Yes.' He paused, not touching any part of her. 'And don't you – cherish me with all your heart?'

'I do not know whether you love me – or not?'

'Of course I love you. Good Lord, girl, do you think I would put myself in this position if I did not love you? I have no doubts about you. If you don't hold me in the same high esteem as I hold you then say so, and I'll take myself off and you will not be bothered by my attentions again.'

'I did not mean . . .'

'What *do* you mean, Cassie?'

She could taste the air on her tongue, the cold air from far away.

Panic left a nebulous trail of doubt in its wake. The marriage proposal was not as she had thought it would be. But then life so far had been nothing but a series of expectations and disappointments and she had no reason to suppose that courtship and marriage were not links in the same chain.

'If you ask me properly, Robert,' Cassie said, 'I will give you an answer.'

'Now, do you mean, right now?'

'Yes, right now.'

'Cassie, will you marry me?'

'Yes, Robert,' she heard herself say. 'I will.'

Todd Brownlee would have had her stay with him, if only to save her the cost of her room in the Arms. When he was sober, which was most of the time now, he was as smart as the next man and, in matters of money, smarter than most. Nancy was tempted to tell him the truth about her lodgings and if it hadn't been for Daisy she might have done so.

She would lie with him in the old iron bed in the fourth-floor room, feel the warmth and size of him and and think how nice it would be to stay here, at least until he got tired of her and went back on the bottle, beat her or threw her out.

So far, though, she had seen no evidence of his violent temper. In fact, Ravenshill's dramshops were packed with men much worse than Todd Brownlee. He had a steady job. He paid his rent regularly every Saturday, cooked his own meat, washed his own clothes and, to her surprise, bathed at the stone sink on the second landing when there was nobody around to see him. It did not take Nancy long to realise that Todd Brownlee was nothing more alarming than a solitary man getting on with the business of living. Perhaps that was why the fancy women and layabouts despised him, because his industry and self-reliance challenged their laziness.

Fondness for drink seemed to be the Beast's only weakness. In spite of it he did not seem to be short of shillings. He was proud of the fact that he had never missed a shift, neither day nor night, and got on well with Mr Dunlop, master of the firm for which he worked. He told Nancy that Mr Dunlop had tendered for the work of clearing middens and cesspits thirty years ago and had kept the contract even after the law changed and the removal of night-soil was restricted by the council to the hours between midnight and five in the morning. He told Nancy that out of the twenty men that Mr Dunlop employed he was the only one who would undertake double shifts, working days on the dust-cart and nights on the sewage tubs, three or four nights in every week.

He also confided in Nancy that he had been raised in the old foundlings' ward on Gracefield Street before they knocked the building down. He did not seem shy about his origins and Nancy was tempted to tell him that she too had come up through the charity system as a workhouse girl. But she was still ashamed to admit that she had been discovered naked under a whin bush near Bramwell eighteen years ago and that if it had not been a warm summer night she would have died soon after she had been born.

She visited Todd every day that work allowed, every day except Sunday. She would wait for him in the early morning, before daylight. He would come around the corner from Rathbone Street with his canvas jacket buttoned tight, his hat pulled down, reeking with the sweetish odour of the pits he had been paid to clean. He would grin when he saw her and his broad shoulders would lose their stoop. 'Aye, lass,' he would say, 'I'm fair pleased to see you but we'll need t' be quick for I'm off on the midden cart at eight o'clock sharp.'

Quick she was too, so brisk that by the time Todd had washed himself in the sink on the second landing, she had sawed up a bread loaf and fried it in slices, had broken eggs and fried them too and had breakfast ready, sizzling, on a tin plate. And he would come in, half naked, with a towel around his shoulders and his soiled clothes cradled in the crook of his arm.

There was precious little in the room, only a fireplace, a cupboard, two chairs and a table, the bed, a pineboard dresser and a kerosene stove. The box-shaped stove gave warmth on cold mornings and upon it Todd fried his meat. Before eating he would take a bottle from the cupboard, pull the cork with his teeth, and would drink from the neck. He would hold the spirits in his mouth and let them trickle down his gullet to loosen the taste of the night work or the dust of the work of the day and when he had finished his breakfast he would turn and put out his hand in a manner she always thought princely and let her lead him to bed.

It did not seem to matter to the dustman that she had rough cheeks and a nose bent a wee bit out of shape. Todd himself was no oil painting. She reckoned him to be about fifty years old. He carried not one ounce of fat on his body, though the hair on his chest was whiter than the hair on his head. His hands and arms were latticed with scars, some small and delicate, others long and deep, like knife wounds. She did not dare ask him how he got those scars. She had troubles enough of her own without taking on Todd Brownlee's burdens.

It was October before things changed.

They were lying under the blankets. It was cold in the room, the smell of kerosene strong, the room lit by the stove's blue-edge flame and a faint gaseous glow in the sky above the ironworks which silhouetted Todd's vest and shirt and woollen combinations, wafting on a drying-line at the window.

Nancy was sleepy, thinking of nothing, when, without warning, Todd said, 'Where is it you come from, Nancy?'

'Not so far away.'

'Across the bridge?'

'Aye, across the bridge.'

'Was it somebody there done for your nose?'

She slipped her arm from about his chest and cupped her hand over her face to hide the blemish. 'Nothin' wrong wi' my nose.'

'Except,' Todd said, 'it's been broke.'

'It happened a long time ago.'

'Who broke it?' Todd said. 'Was it one o' the sailors?'

Nancy sat up. She leaned into him, her small, cone-shaped breasts pressing against his ribs. 'The what?'

'You know what I mean,' Todd said. 'One o' your men.'

'Do you think I'm just a puss that takes on anyone?'

'You took me on quick enough,' he said.

'I took you on when you were so rotten drunk you couldn't even remember who I was from one time to the next.'

'It wasna me broke your nose.' He hesitated. 'Was it?'

'Don't be so bloody daft.'

She suddenly realised that she wasn't afraid of Todd Brownlee and that she was at liberty to give him an earful now and then.

'Well,' he said, 'I was thinkin' – I mean, if it *was* a man done in your nose–'

'None o' your business how I got my nose,' Nancy interrupted.

'I'd do the same for him.'

'You'd what?'

'Point him out to me, lass, an', by God, I'll make sure he rues the day he ever laid hands on you.'.

Nancy hoisted herself on to her knees and peered into Todd's face. She saw that he was serious, that he meant what he said. 'You'd do that for me?'

She could see his teeth, white in his swarthy face. She understood now why they called him the Beast, not for his manner or habits but for the look of him, more dangerous at rest than in motion.

'Aye,' Todd said. 'I would.'

'What,' Nancy said, 'would you do to him?'

'Do y' know who he is, then?'

'I didn't say that. I asked what you'd do to him.'

He glanced at her slyly. She glimpsed something in his eyes which she had never seen there before, something to which she could not give a name.

'Whatever you wanted done,' he said.

'Would you – would you murder him?' she said, half joking.

'If you asked me to, aye.'

She placed her hands on each side of his jaw and held him so that he could not look away. 'Have you murdered a man before, Todd Brownlee?'

'I'm not sayin' I have, I'm not sayin' I haven't.'

'Would you really do a murder just for my sake?'

'Who is he?' Todd said. 'Just tell me his name.'

'His name,' Nancy said, 'was Ferris.'

'Where can I find him?'

'It's too late. He died o' the influenza two winters ago.'

'Who was he then?'

Nancy covered her face with her hands and wept.

Cautiously Todd reached out to her, put an arm around her waist and drew her to him. She felt his fingers in her hair, his hand encompassing her skull as easily as if it were a round Dutch cheese. He patted her awkwardly and made noises in his throat as if he were weeping too.

'Tell me,' Todd said, 'what happened?'

'Ferris took me,' Nancy sobbed. 'He took me before I was a woman. When I wouldn't do what he wanted, he slapped me. When I screamed he hit me wi' his fist. Wi' the blood still flowin' down my face he forced me.'

'Where did this happen, lass?'

'In the Ravenshill workhouse.'

Her cheeks were streaked with tears. Her nose ran, as if confession, her first confession, had wrung blood from the damaged tissues. She shrank from Todd Brownlee before he could shrink from her. He did not thrust her away, however, but continued to hold her firmly in his arms.

'My God,' he said, 'so you're a workhouse girl.'

'See,' she said, 'I'm no better than you are.'

'Aye, an' no worse,' Todd said. 'Ferris was what? A governor?'

'Superintendent.'

'He was never caught, never reported?'

'Not him,' said Nancy. 'Who'd dare clipe on a super-intendent?'

'It's different now,' Todd said. 'There's the Poor Law . . .'

'What law?' said Nancy. 'There's just the same old law, as far as I can see: take what you want if you think you can get away wi' it.'

Why had she told Todd Brownlee something she had told to no other living soul? Perhaps because he had been kind to her. Perhaps because he had been a workhouse bastard too. Perhaps because he had offered to take revenge on Ferris on her behalf. Perhaps she might have let him do it too if Ferris had not been roasting on a spit in hell.

She felt her tears dry and be replaced by an itchy warmth. She rubbed her eyes with her knuckles and almost blurted out the rest of it. But there would be time enough for that later, after Todd had proved himself.

She bit her lip, then laughed, slipped a leg over him and straddled his body. Perched on his muscular belly, she leaned forward and kissed his mouth and rubbed her cheek against his grizzled beard.

'Would you really do that for me?' she asked.

'Do what, lass?'

'Murder a man?'

'Aye,' Todd said. 'Oh, aye.'

'Even a stranger, even a man you'd never met?'

'D' you have somebody particular in mind?' Todd said.
And Nancy Winfield, smiling, answered him, 'Not yet.'

Robert had been to dine in the Vulcan Club in Glasgow
with Sir Andrew Flail.

The brotherhood of gentlemen who had acquired the
handsome Georgian mansion in the heart of Glasgow had
more to gain by the purchase than mere relief from the
fluttery distractions of women and the monotony of home
cooking. The Vulcan Club was bound by few of the strictures
that governed the city's other mercantile societies. Its dinner
parties and luncheons were distinguished by a cosmopolit-
anism that cut against the grain of the times. The only
criterion which one had to meet to join was a powerful
connection with all things mineral, for the club's main
purpose was to put buyers and sellers together and rig the
price of iron products throughout half the civilised world.

Robert felt as much at home in the Vulcan as he had
done in Constantinople's barnyard hotels or the sweltering
alleyways of Jerusalem's gold market and he was far from
bored by Sir Andrew's talk of tonnages, beam loads and
borrowing rates. Looking round the Vulcan's elegant
supper room it had struck Robert that whether trade was
conducted in the fluting tones of Syrian shepherds, in
guttural Russian or in the oatcake and kipper voices of
educated Lowland Scots mattered not, since the basic
human condition was best described by an adage as old as
time itself – that power was money and money was power.

It was late when the men left the club for the ride back
to Ravenshill in Flail's carriage. The coupé had been in Sir
Andrew's family for years. He saw no reason to replace it
with something more modern. The cut-down chariot had
graceful lines, leather-button upholstery and Argand
lamps. It was fast and stable and he used it for all his
journeys to and from the city. Horses and coachman knew
every rut and cobble between Glasgow and Ravenshill and
the drive was conducted at dashing speed.

There was no conversation. Sir Andrew was sleepy and

Robert wrapped up in his thoughts. Sullen-eyed, he watched the road roll by, flanked at first by building sites, waste lots, warehouses and coves of black water where the river showed. Then it was Ravenshill's slums and chimney stacks and Flail's Blazes spewing out smoke and little gouts of fire.

Robert felt on fire tonight too. Longing smouldered in his loins and he nursed a strange sense of danger linked to the frustration that went with being a clergyman in a small parish. He could not do as other men might do, pluck a girl out of an alleyway or send for a serving wench willing to do what he asked of her, to take her punishment and her payment and keep still.

Be patient, Robert told himself sternly. *Damn you, be patient.*

When the coach swayed past the Armitage house he looked up through the trees and saw a lamp still lit behind the mullion window and glimpsed there – or so he imagined – a figure in a filmy white nightgown and he let out such a groan that Flail roused himself and asked, 'What? What?' only to be told that he, the minister, was almost home.

Robert was dropped off at the gate at the bottom of the manse drive. He walked between the evergreens and the rearing oaks with the gaunt outline of the house to guide him. It was not until he reached the spot where the lawn dipped into the shrubbery that he noticed a glint of light in the long window that marked the position of the staircase. He watched the yellow light smear and diminish then reappear in the bedroom.

He darted across the corner of the lawn to the gable wall and into the kitchen yard at the rear of the house.

The faint odours of cattle dung and poultry droppings still pervaded the yard, for the Reverend Calderon had kept cows and hens behind the house, like a Highland crofter or a Palestinian farmer, living cheek by jowl with his beasts. The yard was slippery with mud and Robert picked his way across it with care. Eventually he reached

49

the kitchen door, quietly opened it and slipped into the manse by the back.

Holding his coat about him, he made his way by the servants' stairs to the hall and advanced up the main staircase to the first landing.

There was a sword, pistols too, in his army trunk but the trunk was stored in the cellar and he did not have time to search for it. Besides, there was more eagerness than fear in his belly, a trace of the dream that his young bride-to-be had suffered a fit of longing akin to his own and that she, or perhaps her sister, had come to appease their curiosity.

What really fired his blood, though, was the more credible suspicion that he might find a man upstairs, a robber or thief. In his present mood he would be more than a match for any intruder, would soon have them at his mercy, bound hand and foot, to taunt and torment a little before he stalked off to the gardener's cottage and despatched the gardener's boy to fetch a constable.

Past the first landing, past the gallery, up the narrow staircase that led to the bedrooms and the library where he had last seen the light; he crept stealthily along the passage until he saw the light again, shining, unwavering, below the bedroom door. He paused, removed his hat and topcoat, rolled the coat around his forearm then touched down the polished brass door handle and hurled himself into the room.

Save for a short cashmere robe which barely covered his modesty, the man on the bed was naked. His hair was crisp and fair but thin above the brows. He had a monkish look, ascetic yet at the same time animal.

He was propped up in the narrow iron bedstead, shoulders resting on a horsehair bolster, ankles comfortably crossed on the embroidered spread. He supported a book in his left hand, a cigar in his right and a copper ashtray the size of a soup plate was balanced on his bare chest. He blew out tobacco smoke in a thin, expert plume and grinned at Robert boyishly.

'Heard you a mile off, old chap,' he said. 'I think you're losing your touch.'

'Johnny! Good God!'

'Put down thy shield and buckler, for heaven's sake, and come and give me a hug. Didn't you get my letter?'

'No.'

'Oh! Oh, well, perhaps I neglected to send it,' said Major Johnny Jerome and, putting aside book, ashtray and cigar, rolled blithely from the bed and stood upright. 'What's wrong, Robert? Ain't you pleased to see me?'

'Yes, Johnny. Oh, God, yes,' Robert declared and, without further hesitation, embraced his old comrade warmly, man to man.

Four

It was not cold, hunger or rigid orphanage routines that
eventually turned Nancy against the institution and its
inmates. Even her treatment by the superintendent had
seemed no more than the due of a workhouse girl who was
too young to realise that hypocrisy was a basic human
condition and that the world was not naturally divided up
into those who gave and those who were given to.

The humiliation that Mr Ferris inflicted on her was
certainly a factor in hardening her heart but less so than
the manner in which he separated her from her companions. Sensing that something had upset her, Nancy's
friends were sympathetic at first and offered her plenty of
opportunity to share her troubles. But she could not bring
herself to talk about what Mr Ferris was doing to her
because she was afraid of what Mr Ferris *might* do to her
if she spoke of it.

Out of fear and blind obedience she refused to discuss
the acts that took place in the dank, stone-walled
bathhouse, on the wrinkled rug before the fireplace in the
superintendent's office or in the stuffy little alcove behind
the hall that was used for teaching and for prayers. She had
no choice but to do what Mr Ferris ordered her to do, to
keep mum about their 'friendship', as he liked to call it,

smiling and showing his small, sharp, seed-like teeth. Thus she had been drawn into collusion with Mr Ferris and separated from the community to which she belonged. Except that she was not separated at all. She was still there among them, a number on the slate, a name painted on the bed-end, a tin cup and tin plate, a psalm sheet, a pair of cheap boots, still a burden to the burgh and a blot on the face of decent society and she could only hide the truth by shunning her friends and becoming silent and surly.

Naturally they in turn shunned her. They reckoned that she had become Mr Ferris's 'pet' and had lured him into favouring her over them, though what gain there was for Nancy, what promise of betterment, none of them stopped to think. They turned against her swiftly and thoroughly. They spat into her porridge. They peed into her boots. They smeared her bedsheets with dirt. They tripped her, pinched her, jeered when she cried and, straight-faced and unflinching, they pointed their fingers straight at Nancy whenever Miss Gullion or Mr Beatty looked round for someone to blame.

'Nancy,' they would cry. 'Nancy Winfield done it.'

The situation was no better in the nail factory where Nancy worked. All healthy orphans from the Ravenshill workhouse had their first taste of employment at Chisholm's nail factory. They were hired out as day-labourers by the Parochial Board as soon as they reached legal age and spent ten hours a day standing at the rakes where the nails came shovelling down.

Ten hours a day sorting and counting according to type: clamp nails and clench nails, deck nails, rose nails, scupper, rother, white tacks and brads. Domestic orders packeted and boxed. Grand little workers, workhouse girls. Able to read. Able to count. Nimble. Not given to sucking their thumbs. Hands the colour of gun-metal, nails broken, palms suppurating, fingers bleeding. Earning their keep at last.

Even in Chisholm's, though, Nancy Winrield was ostracised and tormented. Her quota was spilled by accident, her dinner-time tea tainted, her piece of bread and lard dropped on the floor. If she wept the foreman beat her about the ears. If she cried out in frustration Mrs McGonigle, one of the nail-makers, was brought down from the nail press to throw her across the table and switch her calves until they bled.

Nancy had no choice but to choke back her anger and her tears and turn for comfort to the person who had ruined her. She even began to look forward to coupling with him, to having his arms wrapped about her, his belly slapping against hers. She even tried to kiss him now and then but he would have none of that and pushed her face away.

Then, one day, her bleedings started. Mr Ferris noticed it. He grew very angry. He struck her, struck her again and again. He raged at her as if it were her fault. He told her it was over between them and that if she knew what was good for her she would keep her mouth shut or he would send her away. Soon after that he took up with another young girl, Jeanne, and there was nothing Nancy could do about it, nothing she could say or do to get him back. When she looked at Jeanne, though, when she saw how ugly the girl-child was, how stupid, she realised that she had been duped.

'What's Mr Ferris doin' to you?' she tackled Jeanne.

'Nothin'.'

'He told you not to talk about it, didn't he?'

'Never said nothin'.'

'It's wrong. He's supposed to look after us.'

Jeanne stared at her, dumbly. 'He likes me, but.'

'He's got a wife. He's got girls your age.'

'Aye, but he fair likes me.'

'You've seen them at the Sabbath services.'

'I'm no' sayin' anythin' tae you, Nancy Winfield. Mr Ferris telt me you were bad.'

'Oh, aye. I'm bad,' Nancy said. 'I'm bad – an' I'm gettin' worse.'

Sunday meant rest, rest and monotony. It meant trying

not to drowse in your seat on the hard bench in the hall while Mr Calderon or Mr McAlister or one of the other ministers on the workhouse rota conducted the prayer service at eight o'clock in the morning. It meant Bible Class from eleven until noon, psalm-singing in the evening. It meant that Mrs Ferris, a stout, moon-faced woman some years older than her husband, would appear in all her finery and parade at her husband's side, her sons and daughters trotting on her heels like pages.

They seemed so aloof, so haughty, those Ferris children. So well fed and well dressed that they were detested, not for anything they said or did but for what they represented and the fact that they came and *went again*.

Governors visited now and then, councillors, Poor Law inspectors, observers from the charities and the Parochial Board. Christmas saw them all out in force to hear the orphans sing benisons to the Lord. But every Sunday morning, rain or shine, there were the Ferrises, feathered and pantalooned, gloved and scarved, and Mr Ferris with them, the perfect image of a family man. What Nancy saw, however, were girls almost as grown up as she was and a wife with a fat face and a fancy bonnet and a man who had panted and grunted when he had discharged into her and who beat her whenever she disobeyed.

On a rain-wet Sunday in the month of November, two months after he had cast her aside, Nancy finally took a stand.

It was nothing more dramatic than that – a stand. She stood up out of the rows of near-grown orphans. Stood straight up, hands folded as if she were praying, turned her head and when Mr and Mrs Ferris came down the central aisle towards her stared at them, stared at them hard.

'Sit *down,* Winfield, sit *down,*' Miss Gullion hissed.

'Gurl, gurl,' said Mr Beatty in a stage whisper, 'what's come o'er ye?'

Nancy ignored the attendants' injunctions and plucking hands. In the silence that blanketed the workhouse inmates, she remained standing until the Ferrises had passed and then, as abruptly, sat down again.

Mr Ferris sent for her right after service. She knew he would. He had her hauled out of the dormitory by Mr Beatty and marched down to his office.

Sabbath smells, subtly different from weekday odours, pervaded the stone-floored corridors, dampness tinged with sanctity. It was not to this austere building that Nancy had been brought as a new-born infant but to the old pauper ward behind the cowsheds in Andover Street, a ramshackle, cosy kitchen-nursery where babies were weaned, cribbed and coddled, taught to walk and talk by the displaced dames of the parish, kindly old widows and impoverished spinsters who earned their keep by tending the orphans without any 'laws' to guide them.

All that had changed when the councillors had put out money on the building of a new workhouse. Then men and women were rigidly separated, mothers and children were torn apart and babies were reared by so-called nursemaids, employed, it seemed, for their cleanliness and for their severity. It was no longer considered dignified for a superintendent to reside on the premises and Mr Ferris was allocated a trim little half-villa on the toll road. Workhouse orphans were no longer regarded as children cursed by ill luck but rather as cogs in the great machine of council welfare, victims of local politics and its managed charities. No matter what changes were made, though, there would still be a man waiting for you at the corridor's end, someone with more authority than you would ever have, a man with a rod in his hand and scowl on his face.

'That will be all, thank you, Mr Beatty.'

'Aye, right ye are, Mr Ferris,' the deputy answered and, because he knew his place, went out and closed the door without protest.

'Stand there, girl.'

'I've done nothin' wrong,' Nancy said.

'Oh, have you not? Let me be the judge of that.'

'You're not goin' to beat me.'

'Making a display of yourself, an' a fool of me, by

disturbing an act of holy worship. You were warned, Winfield. You can't say you weren't warned.'

'I'll not take your stick.'

He stroked the cane, rubbing his fist along its length. He gave it a little swish in Nancy's direction. In days past she had accepted even this from him, had yielded without protest to his fumbling, had let him throw up her skirts and thrust her down across his arm, had let him rain blows upon her, bruising her flesh and narrow bones, sending pain into all her parts.

But on that Sabbath morning with rain sprinkling the panes and the fire unlit she knew that she had the upper hand.

'What?' Mr Ferris said.

'Put me out to service. I'm old enough,' Nancy told him.

'Who would take you as a servant?' Mr Ferris said. 'Nobody wants a workhouse girl.'

'You can arrange it for me. Find me a place an' I'll be gone.' She hesitated. 'An' you'll feel better.'

'God, but you're a sly wee devil. Is this blackmail?'

'I don't know what you mean, Mr Ferris.'

He was not a handsome man. He was not even clean. The boys in the boys' ward, soaped and scrubbed and shaven-headed, were cleaner than he was. He was upright, tall, his cheap morning coat shiny with age, his waistcoat coarsely repaired. Only the watch-chain, symbol of his office, seemed to have any real weight and substance in the grainy daylight. He twisted the rod in both hands and then flung it down into the brass stand by the door.

'You mayn't know what it means,' he said, 'but you damned well know how to make it work for you.'

'I want to leave here.'

'Leave then. See how you like it, girl, when you're starving in the streets.'

'You can't send me off wi'out a job to go to.'

'Who told you that?'

'It's the law.'

'Mr Chisholm might take you on, if I put in a word.'

'Service,' Nancy said, 'not the nail factory.'

'By God,' Mr Ferris said, 'what makes you think you can demand things of me? What's got into you, Winfield?'

'You have, Mr Ferris,' Nancy answered. 'You have.'

At which Mr Ferris nodded and, to her astonishment, sent her away without a beating.

Six weeks later, just after Christmas, she was abruptly removed from the orphanage and escorted by Mr Beatty to a fine house in Ravenshill where, without interview or inspection, she was put to work as a scullery-maid in the household of Cuthbert Armitage.

Todd had devoured the slice of spiced pork that she had cooked for him and all the cabbage and boiled potatoes too. Now, satisfied, he removed from his trouser pocket one of the flat, black bottles. He uncorked it, not with his teeth but his fingers, slopped the dregs from a teacup, poured a finger-measure of the pale, straw-coloured liquid into the cup and pushed it towards her.

'Don't you want to go to bed?' Nancy asked.

'I want you to have a drink with me first.'

'I'm not much of a one for the drink.'

'It'll keep out the cold, lass.'

'I'll be warm enough in bed,' Nancy said.

'Drink,' he said, 'first.'

'Is that a fresh bottle?'

'Aye.'

'Where did you get it?'

'From O'Toole.'

'That villain,' Nancy said. 'What did it cost?'

'Pennies,' Todd said. 'Try a sup, go on. By way o'celebration.'

She peered suspiciously into the cup and sniffed at the contents. The reek of the stuff that O'Toole labelled 'whisky' made her flinch for, curiously, ever since her nose had been broken her sense of smell had grown more acute.

She said, 'What are we celebratin'?'

'My birthday.'

'How do you know it's your birthday?'

'I looked up the date in the register before I left the workhouse. Besides, it's wrote down on my articles.'

'I didn't know you were articled.'

'Aye, I've a trade certificate somewhere.'

Nancy let this information sink in.

Todd had wheedled an account of her girlhood from her piece by piece. He had cajoled her into talking about the workhouse by recounting his own experiences there. How different the institution had been in his day. The boys slept on a dirt floor then and grub was ladled out from a big pan hung on hooks over an open fire. The older boys were sent out to scrounge for firewood and the daring ones among them snared rabbits on the riverbank and Mr Beatty, father of the Mr Beatty she'd known, turned a blind eye to the origins of anything that happened to turn up in the pot.

In those days, Todd said, casuals, indigents and orphans had all mucked in together, living as jolly as tinkers, before the damned parish council developed a conscience and erected proper buildings for the poor.

'What trade?' Nancy said.

'Carpenter.'

'Why don't you work at it?'

Todd shrugged and shook the flat bottle as if that were answer enough. 'Anyway,' he added, 'these days, there's more money to be made shiftin' dirt than shavin' wood.'

'What age *are* you?'

'Fifty.'

'Fifty?' Cautiously, she said, 'You're not so bad for fifty.'

'Mr Dunlop says I'm well preserved. I think he means pickled.'

'He may be right at that,' Nancy said. 'Fifty, my God!'

She gave a *tut* to show her disapproval but raised the cup to her lips, swallowed a mouthful then, coughing, said, 'If I'd known it was your birthday, Todd, I'd ha' brought you somethin'.'

'You've brought me enough already, Nance.'

'What've I brought you?'

'Yourself.'

'Hah!' she said, pleased. 'You pay for me, though.'

'I don't pay for you. An' if I do, I don't pay enough. None of the other women I've ever had have looked after me like you do.'

'What other women?' She feigned shock. 'I never knew you'd had other women.'

'They never stayed long.' He shrugged. 'They robbed me, some o' them, when I was in drink. They robbed me, then they left me. I suppose it was the drink.' He peeped up at her. 'When I was in drink, I hurt them.'

'You'd better no' hurt me,' Nancy said.

'I'd never do that,' Todd said. 'Anyway, they weren't like you.'

'What were they like, then?'

'More like me.'

'I'm like you.'

'Naw, you're not,' Todd said, then asked, 'Do you know who your daddy was?'

The question caught Nancy off guard. She shook her head.

'I know who my daddy was,' Todd said.

'Who was he then?' Nancy prompted. 'Was he famous?'

'He was a sailor,' Todd told her. 'He was a black man an' a sailor.'

'Black? You mean from Africa?'

'I don't know where he was from, just that he was a black man.'

'But you're not black.'

'I'm black under the skin, though.'

'Where is he now, your daddy?'

'They hung him.'

'Who hung him? For what did they hang him?'

'He murdered my mammy.'

'You're makin' this up, Todd Brownlee.'

'Nah, I'm not. Mr Beatty told me.'

'Then Mr Beatty made it up.'

61

'I've seen the sheet,' Todd informed her.

'Sheet?'

'The broadsheet. My daddy's last confession. The whole story. He murdered my mammy wi' his bare hands on the steps o' the Argyll kirk in the year o' 1809. His name was Lee Brown,' Todd said. 'That's why I'm cried Brown-lee.'

Nancy sat back in the wooden chair. He did not seem to be teasing her. He was fidgety and embarrassed and too large a man to hide his discomfort. He was, or appeared to be, all on the surface.

Once at the Bramwell Fair she had seen a black man dance, his arms and legs going in every direction at once, while he played on a one-string fiddle and grinned at the orphans Mr Beatty had taken out for an hour, grinned and smacked his lips as if he would eat them all up. She had sometimes seen black men on the quays and dusky men, small and solitary, who were sailors on the clippers that brought the tea from India. She did not know if it were possible to have a black daddy and a white mammy, to take after one and not the other but she had a suspicion that Mr Beatty's father had made it all up and that the printed broadsheet referred to somebody else entirely.

'Where did they hang him?' she asked.

'On Glasgow Green. They dragged him out o' the jail an' hung him on a pulley near the old cattle mart. It caused a fair sensation at the time.'

'I see,' Nancy said. 'An' they gave him, this black man, time to make a last confession before they thrawed his neck, I suppose. Where were you?'

'Me? I was . . .' Todd sat back. Obviously he had never asked himself the question before or had it asked of him. 'I was only a babby. Only' – he held his hands out, six or eight inches apart – 'only this size.'

'So you were born before she was dead?'

'What? Aye, aye, 'course I was. I could hardly have been born after she was dead, could I?'

'Oh, I've heard o' that happenin' too,' said Nancy.

'Do you no' believe me?'

'Aye, I believe you. I just don't know why you're tellin'
me these things.'

'In case,' Todd said.

'In case what?'

'In case you have a babby.'

'Eh?'

'In case it's black.'

Nancy began to laugh. She could not help herself. His
solemnity was too much for her. Todd was not pompous,
nor was he trying to elevate himself in her eyes. His
warning was genuine and his belief in his origins would
have been touching if it had not been so obviously a story
made up to console a wee orphan boy. She laughed and
laughed. She rocked in the chair, rocked so wildly that she
was in danger of tipping it over. She braced her knees
under the table and might even have taken the table over
with her if Todd had not been leaning on it.

At length, she wiped her nose with her wrist and
gasped, 'Och, Todd, what a funny chap you are.'

'It's not funny havin' a black daddy.'

'I know that.'

'What for are you laughin' then?'

'I'm not goin' to have a babby.'

'You might.' He paused. 'Unless you can't.'

'Oh, I can,' Nancy blurted out. 'I can. I've got . . .'

This mention of babies brought to her mind the image
of Daisy, Daisy in short clothes and lace bonnet, pink-
cheeked and white as a snowflake, lying in her crib in
Madame Daltry's house.

'Got what?' Todd asked.

She pushed herself away from the table and began to
gather the plates.

He caught her wrist and asked again, 'Got what?'

'Let me go, Todd, you're hurtin' me.'

'Just tell me why you can't have babbies,' he said. 'Is it
because o' what Ferris done to you?'

'Aye,' she said. 'Aye, Todd, that's why, that's the reason.'

She was relieved that he had misunderstood her, so

relieved that it did not occur to her that she might have to live with the lie, that the lie might affect what Todd thought of her. Her intention was only to avoid having to admit that she had borne a child already, that everything she did was for Daisy's benefit, that her reason for being here with him at all was because he paid her so well.

He planted an elbow on the table and stared at her. 'Are you sure, Nancy?'

'Aye, I'm sure.'

'I thought,' he said, 'I thought I'd like to have a family.'

'Why would you want t' bring bairns into *this* world?'

'Because this world's the only one I'm sure of,' Todd told her, 'an' my time here's gettin' short.'

'I'm not wantin' babbies,' Nancy said, adding, 'even if I could have them.'

He reached in his pocket and brought out the bottle again. He pulled the cork with his teeth and, tipping back his head, drank.

He sighed and said, 'I thought we might get married.'

'What!'

'Get married, live here, have bairns.'

She leaned her hip on the table and slid towards him. She put one thin arm about his neck and drew his head against her belly. He neither yielded nor resisted but simply let her do as she wished with him.

'Would you really marry the likes of me?' Nancy said.

'Aye, I would.'

'Huh!' she said. 'Look at me! I'm as ugly as a pug.'

'Naw,' he said, scowling. 'Naw, naw, you're not. You've as pretty a face as I've ever seen. The face of an angel.'

'If you think that you must be blind as well as daft, Todd Brownlee,' Nancy said, though she was pleased by his flattery.

Todd paused then said, 'Nancy, will you marry me?'

And Nancy, quick as a lightning flash, said, 'No.'

Five

The day began with a cracking good fire lighted in the kitchen range, the smell of frying bacon and the sound of eggs sizzling on the skillet that Johnny had lugged through one campaign after another and upon which he could perform such miracles of cooking that there was no saying how many he could have fed from it, given the right number of loaves and fishes and a little seasoning.

That breakfast smell, that wonderfully honest aroma, had hung in the desert air of Syria, had pervaded the spice-heavy verandas of the Indian residencies and had even overlaid the stink of marsh-gas and rotting corpses along the banks of the Alma. What Johnny Jerome and his skillet brought to Ravenshill was a zest that scandal had all but erased from Robert Montague's life. Even the way Johnny crouched on the kitchen flagstones, barefoot and bare-legged, bathrobe clinging to his narrow shoulders and tight buttocks, hair bristling and sidewhiskers uncombed, seemed like a vision from the past.

Robert came down from the bedroom eager for breakfast.

Major Johnny Jerome, late of the Queen's Engineers, would turn his head, would grin and wink, would jerk his wrist and dexterously toss the omelette on the skillet, folding the yolks in on the knob of butter that gave the eggs their special richness. And afterwards, when third cups of coffee had been poured, they would light up the day's first cigars and, with neither cook nor mistress to forbid them, would puff away to their heart's content.

The peaceful idyll would not last long, of course, for the tide of Robert's affairs was on the flow again and he was in no position to back-paddle.

He had explained to Johnny that he had deliberately chosen Ravenshill as a refuge and that he intended to remain here, marry and settle down.

'Have you selected the wife yet?' Johnny asked.

'I have.'

'This Armitage girl you spoke of last night?'

'That's the one.'

'She hardly sounds your type, Robbie.'

'Perhaps not. She is, however, the type expected of the wife of a minister in Ravenshill.'

'I see,' Johnny said. 'Presumably she has the ability to handle a little music, a little drawing and lots of needlework?'

'Oh, she has other attributes, too.'

'Do you mean in a housekeeping way?'

'Of that I'm less sure.'

'And is she a horse that will require but little riding to break to the saddle?'

Robert grunted. 'I'd forgotten how vulgar you can be, Johnny.'

'Vulgar? Why I thought I was being awfully restrained.'

Robert tossed his cigar butt neatly into the fireplace, stretched his arms above his head and yawned.

'Cassie's a pretty girl,' he said. 'She'll not challenge me. She'll make me a home and bear my children and leave me to get on with the rest of it without complaint.'

'Render you free, in other words?'

'Marriage is a far from perfect institution, Johnny.'

'Yes, I have observed as much, which is the reason I choose to remain a bachelor.' Johnny ran his hand over his wiry hair and scratched his chest lazily. 'I take it that your dear, decaying father will approve of your choice?'

'Without doubt.'

'And of her family?'

'Yes. Cuthbert Armitage will pose no threat to my father's notion of what an in-law should be. There are no skeletons in the Armitage cupboard, just a kind of stupidity which, fortunately, does not extend to money matters.'

'Ah, I thought there would be money in it somewhere,' said Johnny. 'When you marry, old boy, do you suppose that your inheritance will be restored to you? Will your dada forgive and forget?'

'I am an ordained minister with a busy little parish of my own,' Robert said. 'All that's required to restore me to full paternal favour is the acquisition of a pious little wife.'

'How much *will* you come in for, old boy?'

'Six hundred a year, or thereabouts.'

Johnny whistled. 'I see why you're anxious to restore yourself in your dada's eyes. Think I might be tempted to give up my fun for a reg'lar six hundred quid.'

'Oh, that's only a beginning,' Robert said.

He took the long-spouted copper coffee pot from the hob and, holding his cup in the palm of his hand, poured a stream of the thick, black liquid into it while Johnny continued to scrutinise him with a queer little wrinkle of interest marking the corner of each eye.

'I thought you were set on penning another *magnum opus*?' Johnny said.

'My commentary on the Book of Enoch, do you mean? Enoch is interesting enough,' said Robert. 'Who could fail to be interested in a prophet who dwelled with the angels and had such marvellous visions of judgement and, by the by, managed to father Methuselah?'

'Enoch will make you no chink.'

'Sadly true.'

'Is the girl worth something?'

'I'm not marrying her for *her* money, only to lay hands

on what's mine by right. She'll come with something, I'll make sure of that. Armitage, her father, is a stockbroker, after all, so he can't be short of a shilling or two.'

'A stockbroker, you say? That's interesting. Who else do you know in these parts that might prove useful?'

'Andrew Flail, my sponsor, is a gentleman of considerable influence,' Robert said. 'So, you see, we already have all the necessary elements ready to hand.'

'Yes, even I can see how certain opportunities might unfold before you.'

'Before us.'

'Us?'

'Unless you have other plans?' Robert said.

'Plans? No, I've no plans at all,' said Johnny Jerome, in surprise. 'I'd half a notion to go south again, seek employment on some engineering project or another and, if that failed, to take passage for the Cape. An engineer can do well for himself in Africa, so I've heard.'

'What of your family?'

'My family,' Johnny said, 'rubs along very well without me.'

'If I asked you to, would you billet here with me?'

'With you and your new little wife?'

'Certainly.'

'In what capacity?'

'I could hardly employ you as my butler, could I?' Robert said.

'Hardly. And I'm the wrong sex to be taken on as a housekeeper.'

'Why don't you just stay on as my friend and companion?'

'What will your wife have to say to that?'

'She'll accept you, as I do,' Robert said.

'And the parish elders, your flock?'

'They may think it a little bit odd at first but they'll soon accept you too. They are, I assure you, very susceptible to charm.'

'When do you intend to marry?'

'As soon as possible.'

'Has the girl . . .'

'Yes, she has agreed to become my wife. All I have to do now is to tackle her father and I see no obstacle in that direction. Eight weeks or so by way of an engagement and then I'll go to the altar.'

'After which you won't need me,' Johnny stated.

'After which I'll need you more than ever,' Robert said. 'During my nuptials you'll have to make yourself scarce, of course. Also while my father's here on his obligatory visit. Then back you come and I'll see to it that you have room and board for as long as you wish.'

'In exchange for what sort of service?'

'You may manage my affairs, if you feel up to it.'

'I see,' Johnny Jerome said. 'Well, it's certainly something to consider.'

'As to exactly what you might do—'

'Servants,' Johnny interrupted. 'You've a fine residence here but not a single trustworthy servant. What sort of staff do you require?'

'A cook, of course, parlourmaid, scullery-maid. But not, emphatically not, from around these parts.'

'Easier said than done,' said Johnny. 'But, yes, you may count on me.'

Robert Montague grinned. 'Pig-iron.'

'What?'

'Pig-iron, Johnny. Pig-iron. What do you know about puddling, rolling and forge-castings?'

'A little, not much,' Johnny admitted.

'Find out as much as you can, as soon as you can.'

'Are we going into financial partnership, by any chance?'

'I do believe we are, Johnny,' Robert Montague said, 'unless you object to making yourself a fortune?'

'Damned if I do,' said Johnny Jerome, grinning too now. 'Damned if I do, old boy.'

Robert Montague's courtship moved to its climax with

remarkable alacrity. It was conducted formally and correctly, of course, but somehow lacked the leisurely pace that Cassie had associated with courtship proper. On the evening of the minister's 'official' visit, when the deed would be done, there was in the Armitage household a decided air of nervous anticipation. Robert had declined an invitation to participate in the evening meal and declared that he would call round later, after the conclusion of his monthly meeting with the Presbytery.

Norah chose to wear brown, a colour that did not entirely suit her. She topped off the ensemble with a hair decoration so bristling with wires and cloth-cut rosebuds that she appeared to be almost twice the height of her husband. Cubby, however, was resplendent, hair sleeked down like sealskin, eyebrows trimmed and nails pared. Polished shell notwithstanding, he had a deflated air, almost as if he were taking part in the last meal of a condemned person and not joyfully anticipating the arrival of a future son-in-law.

Halfway through a dish of Mrs McFarlane's *coq au vin* Norah slapped down her fork, fixed her husband with gimlet gaze and snapped, 'Cuthbert, stop fretting about the dowry.'

Pippa lifted her eyebrows and enquired in a piping voice, 'Why is Papa worried about dower money, Mama? Is somebody getting married?'

'Be quiet, Pippa,' said Cassie.

'But *is* somebody . . .'

'Don't be a fool, Pippa,' Mama told her in a tone so severe that it silenced everyone for the rest of the meal.

At a quarter past nine o'clock, Robert arrived.

Cassie remained in the drawing-room with Pippa and Mama while Mr Montague and Cuthbert took themselves across the hallway into the library where sherry and cut cake awaited them.

Cassie stitched at a sampler that had not seen a needle in six months. At the pianoforte, Pippa picked out a melody with one finger and, leaning her elbow on the rococo shelf, sang to herself:

In the gloaming, oh my darling,
When the lights are dim and low,
And the quiet shadows falling
Softly come and softly go.

Norah sat motionless by the fire, ramrod straight, hands folded one over the other in the lap of the brown velvet dress. Her face was angled towards the window which, though curtained, seemed to draw her gaze out over the hidden garden, over the river, over fields that were fields no more.

In the gloaming, oh my darling,
Think not bitterly of me,
Though I passed away in silence,
Left you lonely, set you free;

Pippa sang in a sweet wistful little voice. Her occasional hesitations while she searched for a key added to the sentiment of the song as if, Norah thought, her daughter was aware of the wraiths of memory and sadness that haunted the house and family; and what, on that night, was being lost.

For my heart was fast with longing,
What had been could never be,
It was best to leave you thus, dear,
Best for you and best for me.

With a final ironic *plink* on the keys, Pippa stopped playing and turned. 'That's all I can remember, really.'
'Where did you learn that song?' Norah said.
'Nancy Winfield used to sing it.' Pippa leaned across the lid of the pianoforte, her body elongated, her waist, lithe and ungirded, twisted under pink silk. 'What are they

71

doing in there? How long does it take to pop the question, for heaven's sake?'

'That's quite enough of that sort of talk, Pippa,' Norah said sternly.

It was as if, Cassie thought, the betrothal of a woman to a man was so girt around with superstitions that it must only be referred to obliquely. She was suddenly impatient for the courtship to be over, for an end to secrecy, to discover what would be expected of her in exchange for Robert's protection.

'Cassie,' Pippa squeaked, standing up, 'behold, he comes.'

When the drawing-room door opened, Cassie could not raise her eyes. She gripped the rim of the sampler with both hands.

Papa entered the drawing room. He moved slowly and looked pale. He turned and closed the door carefully. Robert wore black, all black, except for the lace frill at his collar which was startlingly white. He folded his arms and inhaled a deep breath.

Papa positioned himself by Mama's chair. He cleared his throat.

'Cassie, my dear,' he said, 'Reverend Montague – em, Robert – has asked permission to make you his wife. He informs me that he believes you are not averse to this arrangement. If this is the case then I am willing to give my – em – permission for a union between you to take place.'

Robert came forward.

Removing the sampler from Cassie's hands, he placed it upon the floor. He did not kneel. He did not throw himself before her. He crouched so close to her that she could see nothing but his face. He slipped his hands under her fingers. He lifted them to his lips, kissed her knuckles and said, 'Cassie, will you?'

She could not look away. It was as it had been that very first day in church, except that she had no need to attract his attention now. That was all it had taken, a glance, a moment of contact. So simple, so uncomplicated, it still

72

seemed like one of Pippa's fantasies. Everything she had known would be altered by what she said next and she would be changed in ways that she could not even begin to imagine. And she knew that she had erred, that she did not love him. She could not evade her promise, though, could not take back that first bold glance or deny the excitement that his attention had brought.

'Papa, do you wish me to marry Robert?'

'Yes, yes, that I do,' Cubby said. 'An excellent match, Mama, don't you think? An excellent match.'

Norah may, or may not, have nodded.

'Very well,' Cassie said. 'I will.'

Robert kissed her fingers again and laid his hand lightly upon her knee.

She had said it. She had committed herself. There could be no going back now. Celebrations, congratulations, the reading of banns, invitations, gifts, dresses and flowers were only part of the pretence that their union was divinely blessed, when all it meant was that, at some hour in the future, she must surrender to him in body as well as soul.

Robert got briskly to his feet. He shook Papa's hand. He kissed Mama on the cheek. He embraced Pippa and whirled her about him in a gay little dance.

'First I will arrange a dinner party at the manse,' he said, 'and I will make the announcement of our engagement then. I'll invite Sir Andrew, of course, and my father will come down from Inverness. After which, I'll have the banns declared, attend to all the legal folderol of licences and contracts. We will be married soon after the first of the year, if you're willing, my dearest?'

'Who will officiate?' Pippa asked.

'Mr Salmond.'

Cubby was impressed. 'Will Mr Salmond really do the honours?'

'I'm sure he will not refuse,' Robert said.

'Will there be a ball afterwards, Robert?' Pippa cried.

'Oh, yes, we will have a ball, such a ball,' Robert said

and, taking her by the waist, swung her round again as if she, not Cassie, were really his bride-to-be.

'Are you still awake, dear?' Cubby said.

'Yes.'

'Too excited to sleep, I expect.'

'I was waiting for you.'

'Oh,' Cubby said, unsure.

She lay on her back, arms by her sides, legs extended. The brown dress hung on a rack in the corner and the hairpiece, like a gigantic horse chestnut, loomed large on the dressing-table. Only a flat little candle floating like a rose petal in a glass water-dish gave light. He could just make out Norah's nose above the border of the quilt. He unbuttoned his waistcoat and trousers and struggled out of them.

'Cuthbert, are you drunk?'

'No. No. I admit I had a dram or two. With Robert.'

Without stirring, Norah said, 'What did he ask for?'

Seated on the bed-end Cubby stooped over to furl down his stockings, puffing and grunting with the effort.

'How much?' Norah said.

Cubby sat up, a stocking dangling limp in one hand.

'I offered him one thousand. He seemed satisfied with that. He said he would not trade on my good nature by putting me under an obligation to provide Cassandra with – em – additional goods.'

'He wants something,' Norah said. 'I know he does.'

'Certainly, certainly. He wants a wife and we should thank the Lord that he has chosen our Cassie. I mean, she could ask for no better husband, could she?'

'That,' Norah said, 'remains to be seen.'

'I must say,' said Johnny Jerome, 'I do like this room. You've done it out a treat, Robbie. Reminds me of the consul's hideaway in Constantinople. Was that what you had in mind, old boy?'

'Of course. Do you recognise the ottoman?'

'Indeed, I do. You don't mind me lounging here, Robbie, do you? Here, in your private quarters, I mean?'

'Certainly not,' Robert Montague said. 'You have the run of the house.'

'I wonder what the lady will think of it, though.'

'Of what?'

'This, your Turkish room.'

'The lady will have her own quarters.'

'Has she asked for a separate boudoir?'

'She hasn't asked for anything yet.'

'Is she really such an innocent?' Johnny said.

'Very much an innocent.'

'She accepted you, though?'

'She did.'

'And her papa?'

'Delighted to welcome me into his family.'

'What did he offer you?'

'She comes with a thousand.'

Johnny whistled. 'Not bad for a provincial stockbroker.'

'It's her trust fund, left to her by a grandfather.'

'Didn't you try to beat the price up?'

'No, a thousand will do me for now.'

'All's well, then?' Johnny said.

'All's well.'

Johnny shifted his hips on the red plush sofa. He had placed a gold-embroidered bolster behind his back and a smaller version of the same supported his naked feet. He looked comfortable, indolent, somehow installed.

He poured brandy, added soda water and offered the glass up to his friend, as if he, not Robert, were the host.

'What's wrong then?' Johnny said. 'Why so glum?'

'I'm tired, that's all.'

'Don't lie to me, Robbie. What's really round the back of this black mood?' Johnny laid aside his glass and reached forward to touch his companion on the shoulder. 'I cannot believe it's guilt. I thought you'd done with guilt.'

'It isn't guilt, no. I don't know what it is.'

Johnny sat back against the bolster, wary and no longer

75

relaxed. He knew Robert Montague only too well. These dark moods were part of his character, an expression of the simmering violence that had almost destroyed his career. It had been said in the ranks that Chaplain Montague preached against sin from a knowledge of sin, but what that knowledge entailed few men would ever guess.

There was in Robert a streak of madness that had been hidden by the madness of war but he, Johnny, had glimpsed it on more than one occasion and it had always frightened him.

'Is it marriage itself?' Johnny said. 'Is that the rope that binds?'

'Yes, you may be approaching the truth there.'

'It's not too late to slither out of it, you know.'

'It is, John. Oh, alas, it is.'

'But *would* you? Would you slither out of it if you could?'

'Probably not, no.'

'You're not falling in love with Miss Armitage, are you?' Johnny asked.

'Cassie? Good God, no.'

'Well, that's a relief.'

'It might be easier if I were,' Robert said.

'Easier on whom? You or her?'

'On both of us,' said Robert.

Six

Madame Euphemia Daltry was about as French as an Arbroath kipper and, in the opinion of certain gentlemen, even more tasty.

Conjecture as to her origins was useless, however. She told the same far-fetched tale to everyone and the inhabitants of the riverside village of Greenfield had no option but to accept their most obvious citizen at face value.

Face value was certainly good enough for the gentlemen callers who came along the parkway to brave the slabber of byres and strew from livery stables that ornamented Greenfield's lopsided main street.

The Daltry 'rez-ee-donse', at the far end of the parkway, stood on a prominent knoll, shawled by horse chestnut trees, backed by firs and fronted by a beautifully mown lawn that sloped down to the edge of the river. The house was so elegant that it had become a landmark for lightermen and pilots who would grin and relate to impressionable cabin-boys the story of the mysterious French lady who dwelled therein, as if Greenfield was Circe's island or Madame Daltry one of the Lorelei. The legend was hard to sustain, however, even on gullible Clydeside, for it wasn't pigs that scampered about

Madame's manicured lawns or sinuous maidens who waved to the boatmen from the rocks, only small, toddling children, and, here and there among them, a nursemaid in a starched apron and mob-cap.

Hard of heart you would have to be, though, not to respond to the fluttering handkerchiefs of Madame's little charges who, in short frocks and bonnets, presented a picture more sentimental than sensual.

Much the same could be said for the lady herself.

She was as warm and flowery in December as she was in May and nothing seemed to affect her sunny disposition; not weather, not illness, not stock market ups and downs or tantrums in the children or the frequent calamities that beset her female staff. Madame Daltry greeted each crisis with the same disarming smile as she greeted her patrons, that same soft pursing of the lips, with the tip of one tooth showing, like a tiny piece of enamel.

Gentlemen in the know – that is, butlers and valets and trusted agents of the well-heeled reprobates who patronised Madame's establishment – were to a man in love with her inviting smile. The curious thing was that while they adored her they did not actually lust after her. What they felt for Madame Daltry was a reflection of what she felt for her little charges, a protective loving kindness, unadulterated by ulterior motives.

Madame Daltry was small and plump but her heart-shaped face and almond-shaped eyes were just as appealing now as they had been twenty years ago when she had been married to a French aristocrat with the unpronounceable name which she had later abbreviated to Daltry. He, the French aristocrat, had been the dispossessed heir to lands on the Loire, lands which he sought to reclaim by legal proceedings, lands which, according to Madame Daltry, might well have become his again if he had not been fatally wounded by rival claimants and had died with his head on her lap and her name on his lips.

Her chocolate brown eyes would still become moist when she related this ridiculous story and her smile would quiver when she repeated her husband's dying words, 'Euphemia, Euphemia, *ma chérie*, kiss me and send me to God.' The frequently repeated confession turned butlers, valets and agents weak at the knees and generally prompted them to offer an extra half crown or sometimes even a guinea to put into the Treat Box for the wee ones, an act of charity which never failed to cheer the dear lady and restore her good-humoured smile.

The women who visited the Daltry residence were just as sympathetic to charitable principles but were marginally less impressed by Madame Daltry herself.

Housekeepers, governesses and personal maidservants, however powerful in the domestic arena, somehow lacked the tone of their male counterparts. In them an august bearing or aloof manner seemed like severity and Madame Daltry could not abide people who were severe, even if they carried the half guinea which was her weekly fee for caring for the not-quite-unwanted children of the middle class of society.

Nancy Winfield was certainly no lady and was certainly not severe. She considered Madame Daltry to be the most wonderful person on earth, a woman who deserved every penny that she extracted from her patrons and whose promise to turn Daisy into a lady of quality was accepted without question.

On her route across the parkway or up from the ferryboat steps, Nancy would sometimes pass one of the governesses or butlers. She would squint at them with more interest than they squinted at her, for they sailed past, noses in the air, as if she did not exist.

Nancy had been instructed to enter by the gate of the kitchen yard and to meet with her daughter, Daisy, on the drying lawns or, if it was particularly wet or cold, in the back hall of the staff quarters. There, for exactly an hour, she was permitted to pamper her perfect little lady who, indistinguishable in dress and deportment from other

Daltry charges, seemed far too well bred to have any connection with the wretched creature who endeavoured to hold her attention.

Even by the age of three Daisy had developed an indulgent attitude to her mother and played the silly games with which the woman attempted to entertain her with an air of superciliousness. In little Daisy Winfield there was no endemic warmth. Already she seemed self-assured and self-centred, as if she had been trained only to obey or to command. She hardly ever smiled, was never known to cry and according to Madame Daltry, was the perfect 'little guest', even if she did lack breeding and background.

On the point of breeding, however, even Madame Daltry was unsure of her ground. She had been unable to wheedle from the sad little trollop just who the parents of the child might be and in what precise relationship young Daisy stood to the Winfield girl. Madame Daltry had heard every possible variation on the theme of unwanted pregnancy and her ledgers contained a complete genealogy of such 'indiscretions' and lists of illicit infants one half of whose pedigree was too valuable to taint and who were too precious to somebody just to throw away.

Only Nancy Winfield had managed to evade Madame Daltry's rapacious curiosity for she, Madame Daltry, could not wring from the girl one clue as to who she represented or what injudicious act of love had brought Daisy into being.

At first she had supposed the Winfield girl to be the mother of the child. There was a tenderness there that strongly suggested it. But there was also the matter of the baby's clothing which, though a little old-fashioned, was of very best quality. The child was also clean and healthy, qualities that one did not associate with the offspring of street women.

On the other hand when the conversation took a monetary turn there was enough prevarication on the girl's part to hint that Nancy Winfield was not the go-between for some well-heeled gentleman or a lady of private means.

'The fee is a half guinea per week of keep,' Madame Daltry had told the girl who, at that point in the proceedings, still clutched the infant in her arms like a doll. 'Do you wish to convey that fact to whoever sent you?'

'It's too much.'

'Do you not have a gentleman who will pay?'

'He – we can't afford so much.'

'Is it really not your child?'

'It's my child now.'

'What do you mean by that?'

'She's mine because nobody else wants her.'

'Then convey her, and yourself, to the parish board.'

'No,' the Winfield girl had cried. 'No, I'll not be doin' that. I'll drown her first an' myself along with her.'

Madame Daltry had been taken aback. Enough lies had been thrown at her during her years in business to recognise truth when she heard it.

'He won't pay a half guinea,' the girl had said. 'An' I can't.'

'*Is* she your child?'

'I told you – mine now. I want her kept safe.'

Madame Daltry had studied the baby and then the girl. The girl was not coarse or ugly. In fact, if she had been fattened up a little she would have presented a very pretty picture indeed.

'To whom *does* she belong?' Madame Daltry said.

'I told you, she belongs to me.'

'How much can you afford to pay?'

'Half.'

'Five shillings and three pence? Why, foundrymen hardly take home so much. How can *you* afford such a sum?'

'I've – I've a backer. There is money attached. But it'll not be put out willingly.' The Winfield girl had bitten her lip as if she'd already revealed more than was wise. 'Five shillin' an' three pence can be managed, though.'

Further questioning had led to no firm conclusion.

Madame Daltry had taken in others at reduced fee before, the babies of genteel women who were less than well off. There had also been a vacancy in the nursery at the time. Added to which she had had a queer feeling about the Winfield baby.

'You must pay me by the week,' Madame Daltry had said. 'If you miss a single payment, for whatever reason, you will be expected to take the child away without any argument or tears.'

'She'll not be treated different, will she?'

'She will be treated as the others are treated,' Madame Daltry had promised. 'If, however, you or your "backer" fail to keep up . . .'

'We'll keep up,' Nancy Winfield had said and, to give credit where it was due, had met her obligation faithfully week after week ever since.

In exchange Daisy Winfield was well fed and well dressed. She was kept warm in winter, cool in summer and provided with a rudimentary education in deportment and the elements of social congress which would surely stand her in good stead. In four years' time, however, little Daisy Winfield would be too old for the nursery academy and Madame Daltry wondered what would become of her then. Were there 'relatives' who would adopt a well-mannered little girl?

Money enough in the pocket of the mysterious backer to install the child in a private school? Or would Daisy be sucked down into the bone-biting poverty which had scarred the Winfield girl and from which, no matter how lofty one's ambitions, how fierce one's determination, there was no hope of escape?

The prospect made Madame Daltry shudder.

For months Nancy's visits to Greenfield had been the only constants in a life dedicated to earning Madame Daltry's weekly fee.

Some weeks it was almost impossible to scratch five shillings from an uncompromising world. Some weeks, too many to count in fact, Nancy could not afford to put a roof over her own head or food in her belly.

On several occasions she had been so weak and sick that she had been tempted to steal to make up the shortfall. She was not by inclination a thief, though. She lacked the unscrupulous disregard for others that thieves must possess. She had taken on work, bits of work, any sort of work, to earn a shilling or two and when there was no work to be had she had slunk out on to the streets after dark and looked for earnings there. Her days, in fact, had become one long accounting, a balancing of nourishment against energy enough to do her work, to fetch in enough money to present to saintly Madame Daltry and to keep Daisy safe and secure and as far from the workhouse as it was possible to be.

Every Sunday afternoon Nancy received her reward. She put on her patched dress and darned stockings and polished her shoes with soot and made the trip to Greenfield to see her daughter.

Her spirits soared when she caught sight of the Daltry residence and she ran eagerly towards the kitchen gate to spend one glorious hour with her pretty, well-mannered little daughter. She considered it a miracle that Madame Daltry looked after the child so well and thought nothing of the miracles that she performed to raise the wind to pay for it.

After she took up with Todd Brownlee, though, things changed.

She still visited Greenfield faithfully every Sunday, still played with Daisy on the drying green or in the chilly servants' hall, still kissed her child and was dutifully kissed by her child in turn, and left again, already fretting about the source of next week's fee.

Her relationship with Todd Brownlee did not relieve her of this burden of concern. Todd was no miser but neither was he a millionaire. His wages were good by any standards but Nancy did not dare ask for more than he chose to give her. Consequently her secret, her Daisy, became a blemish on her feelings for the dust-cart man.

'Why will you no' marry me, Nance?'

'Because I don't want to.'

'You could come an' live here.'

'What would I do here all day an' half the night?'

'What you do now.'

'Look after you? Huh, it's just a servant you're wantin'.'

'I wouldn't be offerin' to marry a servant.'

'Because you'd have to pay her more than you pay a wife.'

'I just want to tak' care o' you, Nancy.'

'I know you do,' she would say, softening. 'I know.'

'Is there another man? Somebody livin' in the Arms, maybe?'

'There's no other man.'

'Where do you go on Sundays?'

'I told you, Todd, to the mission to hear the preachers.'

'Which mission?'

'Whichever one I fancy on the day.'

'Tell me the one and I'll come along wi' you.'

'You at a prayer meetin'? The preacher would have a fit if you turned up.'

'I'm entitled to say m' prayers like anybody else,' Todd would say. 'We're all equal in the eyes o' God.'

'When did you last say your prayers, Todd Brownlee?'

'Not so long ago.'

'An' were they answered?'

'Aye, they were answered. God sent me you.'

Nancy would pause. She had heard men say such things when they were less than sober, had heard the whisperings of seducers so unscrupulous that they would descend to any depths of flattery to lure a woman into bed with them, talk being cheaper than cash on the nail.

In spite of all the wicked things she had done, though, Nancy did not regard herself as irredeemable. When she prayed she prayed not for herself but for her daughter and for a blessing on Madame Daltry, who looked after her daughter.

As for attending prayer meetings, she went as often as she could, for she found comfort in being with others of her kind, those who had not yet given up all hope of finding peace on this earth and a place awaiting them in heaven.

Todd's sincerity both pleased and distressed her. She regretted having used God as part of her deception, in having deceived Todd Brownlee at all.

Even so, she put him off again and again in the weeks preceding Christmas. She might even have stopped going to Bengal Street altogether if she had thought less of him in other ways, ways that she could not explain even to herself.

The cook was a spinster in her thirty-ninth year. Until recently she had been employed as first kitchenmaid by the Duke of Arroll in Mackarness Castle. Her dismissal from that position, without letters of reference, had left her not only embittered but practically unemployable.

Johnny had got in touch with her through a domestic agency and had interviewed her in the agency's seedy little anteroom in Edinburgh. With Miss Rundall, as she called herself, came Janey. Janey was a willowy parlourmaid of eighteen or nineteen. She, it seemed, was much attached to the bosomy cook as was a sharp-featured little scullion named Marie. All three had been disemployed from the duke's service at precisely the same time.

'What for?' Johnny asked. 'Embezzlement?'

'No, Mr Jerome, not embezzlement,' Miss Rundall answered.

'He di'n't like us, sir,' the scullery-maid put in. 'He had a down on us.'

'Same as the butler,' Miss Rundall said.

'Butler had a down on us,' Janey said. 'Told fearful lies 'bout us, the pig.'

'Very well,' Johnny said, trying to hide his smile. 'I'll ask no more of you by way of explanation *if* you give me your word, all of you, that it wasn't drink or theft or a-riggin' of the larder bills that got you hoisted.'

'None o' those things, sir, I swear,' Miss Rundall said.

'Hands on hearts, ladies, please,' Johnny said.

They did not look like servants down on their luck. They were neat in person and clean about the fingernails. He suspected that the older woman, the cook, had licked the other two into shape. Their failing – an iniquitous failing in the eyes of most employers – was that they were far too sure of themselves.

Johnny took to them at once. He knew what they were, these three. He offered them terms and noticed how they glanced one to the other before Miss Rundall asked, 'Will we be doin' exclusive for men, sir?'

'You'll be doing for the minister, Reverend Montague.'

'He old then?' Janey asked.

'No, he not – he's not old. He'll marry in January, so there will be a lady to answer to shortly.'

'No butler, though, no footman?'

'Only a stable lad,' Johnny said, carefully. 'He'll have to be fed, of course, but he'll be billeted out of the house. The servants' hall will be yours, ladies, and yours alone.' He paused. 'If, that is, you feel three of you can cope with the proper management of the household. Otherwise . . .'

'Ain't no otherwise,' Miss Rundall said, lifting her bosom with the back of her wrist as if to let oxygen into her lungs. 'We accept the terms.'

'An' we can start immediate,' Janey added. 'If that's to your likin', sir.'

'It is,' Johnny Jerome said. 'It is, indeed. Very much to my liking.'

Even more to Johnny's liking was the stable lad he picked up in Leith that evening, a young orphan named Luke Simmonds who had been trained in horse management. With no kin to hold him in the east, Simmonds had travelled back to Glasgow with his new employer the next morning and had been at work before Robert had come in for lunch.

The women had arrived all together on the one o'clock

train and by dinner time that same evening Robert was convinced that Johnny had turned up trumps. He had gone down to the kitchen afterwards to meet the new cook for, minister or not, he had no 'side' when it came to talking with the lower orders. Besides which, he was only too well aware that he might need the loyalty of these people to help him ride out the difficult first months of marriage when – unless he missed his guess – Miss Cassie Armitage would be all at sea with household management.

They stood behind the cook's board studying him as intently as he studied them: a heavy-set woman, a willowy girl, a ferret-faced maid-of-all-work. Johnny did not have to tell him what they were or speculate on why they had been discharged from the ducal castle. Robert realised immediately that together they formed a female cabal and that in any large household where authority lay strictly with the males their unity would be perceived as a threat.

A broad-chested, fresh-faced young man with a cloth cap clutched in his hand and a muffler wrapped round his neck stood in the corner by the door to the yard as if he might at any moment have to make good his escape. He might safely leave Simmonds to Johnny, along with the purchase of a gig and a couple of horses. He nodded to the young man then turned his attention once more to the domestics.

'Do you have everything here you require, Miss Rundall? I mean in the matter of appliances and utensils.'

'Are we expecting large dinner parties, sir?' the woman asked.

'Three or four in the year, I would predict, with ten or a dozen settings at most,' Robert answered. 'As Major Jerome has no doubt informed you I will soon be embarking on the course of matrimony and there will be a certain flurry of sociability over the next few weeks because of that. I imagine it will not seem unduly strenuous to you after your experiences at Mackarness?'

'No, Mr Montague, it will not. We can manage a dozen without difficulty. I could do with a mortar, though, a big

87

'un, and a pestle to go with it. For a-poundin' of meat, you see.'

'Johnny?'

'I'll see what can be done.'

'Anything else, Miss Rundall?'

'A ice chest. For puddin's and summer drinks.'

'Of course.'

'I like to have a good supply of coal.'

'Delivery has already been arranged. Mr Pollock, the gardener, will call each morning at eight to ask what vegetables you need for the day and to inform you what soft fruits are in season. He will also, I imagine, be able to obtain game at reasonable cost.' He continued, 'There will be morning prayers in the dining-room on Wednesday only, a quarter-hour before breakfast. You will be expected to attend church on Sunday, one service only, and you may also participate in the Bible School meetings if you have a wish to do so.'

'But you don't insist on it?' said Miss Rundall.

'No, I do not insist upon it.'

They glanced at each other, passing some sign, some secret information down the line. He had not encountered such a banding of women before, not in Scotland. He would, he knew, master them. But Cassie would surely find them implacable for she was too young and pretty to find allies below stairs.

'I insist,' Robert said, 'upon punctuality, cleanliness and order, otherwise you will not find me demanding. It is not my intention, nor will it be my wife's intention, to entertain more than is necessary. I prefer a quiet life.'

'Who does we answer to, Mr Montague, now and for the future?' The cook bowed her wrist beneath her bosom and hoisted it above the crimping line of her stays. 'Is it yourself or the mistress?'

'You will answer to me, Miss Rundall,' said Johnny.

'Even when the wife – when the lady comes?'

'Oh, yes, Miss Rundall,' said Johnny Jerome. 'Now and in the future you answer to me.'

The woman's eyes widened. 'Is that how it's to be, Mr Montague?'

'Yes,' Robert answered. 'That, Miss Rundall, is how it's to be.'

Johnny lay back on the sofa. He sipped brandy and soda water and puffed on a cigar. 'Are you pleased with the staff then, Robbie?'

'Very pleased.'

Johnny held the brandy glass to the light and studied the glow within it.

'Listen,' he said.

'I hear nothing.'

'Precisely,' Johnny said. 'We might be upon another planet altogether up here at the top of the house.'

'I expect they're fast asleep.'

'One, two, three – in the same bed?'

'Hardly.'

'Not even for warmth?'

'Well, perhaps,' Robert conceded.

'Which one is in the middle, do you suppose?'

Amused in spite of himself, Robert grunted, 'The little one, the scullion?'

'Cookie, my money's on cookie,' said Johnny Jerome.

'Where's Simmonds billeted?'

'In the hay-loft above the stable.'

'It's frosty tonight. I trust he won't freeze.'

'If you're so concerned about the boy, why don't you tuck him in?'

'No, Johnny, I really don't think I will, thank you.'

Johnny Jerome shrugged. 'Couple of horses and a gig, a pestle for the meat, an ice cabinet, and your nest will be all ready for the bird to take occupancy. When will you show her the wonders you have wrought?'

'In eight or ten days,' Robert said.

'And your dada?'

'He will come down shortly before Christmas.'

'So, I'd better make myself scarce.'

'For a day or two, Johnny, just for a day or two.'
'Will you miss me, old boy?'
And Robert answered him, 'Not much.'

In summer months Greenfield parkway was a popular promenade. The good folk of Glasgow did not venture into the village, of course, where the odours were a mite too rustic to be wholesome and the clabber on the road could ruin your shoes. The broad path which followed the line of the river, however, carried much traffic of the strolling variety and, as a rule, it was not until she reached the last of the alders on the grazing strip that Nancy left the pedestrians behind.

The walk ended abruptly at a fence that overhung the Clyde. Only small boys and dauntless fishermen were ever to be found on the big stones beyond the stave fence, for the drop into deep water was perilous and the spot exposed.

It was upon this rocky outcrop that on a still, cold December afternoon, Nancy Winfield first encountered the weeping man.

The path by the Clyde was deserted. The river was tarnished like old tin, so calm and cold that not a ripple stirred the surface. Frozen to cottage roofs and chimneypots, even the gulls were silent; not a sound to be heard but the groaning of a cow from one of the byres, the melancholy croak of a rook from the elms behind the nursery and, as Nancy approached the parkway's end, faint sobbing.

Curiosity rather than pity drew her towards the sound.

She pulled her patched cape about her shoulders and stepped across the withered weeds to the fence.

She leaned over the paling and saw him below.

He was crouched on the rocks, fifteen or twenty feet above the water. His hands were cupped to his face like a person with a toothache and he was crying so sorely that Nancy's heart went out to him at once.

She called out, 'Sir? What ails you, sir?'

He glanced over his shoulder but did not leap up or change position. She thought she recognised his face, but could not put a name to it. She wondered if she had been with him at some time in the past; if, perhaps, he had taken her in a dark alley in one of the weeks when she had been strapped for cash.

'Go away, girl.'

'Are you sick, sir? Shall I fetch a doctor?'

'I've no need of a doctor. Leave me alone'

'You're not goin' to do anythin'–' she could not conjure up an appropriate word and, frowning, said, 'anythin' *final*, are you?'

'What business is it of yours what I do?'

He was no toff, no swell gent. No more, though, was he a fusty-man, a navvy or common labourer. He was well dressed in a heavy double-breasted Tweedside jacket with big flap pockets, chequered trousers and polished half-boots. His hat, a Bollinger, even had a cloth button on top.

'Go on about your business, girl, and leave me to mine.'

He spoke in a light voice that seemed ill-suited to anger or to despair. Arms resting on his thighs, he swayed dangerously close to the slope of the rock. Nancy gathered her skirts and, just as the bell of Govan Old Parish kirk away across the water clanked out two o'clock, climbed nimbly over the paling and went down through the boulders to join him.

At least he had stopped weeping now. She stood behind him so that he had to adjust his balance to see her and looked, Nancy thought with some relief, more steady and secure.

'What do you want with me?' he said.

Nancy said, 'If you are a-goin' to jump, sir, take the overcoat off first.'

'*What?*'

'I've a man friend could use a coat like that, if you're done wi' it. Aye, an' the hat too. Maybe the boots – *if* you're done wi' them.'

He choked on some emotion between laughter and

91

tears, then he got to his feet and confronted her.

'What makes you think I'm keen for a swim on a cold day like this?'

'I heard you cryin',' Nancy said.

'Can a man not express his feelings without some chit appearing out of nowhere to interfere? Are you from Greenfield?'

'No, I am not.'

'Well,' the man said, 'I am not going to jump, girl. I never had any intention of jumping. So I'm afraid I'll require my coat and hat for a while longer.'

Nancy was not intimidated. He was too soft-featured to frighten her. He had fine, sandy-coloured hair and brows so fair as to be almost white. He was hardly an old man, though. She took him to be about thirty-five and when he gave her a little grimace in lieu of apology she had a sudden glimmer of recognition.

She said, 'You're from over the river, are you not, sir? I think I've seen you somewhere in Ravenshill.'

'Does that give you the right to intrude?'

'I thought you might be in need o' help.'

'Well, I'm not,' then, relenting slightly, he added, 'but I thank you for the kindness, none the less.' He hesitated. 'Who are you? What are you doing here on such a miserable afternoon?'

'Visitin'.'

'A relative?'

'Aye.'

He studied her for a moment then, very deliberately, extracted a large handkerchief from one of his pockets and wiped his eyes with it. He tucked the handkerchief away again and, to Nancy's relief, stepped back from edge of the rocks.

'What's your name, girl?'

'Nancy Winfield.'

'Yes, I have seen you before,' he said. 'I've seen you at Madame Daltry's house. Is that where your relative lives? Your child?'

'How could I afford t' keep a bairn in a school like that?'

'It's where I've been,' the man said. 'To see my son.'

'Is that why you were cryin'? Because o' your son?'

'No, because of his mother. Two years ago, two years to the day – she died.'

'What was her name?'

'Elizabeth.'

'What did she die of?'

'A fever. She was fine when I went off to the works in the morning. By midnight she was past recall and before daylight came again she was dead.'

He spoke calmly, without a trace of self-pity. Nancy wondered at the fickle nature of the man, how he could shift from grief to explanation so quickly. Perhaps he had only needed somebody to talk to, even if that somebody was only a passer-by.

'The works?' she said. 'Do you work at Flail's Blazes?'

'Yes. I'm a manager there.'

'An' you go to Mr Lassiter's meetings on Wednesday nights?'

'Hah! So that's where I've seen you before,' he said.

'I don't get along to the mission much these days,' Nancy said.

'I do,' he said. 'I hardly miss a meeting, as a matter of fact.'

'Do you pray for your wife?'

'I pray more for myself, and for my boy, of course.'

'Why don't you keep him with you?' Nancy said.

'In a lodging-house? I suppose I could employ a nurse to look after him but I've seen what fumes from the flues can do to weakly children and I haven't enough time to devote to him. I mean, I can't be mother and father to him.'

'You could marry again,' Nancy suggested.

'I doubt if . . .' He shook his head. 'How do *you* manage? I mean, how do you afford Madame Daltry's fees?'

'I manage.'

'Does your man friend assist?'

'He does what he can.'

'Is he the child's father?'

Nancy did not answer. She had revealed too much already. He was too easy to talk to and she had learned to be wary of soft-spoken, patient men.

'I'm sorry,' he said. 'I've no right to ask such questions. What time does Madame Daltry expect you?'

'Two o'clock,' Nancy said. 'I'm late.'

'Yes,' the man said. 'You had better hurry along.'

'What about you? I mean, you're not . . .'

'No, no, I'm quite myself again, I assure you.'

He accompanied her to the fence and she let him help her over the paling. He climbed over after her and seemed to wish to accompany her towards the nursery school gate.

Nancy had no idea how Madame Daltry would react if she was spotted in the company of one of Madame's 'proper' clients but she suspected it would not go down well. She moved a step or two towards the lane then stopped.

The man put his hand into his pocket. She supposed that he was going for his handkerchief again but instead he brought out a horseshoe-shaped purse which he flicked open with his thumb.

'I'm sorry about the coat,' he said. 'Perhaps I may be permitted to make some amends.'

She looked at the sovereign in his hand and resisted the desire to snatch it from him. A sovereign would pay Daisy's fees for nearly a month.

'I'm not one to go takin' money from strangers,' Nancy said.

'In what other way can I thank you?'

'I'm no' needin' your thanks. I've done nothin' to deserve it.'

'Oh, but you have,' the man said. 'Believe me, you have.'

He was smaller than she had imagined he would be, lighter in build than seemed right for a foundry manager. She found it hard to imagine him giving orders to the muscular labourers who tended the furnaces. He held the sovereign temptingly in the palm of his hand, leaving the next move up to her.

On impulse she dropped him a little curtsey.

'Good day t' you, sir,' she said. 'I'll have to be goin' now.'

'Of course.'

He put the coin into the purse and the purse into his pocket and stood watching as Nancy hurried down the lane and, cursing herself for being so soft as to turn down charity, scuttled round the corner and headed at the double for the nursery school gate.

Seven

The manse which appeared so commodious from the outside seemed, at least to Cassie, depressingly cramped.

The rooms were not wanting in height nor was there any lack of apartments, but Robert had crowded every available space with his possessions. Hallway, dressing-room, drawing-room, dining-room, even the ground-floor 'facility', were crammed with books and traveller's trophies and packed with pieces of furniture in a wide variety of styles. It was not a woman's house and, Cassie realised, never would be. No matter how courageously she might try to alter it there was far too much of Robert here for her to hope to breathe simplicity into the place and render it less assertively masculine.

As she stood in the door of the drawing-room Cassie felt an irrational urge to turn and run home to Normandy Road and never set foot in the manse again.

Pippa nudged her. 'Oh, my Lord! Isn't it magnificent?'

'Yes, yes, it's . . .'

'Did I not tell you that Robert was rich? What a lucky duck you are, Cassie, marrying such an ideal man.'

Cassie had no stomach to argue with Pippa. She had lost all faith in her sister's judgement and was irritated by Pippa's proclamations. Pippa understood no more than she

97

did about marriage, what it would mean to be here, shut away with Robert and Robert's choice of servants for evermore.

In the mirror above the fireplace she caught a glimpse of herself, Pippa at her side, the pair of them in immature pink, frilly and ribboned and as fey as little flower fairies. They were not alone, however. Opposite them, spilling out of a silk-fringed chair, was an elderly gentleman in full ministerial rig.

Crisp white hair and side-whiskers, a snow-white stock above the clerical vest enhanced the stern lines of the face. Beneath the ascetic countenance, however, was a body of billowing softness, not fat compacted but fat loose, like a monstrous balloon halfway deflated. Each movement of the gentleman's dainty legs or his tiny hands caused his bulk to wobble and if there had been air in the room, a draught from window or door, it seemed to Cassie that the Reverend Angus Montague might have taken off and floated upwards to the ceiling.

The old minister studied Cassie and Pippa for a moment then gave a little nod as if to signify that, initially at least, they had met with his approval.

'My son told me you were a pretty pair,' he said. 'I see that his judgement was not at fault. Which one of you is destined to be Robert's bride?'

'I am, sir. I'm Cassandra.'

'Do you know who I am?'

'Robert's papa,' Pippa put in. 'Reverend Montague, from Cleavers in the county of Sutherland. Robert told us about you.'

'Did he, indeed?'

Angus Montague offered no gesture of greeting. He inched himself forward, the chair creaking under his weight, placed his small, pinky-white hands upon his knees and lifted his head so that the rounded crowstep of chins that hung from his jaw smoothed out into a single plump curve. He continued to inspect the girls as if they were specimens of a rare genus.

Pippa was undaunted. 'Cleavers is a very queer name for a parish, sir,' she said. 'Have you ministered there long?'

'It is not a large parish.' Angus Montague's voice was deliberate and grave, much firmer than his body. 'Nor is it in the least queer. I have ministered there for the best part of twenty years.'

Voices were heard in the hall and Robert ushered Cassie's parents into the drawing-room. He had deliberately allowed the old man and the young women a few undisturbed moments in which to size each other up but there was no cheerful cry of, 'Well, what do you think of her, Papa?' no sign of effusiveness, no apparent bond between father and son.

Robert's introductions were made with curt formality. But Cuthbert Armitage was so grovelling and self-abasing that Cassie was reminded of those devout adherents of the Roman religion who would prostrate themselves before bishops and cardinals and kiss their feet. Her father's obsequiousness stopped just short of throwing himself upon the carpet in front of the Highland minister before Norah was brought forward by the elbow to the velvet chair.

'My wife, sir. My spouse, my better half,' Cubby crowed.

Norah offered her hand and had the satisfaction – which her daughters shared – of seeing the old man struggle to his feet and, rather to everyone's surprise, brush his lips against Mama's gloved fingers.

Robert watched impassively for a moment then slid a hand behind his coat-tails and signalled to the maid who was hovering in the hallway.

The maid, not much older than Cassie, was tall and willowy. Dressed in dove grey, bibbed, aproned and capped, she displayed a confidence which increased Cassie's apprehension.

In response to Robert's signal the girl cleared her throat and announced, 'Dinner is served, sir, at your convenience,' as if the phrase had been rehearsed to bring to an undramatic end the first meeting of Armitage and Montague.

'Thank you, Janey,' Robert said and, extending his arm, politely invited his father to lead the way through to the dining-room.

In the night, in the darkness, while other folk dined by candlelight, Allan Hunter felt most alive. Gone was the despair that wrapped his soul in the daylight hours. With rain lashing the towers, a ferocious wind snarling round the furnace heads, fires roaring in the flues, red dust pouring from the vents, with the stink of sulphurous gases in his throat and the glare of molten metal blinding him, then, and only then, could he put the memory of his sweet dead wife to rest and for an hour or two feel like his old self again.

On the back shift in wild weather Allan did not have time to dwell on where Elizabeth had gone or why she had been taken from him. He did not have leisure to worry about his son lying in Madame Daltry's house across the waters of the Clyde. He was too stimulated to grieve. His senses were invigorated by the battering of the elements and the elemental nature of his work with ironstone, limestone, air and fire.

He understood how the men suffered on a night like this, how they revelled in their ability to endure. In his day he too had slaved in the bunkers, had frozen on the gantries, danced on the high platforms and sweated blood-red drops by the grates. Precious few jobs he had not done before he had come to Ravenshill to sell himself and his skills to the Flails.

Now he was a manager, the man in tweed, who had mastered the chemistry of the transmutations that heat wrought on ironstone and lime. He could read colours and weights as well as anyone, judge the quality of a casting by the way it flowed into the pig-bed. But he knew only too well that atoms and molecules, those measurable particles of matter, were nothing compared to the skill of human

100

hands and the courage required to deal daily with liquid fire.

Now, with Elizabeth gone into heaven and little Tom as safe as money could make him, he had rediscovered the spirit of recklessness which he had thought lost. He would stride brazenly along gantries thick with ice, would dance with the chargers on the high platforms, would snatch the hammer out of a tapper's hand and shatter the fireclay plug to release a river of molten iron. When the wild mood was on him he would even grab a shovel and attack the red-hot slag that spewed from the grates.

The workers respected him for his hard hands and scorched clothing. They listened when he shouted, obeyed without truculence, for in this past year or so Mr Hunter had become a paragon of virtue in their eyes, no tin-pot dictator calling the tune from the cabin on the weigh-bridge but one among them, as reckless and watchful as they were among the fumes and heat and smoke.

On that December night, when the wind brought rain in sweeping clouds and dust lay down in puddles of red mud Allan Hunter felt himself to be all of a piece again.

If he had room in his mind for anything not mineral in origin, it was a hazy recollection of the girl he had encountered on the riverbank on Sunday past; the skinny, half-grown, child-woman who had shown him kindness and refused reward. He did not pine for her as he pined for the dead, of course. He did not yearn for her or plot how he might meet her again. But he thought of her, vaguely, as he attended his business and, with a tar-black oilskin taped over his tweeds, tramped the avenues of the ironworks in teeming mid-winter rain.

Allan climbed the ladder to the weighbridge with a zest that had been missing since Elizabeth had entered – and departed – his life. Taking a firm grip on the railing, he hoisted himself on to the gantry and a moment later flung open the cabin door.

Bremner, the weighman, was seated on an unpadded

stool at the tall desk facing the unglazed window that opened on to the tracks.

Shutters were bolted tight against the rain, for the last of the night's consignments had trundled through more than an hour ago. Tally books and the wagoner's log should have been laid out for Mr Hunter's inspection, along with a pen and a brass inkpot. But the desk was not set out for Mr Hunter's inspection. Instead, Charlie Bremner had turned his stool around, was holding out the tally book as if it were a Psalter and, with an ink-stained, coal-stained finger was pointing out certain items to a man whom Allan had never seen before.

The rich smell of cigar smoke seemed utterly anomalous in the cabin's scoured wooden shell. Allan sniffed and stared and, with rain driving against his shoulders and wetting the floorboards, slapped the door shut with his heel.

Bremner started and leapt guiltily to his feet.

He was a small man, broad-beamed, his features dominated by an untrimmed moustache perpetually wet with tobacco juice. In place of the tar-black clay pipe that usually hung from his lips was a smooth Havana cigar, half-smoked but still bearing a sheath of silvery grey ash that measured it out as very long indeed.

'What the deuce is going on here?' Allan Hunter demanded.

'My fault, sir, entirely my fault,' said the stranger.

He was smoking an expensive Havana too. He did not clench it in his teeth as Bremner did, however, but held it lightly between forefinger and thumb like a person who knew how to savour a good thing. He blew a perfect smoke-ring, then, stepping past Bremner, thrust out his hand. 'Jerome, sir. Johnny Jerome.'

Allan ignored the hand. 'What, may I ask, are you doing here, Mr Jerome?' he said. 'The ironworks are private property and I do not take kindly to strangers wandering about in daylight, never mind after dark.'

'Quite right, sir. Would react 'zactly the same way

myself,' Jerome said. 'However, the password is *Flail*. And my passport is right here.'

He extracted a document from his cape and held it out, shaking it slightly as if he thought that the manager would not see it otherwise.

Bremner, meanwhile, was trying to rid himself of the cigar. He looked this way and that for a place to deposit it but, finding no suitable receptacle, held it out at arm's length and tried to pretend that it did not belong to him.

'He's gotta pass right enough, Mr Hunter,' Bremner said. 'Wouldna ha'e let him in if he didna ha'e a pass.'

Allan took the document and held it towards the oil lamp on the desk. It was a signed note from Sir Andrew Flail sanctioning admission to all parts of the works for Mr John James Jerome, engineer.

Allan said, 'Are you a friend of the Flails, Mr Jerome?'

'No, sir, I have not had the pleasure of meeting any of the family yet. I do, however, have a friend – an acquaintance – who *is* a friend of Sir Andrew.'

'Who, might I enquire, would that be?'

'It's the minister,' Bremner interrupted. 'Mr Jerome knows the minister.'

'Which minister?'

'Mr Robert Montague, of the parish church,' Jerome said.

'I'm not of that congregation,' Allan said, then added diplomatically, 'though I have heard that Mr Montague is a very fine preacher.'

'Aye, he's a' that, Mr Hunter, sir.' Bremner, having found nothing better to do with it, put the cigar back into his mouth. 'Damned fine preacher.'

Allan returned the letter to Jerome.

'Tell me, sir, what sort of an engineer are you and why have you elected to begin your tour of the works at such an ungodly hour here at the weighbridge and not at the gate?'

'Oh, I simply stumbled upon it,' Jerome said. 'Had a notion to see the place after dark. Devilishly dramatic,

103

don't you think? Reminds me of Baghdad, all minarets and pinnacles. I take it you've never been to Baghdad?'

'No, Mr Jerome, I've never been to Baghdad.'

'Or to Constantinople?'

'I've travelled no further than Lanark.'

'I see, I see.' Jerome puffed on his cigar. 'You should have joined the army, Mr Hunter. Fine, strapping fellow like you would have made much of it, I'm sure. And you would have got to see Baghdad.'

'Are you makin' fun of me, Mr Jerome?'

'Certainly not. Oh no, on the contrary.'

'Queen's Engineers?'

'Yes, rank of major. Now retired.'

'Who do you represent?'

'Beg pardon?'

'What partnership do you work for?'

'None, none at all, old boy.'

'Then what's your interest in iron-founding?' Allan Hunter asked.

'Casual.' Jerome nibbled a little bit of smoke from the cigar. 'No, not so casual, come to think of it. I've a mind to invest a small sum in pig-iron stock and, being prudent by nature, I thought it would not go amiss to explore the process before I put out my hard-earned. Do you see, Mr Hunter?'

'I'm not sure I do,' Allan said. 'Are you staying with the minister?'

'He's for gettin' married, so he is,' Bremner put in. 'The minister, I mean. Mr Montague's for gettin' married tae Mr Armitage's daughter.'

'In fact,' Jerome ignored the interruption, 'I'm residing in the Arms for a day or two, just a day or two, while Robbie entertains his father.'

Allan had no interest in the affairs of Bramwell manse.

He had attended services now and then at the parish church when old Calderon had ministered there but had gravitated away from the established Church which had neither consoled nor uplifted him when his need was greatest. He worshipped now at the mission down in the Seaforth Road. What he wanted from a preaching now was to be raised up, offered promises that soothed his concerns about an afterlife and brought him relief from black despair.

'I take it,' Jerome said, 'that you are not acquainted with Miss Armitage?'

'I'm slightly acquainted with the father,' Allan said, 'but I have not, that I can recall, met his daughters.'

'Aye, you'd know it if ye had, Mr Hunter,' Bremner said. 'Since lassies as pretty as yon are no' easy to forget.'

'Be that as it may' – Allan glanced at the brass clock that was screwed to the cabin wall – 'you still haven't explained what you want here at this hour of the night, Major Jerome.'

'Johnny, call me Johnny. Now I've put off my uniform I'm not much given to formality,' Jerome said. 'To answer your question, Mr Hunter, I came at this hour of the night in the hope that I might find you engaged upon your duties which, fortuitously, has proved to be the case.'

'Me? You came to find me?'

'Oh, yes, Mr Hunter. And while I awaited your arrival Mr Bremner was considerate enough to show me how the tally system operates. I hadn't realised that it was quite so complicated. That said, though, it is not so very much different from quartermastering.'

'What interests you most, Mr Jerome?' Allan politely refused the intimacy that the engineer had offered. 'Is it book-keeping or iron-founding?'

'All of it, Mr Hunter, absolutely all of it.'

'That is not something that can be demonstrated in the last hour of the back shift, sir,' Allan said. 'If you are willing to be soaked to the skin and have your cheeks roasted, however, you may accompany me down to watch the furnaces being tapped and molten iron run off into the moulds.'

'I've been soaked to the skin and roasted raw many a time for much less reward.' Johnny Jerome eagerly buttoned the collar of his cape and reached for the half-topper that he had placed on the lid of Bremner's desk. 'I assume that as manager you're obliged to supervise the process, from furnace to furnace?'

'Yes, I am.'

'And afterwards?'

'The moulds are cooled and broken and the pig carted to the stockyard.'

'Which is not something that requires your presence?'

'Not as a rule, no.'

'In that case, Mr Hunter, perhaps you would care to join me for a glass or two at the Ravenshill Arms, which is situated at a not inconvenient distance from your lodgings, I believe?'

'Who told you where I live?'

'Mr Bremner – ah – let it slip, I think. Will you have a snifter with me?'

'It'll be after ten before I'm done here.'

'Time matters not to me,' Johnny Jerome said. 'And the public house is open late. I'd be honoured to have your company.'

'In that case . . .'

'Good. Good. Good,' said Johnny Jerome and, laying a hand on Allan's shoulder, suggested that he do what had to be done to make the books shipshape before they ventured out together to watch the iron run.

By half past ten the servants had been dismissed for the night and Robert and his father were closeted in the library on the upper floor of the manse.

Seated in a big brocaded armchair by the embers of the fire, Angus Montague nursed a glass of brandy as if he hoped to draw from it sufficient warmth to melt the animosity that existed between him and his only child. It had been over fifteen years since they had been alone together and there were many matters of importance to discuss; yet he found himself struggling to make conversation at all.

Whatever turmoil went on within him nothing showed in his face. In this Robert and he were well matched. Behind the glass of the bookcase he could make out the books that his son had foisted upon the world. Daringly frank accounts of Robert's travels rubbed shoulders with scholarly translations and stout theses.

Angus Montague had read and reread them. He had studied Robert's published writings until his eyes ached. Still he could not reconcile the savage accounts of, say, the circumcision rites of Circassian tribeswomen with the epigrams of the Ecclesiasticus or with Robert's arguments for atonement without suffering. He was not inclined to debate these troubling theological problems, for to do so would have meant acknowledging his son's intellectual superiority and the hurt and embarrassment that the publications had caused him.

'You have not yet told me what you think of Cassandra,' Robert said at length. 'Am I to assume that your silence indicates disapproval?'

'Most certainly not.'

'Cassie may not be the sort of woman you would have chosen for me,' Robert went on, 'but she will make an excellent wife.'

'I have no doubt of it,' Angus Montague said.

'But?'

'She is hardly your equal.'

'Only a fool marries a woman whom the world regards as his equal.'

'Is that another of your Hebrew epigrams, Robert?'

'No, just a bit of homespun Scots nonsense.' Robert allowed himself a half smile. 'Do you wish me to dazzle you with ancient proverbs, Father? Very well. "Without a hedge the vineyard is ravaged. Without a wife one is a fugitive and a vagabond for ever." How will that do?'

'I can think of another,' Angus Montague said. ' "All that comes from nothingness returns to nothingness, So the wicked – from emptiness to emptiness." Is that not correct by your translation, Robert?'

'To the letter,' Robert said, still smiling.

'Are you doing all this – by which I mean marriage and a manse – simply to appease me and compensate for your transgressions?'

'Why do you doubt my good intentions?'

'Because I have cause and precedent,' Angus Montague said. 'I do not understand you, Robert. I have never understood you.'

'That, surely, is your fault.'

'Perhaps it is,' Angus Montague said. 'I admit that I was given more to God than to fatherhood. That is a failing that men of the cloth cannot easily mend, for God is demanding of all His servants and those who will best serve Him must sacrifice all else and–'

'Please,' Robert interrupted. 'No sermons, Dada, not tonight.'

'So far, Robert, I have taken you at your word. I am, however, puzzled by your desire to settle in Ravenshill. A college appointment would surely have been more fitting.'

'What fits me, Father, is a parish like this one.'

'So be it,' Angus Montague said. 'It's your decision.'

'Unfortunately the stipend is meagre.'

'Do you not draw income from your published works?'

'Authorship is notoriously badly paid.'

'How did you furnish the manse?' Angus Montague asked. 'I assume that you did not find it so – elegantly appointed?'

'No, I spent money on it, a considerable amount of money.'

'Now you've nothing left?'

'Oh, yes, I've plenty left,' said Robert. 'I have energy and ambition left.'

'Will that be enough?'

'For me,' Robert said, then added, 'but not, perhaps, for my wife.'

'I trust you're marrying out of love, Robert, and not from a desire to convince me how much you've changed?'

108

'Cassie Armitage deserves a measure of comfort. She's used to it.'

'Answer my question.'

'I've considerable feeling for Cassie, if that's what you mean.'

Angus Montague paused and, leaning, set the brandy glass aside. He did not so much lean as list and it cost him effort to restore his body to an upright position.

Panting slightly, he said, 'Where's Jerome?'

'I have no idea.'

'Do not lie to me, Robert. Where is Jerome?'

If the question angered Robert he gave no sign of it. He got to his feet, moved to the bookcase, leaned against it and folded his arms. 'I borrowed money from Johnny, if you must know.'

'So you *are* still in touch with him?'

'Why should I not be in touch with him? There was never any substance to the accusations against us,' Robert said. 'Nor did the threat of a summary court martial come to anything. Don't you understand the mechanics of malice, Father? Don't you realise how spiteful and vicious Queen's officers can be? One is in more danger in an officers' mess than on a field of battle.'

'You exaggerate.'

'I do not. Boredom and monotony inevitably lead to vice. Not the great thundering vices out of which we fashion our sermons but small vices, quite insidious and damaging. Sins of omission accumulate into vendettas that spin out and proliferate until everyone is bristling with grievances and smarting from blows to their insufferable pride. They are worse than women, I tell you.'

'Why did you borrow money from Jerome?'

'Because he is, and always will be, my friend.'

'Why did you not come to me?'

'Because I knew you would not forgive me.'

'How could I?'

'How could you not? There was no harm in anything, Father. The harm lay in rumour and the fact that you swallowed that rumour without question,' Robert said. 'I can't pretend I've been an ideal son but I have done my best to re-form myself as you would wish. I've changed, Dada.'

'But are you *His* man now, Robert? Are you committed to the Lord?'

'Yes, I am.'

'And the girl?'

'Cassie? I will be a devoted and faithful husband to her. There's no question on that score. None.'

'Do you wish me to repay your debt so that you may be free of Jerome?'

'I want nothing of the sort,' Robert said. 'I may owe Johnny money but I am not indebted to him. He'll wait patiently, like the friend he is, until I am ready to repay what I owe.'

'What if he turns up here?'

'What if he does? I'll not send him away.'

'Because you cannot.'

'Because I will not.'

'What will your wife have to say to it?'

'She'll understand. She'll understand better than anyone.'

'You ask a lot of a young girl.'

'In any case, Johnny will not trouble us.'

Angus Montague stroked his chins, touching the soft flesh so lightly that it did not even tremble. He was still panting slightly and there was a faint wheezy rattle in his chest. Decay was within him. Death could not be so very far off.

'What *do* you want from me, Robert?'

'I want you to forgive me.'

'I do.'

'I want you to demonstrate your forgiveness.'

'By restoring your remittance?'

'Yes.'

'What you have now, you will not have later.'

'What changes did you make to your will, Father?'

'None.'

'I beg your pardon?'

'None,' the old minister repeated. 'What did you think, Robert, that I would leave everything to the Cleavers' poorhouse?'

'I thought . . .'

'It's Montague money and you and I both know how it came into the family. I would not have the temerity to pass on the taint of slave-earnings to the Kirk,' Angus Montague said. 'In any case, the interest alone is more than sufficient to see to my needs. The capital remains entirely untouched. If you had been patient, if you had trusted me, Robert, then you would have had what you set your heart upon without having to take on a pulpit and a wife.'

'I'd have taken on the pulpit,' Robert said, 'and the wife, no matter what.'

'It is the remittance, isn't it? You need the remittance now?'

'Yes.'

'It will come out of capital, you know.'

'I understand that.'

'Depending on how many years God grants me,' Angus Montague said, 'there may be nothing but bones left of the fatted calf when the time comes for you to collect. Be that as it may, I have already restored your allowance. I've instructed Mackenzie, my solicitor, to pay you the sum of two hundred pounds per quarter, commencing on the first day of January. Will that satisfy your needs?'

'Admirably.'

'Will it pay off Jerome?'

'Yes, handsomely.'

'Well, I'm glad of that. I want you to be free of him, to start clean.'

Angus Montague stared at his son out of watery brown eyes.

'Of course, I will not be at the wedding,' he said.

'What? Why not? The Armitages will be disappointed. So, indeed, will I.'

111

'Too far. Too cold a journey, Robert. I've given you what you wanted. Another winter trip would be tempting fate. But, aye, I do like the pretty lass and I wish blessings on you both,' the Highland minister said. 'Just promise me one thing, Robert. Promise me you will shake off Jerome.'

'I promise,' Robert said.

'Cleave to your wife.'

'I will.'

'And walk henceforth only in the ways of the Lord.'

'I will, Dada,' Robert Montague said. 'I promise you, I will.'

Eight

Mrs McFarlane had not yet encountered the minister's cook. She had heard talk in the provision merchant's shop that Miss Rundall was a miser when it came to purchases and that her order list seemed to consist of nothing but beans, peas and lentils. With a vision in mind of her master and mistress arriving home from dinner at the manse in a state of near starvation, Mrs McFarlane had thoughtfully baked a batch of cheese scones and had laid them out, along with the cocoa jug, on a tray in the parlour.

Norah, however, was not partial to cocoa and the girls had consumed enough at dinner to nourish them for a week.

Norah was tired and would have preferred to follow her daughters directly upstairs but Cubby insisted that she remain with him while he scoffed scones and cocoa in the hope that a late night snack might sweeten his dreams. Not that his dreams needed much sweetening. He was jovial to the point of uproariousness and chirruped away like a budgerigar until Norah reminded him that there were people trying to sleep downstairs.

'What's wrong with you?' Cubby demanded, slopping cocoa first into his saucer and then on to the rug. 'Did you not have a marvellous, I mean a *marvellous* time?'

On her knees in her best gown Norah mopped up cocoa stains with her handkerchief and did not respond to his question.

Cubby leaned forward. 'Did you ever suppose when you married me, Norah Clavering, that you'd be sendin' your daughter off into such luxury?'

Norah got stiffly to her feet and stood with the damp handkerchief clenched in her fist, waiting for Cubby to finish supper.

'Never thought about it,' she said.

'Never thought about it? Never thought about it? Is it not the ambition of every mother to see her daughters safe into a good marriage? And,' Cubby went on before Norah could contradict him, 'what better marriage could a young woman have than to marry a minister. Especially one who's so well heeled.'

'Is he?'

'Look at it. I mean, look at the house. Look what he's done to it. Foreign furniture or not, I never saw such luxury. I mean, what girl would not be delighted to be mistress of such a house?'

'Cuthbert, you're drunk.'

'No, no. Happy, that's all, my dear. Weddin's have that effect on me.'

'He's not marrying you. He's marrying Cassie.'

'Same thing. Family bonds.'

'I had other things to think about when I married you,' Norah said.

Cuthbert Armitage did not listen.

He rattled on in praise of Robert Montague and all that Robert Montague represented, and dismissed his wife's misgivings as female vagary.

If Cassie had nurtured any inclination to indulge in romantic affectation her first visit to the manse put paid to it once and for all. Any last tingle of excitement which dining with Robert might have occasioned vanished completely when nature, a little earlier than expected, visited upon her solemn reminder of the female cycle as if to indicate that whatever Robert thought of her she was no different from any other woman.

In the hackney on the short drive home, with rain lashing down and the coach shuddering in the buffeting wind, Cassie wanted to weep.

She had no real reason to weep. The fat old gentleman had been kind to her. He had spoken in praise of her and had reminded her of the sacredness of marriage vows and how much a marriage made in heaven was pleasing in the sight of God. Apart from one moment of brusqueness, Robert too had been admirably polite. He had treated her with a respect that he had denied to Pippa who, as usual, was clamouring for his attention.

No reason then to have to fight back tears while the hack's big iron-rimmed wheels dunted over the potholes and shook up her insides like curds in a jelly bag, and her father cackled on about her good fortune and the radiant future that awaited her as the Reverend Montague's wife.

When they arrived home, Pippa, who still made a fuss about 'these things', offered sympathy, put a cold cloth upon Cassie's flushed brow and would have assisted her out of her evening gown and into her nightclothes if Cassie had not pushed her aside. A spat ensued, not much of one but just enough to send the girls huffily to their separate beds and to prompt Pippa to turn off the lamp before Cassie was quite ready.

Cassie climbed into the cold bed in darkness and sought for the warm spot that the stone hot-water bottle had made. Her feet were like ice and cramp dug vicious fingers into her stomach and, as always at this time, she felt weepy and unnecessarily ashamed.

Soon she would have to share this sordid secret with Robert. She would have to find a delicate phrase to indicate that she was – what? – 'not herself'. She mouthed the words under her breath: 'I am not myself tonight, Robert.' They sounded false and haughty, like a lie. She slipped her feet away from the inadequate warmth of the bottle, tucked her knees up to her stomach and, with arms folded tightly across her breasts, tried again: 'Robert, I am indisposed.' He *would* understand. He *must* understand. 'Regrettably, I am indisposed,' she whispered into the sheet.

It was not that, not that at all.

It was the other thing; ignorance of the other thing that she found so upsetting. She could not even begin to contemplate the secret that men shared and that women knew nothing of. She was frightened by it, more frightened than she had been by that first, unannounced evidence that nature and God were not one and the same, that the visitation which came upon her must never be spoken of, not to Mama, not to Pippa, and certainly not to Papa.

In a furtive conversation that had lasted no more than a half-minute, Mama had informed her that nature was at work in her and that it would happen again each month at her time of the moon. Cassie had had no notion of what the moon had to do with her body, how that flat and distant object in the night sky could lodge within her, lolling and liquid, and so her fear had grown.

It had been left to little Nancy Winfield to reassure her.

'Happens t' all us girls. So we won't have too many babies,' Nancy had told her. 'If it doesn't happen reg'lar then there's a baby inside you. So I'm glad to see it an' welcome it like a friend.'

'Is it – is it not the punishment of Eve?'

'That old wives' tale?' Nancy had said. 'Nah! God's no' so spiteful as all that – even if He is a man.'

As she lay in bed racked by pain and fear of pain, Cassie wished desperately that Nancy had still been with them and that she might lay her ignorance before the servant girl once more.

'I am indisposed,' she whispered. 'I am not feeling myself.'

She heard the creak of the mattress, the starchy crackle of sheets as Pippa sat up in the bed next to her.

'Cassie, are you praying?' Pippa said.

She compressed her lips and shut her eyes so tightly that her head ached.

'Yes,' she whispered. 'Yes, I'm – I'm saying my prayers.'

'Are you thanking God for Robert?'

'Yes.'

'Why are you crying then?'

'I have . . .'

'Huh! I wouldn't cry if I was marrying Robert, I might tell you.'

'It isn't that,' said Cassie.

'What is it then?'

'The – the other thing.'

'Of course,' said Pippa sceptically and, with another crackle of bedsheets, lay down again and left Cassie to suffer alone.

History had left few scars on the Ravenshill Arms. After the new workhouse it was the smartest edifice in the burgh and only its situation, hemmed in by ironworkers' tenements, detracted from its reputation as an archi-tectural wonder.

Archie Sinclair, the landlord, was naturally proud of the place. In the morning, when trade was slack, he would dawdle into the street, stand before the building and admire its clean lines and carved sandstone pediments. He would try to put out of mind what it had cost him to transform the property from an old-style tavern to a modern hotel and how much of his not inconsiderable profit was being repaid in interest on the borrowing.

History may not have been apparent from the front of the Arms but if you went down the lane to the backs there was evidence in plenty of what sort of howff the Arms had once been and how, by Archie's efforts and enterprise, it had grown from beginnings more disgusting than humble.

On the acres of waste ground that bordered the embankment the old buildings were still visible sticking up out of the weeds and a litter of wheel-less carts and decaying carriages, broken baskets and barrels and the remnants of an orchard stunted by the fumes from the ironworks. Archie could hardly bear to look out there. It angered him to realise that he had been raised in such squalor and that his father, never mind his grandfather, had done nothing worthwhile with the Arms except reap money hand over fist from improvident farmers and those unfortunate travellers who ran out of steam before they reached the Glasgow bridges.

All that was in the past, of course, but the past did not seem 'past' enough to justify the speed of change that had been wrought on Ravenshill by the building of the railway, the dredging of the river and the expansion of the ironworks.

Archie had met the challenge of commercialism by transforming the ramshackle collection of cottages and sheds into a fine modern hotel, complete with hot water taps, water-closets and a dining-room large enough to host receptions. He had sunk his inheritance into the new building, had borrowed to complete the project but, alas, had never quite had the wherewithal to shake out the junkyard at the back and be rid once and for all of the dire legacy of his ancestors.

He had had sufficient acumen to retain three old cottages for use as a public bar, however; a convenient oasis for parched foundrymen who would have been daunted by, not to say unwelcome in, the hotel proper. There in the backs, Archie took advantage of the special licence that the burgh council had granted him and dispensed drink to working men and kept his grand commercial hotel afloat on the tide of shillings and pence that rolled over the ironworks' wall.

In spite of the fact that he had resided not three hundred yards from the Ravenshill Arms during his all-too-brief marriage and now, in widowerhood, dwelled in lodgings only a quarter of a mile away, Allan Hunter had never before set foot in the low-roofed conglomeration of cottages that had been knocked together to serve as a public house.

It was surprising that Allan permitted his new-found acquaintance, John Jerome, to lure him into the drinking den and cajole him into imbibing far more whisky than his head, or his stomach, could stand. He had no excuse for it, no excuse at all. Except that Jerome was a genial and persuasive chap and the weather so wild that anywhere with a roaring fire and the sound of laughter was to be preferred to Mrs McGuire's boarding-house where, in a room as drab as a hermit's cell, he usually spent his nights.

Manager Hunter's appearance in the hostelry created quite a stir among the regular clientele. It was all Allan could do not to turn on his heel and slink away. Taking him by the arm, Major Jerome led him to a quiet corner by the fire where high-backed chairs and a pineboard partition gave a modicum of privacy.

For a time Allan felt more consoled, more alive, than he had done in months. More so even than in the mission hall, cheering though the preacher's words could be. Here, with the cigar-smoking ex-army engineer the talk was of things other than the wings of angels and the arrival of the soul in paradise. Here he could talk of iron and the making of iron, of his duties as a manager and what volume of profit could be made from pig, how many thousand tons the Flails had piled in their stockyards and how they found markets for it all.

In exchange the admirable Johnny Jerome told him how bridges were built, how gun emplacements were constructed and roads carved across hostile mountain-sides. And while he discoursed he mixed whisky with hot water, sugar and lemon juice, glass after glass, in so easy a manner that Allan was drunk before he quite realised what was happening.

It was almost midnight when he tried to rise. Stumbled and sprawled across the table. Had to be helped to his feet. Had to be helped to the door and pushed outside into the darkness in the general direction of the latrines.

Rain lashed against his face but did not sober him. He did not feel sick. He felt heady, so light and heady that his feet seemed detached from his body and his body seemed to float on the night wind like, he thought irreverently, an angel, an angel in tweeds and half-boots drifting towards the flickering lantern over the door of the shed where, in reeking darkness, he might relieve himself. Only he never seemed to reach the latrine and went on walking, floating, until he realised that he was far from the Arms, adrift in the wilderness below the embankment.

No, he thought, I *am not an angel after all. I am just Allan Hunter, manager at Flail's Blazes, and I am disgustingly drunk and thoroughly lost.*

He fell down.

Grounded on all fours like a dog, trousers sodden, hands grazed by icy grit, he crouched, head spinning, and looked round for jolly Major Jerome, who was nowhere to be found.

And then *she* appeared.

Stiffed as he was, he recognised her immediately.

'Well, if it ish – ishn't Nansh – Nanshy Winfield. What're *you* doin' here?'

'I live here, Mr Hunter,' the girl said.

Kneeling, she put an arm under his chest and helped him to his feet.

'I thought – I thought . . .'

'Are you lost, Mr Hunter?'

'Aye, aye, Mish – Mish Winfield, I'm lost.'

'Then you'd better come wi' me, sir, before you die o' the cold.'

Cold wakened him. Cold and an acrid stench in his nostrils. Cramp in his stomach, a crick in his neck where it rested against the barrel staves. He had no notion where he was or why he could see nothing. He wondered if, like Samson, he had had his eyes put out in punishment for a crime he could not recall having committed.

Pain rolled across his brows when he moved his head.

He opened his mouth and sucked in a freezing breath. The sour aftertaste of whisky encouraged his memory, drop by drop.

He groaned, hoisted himself on to his elbows and peered blearily about him. He could see shapes now humped like tumuli about him. He was covered by sacking and musty straw and lay head and shoulders inside a broken hogshead whose jagged edges curved like an eggshell over his face. He needed to make water.

He leaned forward, groaning again, then flinched as something stirred in the straw beside him and something cold and soft touched his mouth.

'Hush now, sir, hush now. It's early yet.'

'Where – where am I?'

'Here wi' me. But I've got to be away soon.'

'How did I get here?'

'It was here or freeze, Mr Hunter,' the girl told him. 'I wouldna leave a dog out on a night like last night was.'

'I was with someone.'

'Nah, you were all alone,' the girl whispered.

She was very close to him, her lank hair brushing his cheek. Beneath the layer of sacking he could feel her body, fully clothed, against his thigh.

Out in the darkness among the tumuli someone let out a shuddering sigh and a woman's voice croaked unintelligibly.

'Who are they, Nancy? Where have you brought me?'

'Mr Sinclair lets us use the sheds at night. He sends a boy down at six wi' a bucket o' hot tea, then we've all to be up an' out before his gentlemen waken an' see us.'

'Who does these things?'

'Archie, Archie Sinclair. We're in his shed, by the embankment,' the girl whispered. 'I'd have took you back t' your own place but I could get no sense out o' you, Mr Hunter, about where you lived.'

'I was with a man named Jerome.'

'Nobody was with you, Mr Hunter,' Nancy informed him. 'Listen, I'll have to go soon an' you might not be safe

121

here on your own. If you can walk, I'll show you the right road out.'

'What time is it?'

'Five, near enough.'

The pain in his head had receded. There was some warmth in his limbs after all. He could make out the walls and roof of the long shed, see splinters of night sky through the planking, a smear of white, like lace, overhead. He still needed to make water, though, or he might have endured the discomfort and lain there with the girl and persuaded her to talk for a while longer.

'I have to go, Mr Hunter. I have to be off now.'

He sat up and pushed aside the sacking. He felt her hand grope for his arm. He allowed her to guide him, stepping around the hummocks, eight, ten, a dozen of them. He glimpsed a scrawny arm, a bare foot, a clenched hand, the face of a child, its eyes open, staring up at him from a twist of rags on the ground.

Nancy opened the shed door just wide enough to let him slip through and closed it again after him.

The air was bitingly cold but not frosty. Rain had turned to sleet and sleet to snow. Snow rimed the roofs of the decrepit buildings and defined the embankment on top of which the coal wagons would soon roll and from which steam engines would spew smoke down into the wilderness behind Archie Sinclair's hotel.

Allan had walked this stretch of the embankment with the stockyard manager, checking drainage and the linking of the rails. Had glanced down upon the derelict outbuildings often enough but had failed to realise that they were inhabited, that human creatures might be driven to sleep in such conditions.

In mission halls and churches he had listened to many a plea on behalf of the poor and had donated as much as he could afford to charity. He too had experienced life on the knuckle, where unremitting labour was required just to keep soul and body together; but of this other, mongrel level he had no knowledge whatsoever.

If he had not been so fogged with whisky fumes and so shivering cold he might have asked Nancy to take him back again, to let him see how the day began for outcasts and how – God alone knew how – it unfurled.

She stood by him, anxious to be off.

She wore a shawl about her head and shoulders, held her boots in her hand. He wondered how far she would walk before she put them on. In spite of her frailty, she did not seem to feel the cold as he did.

Shivering, he said, 'Where do you go at this hour?'

'To visit . . .' She hesitated, squinting at him. 'To find work.'

'What sort of work?'

'Whatever work there is.'

'To pay for the boy at Daltry's?'

'Girl. It's a girl I have there.'

'Girl then, to pay for the girl?' Allan insisted.

'Aye, that's the reason.'

The gusting wind swirled dirty wet flakes out of a dark sky. He could taste iron in the flakes that melted on his lips. Beyond the ruins of the sheds, behind the stunted apple trees, lights showed in the ground-floor windows of the Ravenshill Arms. Breakfast would be on the go, fires lighted, pans and kettles steaming warm. Allan shivered and rocked in discomfort.

Nancy pointed. 'Over there, there's a path under the embankment that'll take you out near the harbour workin's at the end o' the old Govan Road.'

'What about you? Which way do you go?'

'The other way.' The girl tucked the shawl's ends into her belt and held her boots by the laces. 'You shouldna drink, Mr Hunter. You've no head for it.'

'No, I know it, Nancy,' Allan Hunter told her.

'Good mornin' to you then.'

'Good morning,' Allan said.

He watched her pick her way, barefoot, across the sleety ground, watched her vanish into the mirk with sorrow in his heart, a sorrow that was no longer centred on Elizabeth and his own sad, selfish ends.

123

* * *

During his years in the army Johnny had always disapproved of wives who went campaigning. He had detested the gentility of those regimental marquees which hosted womenfolk, a sex which Johnny regarded as ubiquitous and inescapable. He had been plagued by women even on the stinking plains of Balaclava and had half expected excursion steamers full of waving ladies to arrive from England to picnic on the battery at Sebastopol.

Miss Rundall and her girls were different, though. He felt comfortable with them, perhaps because they were willing to attend to his needs without fuss or false politeness. He congratulated himself on having picked good servants as he sat down to breakfast on an excellent ox tongue garnished with scrambled eggs.

Miss Rundall did not object to sharing her kitchen with the master's friend, an infringement of custom which would have been sufficient to send less astute domestics into a sulk. Nor did Johnny have to point out to the cook the delicacy of the situation which existed in the manse at the present time and explain why he had spent the last three nights sleeping in the hay-loft.

'Did he enquire, Miss Rundall?' Johnny said. 'Did he ask you about me?'

'He did, Major, he most certainly did.'

'In our Mr Montague's presence?'

'In private, Mr Jerome, in private.'

'What answer did you give him?'

Miss Rundall assumed the blankest of blank looks and repeated her answer to Angus Montague in a slow bovine voice. ' "Harmy Captin, sur? Hain't never heard of no harmy captin here, sur, an' no'un name uv Jerome." '

'Did he swallow it?'

'Like a cat swallows cream, Major.'

'What of the maids?'

'He asked the same question of Janey.'

'Which was very naughty of him, wouldn't you say, Miss Rundall?'

124

'Not my place to criticise,' Miss Rundall said in a tone that implied stern criticism indeed. 'It ain't right to annoy the maids, though, is it? Even if you are a Reverend gentleman and knockin' on in years. It's a liberty, my opinion, which I wouldn't accept from a reg'lar member of the household.'

'What did Janey tell him?'

'What I told her to.'

' "Hain't never heard, etceteras?" ' Johnny asked.

'She's a good girl, Janey. Always does what's requested of her.'

'I think it's time Janey had a new bonnet, Cook, don't you?'

'If you say so, Major.'

'What do new bonnets cost these days?'

'Get a nice one for ten and sixpence.'

'And two for a guinea?'

'And two for a guinea,' Miss Rundall agreed and pocketed the coins that he put upon the table. 'Will a wee taste of jugged hare follow that down for you, Major Jerome?'

'Follow it down nicely, Miss Rundall. Many thanks.'

Whisky never had much effect on Johnny. He could not understand why some fellows suffered ill on 'the morning after'. He felt as chipper as he usually did first thing and did full justice to the breakfast that Miss Rundall whipped up for him. The only wrinkle on his brow, in fact, was put there by Hunter's mysterious disappearance. He could not understand why Hunter had gone lumbering out to visit the privy and had simply failed to return.

Still, Johnny thought, as he munched on flakes of hare meat, if he failed to charm and impress one manager he would surely be able to charm and impress another. He was beginning to comprehend what Robbie had in mind and why the financial prospects here seemed so rosy. Ravenshill was a hot-bed of trading and dealing, not all of which, according to Hunter, had been commandeered by the Flails. Crumbs from a rich man's table were not to be sneezed at and, even at a rough calculation, he realised that Robbie would have a sizeable stake to invest as soon as his scheme took shape and form.

Still dreaming of money, Johnny had just lighted his first cigar of the day when the door from the corridor opened and Robert put his head around it.

'Ah, so here you are?' the minister said.

'Well, you didn't expect me to *eat* with the stable lad, did you?'

'With your permission, Miss Rundall?' Robert said.

'Do come in, sir. Will I be makin' you somethin' to break your fast too?'

'No, I'll breakfast with my father at eight, as arranged.'

'Coffee, Mr Montague?'

'If you please.'

Cup in hand, Robert seated himself at the table while the cook shepherded the tall servant and the scullion out of earshot.

'Did it go well with your dada?' Johnny asked, soft-voiced.

'Yes, it seems I'm restored to grace.'

'And favour?'

'Two hundred a quarter.'

'Excellent, excellent.'

'He wants my assurance that our friendship will end with my marriage.'

'Something on paper?'

'No, nothing so binding as that,' Robert said.

'We have it then. Operating capital, I mean?'

'We do,' Robert said. 'Tell me, what have you learned, Johnny, concerning the best means of investing our money?'

'Pig-iron's the stuff,' Johnny said. 'From what I gather the market fluctuations are astonishing. A man might make a veritable killing in a single day if he's clever enough.'

'Have you been to the works?'

'Yes, I'm cultivating Hunter, as you suggested.'

'Will he be of use to us?'

'It's far too early to say,' Johnny replied. 'Particularly as I'm not quite sure what sort of scheme you have in mind.'

'I'm not exactly sure myself yet. Something that will net us a fortune.'

'You already have a fortune.'

'Nonsense!' Robert exclaimed. 'What my father gives me is nothing.'

'And what you will inherit when he shakes off the mortal coil?'

'Nothing, nothing really.'

'There's also the dower money. A thousand, was it?'

'I've taken a loan to pay for the furnishings,' Robert admitted. 'The repayment rates are high. I intend to use the dower money to square that away.'

'Eight hundred per annum from your dad, plus your stipend and whatever you have left from the money your wife brings – it ain't exactly chickweed, is it?'

'It isn't enough.'

'Oh! I see,' Johnny said. 'We're in pursuit of excess, are we? For what reason, old boy, for what purpose do you *need* so much money?'

'Purpose?' said Robert Montague. 'I do not understand.'

'No, of course you don't,' Johnny said. 'Stupid of me to ask. Sorry.'

'It's simply there, there for the taking, Johnny. It would be ungracious of me to ignore the opportunities which the Lord in his wisdom has put in my way.'

'All for the cost of taking a wife on board.'

'There will be compensations to that arrangement,' Robert said, 'in spite of what you may think.'

'I think nothing,' Johnny said. 'By which I mean I think it's admirable that a parish minister should have a wife to satisfy his needs.'

'There's more to marriage than that.'

'Is there?' Johnny said.

'Much more,' Robert Montague said.

Johnny said nothing for a moment. He was conscious of

the nearness of the women. They were tucked out of sight in the larder but with ears flapping, no doubt.

At length he said, 'When will your father depart?'

'I've ordered the hack for noon. He's staying with Salmond in Glasgow tonight and will set off for Inverness first thing tomorrow.'

'If the weather permits,' Johnny said. 'Is it safe for me to move back in, do you think, or would you prefer me to keep my head below the parapet a while longer?'

'Come indoors, by all means, just as soon as we leave. I'm accompanying my father to Glasgow,' Robert said. 'I require to have words with Salmond.'

'About the wedding?'

'Quite!'

'But you will be back by bedtime, won't you?'

'Oh, yes, Johnny,' Robert Montague said. 'I'll be back by bedtime, never fear.'

Nine

In the week that spanned Christmas and New Year Cassie's depression deepened. Anxiety coloured everything she did. She slept badly, tossed in feverish sweats and started out of sleep with nightmare visions lurking in the corner of her mind. There was no one to whom she could turn for comfort.

She attended the services that marked the season and saw Robert from a distance. From the stall to the left of the pulpit she stared at her husband-to-be and drank in his every utterance as if she hoped that he might let slip some phrase that would reassure her. But she found nothing in Robert's oratory to soothe her horrid fears.

His Christmas sermons were original without being controversial. His New Year preaching so stirring that the kirk fair buzzed in response to it. It was universally agreed that if the Holy Spirit ever moved in Ravenshill it would move through the Reverend Montague. Cassie was not comforted by the admiration that was showered upon her fiancé.

When the banns were read and the intention of marriage made public, congratulations showered upon Cassie from all quarters. How fortunate she was to be chosen by a good man like the Reverend Montague, how favoured among women, she was told; how fulfilled and fulfilling her life as the minister's wife would be and how her obedience to his will would mirror his obedience to the will of God.

Cassie listened politely. She smiled, bowed, murmured her thanks and felt nothing, nothing but anxiety.

The manse on Bramwell hill also seemed hostile and threatening.

She sought in vain for welcome in its luxury or some niche which she might be called upon to fill. She found none. The household seemed complete without her.

During the course of convivial dinner parties she would observe Robert without passion or desire and endeavour to imagine how she could relate to this paragon, this stranger. She would sit at Robert's table and eat the food that the maid dispensed so swiftly and efficiently. She would sip sherry wine and toast the nuptials to come, would listen to conversations swirl about her, would respond intelligently while all the while her thoughts were engaged on imagining what lay at the top of the staircase and what might happen to her there.

Being alone with Robert – brief moments, not precious – did not alter her mood. He spoke to her softly and courteously and perhaps, Cassie thought, had an inkling of what lay behind her reserve.

On the other hand, perhaps he did not. Perhaps he was as adamant as he appeared to be in the pulpit, minister and man one and the same and indivisible. But when he touched her, when he brushed her cheek or squeezed her fingers then another element entirely came into play, something as unexpectedly rough as the tongue of a cat.

Christmas came and went.

New Year was greeted with due solemnity.

'The year in which you will be married, Cassie,' Papa reminded her. 'The year in which you will leave my house and assume the responsibilities of a wife. I am very proud of you, Cassandra, very proud to have such a fine man brought into our family.'

January: Robert busy burying old folk and weaklings
that the harsh winter weather had carried away, and the
Armitages, mother and daughters, entering upon the final
phase that would bring Cassie to the altar.

Receipt and acknowledgement of wedding gifts.
Compiling guest lists. Selecting materials from samples.
Fittings and refittings. Pin-pricks and scissor-snips. Last-
minute adjustments. Hothouse bouquets for a winter
bride. Forced roses for Mama, a posy on ice for bridesmaid
Pippa. Meetings with groomsman Ewan Flail. Meetings
with the Reverend Salmond.

All of it and more going by not in a whirl but a daze and
February rushing at Cassie on the breast of a wet, cold
wind and through cold, hard nights when smoke from the
Blazes drifted past the bedroom window, round and
rolling in the empty moonlight.

Mama presented Cassie with a book on marriage, a
plump little volume written by a Dr De Witt. Pippa found
it and read aloud from it, sniggering.

' "The nuptial meeting," ' Pippa read. 'Oh, listen, Cassie,
listen to this. "Isaac is meditating in the fields upon his
passage from celibacy to monogamy. And he sees a speck
against the sky and groups of people and after a while he
finds that the grandest earthly blessing that ever comes to
a man is approaching with this gay caravan." Blah-blah-
blah . . .

'Then Doctor De Witt goes on, "I take it for granted, O
man, that your marriage was divinely arranged and that the
camels have arrived from the right direction, bringing the
one that was intended for consort – a Rebecca and not a
Jezebel." I wonder if Robert is meditating like Isaac?
Perhaps Robbie's wondering how many camels are
coming up Main Street and how many dromedaries he can
squeeze into the stable at the manse. Perhaps,' Pippa went
on, still giggling, 'he's hoping that you're not too much of
a Rebecca but have a touch of Jezebel about you.'

'What else does it say?'

'Oh, nothing, nothing of any value. "You must navigate

through the storms and cyclones of a lifetime. You must run clear of the rocks and icebergs. You have no experience and no seaport now but all aboard for the voyage of a lifetime. I admit" – jolly sporting of him, don't you think? – "I admit that there have been ten thousand shipwrecks on this very route. But do not you hesitate. Tut! Tut! There now. Don't cry. Brides must not cry at their wedding." '

'It doesn't say that, surely?'

'It does. It does. In plain black and white. Astonishing, isn't it? What does Doctor De Witt take us for? Luggers or clipper ships? Perhaps he assumes that all girls marry sailors,' Pippa said, 'or camel-drivers. *You* won't cry at *your* wedding, Cassie, will you?'

'No.'

'Or afterwards?'

Cassie hesitated.

'I say, you're not crying now, are you?'

'Of course I'm not.'

Pippa tossed the book aside. 'I'm sure I'll cry afterwards. I mean, it'll be so different, so – so changed, won't it? No mama downstairs. No papa. No you, Cassie, right next to me. Just a husband, closer than will seem proper. Perhaps that will be compensation for the rest of it?'

'The rest of it?'

'The pain. It's bound to be painful when you think of it.'

'What . . .' Cassie began and then, voice rising, snapped, 'No, no. I don't wish to speak of it. It's not right to speak of it. It isn't decent.'

'Decent or not, it's something you cannot avoid.'

'Stop it, stop it, please.'

'Oh, are you frightened, dear? Do you find Robert terribly frightening? Is that what's got you stuck in this dreadful mood?' Pippa, lying back on her bed, did not await an answer. 'I don't find Robert frightening,' she said, an admission that in months to come Cassie would find hard to forget.

* * *

132

She would be married in white, of course: a dress of white tulle threaded with silver, a veil, a headdress, a white satin sash, milk-white stockings sprinkled with tiny daisies, and new embroidered garters. Because it was February, she would be hugged by a waist petticoat, a crocheted under-waistcoat of fine warm silk and silken drawers. She would be tailed by a light whalebone half-crinoline without steel or springs to weigh her down for she had the shape, the pedestal, to need no other embellishment to her figure and, so the dressmaker said, bridal gowns should not be spoiled by too much fashion.

Cassie endured the fittings with noble patience but because she had never been vain about her appearance she was unable to share the excitement that gripped Pippa and Mama.

Relieved at not having to part with too large a dowry, Papa was generous when it came to footing the dress-maker's bills. Selection and purchase of nice new nightgowns, underclothes, stockings, shoes, dresses and gloves, bonnets and capes for Cassie's trousseau occupied the Armitage women fully, an activity that, along with entertaining and visiting, brightened the short gloomy days of the January month for everyone except Cassie.

Then suddenly it was February, and the eve of her wedding.

Papa came home early from the city. He was fidgety, Mama agitated, Pippa gay as a lark in the chill, drizzling weather that, in spite of all their prayers, did not seem willing to relent. None the less, Papa declared, Cassie would bring enough sunshine to the kirk to cheer all those who would gather to bless her and send her off with Robert on the great voyage of life.

Cassie was sick in the night, sick again in the morning.

She lied to Pippa about it, lied to Mama.

In the mirror the lie stared back at her. Paste-white, circled eyes, blotched cheeks, lips as pale as alabaster. How disappointed Robert would be to discover that she was not pretty at all, that the quality for which he had

133

chosen her had vanished on the steps of the altar. She slipped out of the dressing-room and, holding a towel across the breast of her bridal gown, was sick once more into the basin in the water-closet.

The carrier's men took Cassie's trunks away to deliver to the manse. Pippa giggled saucily and called out to the carrier's men, giving them cheek. Mama was busy dressing. Banished to his room, Papa lay upon the bed, nibbling his thumbnail and pretending to read a newspaper as if nothing untoward was going on and he was not on the verge of trading away a daughter in exchange for a son.

At half past one o'clock the dresser put the headdress and veil on to the bride and told Cassie how beautiful she looked, and then, for three or four minutes, she was left alone.

The wind drove sleek little streaks of sleet against the window glass and knurls of cloud rolled remorselessly over the river and the hills.

Cassie thought of Robert in the manse. How calm he would be, how matter-of-fact, ticking items from his list of things to do. A glass of brandy, a light luncheon in the company of Ewan Flail while the sallow-faced servant girl laid out his clothes upstairs; the same servant girl who would light a fire in the bedroom, turn down the sheets, insert a warming-pan, trim the lamp if lamp there was to be while she, Cassie Armitage, intoned the marriage vows, sipped champagne and danced a *Valse* in Robert's arms.

The bedroom door opened.

Mama said, 'It's time to go, Cassandra.'

On the stairs below, Pippa was shrieking, 'The carriages are here. The carriages are here. Cassie, come along. You mustn't be late. Today of all days you really must *not* be late.'

'Mama,' Cassie whispered, desperately. 'Tonight, Mama, what will happen tonight? What will I do?'

'Robert will tell you what to do,' Norah said quietly. 'The gentleman always knows what to do.'

Then Cassie was taken from her bedroom, escorted

downstairs and led from the house to the carriage. A half-hour later she was joined in bonds of holy matrimony to the Reverend Robert Montague, a man about whom she knew nothing at all.

It was not the first wedding reception that Archie Sinclair had been called upon to host but it was certainly the grandest.

The Ravenshill Arms had never looked so spick and span. Archie had put out a deal of effort to decorate the gloomy ballroom with ribbons and hothouse flowers and to ensure that it glittered with crystal and silver and that the chandeliers shone with a full complement of candles.

As requested by Mr Cuthbert Armitage, he unleashed his finest wines and his least fiery spirits and set out as many tables as the room would take, each draped with the monogrammed napery that he kept for special occasions. How Cubby Armitage had learned of the fad for serving dinner from a buffet was a mystery. Perhaps a word had been dropped in the wee man's ear by one of the Flails who were, of course, exceedingly cosmopolitan.

Sixty-eight guests, mostly drawn from the ranks of the local gentry and the inner wheel of the church, with only a handful of friends of the groom and no relatives at all. It mattered not to Archie. He was out to impress the rich and influential Flails, not humble Cubby Armitage or the temperate new minister. He scoured the countryside for game, for ripe venison and best butcher meat, and hired three cooks from Glasgow for the whole of the day, as well as taking on an army of carvers and servers, pot-boys and bottle-washers to keep things running smoothly behind the scenes.

From the outcasts who slept in his shed Archie hired but one pair of hands, but he would see to it that whatever scraps were left after the staff had had first pickings were carried down to the shed by the embankment first thing tomorrow morning. He might have sold the fat and bones to tallow merchants and the peelings and crusts to pig-farmers but Archie was unself-consciously generous and had a genuine sympathy for those who were down on their luck.

The pair of hands that Archie hired belonged to Nancy Winfield. Archie had a soft spot for the workhouse girl. He gave her work when he could, kitchen jobs mainly, for although she was as clean and neat as could be expected under the circumstances she was still too shabby and unprepossessing to employ on a regular basis.

Archie was aware that Nancy had once worked as a servant to the Armitages and thought it best to warn her not to show her face near the ballroom in case it caused embarrassment.

'She's gettin' married? I never knew she was gettin' married,' Nancy said when Archie informed her of the event that the reception was intended to honour. 'Which one is it? Cassie, or Pips?'

'Pips? Who's Pips?'

'The young one. Nah, she's o'er young for a man yet. It'll be Cassie. Is it a minister she's marryin' right enough?'

'Aye, the new minister from the parish church.'

'Montague?'

'That's the man,' said Archie. 'Listen, I haven't the time to waste gabbin' to you. Are you on for the day, or are you not?'

'How long?'

'Ten o'clock, mornin', 'til we're all cleared away at night,' said Archie. 'You can help set out the tables then go in back to help serve an' wash up. Mr McNair will supervise the cookin' but there's three cooks from Glasgow comin' to help him, so you'll need to be mindin' your Ps an' Qs.'

'Oh, I'm used to mindin' my Ps an' Qs,' Nancy said. 'How much?'

'Half a crown.'

'Make it three shillin'.'

'Get on with you, lassie, I can hire at a shillin' if I've a mind to.'

'Half a crown then,' Nancy said. 'Will I get a chance to see the bride?'

'No, you will not.'

'Just a wee peek, Mr Sinclair. I used to be her lady's maid an' I'd love t' see her all trigged out in her weddin' dress.'

'You can sneak up to the gallery after the dancin' starts,' Archie said. 'But keep your head down an' don't loiter. Understood?'

'Understood, Mr Sinclair.'

For once Nancy had no need to lie to Todd. The chance of a full day's employment was too good to pass up. She told him excitedly who the star attraction would be and, though Todd was polite enough to indicate interest with a grunt and a nod, the cold of a night shift had drained him and he was too weary to listen for long to Nancy's prattle about her time with the Armitages.

On the eve of the wedding reception – a full day's work – Nancy lingered on in the tenement in Bengal Street long after Todd had gone on shift.

She brushed her clothes, patched and ironed them and, when she was done, lifted the garments to her nose and smelled them and tried to imagine what it must be like to be Cassie Armitage, all clean and new and arrayed for the bridal.

She sat on Todd's bed with the petticoat held to her nose, listened to the wind howl about the chimneys and pitied poor Todd out there in the night lugging his soil-tubs and spade and was glad that her daughter was snug in Madame Daltry's house. She thought again of Cassie Armitage in the house in Normandy Road and the love that would await the girl when she was transported to the manse by her husband; and she decided that on such a miserable night she, Nancy Winfield, was better off staying where she was in Todd's room, in Todd's bed. So that night, for the first time, she stayed over to surprise her man in the morning, first thing.

Nancy arrived at the Arms a full half-hour before Archie expected her. She worked throughout the morning at setting tables, stirring pans and turning spits. In early afternoon, she was rewarded with a peep into the ballroom which, with the buffet tables set and the candles lighted, seemed to the scullions as glittering and glamorous as a palace in a fairytale.

Nancy was glad that everything was arranged so perfectly for Cassie Armitage, against whom she bore no grudge. She would have liked to loiter in the hallway, to curtsey when bride and groom arrived from the church, to give Cassie a grin and a wink just to show that she wished her former mistress every happiness. By the time the wedding party scurried in out of the rain, however, Nancy was back in the kitchens, toting coal for the stoves and water for the boiling pans while the hired cooks squabbled with Mr Sinclair and hurled insults at each other through clouds of steam.

At half past six o'clock the orchestra came down from the ballroom to be fed and watered at a side table near the larder. By then dishes and glasses were descending in an avalanche from the buffet tables upstairs, the washing-tubs were sloppy with suds and the garbage pails filling up as fast as the scullions could scrape into them and Nancy, like the others, was red-faced and tousled.

She was anxious not to miss at least one glimpse of Cassie and her man, though, and she was relieved when, about eight o'clock, Mr Sinclair noticed her slaving in the tub-room amid plate racks and sodden duckboards and suddenly remembered his promise.

'Nancy,' he called out. 'Dry yourself an' go up the back stairs to the gallery for five minutes. Five minutes, no more.'

Wiping her hands on her apron, Nancy darted off in the direction of the stairs before Mr Sinclair could change his mind.

She knew where the gallery was, although she had never been up there before. It hung like a swallow's nest in a corner of the ballroom, close to the plaster cornices of the arched ceiling. No visiting orator had ever delivered an address across its wooden rail and it was far too narrow to bear the weight of an orchestra or choir. It existed solely to give access to the anchor points of the chains of the chandeliers, by means of which they could be lowered for cleaning, rewaxing and lighting.

Nancy took the stairs two at a time. She checked before the narrow door, however, fumbled in the gloom for the handle and opened the door cautiously.

The man was kneeling as if in prayer, his back to her. She could see boot heels, a pleated tweed jacket drawn tight across his back and knew at once that this was no footman or lackey stealing time from his duties. She tried to step back but before she could do so the man jerked his head round and stared at her.

'Mr Hunter,' Nancy said, 'what are you doin' here?'

'I came to meet someone by appointment,' he said, 'and then I saw her.'

'Saw who?'

'The young woman.'

'The bride, d' you mean?'

'Yes, the bride.'

He beckoned to Nancy to join him at the railing. She knelt by him and squinted down through the upright posts into the ballroom below.

Even as she did so the orchestra struck up an Austrian medley, couples separated themselves from the flowerbeds of silk and satin that lined the room and swirled out on to the polished surface, so light, so far removed from reality that they seemed not to be dancing at all but skating on ice.

'Do you see her?' Allan Hunter whispered.

'Aye, I see her,' Nancy said.

She looked younger not older, did Cassie Armitage, like a slender white stalk in the arms of the tall, black-garbed man who, Nancy guessed, was the new husband. She tried to catch a glimpse of Cassie's face but it was hidden. All she could see were the young woman's skirts and her gloved hands against the man's black suiting, the

139

husband's face, haughty and severe and handsome as he led his new wife in the dance.

'Do you know her, Mr Hunter?' Nancy asked.

'No,' he answered. 'No, I've never seen her before.'

'Are you not a weddin' guest then?'

'I didn't even realise that a wedding was in progress until I came into the hotel a half-hour ago.' He turned his head and frowned. 'How do you know her? Who is she? I mean, more than her name?'

'I was a servant to the Armitages for a while, an' she's Mr Armitage's oldest daughter. Her name's Cassandra. They call her Cassie, though.'

Allan Hunter rested his brow against the railing and stared at the bride.

'Cassie,' he murmured. 'God, but she's beautiful.'

'What are you doin' away up here, sir?' Nancy asked.

'I came to see her, to look at her.' Allan Hunter shook his head, then, with an impulsive gesture that Nancy did not have the heart to resist, gathered the workhouse girl to him with an arm about her waist. 'Do you see, Nancy, do you see her down there?'

'Aye, 'course I do. I'm not blind.'

'Do you know, she's the living image of my darling, my departed wife.'

'Cassie Armitage?'

'Yes, Cassie Armitage.'

'Well,' Nancy said, nonplussed, 'it's a pity she just got married to another man then.'

And, to her astonishment, heard Allan Hunter laugh as if that grievous coincidence was a trifle which, in the great scheme of things, mattered not at all.

Robert and Cassie Montague left the wedding party at half past nine o'clock. Cassie was still dressed in her bridal. There would be no honeymoon until later in the year. The work of the parish was too demanding in that grim season, Robert told her. Besides, they would be more at ease in each other's company come summer, more able to enjoy a sojourn in France or Italy together.

Cassie did not protest. She was in no fit state to protest about anything that Robert said or did. She had gone through the day in a trance, oblivious to the significance of the service and the rejoicing that followed it.

When Robert kissed her, when Robert touched her, when he danced with her, she felt neither revulsion nor joy, only a numbness that protected her against panic and allowed her to fulfil her role in the ceremonies without making a fool of herself entirely.

The last things she saw as the coach pulled away from the Ravenshill Arms were Pippa standing outside in her skimpy pale blue dress waving her arms and mouthing, 'Good luck, good luck, dearest,' and Papa sheltering in the doorway with Ewan Flail, more drunk than not, swaying at his side. And a man, a bystander in a pleated tweed jacket positioned on the pavement ten or twenty yards from the door of the Arms who raised his hat and smiled at her as she stared balefully out of the coach window.

'Robert,' she said, 'who is that?'

Robert was not concerned with strangers or the passing scene. He had slumped back in the leather seat, drained by the effort of being sociable. He made no attempt to rise and look from the window. Then the man and the bright lights of the Ravenshill Arms were gone, and Cassie was left with the glimmer of tenements and the thud of wheels on the cobbles and the sounds of the wet wind, mellowed now by snow.

She peered out at the shapes of Ravenshill and the landmarks of the Bramwell Road as if she had never seen them before. She rested her brow on the rattling glass, and did not dare face him. She heard him move. She heard the creak of leather, the rustle of her skirts as he leaned towards her. She stiffened. He pulled himself against her. He put his hand to her throat and gently turned her face away from the window and kissed her. He kissed her full on the mouth, letting his lips linger and his tongue touch hers. She felt his hand upon her breast, against the surface of her dress and wondered if this was what intimacy meant, if it would be no worse than this.

'You're cold, Cassandra.'

His breath smelled of peppermint cordial, not sweet but sharp.

She shook her head. His hand rested against her throat. She could feel a cold pulse in her neck beating against his fingertips.

He squeezed her breast gently. 'I will soon warm you.'

The coach rolled a little, tilting her towards Robert. He laughed and caught her in his arms. He held her against him. She remained protected by full skirts, silk scarves, his topcoat.

The road opened along the riverside. Snowflakes plastered the glass, softened the angry wind and laid upon the cobbles a grey-white carpet that deadened the sounds of hoofs and wheels. She could hear the driver crying to the horses. She felt the coach sway and slither dangerously.

She heard Robert laugh once more. 'I told the fellow to make all the speed he could. He's obviously taking me at my word.'

Cassie did not ask why Robert had instructed the driver to hurry. She sensed that his answer would not be decent. She vowed that she would give him no opportunity to dismay her more than he had done already, and for the rest of the short journey she lay like lead in his arms.

The manse gate was open. The coach rolled through.

Its wheels were muffled by lying white snow. She saw the house ahead, gaunt against the sky. Then she was being helped down by a jovial stranger and – on his arm, not Robert's – she was led into the hallway where the servants were lined up to greet her. Two grown women and a girl. Cook, maidservant and scullion. They curtsied politely. The stranger introduced her to each of them by name but neglected to inform her who he was and what role he filled in the household.

'Johnny,' Robert said, urgently, 'where are the lady's trunks?'

'Laid out, Robbie, and everything laid away.'

'Janey, are the fires lighted?'

'Just what you asked for, Mr Montague.'

'Hot water?'

'In the brass jug.'

'Good.'

'Will you be going up directly?' the wiry little man asked.

'At once,' Robert said. 'Cassandra, my wife, is naturally very tired.'

'Sure she is, poor soul,' the cook said. 'Will she be requirin' Janey's assistance, Mr Montague. Now or later?'

'No, we need nothing further, thank you, Miss Rundall.'

'Goodnight then, sir. Goodnight, ma'am.'

'Goodnight,' said Cassie, automatically.

Robert took her arm, steered her from the hall and up the carpeted staircase.

From the half-landing she glanced back. The wiry little man and the three females stood in a semicircle at the bottom of the stairs, watching her. Cassie took no comfort from their presence.

'Robert, who is that man? Is he the butler?'

'He is my friend. Johnny Jerome.'

'Why was he not at the wedding, and why is he here now?'

'He lives here, dearest, he lives here,' Robert said.

He guided her up a second flight of carpeted stairs that led to a lofty corridor and a pair of oak-panelled doors. He opened one of the doors and ushered her into a parlour.

'Our rooms, Cassie,' Robert told her. 'Our private rooms.'

She took in the sight of satinwood cabinets, inlaid secretaires, armchairs with barley-twist legs, couches upholstered in gros-point needlework, a tall iron fireplace with marble insets, a fire burning brightly in the grate. Also off the parlour was another room, hardly larger than a closet, furnished, as far as Cassie could make out, with nothing but a basin-stand and a single iron bedstead.

143

'No, that is not your room, Cassie,' Robert informed her. 'That is my study. Here is your room. You will find that your clothes and accessories have been laid out for you.'

A brass-based oil lamp with an engraved globe lit the apartment to the left of the parlour. She could see a bed reflected in a standing mirror, washing apparatus, a huge breakfront wardrobe, a window draped with velvet curtains swagged by an embroidered sash.

Robert closed the door to the corridor.

'Are you hungry?' he said.

'No.'

'Then I will leave you to arrange yourself.'

'Where will you be?'

'Here,' Robert said. 'I think I'll have a little of that chicken. Are you sure you do not care to join me?'

He spoke with a strange vibrancy, already peeling off his black coat and unbuttoning his waistcoat. Suddenly Cassie wanted to be sick again. She swallowed and looked towards the bedroom.

'What – what will I – what will I do, Robert?'

'Whatever you wish,' Robert said.

She forced herself forward, forced herself to kiss him. He closed his arms about her waist, drawing her hard against him, crushing the skirts of her bridal gown, crushing her breasts, crushing the breath out of her. She gasped and drew back. She could feel her stomach cramping, the numbness that had possessed her beginning to melt, not into liquid passion but into a hard lump of terror.

She turned abruptly from him, passed into the unfamiliar bedroom and closed the door.

The bed had upon it a thick feather mattress covered by layers of blankets, spotless linen sheets and pillow cases and an embroidered quilt cover. On a rug by the wash-stand was a copper hipbath which had been filled with hot water. Steam still rose into the air of the bedroom and combined with the smell of new linen and new carpeting to give a queer strong musky odour. Across the top of the

144

quilt someone – the thin maid, perhaps – had laid out her nightgown and, like a pure white stain on the plum-coloured silk, a towel.

Cassie discovered her dresses from home hung up in the wardrobe and in the drawers of a mahogany tallboy her underclothing. In the bowls of the jewellery drawer were all the little trinkets that had been collected and packed in Normandy Road. The presence of familiar objects gave her no comfort.

She seated herself on the edge of the bed and took off her shoes. She stood with her back to the painted mirror and removed her headdress and bridal gown. She shook the gown and put it and the headdress away in the wardrobe, and closed the door on them.

She had bathed that morning. She was clean, pink-white clean. None the less she felt dirty. Stepping out of her underthings and floral stockings, she stepped into the bath. With a sponge from the wash-stand, she laved her body with tepid water, let it run and trickle over her skin, while the terror that had gripped her receded a little and she felt, if not calm, at least resigned.

She would put on her gown. She would slip into the bed and wait for him there. What lay beyond that she would have to wait and see. She was a plain slate upon which Robert would write the story of the beginning of their marriage according to his wishes.

She stepped cautiously out of the bath.

He came into the bedroom without warning.

He was there before Cassie quite knew what was happening.

He wore a flowered silk robe, open at the front. He was naked beneath it, naked and aroused. His body was downed with dark hair. A great spear of it ran from the forest of chest hair down his stomach to his thighs. His legs were muscular. His feet were long with thin high arches so that he appeared to come at her on toe-tip, walking daintily and swiftly.

He said nothing, not a word.

145

He caught her by the arm and pulled her to him as he had done in the parlour. This time there were no waistcoats or skirts to separate them. She felt his hands upon her hips, her spine. He pulled her hard against him. He chafed her breasts with the palm of one hand then, before Cassie could cry out in protest, he pushed her across the side of the bed and pinned her with a hand to the back of her neck.

There was no apparent cruelty in his action. She was his wife now and had no right to resist.

Robert was firm with her, as firm, swift and uncompromising as if he were administering justice. He placed her in the position he favoured and entered her suddenly, while Cassie, livid with pain, buried her face in the pillow and bit her lip till it bled.

BOOK TWO

The Marriage

Ten

Friendship was such a feature of mission preaching that the folk who gathered in the tin hut in Seaforth Street on Wednesday evenings exuded a cheerfulness that was entirely at odds with their circumstances. The dispensing of tea and buttered bread attracted those poor souls who required more than the hand of friendship to keep them going from day to day but even the drunkards who shambled in to partake of a free supper were soon affected by the optimism that flowed from Mr Albert Lassiter and his big, raw-boned wife.

Mr Lassiter had started out in life as a brewery hand but had gravitated into mission work because of natural loquaciousness and a faith so strong that it could not be denied. He had never been trained and never ordained and yet he spoke with the assurance of one who had found the secret of true happiness.

'Good tidings,' he would cry from the platform as the evening crowd assembled. 'Good tidings and good news. That's what I'm a-here to bring to you people. I'm a-here to bring you witness of what the Lord can do.'

'An' bread and butter, Mr Lassiter?'

'And bread and butter too, sir, have no fear.'

Albert Lassiter admitted no affinity with the joyless

149

brethren of the Conventions. His simple, self-appointed mandate was to proclaim the Gospel and induce trust in God; nothing that could not be understood by the humble citizens who filled the mission two or three nights in the week. Behind Mr Lassiter's uncontroversial agenda, however, lay grievances particular to the man himself. Empathy with the poor, the hungry and oppressed had led him perilously close to conflict with those salvationists to whom social ills were simply part of the divine order and the poor mere stones in the great pyramid of power by which society was governed.

Mr Lassiter was not tall but he was as muscular as a navvy. Brow, cheekbones and chin formed a square-box shape from which his smile and animated eyebrows seemed always on the verge of breaking loose. His hair was tufted like heather and in spasms of enthusiasm he would rub his hands over it and release quite a blizzard of dandruff on to his clothing. Fortunately he was not endowed with black vestments but wore a rumpled coat of coarse grey fustian with a scarf tucked into the collar in lieu of a stock.

His wife played the harmonium. The instrument was bolted to a plank bed attached to iron wheels. It had been shoved about the highways and byways of Scotland for so many years now that it was as battered as a siege weapon. Much the same could be said for Agnes Lassiter. A big, haggard woman, she combined love of her husband with a love of music and when she rendered her sacred solos in a harsh, tuneful voice she would gaze up at Albert with a rapture that would have shamed a courtesan.

The Lassiters had travelled the roads and lived rough for many years. They had preached, prayed and played the old harmonium on windswept beaches, in fields, in tents and halls in country towns and villages from Jedburgh to John o' Groat's. They had brought the Word to the worldly and spread the glad tidings that the Lord was with them and would be with you too if only you would trust Him with your life.

Albert would have taken off for the mission fields in Africa or India if one of the societies would have paid his fare. Agnes, though, would not allow him to consider it. She refused to concede that their work at home was done and, still pushing the harmonium, had led him out of the countryside into the darkness of pit towns and the sore places of the cities. There she had pointed out the sickly mill girls and starving weavers, the wretched waifs and prostitutes, whole families living on dust and ashes under railway bridges and along the iron embankments.

She had held Albert in her arms when he wept, had soothed him when he raged against the plight of the neglected poor. She had knelt by his side to pray for strength to help those who had lost everything and who needed the comfort that the love of God could bring.

When poor Albert had fallen ill it was Agnes who had nursed him back to health, though she too was dying inch by inch.

It was Agnes who had first stumbled on the empty building in Seaforth Street. Driven and desperate, filled with love of God and Albert, she had searched out the factor and begged him to allow them free use of it for six months; a place to lay their heads and rest for a while and to preach the Word of God and sing His praises while they still had breath in their bodies.

If the property had belonged to Sir Andrew Flail the Lassiters would have whistled for an answer.

Fortunately the corrugated iron hut was owned by Edward Hounslow who, in his own small way, was an ironmaster too. The 'tin hut' was all that was left of Hounslow's holdings in that part of Ravenshill, for he had moved his interests closer to the coalpits and steamship yards and Hounslow's hut was currently a store that stored nothing.

Edward Hounslow was sufficiently intrigued by Agnes Lassiter's request to interview the couple in person. He spoke with them at length and was impressed by the simplicity of their faith and by their desperation. He had

151

dozens of men in his employ, of course, and held the fate of hundreds more cupped like water in the palms of his hands; yet he was moved by memories of his own boyhood training in the Wesleyan missions around Durham and had just enough of the Calvinist in him to seek redemption by good works. Consequently he donated the use of the hut to the Lassiters, along with a stove and benches, pans, pots and bedding and even sent in a crew to resheet the roof and erect a little platform to elevate the preacher and support the weight of the old harmonium.

Now, two years on, shawled wives and workmen far from home hurried to the Seaforth Mission along with the local poor. Certain well-known citizens from the other side of the street would also steal in to do themselves a bit of good in the paradise stakes and even Edward Hounslow, the mission's benefactor, would slip in unannounced whenever he could get away from his forge and his rolling mills.

'Good tidings, Edward,' Albert Lassiter would bawl from the platform. 'Good news. Are you in health, sir? Are you fit?'

'I am, Mr Lassiter,' Edward Hounslow would reply, folding himself down on the nearest bench and covering his face with his hand as if he were embarrassed at being recognised. 'I am very fit.'

It was a mischief on Mr Lassiter's part that the more important the man the less formal the welcome.

'Miss Winfield, we've missed you these weeks. Are you well?'

'I am, Mr Lassiter. I'm very well.'

'Mr Allan Hunter, sir, have you come to hear the good news?'

'That is my purpose, Mr Lassiter.'

'Did you leave a fire on in your furnaces?'

'A peep to keep them going, aye.'

On that Wednesday evening in March, with a mild spring wind melting the snow in the gutters, Allan Hunter and Nancy Winfield arrived at the mission together. Not arm-in-arm, of course, not attached in any manner that would suggest impropriety but with an easiness between them that did Mr Lassiter's heart good to see. What Nancy Winfield was, or had been, was no mystery to the Lassiters. Even so, they were pleased that Mr Hunter had found a companion. He had been a man much in need of a friend. If the friend-in-need turned out to be a workhouse girl who spent her nights huddled in the straw in Sinclair's shed what did that matter? The pleasure each took in the other's company was palpable and, unless Mrs Lassiter's judgement of character was sadly out of whack, quite definitely innocent.

Every seat was occupied. Over by the coke stove several elderly outcasts gathered to absorb a little warmth into their bones. In the body of the hall was the customary assortment of working men and women, husbands with wives, daughters with mothers, and girls and boys old enough to be kept up late.

Agnes Lassiter was seated at the harmonium, a sheaf of sacred music pegged to the fretwork stand before her. Her cheeks were flushed, her eyes bright with the consuming fire of the lung disease that would surely carry her to heaven before her man.

On the platform's edge Mr Lassiter swayed back and forth, square face ruddy with the pleasure of doing what God had summoned him to do. He sweated heavily in the warm air and the old walls and iron roof sweated along with him and dripped condensation like a blessing on the heads of the folk below.

Edward Hounslow sat alone, a little space on either side of him as if decent clothes and white hair invited respect. He was a handsome, serious man in his sixties, as affable as his position allowed. He politely raised his hat to the whiskery widows who shared the vintage years with him and who admired him for living as long as they had, albeit with more distinction. He was just as surprised as anyone, however, when, a moment after Agnes Lassiter had coaxed the first long chord from the harmonium, the door to the hall was flung wide open and the Reverend Robert Montague, accompanied by his wife, stalked in unannounced.

Agnes Lassiter let the long chord fade into oblivion. Albert Lassiter opened his mouth and closed it again.

Heads turned and a grumbling murmur of comment and curiosity rose into the warm, moist air.

Frowning, Edward Hounslow turned to face the door. Nancy Winfield did likewise. At her side Allan Hunter swung round too. He, though, seemed less dismayed than delighted at the unexpected intrusion. He beamed at the sight of the Ravenshill minister or, more accurately, at the minister's brand-new wife and nudged Nancy with his elbow, urging her to make room for the late-comers on the end of the bench.

Reverend Montague would not be rushed. He studied the occupants of the hall as deliberately as if he were counting sheep and betrayed no hint of what he thought of the rough gathering. Only after he had completed his survey did he remove his hat and, hand upon her arm, steer young Mrs Montague towards the space that Allan Hunter had made for them.

'Good tidings, sir,' said Albert Lassiter. 'Good news.'

'Do you know who I am?' Reverend Montague called out.

'Indeed, sir, I do know who you are. You are the minister of Ravenshill Parish church.'

'My wife and I have come to join you in worship. I trust you do not object?'

'Why should I object?' said Albert Lassiter. 'You are most welcome.'

'Pray then continue, sir,' Robert said, while Mrs Montague, cheeks pale and eyes cast down, crushed her voluminous skirts into the seat beside Allan Hunter and gave a little grimace of apology as if her husband's ill-mannered interruption had somehow been all her fault.

Cassie's delight at encountering Nancy Winfield again was

154

dampened only by her fear of Robert's disapproval. Everything Cassie did these days was governed by the need to please her husband. She spoke in a timid voice, glancing nervously at Robert who, teacup in hand, was engaged in a discussion with Mr Lassiter and Mr Hounslow and paid her no attention at all.

Throughout the service she had tried not to stare too hard at the poor old men and shrivelled old women or at the more youthful men and women who sang so lustily that they almost drowned out the wheezing harmonium. The singing was not dolorous. The unfamiliar mission hymns were so gay and rousing that Cassie would have found herself uplifted by them if she had been capable of being uplifted by anything. She was, however, cowed by the suspicion that there was some purpose other than worship behind her husband's visit to the mission. She had already deduced that Robert was a man without principles who performed his duties as preacher and pastor with intellectual rigour but without devotion. His hypocrisy did not shock her any more. Nothing about him shocked her and she bore the humiliations that he inflicted upon her like leaking wounds.

She was so afraid of offending Robert that she spoke to Nancy Winfield in furtive whispers in spite of the fact that when she had first recognised the girl she had experienced a longing to reach out and clasp her in her arms as if Nancy had once been someone dear. She struggled to remind herself that Nancy Winfield had not been a friend but only a servant and that she had passed through the house in Normandy Road as fleetingly as a draught of air and that the little intimacies they had shared had no relevance now.

Even so, when Nancy spoke to her Cassie's heart gave a skip and, in spite of her fear of Robert, she responded eagerly.

'Nancy, how good it is to see you again. How have you been? Where are you living? Do you still work as a servant?'

She felt rather than saw Robert's flinty smile and, stiffening, refused the hand that the servant girl offered.

'I saw you married, miss,' Nancy told her. 'I was there, up above, in the Arms when you were dancin'.'

'Oh, are you employed at the hotel?'

'Not me,' said Nancy, cheerfully. 'I was with Mr Hunter. We were up in the gallery, watchin' everybody dance. You looked lovely, so you did.'

'Mr Hunter?'

'Aye, this is Mr Hunter. He's a manager at the Blazes.'

'Madam,' Allan Hunter said, bowing.

Cassie raised her gloved hand and let him touch it in greeting.

She heard Robert laugh and, glancing round, saw that he was observing her again. Mr Hunter was not forward or pressing but in Robert's book of rules the simplest gesture might be construed as incorrect and demeaning to her status as a minister's wife. She withdrew her hand quickly and shook her head as if to warn Mr Hunter that she was not as other women were.

'I take it, Mrs Montague,' Allan Hunter said, 'that your husband is non-sectarian?'

'Pardon?'

'That he believes in free worship.'

'Oh! I'm not sure what he believes,' Cassie said.

'Did you enjoy the singing?' Nancy asked.

'Yes, it was . . .'

'Mr Lassiter's a fine advocate for the Lord, isn't he?' said Allan, pushing the conversation past Cassie's hesitation. 'I never tire of hearing him. I come here jaded and go away refreshed.'

'Are you an evangelist then, Mr Hunter?'

'No, alas.'

'You can be what you like here. You don't have t' be anythin' special to be welcome in the mission,' Nancy said. 'Do you live in the manse, Miss Cass . . . I mean, Mrs Montague?'

'Yes.'

'Is that the big house on Bramwell hill?' Nancy said.

'It is.'

'I'm no' a servant any more,' Nancy said, 'or I'd come an' work for you.'

'Do you not work for Mr Hunter?'

'What would I do for him?' Nancy said. 'He lives in lodgin's.'

At the trestle tables Agnes Lassiter and two young women were tapping tea from a copper urn and handing out slices of bread and butter. Many members of the congregation had already departed but the ragged element remained. They devoured the bread hungrily and slopped tea from big coarse cups. The children were herded together on a long bench behind the tables where Mrs Lassiter could feed them without fuss and supplement buttered bread with cups of fresh milk and great crumbling slices of fruit cake.

The children ate without manners, cramming cake into their mouths as if they were afraid it would be taken from them even after it had been given. They were not awed by the hall nor frightened of Mrs Lassiter, Cassie noticed, and they hummed and chuckled and sat neatly all in a row, rickety legs sticking out and grubby bare toes wriggling.

'Who are they?' Cassie heard herself ask.

'Waifs,' Allan Hunter told her. 'Outcasts, mostly.'

'Who looks after them?'

'They look after themselves,' Nancy said.

'Do you know them?'

'Some o' them, aye.'

'Where do they sleep?'

Allan Hunter glanced at Nancy who gave a little frown to deflect him from blurting out the truth. There was a secret here, Cassie realised, a different sort of secret from her own.

'Wherever they can,' said Allan.

'Do you mean – out of doors?'

'Sometimes, aye,' said Nancy.

'Even in winter?'

'They usually manage to find shelter of some sort,' Allan said.

'I'm surprised they survive,' said Cassie.

'Oh, that's somethin' you have to learn, Miss Cassie,' Nancy told her.

Cassie knew that Nancy had been raised in the workhouse but until now she had failed to appreciate what hardships such an upbringing entailed. The girl was hardly larger or more sturdy than a ten-year-old child. Her pretty little face, with the bend in the nose, was drawn and pale. Her clothes, though carefully patched and perfectly clean, were threadbare.

Cassie said, 'Is that what you've had to learn, Nancy?'

'I couldna come to work for you even if you had a position open,' Nancy Winfield declared. 'An' by-the-by, I don't have to come to Mr Lassiter's for to get my bread. I'm not starvin'.'

'I'm sorry. I didn't mean . . .'

Tears welled up in Cassie's eyes.

In six weeks of marriage, six weeks of silent humiliation, she had shed not a single tear, but now she saw how it was with other women and realised that they would consider her pampered.

'I'm sorry, Nancy. I didn't mean to offend you.'

She brushed her lids quickly with the edge of her glove.

She felt as if they were judging her, not just Nancy but all of them, rickety children with their mouths full of cake, old women twisted by unremitting childbearing, old men crippled by a lifetime of hard labour.

Allan Hunter's square, competent hand closed on her arm. She felt pity in him, the same pity that had been in her but changed somehow, somehow made tender and loving.

'*Cassandra?*'

She smelled Robert's smell, that dry, powdery cat's fur smell and from the corner of her eye saw him loom behind her but, curiously, she no longer feared him quite as much as she had done a half-hour ago.

'Who is this, Cassandra?' Robert said. 'I do not believe I know these people.'

'Allow me to do the honours, Mr Montague,' Allan said and duly made the introductions.

'I believe we have a mutual acquaintance,' Robert said.

'Major Jerome, do you mean?' Allan said.

'Yes.'

'Well, I can hardly say that Major Jerome is an acquaintance of mine. I've met him once or twice but, if you will pardon me, he has the disconcerting habit of not keeping appointments,' Allan said. 'Is he still here in Ravenshill?'

'He is,' said Robert.

'He lives in the manse with us,' Cassie heard herself say.

'Does he?' said Allan. 'While he learns the ropes, I suppose?'

'Ropes?' said Cassie. 'What do you mean?'

'Johnny's studying the process of iron-making, my dear.'

'He said nothing to me about it,' Cassie said.

'Of course he did not,' Robert said. 'It is business.'

An hour ago Cassie would not have dared question her husband but in the low-beamed, sweating tin hall with its reek of tea and stale sweat, she felt strangely protected. She heard herself say, 'Is Johnny going into business on his own account? Does it have to do with—'

Robert interrupted. 'What do you think of the mission, my dear?'

'I – I'm much taken with it.'

Nancy said not a word but she did not let her gaze stray from Reverend Montague and she uttered a little '*uh*' as if she expected more from Cassie.

Robert rounded on her at once. 'Who are you, girl? In what manner or capacity are you acquainted with my wife?'

'Nancy was a servant in our house, Robert,' Cassie explained. 'She was our maid for a while.'

'A wee while,' Nancy added.

'Oh, I see. You're a servant, are you?'

'I was, sir, but not now.'

'What are you now? Are you married? Are you somebody's wife?'

'Not me, Minister Montague,' Nancy said. 'I'm just one o' them.'

'Ah!' Robert nodded. 'In that case, Miss Winfield, you may be interested to learn that I am very impressed with what Mr Lassiter does for you people. In fact I'm exploring the possibility of offering similar assistance to those in need.'

'What sort o' assistance?' Nancy asked. 'More bread and butter?'

'More than that. Much more,' Robert said.

'Really?' said Allan.

'It's only an idea at the present time,' Robert said. 'And I prefer not to discuss it just yet, if you have no objection.'

'I've no objection,' Allan said.

'Will you really try to help them, though?' Cassie said.

And Robert told her, 'Yes.'

He was merciless that night. He seemed intent not only upon appeasing his desire but upon uncovering the sullen particle in her that had so far eluded him.

Cassie had already learned that Robert was just as dedicated to order and ritual in private as he was in public. He would organise their marital encounters with the same formality as would organise a Session clerks' meeting. His love-making was never uninhibited and the ceremony would always conclude with Cassie sprawled face down across the ottoman in the parlour that Robert had taken to calling the Turkish room. He even instructed her what to wear before he summoned her from the bedroom.

Obediently, she would put on lace drawers, a short waist petticoat with an edging of broderie anglaise, a tight front-lacing corset with soft whalebone inserts that pushed up her breasts until they seemed to spill from the ruffle of lace that hid the garment's hard steel clasps and chamois leather sleeves. When Robert called her she would step

160

barefoot and bare-legged out of the bright, white light of her bedroom into the firelit parlour, would advance reluctantly towards the Egyptian chair where Robert waited, his legs thrust out and his embroidered robe thrown open.

He would command her to parade before him, directing her this way and that with his forefinger so that he might observe the precise effect of each revelation; all done with the same patient solemnity, the same expressionless absorption that gripped him when he read or wrote or prayed.

For five or ten minutes he would put her through a repertoire of poses, would watch without apparent pleasure or arousal and then, and only then, would he beckon her to come to him.

At least when they were linked together Cassie could pretend that what her husband did to her was done out of passion and out of passion, love.

If he had kissed her or caressed her she might have learned to respond to his sudden, calculated intrusions. But, saying nothing, he merely pulled her on to the floor or thrust her across the ottoman where he would draw up her petticoat, carefully part her drawers and uncouple the clasps of her corset.

When he was done, there was nothing to show that the act of love-making had meant anything to him. He would observe her disinterestedly for a moment or two and would then take himself into the narrow bedroom at the rear of the parlour to wash and, she presumed, to sleep, leaving her to crawl away into the bright, white bedroom, too numb, too dispossessed to weep.

'Why,' Pippa would declare, 'you look quite pale, Cassie, dearest. Does marriage not agree with you?'

Cassie would assume a cultivated smile and repeat as if by rote, 'Marriage agrees with me very well.'

'Is Robert all that a husband should be?'

'He takes care of me, Pippa, if that's what you mean.'

Even when Pippa and she were alone, she could not

admit what really went on in the Turkish room. Such acts, she knew, were not the fruit of a proper marriage. Somehow, though, she could not separate Robert's actions from her own, his mastery from her meekness. It was as if her skittishness before marriage, her foolishness and naïveté justified her husband's perverse behaviour. Therefore she told Pippa nothing, gave her sister no warning about the perils of the marriage bed.

There was also the ever-present Johnny Jerome to contend with. Cassie detested him, for he exuded an air of sympathy and collaboration, as if his position in the household were somehow equal to her own.

'Good morning, Mistress Montague,' Jerome would croon when she joined him in the dining-room for breakfast. 'Did you spend a good night?'

'Yes, Mr Jerome, thank you.'

'You don't seem awfully rested, if I may say so.'

'I am very rested, thank you.'

'Where's Robert?'

'Dressing, I believe.'

'What will you have? I can recommend the kedgeree.'

'What is that?'

'Fish, hard-boiled eggs and rice. I taught Miss Rundall how to prepare it,' Johnny Jerome would say. 'It's Robert's favourite dish. Did you not know?'

'There are many things about Robert I do not know.'

'Ah, well, you'll learn. In time, Mistress Montague, you'll learn.'

During the long hours when Robert was off about his business or closeted with his books, Cassie felt even more isolated.

Cook and maids were not hers to command. They communed with her stiffly and if, seeking company, Cassie was thoughtless enough to wander into the kitchen they would immediately raise a hullaballoo and complain to Major Jerome about the unwarranted intrusion and it would be up to Johnny to placate them and explain to Cassie how touchy cooks could be and how certain foibles in servants' behaviour must be excused.

He said that he would see to it that she was given 'her place', but that in the interest of harmony it might be as well if she steered clear of the kitchens and left the choice of menus and the checking of the domestic accounts to him. After all, he had to do *something* to repay Robert for his hospitality, at least until Robert found other work for him to do.

'What sort of "other work"?'

'Oh, this and that, Mistress Montague, just this and that.'

'To do with the iron works?'

'I'm exploring, shall we say, that branch of engineering, yes.'

'On Robert's instruction?'

'Out of interest, Mistress Montague, purely out of interest.'

Cassie did not believe him. It seemed to her that Johnny Jerome's only role was to provide companionship for Robert.

In early spring, when snow was still upon the ground, the men would walk out together. From the upstairs window Cassie would watch them tramp away across the moorland or stroll upon the back lawn, trails of cigar smoke hanging behind them, like whispered breath. What did they converse about? she wondered. Did they reminisce about their army days or discuss religious matters or the book that Robert was writing? Did they talk, perhaps, about her and her inadequacies as a wife?

When March came, though, and grass showed again, out came bat and ball and the men occupied the back lawn almost every afternoon, batting and bowling with a competitive vigour that brought a glow to Robert's cheeks and dewed the brisk little major's brow with sweat. Sometimes Luke Simmonds, the horse boy, would be pressed to serve as fieldsman or a keeper of the wicket; and all three would play the game, shouting and laughing like schoolboys until Robert's pastoral duties called him away.

Meanwhile Cassie confined herself to the top of the house or loitered in the ground-floor rooms that were dedicated to Robert's history and Robert's pursuits.

She was at liberty to visit her family at any time, of course, or put herself back on to the circuit of visits to the elderly. But Cassie could not bring herself to leave the manse except on those occasions when her role as the minister's wife demanded it. She was afraid of what she might reveal, afraid that one kind word might release the flood of tears that lay within her.

On that March night, however, there was a shift in the relationship, a subtle and unexpected change.

When he had made love to her Robert did not pull away. He continued to lie upon her, arms braced on either side of her head. He put his mouth close to her ear and whispered in a voice so hoarse that she almost mistook it for tenderness.

'Why do you not love me, Cassie?' he said.

She stirred beneath his weight, tried to look over her shoulder at him, to see his face. He was too close, humped over her, his face in her hair.

'Is it because of what we do here at night?' he said.

'I'm your wife, Robert.'

'Then why do you not love me?'

The truth lay on her tongue like the taste of him, curled like an irritating hair on the back of her throat. She was wet with him, worn by him, yet there was in her a sudden little spark that had not been there before, an absence of meekness, that prevented her from giving him the answer he expected.

'You are not hurt by what we do,' he said, 'not now, surely?'

'No.'

'Then why do you not love me?'

'I do not think that you love me,' she said.

He released his weight carefully.

Cassie sank against the contours of the ottoman. She wanted him to go, not to probe and penetrate her thoughts as efficiently as he probed and penetrated her body. She was determined that she would not lie to appease him.

'I begin to think, Cassie, that you are incapable of love.'

'If this is what you mean by love, Robert, then perhaps I am.'

'Do you admit it?'

'What do you wish me to admit?

'No,' he said, holding her. 'No, you must tell me. You must say it.'

'I have nothing to say.'

'You're not incapable of love, are you?' he insisted.

Then she realised that he was asking the question not of her but of himself. She felt the desire to placate him wane away to nothing. At last it dawned on her that Robert did not possess her completely, that while she might belong to him, she still had a self, changed by marriage but not detached.

'You must learn to love me, Cassie.'

'Why?'

'Because I'm your husband. Because I chose you to be my wife.'

'What if I cannot?' she said. 'What if I am incapable of giving you love?'

'I won't let you go,' he said again.

'Will this satisfy you then, this and nothing else?'

'What?'

She tilted her shoulders back so that the line of her body was exposed before him; not done to please or taunt him but to turn what he had taught her back against him.

'This,' she said.

He pulled her abruptly to her feet. 'Go to bed.'

'My bed or yours?'

'Go to bed, damn it.'

She glanced at the garments that lay strewn about the ottoman and resisted the temptation to pick them up and carry them away to hide, like her shame, in the bright, white, feminine bedroom that Robert could not bring

165

himself to enter in daylight let alone after dark.
'Goodnight,' she said tersely, and walked away.

Eleven

'None of my affair, of course, old boy,' said Johnny Jerome, 'but what's got into the little lady these days?' He paused and amended the question. 'I mean, she does not seem as sulky as she was. Is she settling into a life of wedded bliss?'

'What has Cassandra been saying to you?'

'Oh, nothing, nothing,' Johnny assured his benefactor. 'It's just that she seems more self-assured.'

'Has she been squabbling with Miss Rundall again?'

'Not to my knowledge.'

'No love lost there, I fear,' Robert said.

'No, none at all,' Johnny agreed.

Side by side the men strode along the stony track that led from the rear of the manse up on to the moorland.

To the west were the trees and rolling parklands of Sir Andrew Flail's estates, all tame and cultivated. Ahead, rising through heather and birch scrub, lay the ridges of Bramwell Moor, divided by drystone dikes into rough pastures that Flail leased out to cattle grazers and shepherds who could afford no better pickings for their beasts.

Here the minister and the major would walk whenever time and weather permitted the luxury of 'a constitutional'. They would linger beneath the pines, gaze out

167

across the moorland or back at the hills, at the thatches of Bramwell village and the chimneys of Ravenshill, all miniaturised by space and distance and they would listen to the desolate cries of curlews and the *kee-ing* of the buzzards that circled high overhead and because they were modern gentlemen they would resist the tug of wild nature, would light up a pair of thin Havanas, blow smoke across the landscape, sip brandy from Johnny's silver hip-flask and pose against the skyline as if they owned everything that the eye could see.

'You know, old boy,' said Johnny, out of the blue, 'I really rather admire your sweet wee wife.'

'I thought you did not care for women?'

'Never said that, never in my life. I do not care for certain women, that's true, but then no sensible man actually cares for the sex as a whole, do they?' Johnny sipped from the flask, tapped cigar ash on to the ancient grey stones at his feet. 'I wish she would take to me, though. It would be more comfortable for all concerned if we could be friends.'

'She's jealous of you, John, that's all,' Robert told him. 'Why do you say that you admire her?'

'Well, it can't have been easy for a young girl to be suddenly pitched into marriage with a fellow like you.'

'A fellow like me?' said Robert, not displeased.

'I mean, brought among strangers. I believe she's adjusting very well, all things considered.'

'Does she ever talk to you about how she feels?'

'No, no. Hardly talks to me at all.'

'She is, by nature, too modest for her own good.'

'I don't think she even knows what's going on,' Johnny said.

'Of course she doesn't know what's going on,' Robert said.

Johnny paused then asked, 'What is going on, by the way?'

'Hah!' Robert flung an arm about Johnny's shoulders and gave him a brusque, affectionate hug. 'Are things too slow for you around here, is that it? Do you yearn for something more exciting than lolling around a manse all day?'

'Now that you mention it, old boy, I do feel rather – what? – excess to requirements.'

'Not for much longer, my friend,' Robert said. 'It will soon be April.'

'April? What happens in April?'

'My account with the Highland Bank will be fatter by two hundred pounds.'

'Ah, yes, your quarterly emolument from dear old Dada?'

'From dear Dada's agent, to be precise.'

'The Highland Bank?' Johnny said. 'Never heard of it.'

'Head office in Inverness. Branch office in Glasgow.'

'Is this your father's banking house?'

'In every sense.'

'Is it safe, old boy? I mean, what with one crisis after another shaking the confidence of the city one can't be too careful,' Johnny said.

'The Highland Bank is as solid as Stirling Castle. My father's been a shareholder for many years. It's where the family fortune's deposited.'

'Have you a reason for entrusting your money to the Highland?'

'Indeed, I have,' Robert said. 'The Highland is also the depository of Ravenshill Parish funds.'

'Have you invested Mrs Montague's dowry there too, by any chance?'

'Safely tucked away, yes.'

'I had better be careful,' Johnny said, ruefully. 'You'll be after my army pension next. Tell me, have you decided how to use this accumulated capital?'

'I intend to open a Home Mission fund.'

'A what?'

'A fund to finance a programme of Church Extension.'

'Dear Lord, don't tell me you're going to build churches?'

'Yes, iron churches.'

'Where?'

'In Ravenshill.'

'For that you'll need land, land and backing.'

'Oh, certainly, a very great deal of backing.'

'And a committee?'

'Boards and partners, yes.'

'And an agent, old boy?'

'I already have an agent.'

'Do you?' Johnny said.

'Of course I do.'

'Yours truly, do you mean?'

'Who else can I trust?'

'True,' Johnny said. 'What about partners?'

'A fellow called Hounslow, the Lassiters, and your friend Allan Hunter.'

'Hunter's hardly my friend,' Johnny said, frowning. 'Besides, what can Hunter possibly contribute to a financial partnership?'

'Expertise,' Robert said, 'and respectability.'

'Oh, I can vouch for his respectability,' Johnny said. 'Who else?'

'My father-in-law. We'll need Cuthbert on our side when the time comes.'

'When the time comes for what?'

'To make a killing,' Robert said.

Johnny pursed his lips and let out a little *phew* that may have signalled admiration but, in fact, inclined more to apprehension.

'I do hope you know what you're doing, old boy.'

'Feathering my nest,' Robert said, with a shrug.

'Gilding the lily, more like,' Johnny said, anxiously.

'That too. That too,' said Robert.

Robert was firm about it, quite adamant, in fact. He issued the command over breakfast. When Cassie looked startled Robert became quite cross with her.

'Do you wish me to go alone to Seaforth Street?' Cassie asked.

'Have I not just said as much?'

'Will you not be with me?'

'I have a meeting to attend, in Glasgow.'

'What sort of meeting?'

Robert seemed about to deny her even that innocent bit of information, then, relenting, said, 'I'm addressing the Glasgow Association.'

'On what subject?'

'The position of women in heathen societies.'

'How interesting,' Cassie said. 'I'd like to hear you speak on that topic.'

'Women are not admitted to the University College.'

Cassie toyed with the remnants of a kippered herring. She had eaten most of what had been put before her, for her appetite had improved. Mama would have put it down to spring but Cassie did not believe in the affective powers of weather and season.

'Is it proper for me to attend the mission service alone?' she said.

'Quite proper. Unless your sister would care to—' Robert began.

Cassie interrupted. 'What about you, Mr Jerome?'

'Me? What about me?'

'Would you not care to hear the Word of God?'

'I've heard the Word of God,' Johnny said, glancing at Robert.

'Johnny has other things to do,' Robert said.

'What things?' said Cassie. 'What *do* you have to do, Mr Jerome?'

'I – I really . . .'

'Simmonds will drive you to Seaforth Street and drive you home again,' Robert stated. 'You'll be perfectly safe.'

'I know I will,' said Cassie. 'I can think of few places safer than the Seaforth mission. The point is why do you wish me to go at all?'

'Do you not enjoy Albert Lassiter's oratory?'

'Certainly. I find his enthusiasm very inspiring.'

'Well, then?' said Robert.

What, apart from porridge, a kipper and several slices of brown bread, had got into her today? She felt stronger than she had done in weeks. The spark of rebellion that had been kindled in the Turkish room had flared up in her again but she gave no sign to Robert that she longed to return to Seaforth Street, to the damp iron building where men like Albert Lassiter – and Allan Hunter – gave forth a sentiment that could not be measured in pulpit platitudes.

'You still have not told me why you wish me to go,' Cassie said. 'Am I not entitled to request an explanation?'

Johnny Jerome shrank a little in his chair. He clasped his coffee cup in both hands as if it might ward off the evil spirits of domestic quarrel. His gaze slid from wife to husband, from husband to wife. For the first time since his arrival in Bramwell he felt like an intruder.

'I thought you might be bored staying at home,' Robert said.

'How considerate of you.'

'Besides, I have it in mind to form an association between Mr Lassiter and myself in the matter of poor relief. That is all there is to it,' Robert said thinly. 'Now will you do as I ask?'

'With pleasure,' Cassie answered him.

The night was dry and brisk. The streets of Ravenshill were brushed by a little wind that, while not chill, had a crispness to it that increased Cassie's exuberance. Her triumph at the breakfast table had been a minor skirmish in a war that she could not possibly win. She had learned, however, that it was possible to challenge Robert and, in the process, discomfit Johnny Jerome and the glow of her achievement had been with her all day long.

She had even invited Janey, who aspired to be a lady's maid, to assist her in selecting a suitable dress, nothing too grand or too expensive, and had gone so far as to allow Janey to help her hook up her crinoline.

The girl was annoyingly ingratiating but, Cassie had to admit, very dexterous when it came to taping the awkward hoops of the 'cage' in which fashionable ladies, even ministers' wives, were expected to appear in public these days. Beneath the swaying skirts Cassie wore a pair of magenta-coloured drawers that Robert had purchased for her through the Swansdown Catalogue. Devilment, a kind of mischief quite devoid of vanity, had prompted her to wear them for her visit to the mission hall.

As she rode the gig through the streets of Ravenshill, however, she was acutely aware of the clinging silk things, felt the garish hue through the pores of her skin and wondered if Allan Hunter would sense that she was not as prim as he had judged her to be, not all through at any rate.

There was a faint glow in the sky above the mission hall. Scudding cloud chased across the heavens and mingled with smoke from the chimneys and, so Cassie thought, delineated the scene like a gloomy etching.

Luke Simmonds was oblivious to the unusual quality of the night. He was a big, blond boy with a frisk of fair hair bobbing under the brim of his hat and shoulders that bulged, ox-like, under his coarse woollen jacket.

'Is this the place, Mittress Montague?' he said.

'It is. You may let me down at the door.'

'No' verra nice, is it? Am ah tae come inside wi' you?'

'Did Mr Montague not give you instruction on that score?'

'Nah, Mittress Montague, he didna.'

'Or Mr Jerome?'

'Nah, nor him neither.'

'Do you wish to join in the hymn-singing?'

'Ah – em – ah'em no' sure.'

He had brought the horse to a halt, the wheels of the gig slotted neatly against the curve of the cobbles. He was a bumpkin, no question of that, but he was exceedingly good with horses which, Cassie supposed, was why Johnny Jerome had employed him in the first place. Twisting the reins in his big hands, he squirmed with indecision, in sore need of an order to put him at ease and steer him from one action to the next.

'Is there a public house in the vicinity, a respectable house?'

'Ah – eh – ah – em . . .'

'If I give you sixpence will you promise to drink no more than two pints of ale and to be back here in good order by half past nine o'clock?'

'Where, Mittress Montague?'

'Here, right here in front of the mission hall.'

'Aye, ah will.'

'Without fail?'

'Aye.'

She gave him sixpence from her purse.

He would have smacked the reins against the horse's crupper and been off in search of refreshment at once if she had not ordered him to stop and come around to the rear of the vehicle and open the gate for her, lower the step and give her his arm while she squeezed her skirts through the gate and alighted, floating on a cushion of air, on to the pavement.

From the doorway Allan Hunter watched her descent.

The manager was not the only witness to the arrival of the minister's wife. Six or seven old women and two or three rough-looking men were loitering along the wall, taking a last chew of tobacco, a last puff at a pipe, a last swig from a bottle before they braced themselves and entered the tin hut for a dose of redemption and a slice of bread and butter. They said nothing, did not growl, chirrup or applaud when the energetic little wind caught the edges of the lady's skirts, lifted them up and exposed the fancy magenta drawers beneath.

'Are ye down, Mittress Montague?'

'I am, thank you.'

'Can ah go now?'

'Half past nine o'clock, Simmonds, no later.'

'Aye.' He vaulted over the side of the gig and plucked up the reins before 'Mittress' Montague could have second thoughts.

Blushing, Cassie pushed down the wires of her crinoline

and gave herself a little shake as the gig jolted away from the pavement's edge and left her there, with all eyes on her.

'Is Mr Montague not with you tonight, ma'am?'

She blushed deeply. It seemed ridiculous that after all she had endured in the Turkish room she could still blush at the sound of a man's voice, yet the humiliations that Robert had inflicted upon her faded when she swung round to confront Allan Hunter.

'No, my – my husband is otherwise engaged.'

'In that case, if I may offer you my arm . . .'

She took it as once she had taken Robert's arm. But now there was no conceit in the gesture, for she felt in Mr Hunter an affection so subtle as to be almost undetectable. They loitered together while the gallery of outcasts glowered and then, with a little nod, Allan led Cassie into the lighted hall.

Cassie said, 'I thought that Nancy would be with you.'

'Why would you think that?'

'You seem to be such good friends.'

'We are – but she is in some ways a secretive girl.'

'Secretive?' Cassie said. 'I always found her most open.'

'Perhaps "shy" is a better word. She keeps herself to herself.'

'How does she live?'

'From hand to mouth, I gather,' Allan said.

'If it's a matter of money . . .'

'Is it not always a matter of money, ma'am? But I doubt if she'll accept charity,' Allan said. 'She'll certainly take nothing from me.'

'Except your friendship?' Cassie said.

'Oh, that is freely offered and freely received.'

'How did you meet Nancy?'

Hesitation suggested that he might not be telling the truth.

'Here,' he said, 'at the mission.'

'It is a famous place for meeting people, it seems.'

'And for making friends,' Allan said.

'I have not been here often enough to make friends,' Cassie said.

'How long does it take to make a friend?' Allan said.

'Some considerable time, surely.'

'I'm of the opinion that it can happen suddenly.'

'How would one then know if the friend is to be trusted?'

'You wouldn't. You would have to take trust itself on trust.'

'Oh, that is too profound for me,' Cassie said.

'I do not mean to sound pretentious.'

'I know that you do not,' Cassie said and, as if to reassure him, gave him a soft little tap upon the forearm.

Seated together on a bench near the rear of the hall they conversed as if stiltedness was an essential ingredient of decorum.

'I am not an educated person, Mrs Montague, not like you.'

'Me? What makes you suppose that I am educated?'

'The fact that you are married to a minister.'

'Reverend Montague did not marry me for my education,' Cassie said. 'I believe he married me because he fell in love.'

'I cannot blame him for that.'

'Mr Hunter! Really! The remark does not seem suitable for such short acquaintance.'

'It was forward of me. I should not have said it – even if it is the truth.'

'I'm sure your wife would not like to hear you pay compliments to a woman you hardly know.'

'My wife is dead.'

'Oh, I'm sorry.'

Cassie felt sympathy for him and at the same time relief that there was no woman at home to whom he might compare her as she compared him to Robert.

'She has been dead for some time now,' Allan said.

'Do you have children?'

176

'I have a son. He is boarded out.'

'Is he far away? Do you not see him?'

'I visit him every Sunday afternoon.'

'And you? Where do you lodge?'

'At Mrs McGuire's boarding-house, not far from here.'

'Is it comfortable?'

'It suits my needs.'

'I would like to meet your son,' Cassie heard herself say.

'Why?'

'To see if he is like you. What is his name?'

'Oh, he's better than I am, a proud and sturdy lad. His name is Tom.'

In spite of the clear weather there were a few empty spaces in the hall tonight. The children were all ranked against the wall, however, legs sticking out, faces eager, not so much for preaching to begin as for a share of the peppermint candy that one of the young women passed out from a brown paper bag.

Though it was now some minutes after eight o'clock Mr Lassiter had not begun his customary speech of welcome and praise to the Lord. He appeared to be concerned for his wife who, though smiling, did not seem to be quite herself.

She was seated at the harmonium, her long body in its sparrow-brown dress raked away from the keyboard as if she were about to take flight. Her shoes, brown too, were worn down at the heels and her brown stockings were wrinkled. She smiled and shook her head while Mr Lassiter addressed her anxiously and, with a hand upon her back, offered her first a glass of water and then a large red-spotted handkerchief.

Cassie was unaware of the little drama that was being enacted upon the platform before her. She was too wrapped up in feeling sorry for the lonely widower with his son put out and no consolations in his life except the mission hall and, perhaps, his friendship with Nancy.

Allan Hunter frowned in the direction of the platform then turned to Cassie, cleared his throat, and asked,

'Who's the fellow who lives with you? Jerome, I mean? Is he a particular friend of yours?'

'No friend of mine,' said Cassie, bluntly. 'A friend of my husband's.'

'He does reside in the manse, however?'

'Unfortunately, yes.'

'I gather that you do not care for Major Jerome.'

A certain caution stole over Cassie, a feeling that to complain about Johnny Jerome to a stranger might lead her into other confessions. She chose her words with care. 'Major Jerome and my husband served in the army together.'

'Jerome spends an inordinate amount of time nosing about the works. He has a letter of access from Andrew Flail which seems to give him the right to turn up at all hours,' Allan said. 'I thought perhaps he was a friend of yours.'

'If you mean, Mr Hunter, do I know why Johnny Jerome is interested in iron-founding I'm afraid it is as much a mystery to me as it is to you.'

'He talks of investment,' Allan said. 'He questions me closely about the quality of iron and what various grades are used for. He's an engineer, I gather, and understands everything I tell him.'

'Then you know more than I do,' Cassie said.

'Your husband, Mrs Montague, may I ask what he wants from Albert Lassiter and what plans he has in mind for the mission?'

'I have no idea what you're talking about, Mr Hunter.'

Allan seemed to be on the point of asking more questions about Jerome, possibly about Robert too. Cassie wondered if his attentiveness was simply a manifestation of the calculating instinct which drove men on and reduced most of their relationships to dealings of one kind or another.

She began to wish that Nancy had come after all, if only to relieve her suspicion of Mr Hunter's motives and her disappointment in the turn that the conversation had taken.

'If any information does come your way, Mrs Montague, perhaps . . .'

She stifled her anger and, sitting higher still, exclaimed gaily, 'Oh, look. I believe we are about to begin.'

She was still angry, as much with herself as with Allan Hunter. The service had not soothed her. She had said her prayers, chanted the hymns, listened to the missionary's inspiring lecture and the missionary's wife's rather gasping rendition of 'The Weary Draw to Rest', with no lessening of the bitter feeling that she had been played for a fool.

As soon as the final blessing was called and Mr Lassiter reminded them where the poor box was situated and where the tea urn was to be found, Cassie rose, squeezed past the ironworks manager and bustled out of the hall.

The wind had freshened. It aerated her skirts and tweaked the scarf with which she had secured her hat for the ride home. She stood hesitantly on the pavement's edge, hands thrust down to restrain the twirl of wire and cloth.

'Simmonds,' she called out. 'Simmonds, where are you?'

She told herself that she wanted to escape from Seaforth Street, never to clap eyes on Albert Lassiter or, for that matter, on Allan Hunter again.

'Sim-*monds,* bring the gig here at once.'

Her voice sounded shrewish and spoiled. She looked this way and that, desperately, but when the hand touched her shoulder she was instantly still.

'Why are you running away?' Allan said.

'I told the boy to be here at half past nine o'clock.'

'It's barely that now.'

'He should be here. I told him to be here with the gig.'

He was still touching her, a hand upon her shoulder as if to hold her down. She felt the wind maul the ridiculous hoops, lift her skirts in front and then at the back. She wrestled with them, patting and slapping at the flounces.

'Come inside,' Allan said. 'Wait for him inside. Drink a cup of tea.'

'I don't want to drink tea. I want to go home.'

'Something's upset you. What is it?'

'I do not like being interrogated, Mr Hunter, if you must know.'

'I'm sorry. I didn't intend to interrogate you. I simply wondered . . .'

'I'm not privy to my husband's business. And if I was, I would not betray his confidences to a total stranger.'

'I see.'

'What do you see, Mr Hunter?'

'Come inside. Your man will turn up in due course.'

'What if he doesn't? What if I am stranded here?'

'We'll find him, never fear. He can't be far away.'

'Stop it,' she said. 'Stop patronising me. I'm not a child.'

'He'll be in the tavern, I expect.'

'I know he'll be in the tavern. I told him to go to the tavern. I gave him sixpence to buy refreshment.'

'Ah!'

'Ah? What does "ah" mean, Mr Hunter? Does "ah" mean that you consider me a fool for trusting a servant?'

'Perhaps we should go in search of this lad of yours,' Allan suggested.

'I would not know where to begin.'

'No, but I do,' Allan said.

'Do you expect me to enter a public house with you?'

'I don't know what your boy looks like.'

'Fetch me a hackney, that's the simplest solution.'

'The nearest rank's half a mile away. The simplest solution is for me to accompany you around the corner, find your gig and let me unearth your servant from the public house while you wait outside.'

'In the street?'

Allan sighed. 'It's no use, Mrs Montague.'

'What, what's no use?'

'You're stuck with me.'

'I – I – I can't loiter in the street,' Cassie stammered, 'like a – a . . .'

When he laughed it all changed. His laughter should have roused her to fury. Instead it caused her to recognise in herself the wilful streak that she so despised in her sister, a childish petulance bred into them in Normandy Road where obedience was paper-thin and, in small things if not in large, Pippa and she had had everything their own way.

He laughed again. He drew her round to face him and took his hand from her shoulder. 'You'll not be mistaken for one of those ladies, Mrs Montague,' he assured her, 'not even in magenta drawers.'

'Mr Hunter!'

'Enough,' he said. 'Come along, take my arm. Let's see if we can locate this boy of yours and find out if he's sober enough to drive you home.'

'And if he's not?'

'I'll do it,' Allan Hunter said.

Johnny's rooms were on the first floor of the manse. There he could put his feet up and tuck into the latest novel by Surtees or Reynolds, curl his hair – what was left of it – by reading sensational accounts of vampires and werewolves or by browsing through *The Newgate Calendar*, that vast compendium of crime and punishment which, to the major's way of thinking, better reflected the human condition than a whole shelf of theological tracts.

With both master and mistress away for the evening it was incumbent upon him to remain 'at stations', until one or other of them returned. Robert, in fact, would not return at all. At the last minute, he had decided to accept the offer of accommodation in one of the colleges and stay overnight in Glasgow. Consequently, Major John Jerome was officer of the watch and obliged to stay fully clad and moderately sober until Mistress Montague returned from town.

It was after half past ten o'clock before the clang of the

181

doorbell echoed through the house. Johnny, leaving nothing to chance, bounded out of his armchair and pranced downstairs to let the lady in.

She bustled into the hall with her idiotic skirts puffed out and her hat tipped back. She looked, Johnny thought, like one of those idealised shepherdesses that the kings of France had hankered after and painters like Boucher had immortalised. Nothing idealised about Mistress Montague, though. She was far too sparky to pass for a winsome maiden and the angry glint in her blue eyes put Johnny on his guard.

She left the front door wide open behind her and when Johnny made to close it, rounded on him instantly.

'Wait,' she snapped, as if the absence of her lord and master had elevated her to a position of authority. 'Leave it.'

Johnny peeped outside. 'Why?'

'Because you will be obliged to put away the gig and do whatever it is you do with the horse,' Cassie told him.

'Where's Luke?' Johnny asked with just a faint hint of panic. 'What's happened to Simmonds?'

'Your lad's in the back of the conveyance. If you look over the rail you will see him, dead drunk, sir, and snoring like a pig.'

'Oh, God!' Johnny said. 'Did you have to drive yourself home?'

'Most certainly not.'

She was still mad, still glowing.

There was something strange about her, though, something upon which Johnny could not quite put his finger. He was used to the inconsistencies of womankind, to their moans and groans, to moods that veered from ecstasy to despair in the space of half an hour, to moon madness, mockery and coquettish flirtations – but not to this sort of glowing bossiness.

'How did you get here then?' he asked.

'A friend, an acquaintance, did the honours.'

'Who would that be?' Johnny said, then, with a little

182

twitch of the brow, added, 'I know – Hunter.'

'It was indeed Mr Hunter.'

'Where is the fellow?'

'Gone,' Cassie said. 'He tethered the horse and braked the gig, then, in spite of my entreaty that he take supper with us, doffed his hat like a gentleman and set off to walk home to Ravenshill.'

'Well, that won't kill him,' Johnny said quietly, hiding the little wavelet of anxiety that lapped within him. 'I assume you met Hunter at the mission?'

'Of course. Do you suppose that I would meet him anywhere else?'

'What? No, no, no.' Johnny reached out for the bell rope. 'I'll fetch Janey. She'll take care of you.'

'I do not need taken care of, Mr Jerome. I suggest that you take care of your boy, however, before he vomits over the upholstery again.'

'It's that bad, is it?'

'It took us a half-hour to find him. In some gutter of a public house behind the hotel. He was in the company of two sailors.'

'Oh, no!' Johnny groaned.

'Two sailors who seemed manifestly reluctant to yield him up to us. Fortunately Mr Hunter seems to be quite an exponent of the fisticular art and soon put those sailors in their place.'

'Flat on their backs?' Johnny said.

'Yes, quite! He also had to "lay out" – is that the phrase?'

'It'll do,' said Johnny.

'Lay out Simmonds too, for Simmonds seemed disinclined to accompany us home. He was certainly in no fit state to take charge of a horse.'

'A sorry state of affairs, indeed,' Johnny said. 'I'll give the lad his marching orders first thing in the morning.'

'No need for that. Just make sure he is severely reprimanded.' Cassie wagged her hat and scarf at Johnny so forcefully that her skirts shook and the invisible wires creaked in sympathy. 'If my husband is inclined to dismiss him then be good enough to tell him that I do not wish the boy sacked, only scolded. Where is Robert, by the way? Is he not back yet?'

'He's staying in Glasgow overnight,' Johnny said.

'When was this decision made?'

'This morning, I think.'

Blue eyes glinted, the colour in her cheeks intensified.

Johnny was almost intimidated. He was also anxious about Simmonds, for young lads not used to strong drink were liable to choke while insensible. The last thing he wanted was a corpse on his hands. He would have enough explaining to do to Robert without that.

'I see. I see,' Cassie said. 'Very well.'

She moved towards the stairs and Johnny towards the open door.

'Mr Jerome?'

'Madam?'

'I will take tea, tea and hot buttered toast. Will you attend to that too, please, after you've seen to Simmonds?'

'I think the cook's in bed, Mistress Montague.'

'In that case – wake her. Or do the job yourself.'

'Me?' Johnny was about to protest. Then he thought better of it. 'Tea and toast, Mistress Montague. Dining-room or downstairs parlour?'

'Upstairs, Mr Jerome. In my bedroom.'

'I'll wake the maid.'

'No, on second thoughts bring the tray yourself, please,' Cassandra Montague said. 'I want a private word with you and, with my husband gone, this is an ideal opportunity.'

'A word? What sort of a word?'

'All in good time, Mr Jerome. I shall not be asleep.'

Johnny opened his mouth. He might not object to being Robert's agent, to putting in a bit of time as Robert's steward, but it riled him to be ordered about by a chit of a girl.

He sucked in breath, then nodded. 'As you wish, Mistress Montague.'

She swung away and with an energy that reminded him

184

just how young she was, bounded upstairs, her skirts kicking up behind her.

Johnny glimpsed the drawers that Janey had told him about.

Magenta drawers, for God's sake! What next?

He dallied a moment longer, watching the minister's wife sweep up to the landing. He was puzzled by the fact that Robert had so far failed to break her spirit and afraid that somehow a spark, that frightful feminine spark, had been struck and a termagant released in the household.

'Mr Jerome?'

He looked up.

She was leaning over the rail of the second-floor landing.

'Madam?'

'Don't shilly-shally, if you please. I *would* like my tea before midnight.'

Twelve

Gambling had always been foreign to Cuthbert Armitage's nature. Offered choice in the matter, he would not have elected to trade in stocks and shares and to put himself at the mercy of foreign powers, the vagaries of wind and weather in the China Seas or the progress of wars in India or Mexico. Cubby had inherited a ready-made career from his father, however, and had simply remained a partner in the brokerage firm of Armitage & Smalls, installed in chambers in a sandstone building in Glasgow's Kennoway Square.

The city had never held much excitement for Cubby. Unlike his partner, Charlie Smalls, Cubby did not travel out to confer with correspondents and develop investment opportunities on the far side of the world. Cubby hardly ever saw Smalls, and Smalls avoided all direct contact with Cubby, an arrangement which suited both of them admirably.

Charlie was currently off on another voyage of financial discovery. He had been in America for two months now and showed no signs of wishing to return. His bills were heavy, his expenses immoderate but Cubby co-signed every demand for more credit without a murmur of complaint, for Charlie, whatever his faults, did his job with

187

a thoroughness that even Cubby had to admire.

Regular letters arrived from Baltimore, from Philadelphia, from Washington and New York, together with sealed packets of financial information. Detailed reports of land deals and companies on the rocks and something that Charlie referred to as 'market tendencies' tumbled out of the big waxed envelopes daily, a flood of data which Cubby summarised and channelled to all the plummy names who did business with and for the Flails.

On that bright, blustery Thursday morning Cubby gave every appearance of being a man on top of his trade. The train ride from Ravenshill and a brisk walk from the station to Kennoway Square had brought a glow to his cheeks and in his workaday uniform of striped trousers, morning coat and cutaway waistcoat, he looked every inch a stockbroker.

Outside Cubby's office, in a lofty windowless chamber, his clerks scratched out the latest reports and toted up the rise and fall in interest rates. Gas lamps hissed and the smell of stewed tea and burned toast adulterated the freshness of the spring morning so that the Reverend Montague, spry as he was, gasped just a little as he completed his climb of the stairs and, without knocking, entered his father-in-law's domain.

If he had not been a minister in full rig the clerks would have permitted him to pass no further forward than the bull-gate. But when Reverend Montague announced that he was Mr Armitage's son-in-law there was a scramble to fling open the door that defended the partners' offices and to usher him without delay into Cubby's presence.

'Robert?'

Cubby, surprised, rose from his chair behind the desk.

Executing a neat little *pas-de-bas,* he side stepped the globe on wheels, the cabinet on wheels, the slanted racks in which his correspondence was placed and offered his hand to the unexpected visitor.

'Robert, what a pleasure. How good to see you.'

Handshakes, relieving of topcoat and hat, offer of chair,

proprietorial gestures on Cubby's part, a sending out for and instant delivery of stewed tea.

Cup and saucer in hand, Cubby stood by the imposing desk and, with a frown, enquired. 'Is anything wrong?'

'Nothing at all.'

'Cassandra, she's – I mean, is she well?'

'Perfectly well.'

'Mama – her mother – thought she looked rather . . .'

'It's just the strain of the wedding. She's settling well to married life.'

'Is the patter of tiny feet imminent, perhaps?' Cubby said.

'Regrettably the patter of tiny feet in not imminent.'

'We haven't seen Cassandra down Normandy Road lately.'

'She has much to do, what with church affairs and household duties.'

'Quite! Quite!' said Cubby.

'What brings me here,' Robert said, finally terminating the niceties of casual conversation, 'is not a matter domestic but a matter of business, if you will be good enough to spare me ten minutes of your time?'

'Certainly, certainly.' Cubby scuttled behind the desk again, set down teacup and saucer, folded his plump little hands and leaned forward.

'Put simply,' Robert Montague said, 'I wish to purchase shares.'

'Now,' Cubby kneaded his hands together nervously, 'if the purpose of the investment is to secure a regular income then I would recommend . . .'

'I wish,' Robert said, 'to turn a profit as speedily as possible.'

Cubby sat back. 'On what sum?'

'Five hundred pounds.'

'That,' Cubby said, 'is different.'

'Oh, indeed,' Robert said, 'I'm well aware of just how different it is.'

'Why have you come to me?'

'Really,' Robert said, 'who else would I go to?'

'Robert' – Cubby was flustered – 'I must ask if this is how you intend to spend my daughter's dower money? I mean, the gradual accumulation of interest is one thing, but speculation is quite another.'

'Come now,' Robert said, 'do you not gamble all the time? Is that not the nature of your profession, to wager on the fluctuations of the market?'

'Partly, partly,' Cubby conceded.

'As to the capital being a portion of Cassandra's dowry – well, sir, that is not strictly the case. What is strictly the case is that I am in urgent need of a capital sum in excess of that which I can raise by borrowing.'

Cubby said, 'I thought you were – I mean, I thought you had . . .'

'Unlimited resources?' Robert said. 'For my own humble needs and requirements what I have is more than sufficient. For the Lord's work, however, it is not nearly enough.'

'Pardon?'

'I have devised a scheme to bring relief to the unchurched souls who crowd our community.'

'What sort of scheme?'

'To build churches.'

'Churches?'

'Churches not of stone but of iron.'

'Ah!' Cubby said, vaguely.

'There is a precedent.'

'Oh!'

'I have purchased a design which has never been taken up and never acted upon. It is, I am assured, a thoroughly practical design which involves the casting of the parts of a building in iron and the assembling of those parts upon a prepared site.'

Cubby, sensing flaws, said, 'A purchased site?'

'Of course.'

'In Ravenshill?'

'Where else?'

'There's no land to be had in Ravenshill. Even the Flails cannot find free land to develop and expand their works.'

'If God could give the land of Israel to the Jews then cannot God find land for unsaved souls in Scotland?'

Even Cuthbert Armitage was not inclined to swallow that analogy without choking a little. 'The children of Israel were, as I recall, in exile.'

'In exile, yes, and are not we in exile from God's grace?'

'It's not my place to argue, Reverend – I mean, Robert – not on such profound matters as God's purpose. But when it comes down to it what you're talking about is a business venture, a complicated business venture. Churches?' Cubby shook his head. 'Iron churches – well, I mean to say.'

'Have you ever been to the Seaforth Street mission?'

'No, of course not. We all know that missions are – well, different.'

'Why are missions different? Why can an untrained, uneducated man like Albert Lassiter fill his little tin hut night after night? Is it because he feeds the flock on buttered bread? No. It's because he has brought himself to them. Put himself on the spot.'

'We have already schools, assemblies, institutions,' Cubby said. 'I ask myself, do we need more?'

'If I said that I required funds to build churches in China would you be so damned – so exceedingly reluctant to help?'

Cubby was less than convinced and his agreement was not entirely sincere. 'Yes,' he said, 'I see what you mean, Robert. I do see what you mean.'

'I will put up five hundred pounds of my own money to start with. It is all, alas, I can afford without hardship.'

'Am I to take it that you will be seeking investors?'

'Of course.'

'How will you – em – attract them?'

'I will have one iron church constructed as an example.'

'What will that – em – cost?' Cubby enquired.

'More than I can afford.'

191

'More than five hundred pounds?'

'Yes.'

'You seem very set on this scheme, Robert.'

'I am fired with it. I do not ask it for my sake, you understand, not for my own glorification. I have seen the poor out there, the Godless souls that languish in the tenements. I would have them served by Mother Church and I'll use any means to accomplish that end. Now, are you in with me or are you not?'

'I'm in with you, Robert, I'm in with you,' Cubby said. 'In principle, at any rate.'

'In principle? What does that mean?'

'What if I – em – what if the five hundred pounds is lost?'

'It will not be lost, Cuthbert.'

'How can you be – I mean, speculation is risky.'

'God will move through you, Cuthbert. You will be His instrument.'

'Really?' said Cubby again, with more conviction this time. 'Do you mean He will guide my hand?'

'Be sure of it,' Robert said. 'Shall we pray together for guidance?'

'Oh, indeed, yes, perhaps we'd better. Do you wish me to kneel?'

'No,' Robert answered him, 'just bowing your head will do.'

It was noon before Robert arrived back in Bramwell. He was satisfied with his morning's work and thought more of it than of the ovation he had received from the university audience the previous evening or the grudging praise that Matthew Salmond had heaped upon him for his 'sane and substantial' approach to the vexed subject of women's place in heathen societies.

Robert had not told them a half, not a quarter of what he really knew about slavery. He had shaped his lecture to feed enduring prejudices and titillate his audience with descriptions of pagan promiscuity and female slaves purchased for sexual purposes. He could have told them much more about the slave trade, for his grandfather and his grandfather's father had established the Montague fortune by running black beef across the Atlantic and from the seas of the Caribbean.

As a child Robert had often eavesdropped on his grandfather's gleeful discourses about Jamaican women and the crossbred mulatto girls whose virginity was so highly prized in the brothels of Liverpool and Marseilles. Old Bob Montague, crippled by syphilis and heart disease, would boast how a child broken and trained by old Bob Montague was never the same again.

Eventually, though Old Bob was sicker than ever and hardly more than a husk, Robert's father had revolted against the old man's crowing and had had him committed to a lunatic asylum.

Robert's uncles had complained about such heartless treatment but had signed the charges and certificates that had put the old man away none the less and had thus gained control of the old man's considerable fortune even before Old Bob was dead.

When at last he had passed away his sons had had him buried in a public grave in the seamen's cemetery in Liverpool among mates and cabin-boys and the skippers of bum boats who weren't fit to lick his boots. Soon after, they had divided among them the huge sum that Bob had amassed from slaving and had gone their separate ways never, to Robert's knowledge, to meet again.

From an early age, then, Robert had known what sums men were prepared to pay to be rid of ancestral guilt, of the sins of a past that was still attractive no matter how vociferously they denied it.

Robert did not doubt that scheming, venal and unrepentant old Bob Montague stood close behind him, that old Bob's blood still raced in his veins. Sometimes, when the madness was upon him, he wondered if he had not been taken over and procured by the barbaric spirit of his grandfather just to challenge the conservatism of the times.

Robert's mind was filled with more immediate matters as he walked uphill from the railway halt that served the parish of Bramwell.

When he reached Main Street the minister was immediately recognised. He touched his hat to the simpering female parishioners who wished him good morning, waved to wealthy farmers who rode their trotting carts along the old market route to purchase feed or seed corn from the store at the railhead or to supervise the return of milk churns from the dairyman in town.

He walked at a steady pace, scuffed leather bag gripped lightly in his left hand. When he reached the hill that wended up to the manse, though, he quickened his step for he was eager to reach home, to consume a spot of lunch and confide in his friend Johnny Jerome what had occurred that morning.

The front door of the manse lay open.

Robert entered the hall.

He called out for Johnny but Johnny did not answer.

Dropping his bag and peeling off his topcoat, Robert hurried upstairs.

The house was quiet, too quiet. A sense of unease stole over him and he took the last of the stairs two at a time.

He called out, 'Cassandra, where are you?' flung open the door of the Turkish room and strode across it straight into his wife's bedroom.

The curtains were open and a fire burned in the grate. The room was bright with sunlight and the snowy reflections of bedclothes. Cassie was still in bed, propped up by two huge lace-covered pillows. She wore a lacy cap and a light, lacy *robe-de-chambre* through which he could see her breasts.

'Ah, Robert!' she said. 'You're back.'

'What – why are you – are you unwell?'

'Not at all.' She stretched luxuriously. 'A little fatigued, that's all.'

'It's after noon, Cassandra. You should be up and about.'

'Are you looking for Johnny? I thought I heard you call for Johnny?'

'Yes, yes, I am. I did.'

'He's probably down in the stableyard with Simmonds.'

'Why, what's happened?'

'Nothing of any great consequence,' Cassie said.

She wore a dreamy expression, one that he had not seen on her face before but which he remembered from his days with the girls of the horse-riding set who had often worn similar sleek little smiles in bed of a morning.

Robert jerked his head and, coming forward, leaned his fists upon the quilt and peered into Cassie's eyes.

'What is wrong with you?' he said.

'Absolutely nothing.'

'Are you – is it your – your . . .'

'No,' Cassie said. 'No, not for a week yet.'

'So you aren't – I mean . . .'

'You seem rather tongue-tied this morning, dearest,' Cassie said, annoyingly smug. 'It isn't at all like you. Did the lecture not go well?'

'The lecture went perfectly well. Are you – have you conceived?'

She laughed.

It came home to him that he had not heard her laugh since their marriage. He was not pleased by it, not pleased at all. She had no right to be so gay and happy, not without a reason.

'Cassandra, are you expecting a child?'

'Don't be silly.'

'It isn't silly. It's – what . . .'

'I'm not. Really, I'm not.' She reached out and touched his sleeve. 'No need to concern yourself. Johnny took care of it.'

'Took care of what?'

'He was very helpful, very comforting.'

'Damn it, Cassandra, what's been happening here?'

She patted his hand, soothingly. 'I was more distressed than I should have been. Promise me that you won't

195

punish him too severely. After all it was as much my fault as it was his.'

Robert was not entirely unaware that she was playing a game with him, a more subtle game than any that he had played with her. It seemed that his maleness had not touched her, that all his attentions had done was to release this dormant silliness, a fluttery, flirtatious quality which had not been apparent before.

He peered into her blue eyes, watched her give herself a complacent little shake that made her lace frills quiver and her breasts tremble.

He spun round and, at the top of his voice, yelled, '*Johnny.*'

Wrinkling her nose, Cassie stuck her fingers into her ears.

'Not so loud, dearest,' she said. 'Johnny can't hear you.'

'What did he do to you?'

'Hmmm? What? Johnny do you mean? Oh, no, no. Not Major Jerome.'

He gripped her by the shoulders. Under the slippery layer of material her flesh felt solid, almost muscular.

She did not resist. She lifted herself from the pillows so that her breasts pressed against his forearms. He could smell perfume, a musky, aromatic odour, warm as spiced wine. Not Major Jerome, he thought. No, not Johnny. Of course not Johnny. Dear God, how could he even contemplate it? How, for a single moment, could he have fallen for her trickery?

He pushed her back against the pillows, pushed himself from the bed.

Nothing wrong with her. Nothing had happened. She was teasing him, tricking him. He said, flatly, 'Did Simmonds insult you?'

'He got a wee bit drunk, that's all.'

'Did he molest you?'

'Certainly not. He is only a lad, Robert. He was in no fit state to do – well – anything. Mr Hunter was kind enough to drive me home. Johnny saw to the rest of it.' No dreamy haze in the blue eyes now. She studied him carefully, calculatingly. 'I trust you won't be too hard on poor Simmonds. Major Jerome has probably warned him what will happen if he forgets himself again. Now' – she smiled – 'tell me about your evening.'

'I'll tell you at luncheon,' Robert said. 'As you are apparently not unwell, I would be obliged if you would join me in the dining-room in half an hour.'

'I haven't long had breakfast.'

'In half an hour.'

'Very well.'

'Will I send for Janey to help you dress?'

'No,' Cassie said, prim again. 'That will not be necessary.'

He turned on his heel and stepped towards the door.

Hand upon the knob, he hesitated.

On the rack by the chair, and on the chair itself, her clothing lay scattered. She was usually so neat and so meticulous and yet last night she had tossed her dress across the rack as if it were a rag. The half-hooped skirts had slid from the wires and the tapes, like little worms, writhed on the brown linen liner. Her longcloth slip trickled like water over the chair-back and on the floor beneath, as if she had stepped hastily out of them, lay the coloured drawers.

He glanced round, frowning.

Cassie was seated upright in bed, watching him, waiting almost expectantly for his reprimand.

He clenched his teeth, said nothing and, a moment later, left the bright, white bedroom and made his way downstairs to have it out with Johnny Jerome.

The day which had begun promisingly had deteriorated rapidly. The stable lad had wept in a manner that neither Johnny nor he had found in the least becoming. When Johnny had suggested that a beating would do the boy least harm he had yielded less to pity for the fair-haired lummox than to fatigue and had done no more than bawl him out.

Then there had been Johnny to contend with, Johnny nervous, Johnny hopping about like a flea on a hot stone, Johnny apologetic, Johnny tense and uncertain.

Lunch had been a dour affair.

Cassie had presented herself as instructed, buttoned into her best dress, all ready to attend the afternoon's Bible Assembly. She was no longer dreamy but mischievous, more like her sister than herself.

Robert said nothing about his interview with Cubby, about the lecture, about anything of any consequence. He listened to his wife's account of the mission service with only half an ear.

He was thinking of what he had done last night, how differently he had been treated. He had supped with Matthew Salmond and had discussed the latest translation of *Ecclesiasticus*, had been a man of restraint and intellect. Afterwards he had lain in bed in the gloomy college guest room, his head filled with Greek and Hebrew, those strict old languages of dominance and subjugation, knowledge of which separated him from the life he had created in Ravenshill. From Johnny. From Cassie. From memories of Balaclava and the Barrack Hospital at Scutari where he had finally surrendered all belief in atonement and redemption.

Somehow he struggled through the afternoon. He endured the dreary hours of Bible Assembly, the chatter of womenfolk, the walk home again, with Cassie still in that strange rebellious mood bickering away at him.

As soon as dinner was over he took himself upstairs to his study where he felt decidedly more secure. Collar and waistcoat removed, he began work on his Sabbath day sermons. He was soon soothed by the scrolling of the soft steel pen-nib across the foolscap. Words came easily to him, words which the power of his voice would endow with authority. He drank a little brandy, smoked a cigar, thought of Cassie and Johnny together in the drawing-room downstairs and wondered if they were talking about him, conspiring against him.

He was so occupied with his work and his thoughts that he did not hear Cassie enter the Turkish room and it was late into the evening before he became aware of light beneath the door.

He put away his sermons and concordances, sat back in his chair and contemplated what he might do to punish her and how a sea-changed Cassandra might be expected to respond, then, not knowing what he would find, he quietly opened the connecting door and looked out into the Turkish room.

The fire in the grate raged wastefully. Hot cinders spilled into the hearth. He could smell coals burning and hear the roar of flames in the chimney.

The door to Cassie's bedroom was open.

Cassie was seated on the side of her bed, hands folded into her lap, bare knees pressed together. She was naked except for the garish under-drawers that he had bought for her and had obliged her to wear, not because they appealed to him or excited his desire but because they embarrassed her.

She did not appear to be embarrassed now.

She looked up, met his eye and got to her feet at once. She lowered her hands to her sides and stood to attention like a private awaiting inspection. For one irrational, almost laughable, moment Robert almost expected her to salute.

She was so beautiful, though, so female, so *other* that the last remnant of his desire waned away. He experienced a queer pang of awe and envy when he looked at her completeness. The garment which he had bought to demean her seemed so insultingly vulgar that he was ashamed of what he had done.

'Do you want me?' she said, coming forward.

'No.'

'Do you not want me?'

'No,' he said, thickly. 'No. You may go to bed now.'

She nodded and turned and, while he watched, moved away from him, out of the hot stippled firelight into the shadowless light of her bedroom. And closed the door.

199

Thirteen

Madame Euphemia Daltry was not well pleased. Order in all things was her preference and order in the observance of social demarcation her demand. She liked to be able to put people into boxes, pigeon-holed according to income, breeding and connection.

Somehow she felt more in control when she had the mark on her betters and the strongbox was the symbol of her authority, the secrets stored therein her insurance against the future. There was something infinitely comforting in having so much information accumulated against so many and so many 'little ones' who, in due course of time, might feel they owed her favours.

Meanwhile Madame Daltry was discreet and charming and did truly care for the children who had been placed under her care. She stood for no bullying on the part of the girls whom she had trained to attend her charges, nor did she cut her cloth tight when it came to providing food, clothing or medicines. What Madame Daltry expected in exchange for good service, however, was candour on the part of her clients. When this was not forthcoming she tended to become less mild and sweet and to believe that she was being unfairly denied something that was hers by right.

Such was the situation with her 'charity case', Nancy Winfield, who had steadfastly refused to divulge the identity of the man who had fathered her child.

So far all Madame Daltry had learned was that the Winfield girl had once been a servant to Mr Cuthbert Armitage but had proved too flighty and had been dismissed because of it. Euphemia Daltry knew Mr Armitage fairly well for she kept an account with the stockbroker and allowed him to handle certain of her investments. She was not sure if Cuthbert was telling the truth about the Winfield girl's dismissal or if it was merely a presentation of the truth which suited Cuthbert's purposes.

What Madame Daltry knew that Nancy Winfield did not, however, was that Mr Allan Hunter was rather well off. He was not, of course, a true gentleman – never would be – but he belonged to that class of educated artisan whose income demanded respect. For this reason she was snobbish enough to disapprove of Allan Hunter's choice of *une petite amie* and certainly did not appreciate his conducting the squalid little affair on her premises.

Eventually Madame Daltry could endure it no longer. She tackled Mr Hunter about his unsuitable friendship with the Winfield girl and his insistence that Miss Winfield be treated as if she were a person of status and not, as Mr Hunter put it, a charity case.

'But, Mr Hunter, she *is* a charity case,' Madame Daltry said. 'She is the recipient of *my* charity. I allow her a considerable reduction on the weekly sum for the upkeep of her child. Has she not thought to tell you that?'

'Certainly she told me. She is very grateful.'

'In that case,' Madame Daltry said, 'is it too much to ask that she confines her visits to the kitchen garden or, if wet, to the hall? I really do not like to see her parading about the front gardens on your arm.'

'What does Nancy pay you?' Allan asked. 'Half fee, is it?'

'I never betray a confidence.'

'What,' Hunter said, 'if I were to make up the difference?'

'Pardon?'

'If I were to pay the additional half fee, would that alter your attitude, Madame Daltry?'

'My attitude, Mr Hunter?' She tried her sweet smile but found that it wouldn't form on her lips. 'There's nothing untoward about "my attitude" to Miss Winfield.'

'Yet you object to Miss Winfield being seen.'

'In your company, Mr Hunter, in your company.'

'Oh, so it's me you object to, is it?'

'Really, Mr Hunter, that remark is uncalled for.'

He had come early, about half past the hour of noon. Morning prayers and the brief service which Mr Proudie conducted each Sunday were long over and the clatter of crockery and the chatter of little voices rose from the dining-hall that lay down the corridor from Madame Daltry's parlour.

'I asked you a question, ma'am?'

'I'm sorry. I did not hear it.'

'Is it me you object to?'

'So far – I say so far, Mr Hunter – you have been a model client.'

'And Miss Winfield has not?'

'Nancy Winfield understood what was required of her from the beginning. No matter how attracted you are to the Winfield girl she is not – I say not – the equal of my other clients.'

'Not my equal, do you mean?'

'It isn't right for the children to see you in the company of an unmarried young woman who is neither your sister nor your betrothed. Who has, in effect, already shown herself to be less than morally scrupulous when it comes to consorting with gentlemen.'

'Would it be morally less offensive,' Allan said, 'if I matched your fee?'

'No, it would not.'

'Are you refusing my money?'

'Are you a friend of Daisy's father, Mr Hunter? Are you offering the contribution on his behalf?'

'I most certainly am not.'

Madame Daltry did not require to exercise her considerable powers of deduction to realise that the fellow was telling the truth. He could not help himself. He was, perhaps, too transparent for his own good.

She said, 'Do you expect me to believe that the friendship you've developed with Nancy Winfield is not one of obligation but of choice?'

'This is daft,' Allan said. 'I don't know who the father of Nancy's child is, nor do I care. I'm not for making the girl my bride, you know.'

'I'm relieved to hear it.'

'It's no business of yours, whatever I choose to do.'

'If it affects your son then it is business of mine.'

'Oh?'

'If you wish to remove young Tom . . .'

'That's not on my mind, at all.'

'Then,' said Madame Daltry, sensing victory, 'I would be obliged if you would not meet with Nancy Winfield on my time and upon my property.'

Allan Hunter drew in a lungful of air, and capitulated.

'I understand,' he said. 'Will you inform Nancy of your decision?'

Outside in the corridor the clatter of crockery had been laid over by the patter of Sunday-best shoes and the wails of infants whose appetites had not been quite satisfied.

'Perhaps,' said Madame Daltry, 'it would come easier from you.'

'Very well. I'll tell her today – if that's permitted.'

'That is permitted, Mr Hunter. You have my thanks.'

'For what?'

'Your kindness and understanding, sir,' Euphemia Daltry said.

Snowdrops and crocuses had gone but daffodils had exploded through the borders of the lawn and it was a pretty day to be out and about and Nancy lingered on her walk along the parkway to enjoy the fresh spring air.

She had worked all week in the soda factory, scooping up the caustic substance with a wooden trowel, measuring it out in three-pound bagfuls, hour after hour, at a rate of a quarter pence per bag. Nancy had learned to work rhythmically and precisely. Even so, at the end of each shift when the bags were tallied, her arms and shoulders were so stiff and sore that she could hardly lift the broth pot to make Todd's supper and had no energy left to couple with him.

She was better off than the other women, though. Two of them were big with child and two had already developed wet, phlegmy coughs that would eventually render them unfit to work. She was better off than they were because she had a fine little lady for a daughter, a man who loved her, as well as a dependable well-to-do friend in Mr Allan Hunter.

On that Sunday in April, though, Mr Hunter was not waiting for her on the front lawn. He had been put round the back in the kitchen garden which was draped with drying sheets and napkins and lines of little shirts and bits of undergarments and ringed around with basins and coal heaps and sawn logs. It was not an elegant place and had no view across the river.

'I'm sorry, Nancy,' Allan Hunter said. 'Madame's instructions.'

Nancy nodded. She was not surprised. In fact, she'd been expecting it. She looked past him to the place where the children played under the drying-ropes. It was hardly play, hardly the airy freedom of the wide and open lawn by the river; too much like the yard of the new workhouse, Nancy thought, to be fit for a young lady and young gentleman like Daisy and Tom.

'I had little choice in the matter, Nancy,' Mr Hunter told her. 'In fact, I'll not be coming on Sundays any more.'

'Madame Daltry doesn't like me, does she?'

'It isn't a question of liking,' Allan Hunter said. 'She has her own set of stupid rules. We'll still be able to meet at Seaforth Street.'

'Aye, we will.'

The bench, in shadow, was sprinkled with bird droppings. Allan Hunter looked at it for a moment and contemplated putting down his pocket handkerchief to protect the girl's skirt but then, too eager and anxious to remember his manners, placed his foot upon the seat instead and asked, 'Have you seen her this week?'

Nancy nodded. 'At the mission last Wednesday.'

'Was Montague with her?'

'Nah,' Nancy said. 'She came on her own.'

'Did you speak with her? Did she ask about me?'

'First thing.'

'What did you say – about me, I mean?'

'She's fair taken with you, Mr Hunter.'

'Did she say as much?'

'Nah, nah,' Nancy answered. 'She's too much the lady.'

'What *did* she say?'

A grown man Allan Hunter might be, Nancy thought, with responsibilities piled on him up to the sky but when it came to understanding women he was worse than a boy.

She would have been a more willing and light-hearted go-between, however, if Cassie Armitage had not been wedded to the minister of Ravenshill. Nancy had enquired about Reverend Montague, had heard how respected he was, how, in a short space of time, he had got his parishioners into the palm of his hand and how, when he preached, there was not an empty pew in the kirk.

'She said she was sorry not to see you there.'

'Did she? Did she now?' Allan beamed.

'She said she would see you another time.'

'Oh, she will, Nancy, she will. You can be sure of that.'

Nancy said, 'Why does he do it, do you think?'

'Do what? Who?'

'Reverend Montague – why does he let her go alone to the Seaforth?'

'He sends her there,' Allan said, shrugging. 'Who knows why?'

Nancy watched the children in silence. They had

retreated to conspire in whispers behind the dripping sheets, nothing visible but skirt hems and little brown shoes. She would love and cherish her daughter until her dying day, of course, but these past weeks she had learned to regard her baby as something separate, as an individual over whose development she had little or no influence. But when she saw how a manager's son and the daughter of a workhouse girl could play together, how they made no division between themselves, then she knew that she had been right to make the sacrifice.

'Miss Cassie wants me to be her lady's maid,' she said.

'That's wonderful news.'

'It's not settled yet,' Nancy said. 'I'm not sure I want to go there.'

'You must, you must.'

'For your benefit, Mr Hunter, or mine?'

It was not concern for her welfare that moved him so much as the thought of having someone close to the young woman he had fallen in love with, the woman who reminded him of his wife.

'I don't mind the life I've got. At least I'm at nobody's beck an' call.' Nancy shrugged. 'Mr Montague may not want me workin' at the manse.'

'When did she ask you?'

'Last Wednesday.'

'When will she put it to her husband?'

Nancy shrugged again, still looking at the legs of the children under the sheet. 'It might just be wishful thinkin' on Miss Cassie's part. She was always quite fond o' me, I think. But that was before.'

'Before what?'

'Before I had Daisy.'

'Is that why you were dismissed – because of Daisy?' Allan asked.

'Mr Armitage spotted my condition an' gave me my marchin' orders. Handed me a guinea instead of severance an' sent me packin' there an' then.'

'Back to the workhouse?'

'Nah, nah. Not even Mr Armitage could force me to go back there.'

'Where was Daisy born?'

'On the banks o' the Clyde, same as I was.'

'Nancy, for God's sake! Had you no one to turn to, no one at all?'

'Not then.'

'The father . . .'

'How could I turn to one man when there'd been so many?'

'There are charitable societies that would have given you assistance.'

'Aye, an' taken my baby away. Nah, Mr Hunter. I had one thing that nobody could deny was mine. Nobody was takin' Daisy away from me.'

'But you gave her over to Madame Daltry?'

'That's not charity. You don't have to pay for charity, leastwise not wi' money. Anyway,' Nancy said, half to herself, 'what would I do in a minister's house, wi' all those holy folk scowlin' down at me?'

'Look after Cassie?'

'Aye,' Nancy said. 'Well, we'll see. We'll see.'

Rendell Wilks turned up in Armitage & Smalls's office in the middle of the morning and, like any lawyer worth his salt, swiftly wheedled his way into the inner sanctum.

Cubby's initial impression of Mr Wilks was of a man so nondescript as to be almost invisible. Wilks had in fact been in the room for several seconds before Cubby even noticed that he was there. He had the quality of a hat-rack or coat-peg, never noticed until needed. He wore a single-breasted lounge suit in what was called the 'ditto' style – coat, waistcoat and trousers all of a piece – and his voice exactly matched the tone of his suit, so grey-brown that Cubby could not be sure that it actually emanated from the person who stood before him and had not been 'thrown' by some wag in the outer office.

'Pardon?' Cubby said, blinking.

'Rendell Wilks at your service, sir.'

Cubby peered into the planes of shadow, saw something stir. And, lo! Mr Rendell Wilks was offering him a grey-brown envelope which Cubby gaped at as if it were a bailiff's notice.

'What's all this?'

'Do you not know, sir?' the lawyer whispered. 'Are you not the agent of a certain party?'

'I'm the agent of several certain parties.' Cubby struggled to his feet. 'To which particular party do you refer?'

'A certain clerical party.'

At last Cubby managed to focus not only his eyes but his brain and saw in Wilks exactly the sort of legal ambassador that Robert would choose to do business for him. 'A clerical party by the name of Montague, by any chance?'

'Ah-hum,' said Rendell Wilks; a nod made audible.

'Are you acting as Robert's agent?'

'Ah-hum.'

Cubby took the envelope, broke the seal and slipped out the document, a banker's draft. He looked down at it then up again. 'The Highland Bank?' he said. But Mr Wilks had already departed, leaving nothing visible but a grey-brown coat-tail vanishing through the door.

Cubby groped behind him and rested his bottom on the edge of the desk. He sighed and stared into the outer chamber. Then he lifted the banker's draft in both hands and angled it towards the light. Five hundred pounds drawn in his name. He lifted the note higher, peered at the copperplate handwriting and felt a little stab of apprehension in the pit of his stomach. The account of origin was given as *The Ravenshill Church Extension Fund*, but the sole signature was that of John James Jerome.

Robert Montague's name was nowhere to be seen on the document.

'Spratt,' Cubby shouted. 'Spratt, come here.'

The summons brought his most senior authorised clerk

hurrying into the room. Cubby offered Spratt the banker's draft, flicking it impatiently as if he could not wait to be rid of the thing. 'New account, Spratt. Cash the draft personally before you enter it in the new accounts' ledger.'

'Yes, Mr Armitage. Anything else, Mr Armitage?'

'Spratt, what's bullish these days? Is rail still up?'

'Great Western Ordinary seems safe.'

'Foreign rails, I mean?'

'Oooh, Mr Armitage. Risky, very risky.'

'Fetch me the market prices, Spratt, and – em – bring me the word from the street while you're at it.'

'From the street, Mr Armitage?' Spratt said, eyes widening. 'Foreign rails bought off the street . . . Oooh!'

'You don't have to like it, Spratt,' Cubby said, 'just do it.'

'I will, Mr Armitage,' the old clerk promised. 'I'll do it right away.'

Fourteen

In Ravenshill, as everywhere in God-fearing Scotland, the landmark of the congregational year was the April Communion.

Robert did not shirk the heavy duties of Communion week, its Thursday fast-day, its Saturday afternoon diet of preparation, three long Sabbath services or even Monday's forenoon thanksgiving. To the menfolk of the community the worship was both solemn and rousing and marked by a stately dignity to which the new minister seemed to add the final stamp. Every pew was filled for every service and no 'driving of the flock from the corners of the field' was required as far as Robert's congregation were concerned. Men and women, young and old, rich and poor gazed up at the new minister with an admiration that made Cassie queasy and rendered every hour in church a trial.

She managed to fake the role of meek and doting wife, however, to listen to her husband's praises sung time without end and to accept without quibble the breathless compliments of susceptible womenfolk to whom God and Robert Montague were in danger of becoming one and the same.

Pippa was the personification of a Montague disciple, a

trusting, enamoured, shining-eyed acolyte for whom Robert could do no wrong.

Whatever bond Pippa had shared with Cassie had been broken long since and her intimacies now had a sly, wheedling quality. There were, indeed, times when Cassie suspected that Pippa was no more than Robert's puppet or, perhaps, his spy.

'Why, my dear,' Pippa would say, 'you're looking a little pale this morning. Are you getting enough sleep?'

'Yes,' with a patience she did not feel.

'Are your nights disturbed?'

'Of course not. I'm perfectly well, Pippa.'

'Perhaps an event is about to occur, hmmm?'

'No, Pippa,' almost wearily. 'An "event" is not about to occur.'

'It will in time, will it not? I mean, in the course of nature?'

Cassie would busy herself with a trivial piece of embroidery or, more often, put down the book that she had been pretending to read and look away across the garden from the window of the drawing-room.

Pippa had been upstairs in the manse. There had been no means of preventing it. Even Robert, to whom the Turkish room had a sanctified air, did not dare deny his nosy little sister-in-law access to the upper floors.

Pippa had poked about the frilly white bedroom, had seated herself on the bed, had admired the oppressive furniture of the Turkish room, had done her impersonation of a harem wife by lolling on the sofa and kneeling on the ottoman until Cassie had snapped at her to get up.

Pippa had peeped into the back room too, that plain, dull, book-lined study which was Robert's private retreat. Not unexpectedly, she had remarked upon the narrow iron bed there.

'Oh, I say, Cassie, is that a bed?'

'When Robert's working,' Cassie had told her, 'he sometimes likes to lie down – to think.'

'It must be very hard work composing sermons.'

'It is.'

'Does he sleep there too? I mean, nap there?'

'Sometimes.'

'Do you waken him with a little kiss, hmmm?'

'No.'

'It's a very "manny" sort of room. Do you have guests to sleep there?'

'Of course not.'

'Where does Mr Jerome sleep?'

'Downstairs.'

All innocence: 'If I stayed over, where would I sleep?'

'In the guest bedroom on the first floor.'

'I could sleep here, couldn't I? I wouldn't make a sound.'

'Pippa, kindly stop this nonsense.'

'Nonsense? Oh, yes, I suppose it is.' A rosebud smile. 'I'm so envious of your happiness, Cassie, that I long to share it. You are happy, aren't you? I mean, in ecstasies?'

Cassie would pause, tempted by the habits of childhood to confess the truth. She would feel the words form: *Do you know what he does to me? Do you know what he makes me do to him? There is no ecstasy, only pain and humiliation.* She said nothing, though, gave Pippa no warning of what was to come. She realised that such things might not seem wicked to her sister but might indeed fill her with unrealisable longings.

When spring came and daylight spilled over into the evenings, Pippa took to 'dropping in' with a casualness that could only be forgiven in close relatives.

'If you tell her not to come, Robert, I'm sure she'll listen.'

'Why would I tell her not to come? It is no inconvenience to me. It cheers me to have her about the place. Johnny, what do you say?'

'I say – fine,' Johnny Jerome would answer. 'I say fine, old boy. If it suits everyone else, it suits me too.'

'I do not think Papa likes her spending so much time here.'

'Cuthbert has said nothing to me.'

'Perhaps not, but then . . .'

'What, Cassandra? What do you have to say now?'

'Nothing,' Cassie answered for she recognised, even then, that her father was also under Robert's spell. 'If Pippa doesn't bother you . . .'

'She doesn't,' Robert said; and that was the end of that.

Johnny Jerome knocked out the little legs that were hinged to each corner of the breakfast tray and leaned across the bed and placed the tray over Cassie's knees. He did not like being so close to her. At this range he could smell the warm womanly smell that some men found attractive and he could see her ungirdled bosom beneath her half-open robe.

He stepped back, stepped forward again, quickly adjusted the cream jug and sugar basin and removed the silver lid that covered the plate, then retired to a safe distance.

'What is it, Mr Jerome?'

'Omelette, as you requested.'

'Thank you, Mr Jerome.'

He turned away, nether lip caught between his teeth then he swung round again. She had already picked up a fork and was sampling the omelette delicately. He could see the slippery pink tongue in her mouth, the movement of the skin of her throat as she swallowed.

'At the risk of seeming impudent, Mistress Montague,' he said, 'may I point out that I'm neither kitchen boy nor lady's maid. If you want breakfast in bed of a morning then Janey will bring the tray up to you.'

'I prefer you to do it, Mr Jerome.'

'Prefer away, Mistress Montague,' Johnny said. 'I'm not your servant.'

'Do I embarrass you?'

'Yes, damn it, you do embarrass me.'

'Complain to my husband, then.'

Johnny darted a glance at the bedroom door. The room beyond was bland and sunless and Robert's study was as shadowy as a cave. Johnny had eaten breakfast long ago. He had been out in the stable watching Simmonds groom the horse when Janey had come to fetch him. He was dressed in a collarless striped shirt with sleeves rolled up and patched breeks. He had answered Cassie Armitage's summons, of course, but he was damned if he'd doll himself up like an embassy lackey to do it.

His eyes narrowed. 'No, Mistress Montague, I do not think I will.'

'Is it the stairs that bother you, Mr Jerome?'

'The stairs?'

'Stairs can often be a trial at your age.'

'My age?' He opened his mouth to protest and then, instead, grinned. He suddenly realised what she was up to and was more entertained than angered by it. 'Oh, no, Mistress Montague. I can still manage the stairs without a tremble. It's the principle of the thing.'

'Where is my husband, by the way?'

'At a burial.'

'He said nothing to me.'

'Why should he? Burials are ten for a penny.'

'Who is it today?'

'Durning's the fellow's name, I believe.'

'Old Daddy Durning,' said Cassie, 'the ferryman?'

'Probably.'

She remembered Daddy Durning from her childhood, an evil-tempered old freemason with a ragged moustache who, it was rumoured, used to beat his wife with a leather strap. She felt no regret at the passing of that unsavoury denizen of old Ravenshill.

'What will Robert say about him?'

Still with a grin on his face, Johnny pondered for a moment, then answered, 'He'll probably quote Tacitus: "May it be given us to remember the departed by imitation." Something along those lines.'

'By imitation?' Cassie laughed. 'Obviously Robert didn't know the man.'

'Probably not,' Johnny said. 'It's Robert's stock

quotation for folk he didn't know. Can you suggest a better?'

Cassie said, 'God will judge him according to his lights, perhaps?'

'Yes, well, I wouldn't wish that on anyone,' Johnny said.

'Would you not care to be judged according to your lights?'

'Emphatically not,' Johnny said.

Cassie tipped her chin and regarded him from the tops of her eyes.

In spite of her youth she reminded Johnny of a school teacher he had had when he was six or seven years old: a fearful dame, never loud, never hurried, never apparently out of temper, whose power lay in her calmness and whose look – that tops-of-the-eyes look – presaged a reprimand so sarcastic that it did more damage than the cane.

Cassie slipped the last fragment of omelette into her mouth, wiped her lips with a napkin and gestured with her fork. 'Sit down, Mr Jerome.'

'I have work to do.'

'No, you don't. Sit down. I wish to talk with you.'

Johnny paused, arms folded, fingers wrapping his elbows. 'Not about theology, I take it?'

'No, not about theology. Sit, please.'

What made him nervous was not just the woman but the appurtenances that women scattered about them. He had never had any desire to be a woman and, unlike one or two of his companions at the officers' club, he had never been attracted to items of feminine apparel. With finger and thumb he carefully removed an embroidered petticoat from a shell-backed chair then seated himself and waited.

'I gather that you do not like attending me?' Cassie said.

'I told you, Mistress Montague, I'm not a lady's maid.'

'Well, I would like a lady's maid.'

'Ah! I see. Janey . . .'

'Not Janey. And not the wee creature from the scullery either.'

216

'No, Marie's hardly suitable, I'll admit,' Johnny said. 'If you ask Robert I'm sure he'll find someone to fill the bill.'

'I think, under the circumstances, I prefer to pick my own servant.'

'By all means,' Johnny said, cautiously. 'I can provide you with the name of a very good agency which will supply a list of qualified candidates.'

'I already have someone in mind.'

'Thought you might,' Johnny said. 'Why tell me about it, though? Why not simply ask Robert?'

'I want you, Mr Jerome, to suggest it to him.'

Johnny got to his feet. 'Who do you have in mind? A local girl?'

'Yes.'

'What's the girl's name?'

'Nancy Winfield,' Cassie said. 'She used to be a servant at our house in Normandy Road.'

'What happened to her?'

'She was dismissed.'

'Dismissed for what reason?'

'I have no idea.'

Johnny studied her for a moment, then nodded.

'Very well, Mistress Montague,' he said. 'I'll see what I can do.'

Mrs McFarlane had been tipsy for most of the afternoon. In fact, Mrs McFarlane had been tipsy for most of the month. Since the arrival of what she referred to as 'the hot weather' the Armitages' cook had been engaged in intricate experiments involving sloe gin and raspberry cordial; harmless enough concoctions in the small quantities required to flavour jellies and trifles but, taken by the glassful on top of burgundy, more than sufficient to keep the woman permanently inspired.

Cubby closed his eyes in rapture. 'What is this, Norah?'

'No name.'

'It's beef, isn't it? Beef in a rich, red sauce?'

'Probably.'

'She must be – em – under the influence again.'

'Yes,' said Norah without inflection.

'Whatever it is' – Cubby tucked in – 'it's delicious. Give the old bird my compliments.'

Norah picked at the pickled cabbage that she had heaped upon the side of her dinner plate and dourly watched her husband demolish a second helping of McFarlane's alcoholic creation. She had no intention of passing on Cubby's message. It had been weeks since Norah had ventured into the kitchen. It set her teeth on edge to hear McFarlane yowling rebellious Scotch songs.

Domestic bills were brought upstairs by the latest addition to the Armitage household, a little maid-of-all-work hired in from the workhouse, a child so reticent that Norah could find no fault with her.

The mousy child seemed well able to control McFarlane, though, to rescue pots from burning and pans from scalding and even to steer the tipsy old cook in the direction of the downstairs water-closet when Jacobite chants changed to cries of 'Pee. Ah'm needin' a pee. Whar's the bloody pottie these days?'

Rowdy sounds from the kitchen did not compensate Norah for the absence of family bustle. Since Cassie had departed, the house had become depressingly dull. Even gay, chattering, infuriating Pippa seemed to have slipped away in her sister's wake, leaving a woman as demure and brooding as Norah herself. Pippa was still dutiful but she was no longer communicative. She sought her own company, kept to herself in her room or in the garden and, whenever she could find excuse, went off to visit the manse.

The arrival of summer only contributed to Norah's gloom.

May was a month too full of memories. Blossom frothing on the trees, fresh vegetables, the fragrance of spring flowers; none of these signs of rejuvenation affected Norah Armitage's mood. Even lengthening days and clear summery twilights served only to recall that month – a thousand years ago it seemed sometimes, and sometimes only yesterday – when she had been delivered of her first child, a child conceived in love but not in wedlock.

'God's benison,' Cubby had declared when the infant had been born dead and, being the man he was, had taken away the remains to dispose of in secret, to pretend to the world that his new, much-loved wife had failed to run her term, that, in fact, the dead child had been his all along.

She owed Cuthbert that much, if nothing else.

When spring bled into summer and the stars shone like marigolds then Norah could not help but remember how it had been before Cubby, when Samuel Taylor had lain with her in the whins on the riverbank above Renfrew and had made love to her, softly, so softly that she had experienced no pain and no guilt, and had floated free as a summer cloud, for she had assumed that next time Sam came ashore, slim and brown and eager, he would show her a wedding ring and a map of the world and would put the ring down on the map and say to her, 'There, there we'll live, my honey, you and I, after we are wed.'

Cubby laid his meat plate to one side and reached for the cut-crystal bowl into which Mrs McFarlane had breathed a creamy syllabub.

'Norah?'

'Hm?'

'Shall I serve?'

'I want nothing.'

'I'll serve myself then, shall I?'

'Hm?'

'Norah, what is wrong with you? You're hardly here.'

Frowning, Cubby dipped the silver spoon into the dish and extracted a generous helping of pudding. It came out of the bowl with a sweet sucking sound and the spoon dripped sherry as Cubby transferred it to a dish.

In the side light from the window he looked so plump and self-satisfied that Norah experienced a sudden hatred of her husband, as quick and stabbing as the lancing of a boil.

219

She hadn't told him about Samuel Taylor.

Cuthbert had jumped to the conclusion that the baby had been put there by one of the Flails and for that reason had agreed to continue his courtship of the governess and accelerate its meandering progress into marriage. Ewan Flail, hardly more than a boy at the time, had given her away. Old Sir Andrew, already a dying man, had allowed Flail House to be used for the wedding reception and had publicly commended Cuthbert for his Christian forbearance; gestures which confirmed Cubby's belief that he was doing the right thing, not by the governess but by the Flails.

'I really do not know what gets into you in summer,' Cubby said.

'Concerned about Cassie,' Norah said.

'For what reason?'

'Changed.'

'Of course she's changed. She has responsibilities,' Cubby said. 'Aye, and she may have more of those before she's much older.'

'What?' said Norah, sitting up a little. 'Is she . . .'

Cubby swallowed a mouthful of syllabub. 'No, not that I've heard. I mean – em – I wouldn't be the first to hear. Have you heard anything?'

'Nothing,' Norah, disappointed, said. 'What responsibilities?'

Cubby was defensive. Perhaps the quantity of alcohol in the meal had affected his judgement. 'That I cannot tell you, Norah.'

'I am your wife.'

'It's business, just business.'

'Dowry business?'

Cubby forced down another creamy mouthful and wiped his mouth on the napkin. It was all he could do not to tell Norah of Robert's bewildering entry into speculative investment and of the success that he had made of it so far.

Foreign Rails had netted profit and the profit had been

put out again, this time on shares in an American mining company which, according to Charlie Smalls, had struck gold in the north-west. Armitage & Smalls had been into that one and out of it in twenty-two days flat, three trading days before the price plummeted, literally to rock bottom.

'Dowry?' Cubby said, as if he had never heard of the word. 'Oh, you mean Cassandra's marriage portion. Well, that's Robert's to do with as he wishes. Hah, hah' – a nervous laugh – 'do you suppose that our minister is – em – dabbling in the market? Hah, hah, hah.'

He squinted at his wife in expectation of more questions. None was forthcoming, which was probably just as well. Cubby had enough speculation going on in his chambers to last a lifetime.

He was currently sitting on an account worth eight hundred and twelve pounds. And Robert, through Rendell Wilks, had insisted that he put the entire sum out again. All forenoon Cubby had pored over Charlie Smalls's reports in search of an American bubble that would not burst at a touch and he was filled with trepidation at what his son-in-law had ordered him to do.

Norah appeared to have lost all interest in Cassie and Robert and gazed vacantly through the long window at the fading of the light.

Cubby knew that her melancholy would last throughout the summer and that autumn would bring but little relief. His wife had become so taciturn that he had begun to wonder if he should summon a medical opinion on her state of mind. It was not that she was vague or irrational, just silent.

Cubby toyed with the remains of the pudding. He 'hemmed' for a moment, then said, 'I'm doing business for Robert, if you must know. He has an interest in market affairs – not for his own sake but for the sake of a – em – a programme of advancement that will benefit the poor of the town.'

'He told you that?'

'Yes.'

'And you believe him?'

'I've no reason not to believe him.'

Norah turned her gaze from the window.

The light from the evening sky honed her profile, whittled it away until it seemed to Cubby that there was nothing left but a gaunt, enquiring nose and high-piled, frizzy hair done into buns.

'More fool you, Cuthbert,' Norah said. 'More fool you.' Then, without seeking his approval, she rang the handbell to summon the mousy little maid to come and clear away.

In Bramwell the air was balmy and smelled of gardens. Under the Ravenshill embankment, the atmosphere was considerably less pleasant. It would grow worse as summer's heat increased and in humid August would become almost unbearable. For those who slept in Sinclair's shed, however, summer did bring some compensations.

To the rear of the shed, against the face of the embankment, fires were lighted, soups and stews were cooked in crusted pots as the homeless gathered in the warm night air. Not for them the casual ward's coffin-shaped cubicles, carbolic baths, doles of gruel and bread so stale you could hardly break it with a pick-axe. There was no sense of community in the workhouse, only enforced cleanliness and a system whereby you were numbered, ticketed and packaged like so many nails in Chisholm's factory.

Nobody sang in the workhouse dormitories. Nobody played the fiddle in its high-walled yards. In Ravenshill workhouse you faced life square and, by order of the Parochial Board, left all your aspirations outside on the doorstep.

No matter how late Nancy arrived in from Bengal Street someone was bound to be up, a tramp or a traveller or a navvy down on his luck. Nancy would crouch contentedly by the embers and listen to the laughter and the crooning of songs and the patter of old men who had tramped the roads for fifty winters and women who had survived as many years on fortitude alone. She felt linked to the outcasts by a bond that only Daisy could break, like a link in a paperchain, and when the last pot had been scraped, the last bottle drained, Nancy would gather her bundle and find her corner and lie and listen to the snores and the mutterings of those who still dreamed of better days.

It was after midnight. Nancy was fast asleep when the door of the shed was flung open and loud voices wakened her.

They were not the voices of the men who sang the songs and told the tales but the voices of strangers.

Nancy sat up. She had enough sense to hug the curve of the old hogshead and hide from the prying of the carbide lamp that cut through the gloom. A baby screamed, a child wailed. Somebody swore obscenely. The shed door crashed against the wall as one fugitive, faster on his feet and quicker of wit than his companions, bolted past the greatcoats and sprinted out into the night.

'Stay,' a voice called out. 'Stay. We mean you no harm.'

Nancy could see nothing beyond the beam. It was not a natural light, not like a candle flame or oil lantern. It shone hard and white and hissing. It probed the hummocks like the spear that fishermen use to spike fish in the shallows and bring them, wriggling, to the net.

Nancy leaned into the shadows and uttered no sound at all.

'We will be with you only a short time, I promise, then we will leave you to your rest.' She recognised the voice. She had heard it before. At the mission.

She could see him, the leader with the bright, white lamp. In the silvery aura he looked like a giant in his tall hat and black coat.

The others held back as if the smell of human flesh offended them.

'Do you see, Andrew? Do you see how pathetic they are?'

There was no answer from the gentleman at the rear or

if there was then it was lost in the moans that rose from the occupants of the shed. They were cowed by the authority of the gentleman who towered above them, the man who controlled the light.

'Come closer, Andrew, and look at this fellow.'

'Must I? I will if you think I must.'

'Edward, did you know that such a state of affairs existed?'

'I've seen the like before, though not in Ravenshill.'

'Lea's alane,' a woman cried out. 'We've done nothin' wrang.'

The beam rounded on the speaker. She was a shaggy creature, neither old nor young. She crouched on all fours like a lioness, a small, naked child still sleeping between her knees.

'I am Robert Montague, minister of the church in Ravenshill. You have nothing to fear from us. It is God's work we do here.' He turned, the lamp swinging with him. 'Will you pray with me, gentlemen, before we leave them to their rest.'

'Aye,' Mr Hounslow said. 'That's the best idea.'

Nancy shrank back into the hogshead.

She listened to the prayer, to the plea for patronage, and felt a sudden loathing of Cassie Montague's husband. The other man she recognised as Andrew Flail, owner of the ironworks, owner of half of Ravenshill. She had seen him too, though not often, and he had been once to visit the new workhouse when it had first opened its doors. She had thought nothing of him then, for he had seemed as remote as a saint in heaven and not quite real. Now here he was, walking among them and even the presence of Mr Hounslow from the mission did nothing to reassure her.

She did not want to be seen. She did not want to be recognised. She might belong here but she did not want them to know that she belonged here.

She heard the minister say, 'May God grant you all a good night's rest.'

She saw his face clearly as he swept the lamp around: a hawkish face, cold and dark and dead about the eyes. She was not taken in by his piety and when he held his right hand poised above them she heard the woman with the baby snarl as if she too sensed danger in the man.

'Come, Robert. Surely we have seen enough.'

'Aye, let the poor creatures sleep in peace.'

'Amen,' said Robert Montague. 'Amen.'

The light flickered over her and was gone.

She saw the shape of the door, the shapes of the men, then they were gone too. She let the sacking fall from her face.

'Bastids!' the woman shouted. 'Bastids!' and plucked the baby from between her knees and, hauling down the neck of her dress, applied its dumb mouth to her breast. 'Lea's alane. Lea's alane. Aye, damn ye, lea's alane.'

Sitting upright, knees cradled by her arms, Nancy had a feeling that nobody, least of all Robert Montague, would listen, that somehow it was all up for the folk who slept in Sinclair's shed and that everything, for all of them, was about to change for the worse.

Although they were birds of a feather and had shared experiences that no civilian could imagine, Johnny Jerome never ceased to be wary of Robert Montague. Throughout the years Robert's unpredictability had lent a kind of fillip to the relationship but now, with wars and expeditions far behind them, Johnny found himself increasingly disturbed by his old comrade's behaviour. He had no reason to expect the worst; and yet he could not help but suspect a hidden motive when Robert suddenly began to pamper his dear young wife and surrender to her every whim. He had seen Robert act this way before and the result had been a tragedy that had almost ruined them both.

Cassie Montague might be a bit wilful but she was intelligent too and he had developed a certain amount of respect for the girl. He was not prepared to side with her against her husband, though, not just yet. He had too much

225

invested in his friendship with Robert to risk losing it because of a mere woman.

He approached the sticky situation cautiously.

'Your wife . . .'

'What about my wife?' Robert said.

'She seems to feel that she is in need of the services of a lady's maid.'

'Oh, I'm well aware of that,' Robert said.

'Has she discussed it with you?'

'No.'

'She has, I believe, someone particular in mind.'

'Girl from the mission by the name of Winfield?' Robert said.

'Why, yes.'

'She was servant to the Armitages for a short time, some years ago.'

'Are you willing to employ her?'

'If Cassie wishes it.'

'Won't Cubby feel slighted?'

'I expect he will,' Robert said. 'I'm not concerned with Cuthbert's feelings at present.'

'Robbie, what *is* going on?'

'I told you, Johnny, I just want to build churches.'

'Come now, I know you too well to swallow that one.'

Robert smiled. 'One iron church to be precise. Hunter will oversee its design and construction, and you will oversee Hunter.'

'Where will this church be erected?'

'In Ravenshill.'

'On Sinclair's land, do you mean?'

'Probably.'

'How much land is there?' Johnny asked.

'Seven acres.'

'How much will be occupied by this iron church of yours?'

'An acre and a half.'

'And the rest?'

'Will be sold on.'

'Flail wants it, doesn't he?'

'Yes, but Sinclair won't sell to Flail,' Robert said. 'On the other hand, Sinclair might be prepared to have it taken off his hands, if the cause is good enough. The site will then be levelled as far as the embankment.'

'How much will Flail pay for prime land in the heart of Ravenshill?'

'Approximately eleven thousand pounds.'

'Good Lord! And what will become of that money?'

'It will be put to further expansion.'

'To buying another site, you mean?'

'Precisely.'

'Where's the other site? It wouldn't, by any chance, be the acres that the Seaforth Street mission stands upon, would it?'

'It would, indeed.'

'Hounslow will never part with it,' Johnny said. 'He's much too shrewd. Quite a different kettle of fish from Sinclair.'

'I'm well aware of that. Hounslow is the key, however. If the honest Mr Hounslow can be made to part with his little piece then Sinclair will jump to follow suit. This is a kirk burgh, Johnny, and it's kirk work I'm engaged in.'

'*Will* you build this iron church?'

'Certainly. It will accommodate about two hundred people and will be the pride and joy of all those who are involved in its construction. Once the castings and forgings are made it will be a simple matter to build more. This burgh alone could accommodate three and the sale of parts and pieces to missionary societies and unions across the length and breadth of the country would be unlimited. Pack it in straw, piece by piece, ship it out to the far corners of the globe and you could have it erected in a couple of days at the cost of thirty shillings or less.'

'Where did you discover the design, old boy?'

'I had it from an Anglican friend.'

'Is it pretty?'

'Very pretty, and very practical.'

'One final question, for the moment,' Johnny said. 'How will the sums raised – presumably by subscription – find their way into your coffers, Robbie?'

'My name will head the subscription list.'

'Yes, of course it will but how . . .'

'The church will belong to the Church,' Robert said. 'But the land will belong to me.'

'And when you have this ten or eleven thousand pounds, what will you do with it?' Johnny asked.

'Use it to make more,' said Robert.

'More? But how?'

'That,' Robert said, 'is where my father-in-law comes in. Meanwhile you may inform Cassie that she can have her lady's maid.'

'The Winfield girl, do you mean?'

'The very same,' said Robert.

If she had not wept so sore when she told him he might have lost his temper and struck her down. But he had felt all along that he could not keep Nancy and that like those who had gone before she would eventually weary of this sort of life, would slip away some night and never be seen again.

At least, Todd thought, she's been honest enough to tell me where she's going and the reason for it. He believed her when she said that she did not want to leave and would never have left if it hadn't been for the offer of a position in a good house, because she needed something secure for a while, because she was tired of rubbing along hand to mouth.

She clung to him, sobbing. He soothed her, told her he understood and that he wouldn't stand in her way if that was what she wanted, told her he would always be there if she needed him. She promised she would come every Sunday, if she could get away, assured him she wouldn't take it badly if he found another girl to look after him. She wept when she said it, almost as if parting from him would break her heart.

Todd had never been sure what love meant. He wasn't sure now. He was sure, though, that he could hardly bear the thought of her being just three miles away in Bramwell, out of reach, while he stayed here alone, chained to the dust-cart, to the tenement that had been his home for so many years that he couldn't remember another. He wasn't even sure that he could bear to have her flutter in and out of his life like a swallow. But there was no help for it. He would have to take that, or nothing. Nancy was not the marrying kind. He had known all along that she would never be his. Even though he cared for her more than he had words to say, he must let her go, must let her take up the post in the minister's house, raise herself above him, for he had nothing better to offer.

He held her tight when she wept.

He might have wept too if he had not been the man he was, and sober; too damned sober.

'I'll come back, Todd. I'll come back whenever I can.'

'Aye,' he said. 'Aye.'

'I mean it. I'll not let you down.'

Soon after, her face blotched with tears, she went away.

Todd stood by the window and looked down into Bengal Street. He watched her pass under the lamp. Watched long after she was out of sight then, because he had no shift until morning, he flung open the cupboard, pulled out the bottle and deliberately and without conscience drank himself to sleep.

Fifteen

She drank tea from a mug dipped in the bucket that Mr Sinclair had sent down. She washed at the tap in the yard by the pub. She had ironed her dress and pinafore the night before at Todd's table and had made up her bundle for the short journey that would carry her to the minister's house on Bramwell hill. There she would be fed three times a day, would sleep in a bed and be paid enough to see Daisy through. Cassie Montague would look after her and she would look after Cassie.

Even so, Nancy felt a pang of guilt when she looked back at the shed in the dawn haze, at men and women who had squandered the best part of their lives waiting for something better to turn up and who would drift through Ravenshill and leave nothing of themselves behind. What did the powdered ladies know of the struggle that went on in the streets? What did the gentlemen who came prying with their lamps in the dead of the night know of despair? Did it not occur to them that poverty was not sentimental and that triumph over it was as rare as a miracle?

Mr Sinclair was taking a breath of morning air in the street in front of the hotel when Nancy emerged from the lane. He wore flannel trousers and broad braces over a striped shirt and had not yet put on his collar.

He looked round at her, unsurprised.

'I've no work for you today, lass,' he said, shrugging. 'Sorry.'

'I'm no' needin' work, Mr Sinclair.'

'Are you not?' he said. 'Are you fixed at the soda factory?'

'I'm fixed as a servant.'

'A servant? Where?'

'In Bramwell, at the manse, wi' Mrs Montague.'

'Well, well!' Archie Sinclair folded his arms and cocked his head. 'When did this happen?'

'I was asked on Wednesday night if I wanted the position.'

'Who did the askin'?'

'Reverend Montague came to the mission in person.'

'Did he now?'

'Are ye no' pleased for me, Mr Sinclair?'

'Aye, I'm pleased for you, lass.'

'I'll be sayin' cheerio then.'

The innkeeper squinted at her for a moment longer and then, for no reason that Nancy could fathom, he reached out an arm and hugged her as if she were setting off for Australia and not just up the hill to Bramwell manse.

'Take care o' yourself, Nancy,' Mr Sinclair said.

'I will, Mr Sinclair,' Nancy said. 'I'll be all right now.'

'Aye, I reckon you will,' said Archie and kept his doubts, such as they were, to himself.

Cassie had no clear idea why she had invited Nancy Winfield to be her lady's maid. At first it had seemed like a whim, a stick to beat her husband with. When she considered it carefully, though, Cassie realised that all she really wanted was a companion, someone she could trust, but she was not unaware that by hiring Nancy for the job she might see more of Allan Hunter too.

She had come into the bedroom late in the afternoon to change her dress before dinner and Robert had been there, stretched at full length upon the ivory bedcover, clad in the black Geneva gown in which he preached and a tight black serge suit. He looked, Cassie had thought, like the corpse of a dead bird, a crow, say, with the gown wrinkled about him. For an instant she suspected that he had devised some new perversity with which to torment her and she had loitered by the door, trying not to let her fear show.

He had beckoned her to him by lifting one hand and flapping it, too weary and indifferent even to raise his head.

'What do you really know of the Winfield girl?' he had asked.

'She was raised in the orphanage.'

'Do you know why your father dismissed her?'

'No.'

'Is she capable of doing those things which are required of lady's maids?'

'She will attend to my wardrobe and help me dress.'

Robert had lifted his head an inch from the bedcover and had squinted at her obliquely. 'You may employ her if you wish. I have no objection.'

'She will need to be paid, and clothed.'

'I am aware of that.'

'Will I offer her the position, or will you?' Cassie had said.

He had laid his head down again, hawksbill nose pointing straight at the ceiling. 'I will.'

'What will it cost, her wage, I mean?'

'Twenty pounds a year.'

'I would not have you employ her simply because she's cheap, Robert.'

'Of course not. Is this the girl you want?'

'It is.'

'Then you may have her.'

'Thank you.'

'No thanks are necessary.' He had rolled suddenly from the bed, the black gown flapping. 'I will have a paper of employment drawn up for her to sign and will make the offer when I visit the mission on Wednesday evening.' He had looked into her eyes for a moment, expressionlessly. 'It is no less than you deserve, Cassandra.'

'Perhaps not,' Cassandra had said. 'But thank you none the less.'

'I hope you do not regret it.'

'Why should I regret it?' Cassie had said.

Robert had given her no answer. He had swept out of the bedroom into the corridor with a kind of jauntiness that had made Cassie's blood run cold.

Now it was Monday morning. Cassie loitered by the window on the ground floor of the manse, scanning the drive that led down to the gates. She needed a friend so badly, someone in whom she could confide. Without rhyme or reason, she already trusted Nancy Winfield and felt an affinity with the girl that was impossible to explain.

Nancy had not appeared eager to take up the offer of a position at the manse. It had been Allan Hunter who had finally persuaded her to accept and who had negotiated the terms of employment with Robert on Nancy's behalf. Cassie had said nothing to Mama or Papa about it yet. She knew that they would not approve. She had not dared tell Pippa, for Pippa would sneer and mock her for being sentimental.

Through the gates below the beech trees, Cassie glimpsed the solitary figure, small as a child, a bundle held against her hip, her bonnet brim raised up and at that moment she knew that she had been right to bring Nancy here. It was all she could do not to run out through the hall and down the path to greet the workhouse girl as if they were sisters, not mistress and servant. She restrained herself, however, and watched the girl come up the drive and vanish around the gable towards the kitchen yard.

It was still in the manse, a soft, warm, grey morning, the sounds of shipyards and ironworks muffled by leafy trees. Robert had left early for a round of pastoral visitations and Cassie found the house on Bramwell hill strangely tranquil. She waited in the drawing-room, sipping tea poured from the little silver after-breakfast pot that Janey had brought in.

After ten minutes or a quarter of an hour, there was a tentative knock upon the door. Cassie gathered herself.

'Enter.'

She looked up, not hurriedly, playing the lady for Johnny's benefit. There was no need for it. Major Jerome had sent Nancy in alone.

Cassie smiled. 'Come in. Come in and close the door.'

In the setting of the manse drawing-room Nancy seemed shabby. Dresses must be sewn up for her, petticoats bought, new stockings from the draper, new shoes too, two short aprons and a pinafore, a Sunday-best bonnet and, before winter came, a cape or topcoat to wear out to the kirk.

Cassie rose. 'Have you had breakfast?'

'I had a bite, miss, aye.' She gave a little shrug. 'What – what should I call you? I mean, what's right?'

'Mistress Montague in company but, when we're alone, Miss Cassie will do very nicely.' Cassie poured tea into a cup and offered it to the girl. Her small hands encompassed the delicate china cup as if they had been made for it. 'Have you met the other servants yet?'

'Aye, Miss Cassie.'

'What do you think of them?'

'I don't think they like me much.'

'No, that was to be expected,' Cassie said. 'But what do you think of them? Come along, Nancy, if we're to get along, you and I, we must have no secrets between us.'

Nancy put the teacup down and, with a grin, said, 'Rum, Miss Cassie, very, very rum. 'Specially the big wifie wi' the whiskers.'

For the first time in weeks, Cassie laughed out loud.

Making calls on his parishioners in their domiciles was not high on Robert's list of priorities. He did what was necessary to maintain face. He called upon the sick and prayed over them and galloped round the aged and infirm on one or two mornings each week. He had an aloof and scholarly air which was generally accepted as an excuse for neglect by the humble folk of the parish who, in honesty, preferred 'their man' ranting in the pulpit rather than kneeling on their hearthrugs.

On that particular morning Robert whisked through the morning visitations and was on the train and up in Glasgow by a quarter past one o'clock.

He paused long enough to partake of a dish of liver and onions and a glass of burgundy at a lawyers' tavern near the court buildings, then, striding out, went in search of the narrow, crow-stepped block in the Candleriggs where Rendell Wilks had his chambers.

Wilks's chambers had turned out to be as elusive as the gentleman himself. It had taken Robert the better part of half an hour to explore the vennels and close-mouths of that insalubrious neighbourhood and to make his way via an ill-lit interior staircase to the top floor closet that Mr Wilks called an office. It opened directly off the staircase, had no outer apartment and no clerk or apprentice, and was contained entirely within a single slope-roofed attic.

Robert had not selected Mr Wilks for his flash but rather for his lack of scruples and his love of money.

There were some framed hunting prints upon the wall, two or three licences too dusty to be decipherable, and a gigantic plan of the city which, like a military map, Mr Wilks had adorned with tiny paper flags as if to show where his forces were accumulated and how, on summons, they might be rallied to the benefit of the client. Also within the room were two large oakwood cabinets above one of which hung a brace of pheasants, shot out of season but gamy enough to fill the room with their odour. A case of Spanish wine and a cask of Algerian brandy were stacked beside the rackety table that served Mr Wilks as a desk and on the desk itself, bedded in straw, were six large goose eggs and a small flitch of bacon.

Mr Wilks was waiting for him, a shadow in the gloom.

A sarcastic question hovered on Robert's lips but he said

nothing about the quantity of provender in the lawyer's office for he guessed, rightly as it happened, that the comestibles had been traded in lieu of fees and that Mr Wilks's regular business was done not with gentlemen but with that rougher element of society to whom a goose egg or a cask of undrinkable brandy were as good as, if not better than, gold.

'I will come to the point, Mr Wilks.' Robert began.

'I will too,' Rendell Wilks interrupted. 'Cuthbert is nervous.'

'Oh, I do not need your observation to tell me that.'

'You have it, none the less,' said Mr Wilks. 'What you also have, sir, is the means of a-makin' him even more nervous.'

'Do you say?' Robert was seated on a narrow stool before the desk and had the sensation that something in the straw of the wine crate was trying to wriggle out and bite his leg. He shifted position, holding the stool steady with one fist thrust between his thighs. 'To do with the Winfield girl?'

'No, Mr Montague, to do with the wife.'

'Wife? What wife?'

'Cuthbert's wife.'

'I do not understand. What of the Winfield girl?'

'It *is* the Winfield girl,' said Mr Wilks.

Robert was no longer distracted by the rustling in the straw of the wine crate and his attention was fixed, limpet-like, on Wilks.

'Got no evidence, none as would stand up in a court o' law,' Wilks went on. 'Given the circumstances and the fact it happened twenty years since, we might never be able to prove it. I, for one, wouldn't want to go a-pleadin' the case if she was a claimant.'

'If who was the claimant?'

'The Winfield girl.'

'Wait,' said Robert. 'I asked you to discover if the Winfield girl had borne a child, where that child might be lodged and who the father of that child might be.'

237

''Cause you thought the father might be Cuthbert?'

'Yes, because he dismissed the girl suddenly and without explanation.'

'The Winfield girl does have a child, a daughter, lodged with Madame Daltry in a nursery school in the Greenfield. The Winfield girl pays sweet for the upkeep but it would take a better man than me, Mr Montague, to winkle the name o' the father out of Euphemia Daltry. She is a clam, sir, a veritable clam when it comes to spittin' out information.'

'So Cuthbert Armitage *could* be the father?'

'I doubt it. If he is, though, we have a scandal most unnatural.' Rendell Wilks paused. 'It ain't the father that's the issue, Mr Montague, it's the girl herself. I've sound reasons for believin' that she's Norah Armitage's child, born out o' wedlock.'

'Norah? I find that hard to believe. Where is your proof?'

'Told you, Mr Montague, no proof. What I did, though, was start right at the beginnin'. I went to talk with Mr Beatty.'

'The workhouse superintendent?'

'Not the present Mr Beatty, the past Mr Beatty. In a word, the father.'

'I thought he was dead.'

'He's still alive, if you can call it that. Lives down Lanark with his sister who is even older than he is. I asked him what he remembered about a foundling, found in the whinfield twenty years ago. He remembered her. He remembered her 'cause he had a letter – unsigned o'course – tellin' him where the new-born infant was to be found. Only, before he read the letter the salmon-fishers found her and brought her in. Some catch, eh?'

'But Norah Armitage was married to Cuthbert by then. Why did she have to abandon the infant?'

''Cause Cuthbert took her on as damaged goods.'

'She was governess to the Flails, was she not?'

'She was.'

'If Cuthbert took her on knowing that she was damaged

238

goods why did he discard the child after it was born? Surely it would be part of any bargain with the Flails that he would raise the infant as his own.'

'If it was a Flail child in the first place.'

'Yes, or if Cubby *thought* it was,' Robert said. 'The letter? What happened to the letter?'

Rendell Wilks allowed himself one of his transient smiles. He reached a hand between the goose eggs and the bacon and produced a cardboard portfolio which he passed across the table to his client.

'It's right here,' he said, smugly.

Robert opened the portfolio and looked down at a small square of quality stationery which had been creased and folded so many times that it had the appearance of parchment. The message was terse: *Baby abandoned on the bank by the Ravenshill whinfield. Please to redeem at your convenience.* No signature.

'At your convenience: is that not rich?' said Mr Wilks.

'Please to redeem: even richer, like a pledge.' Robert glanced up. 'How did you persuade old Beatty to part with it?'

Mr Wilks lifted a hand like a tendril and twined his forefinger and thumb together. 'Chink.'

'How much?'

'Five pounds,' Mr Wilks said, 'And cheap at the price. I take it you can make good use of it?'

'Oh, yes,' said Robert. 'Yes, indeed.'

'To make Cuthbert more nervous?'

'When the time is ripe,' said Robert and, after paying Wilks his fee, left the office with the cardboard portfolio tucked securely beneath his arm.

Nancy did not know what to make of the manse. It reminded her of a time when Mr Beatty had taken some of the orphans to the Glasgow Fair Exhibition in the High Street and there had been a tableau of the bedchamber of Mary Queen of Scots; how she thought at the time that it must be a fine thing to be a queen and have a bed of your own to sleep in and carpets on the floors. But the showman's exhibit had not seemed quite real, whereas the rooms in the manse were all too real. At first she tiptoed among the ornaments and trophies and wondered how long it would take her to gain confidence enough to be natural.

She did not know what would be expected of her, not just by Miss Cassie but by the minister and the man called Jerome and, most of all, by the three glowering females in the basement.

Her duties, however, were well defined. She was Mistress Montague's maid, not a general servant to the household.

She would sew for the mistress, learn to use curling tongs, ensure that her lady's dresses were properly aired. She would bring up any meals that Miss Cassie might wish to have in the privacy of her room. She would attend Miss Cassie when she went out shopping or on visitations; and she, no other, would accompany her mistress to Wednesday night mission services.

Her room was in the basement, a tiny wood-panelled cubicle off the corridor between the kitchen and the laundry room. It smelled, oddly, of horse manure and leather and Major Jerome told her it had been used as a tackroom before Mr Calderon had had the stables built. It was pleasantly musty and dry, though, except on those afternoons when the tubs were filled and the boiler stoked and the week's wash done in the stone-walled room next door; then it would have the same smell as the workhouse dormitory, except warmer.

From the first she was comfortable there, snug in her wee bunk bed. And if she grew restless she could slip out into the yard without bothering anyone and stand by the kitchen door and look up at the moon over the wall and catch the scents of the moor and breathe in the clear, untainted air.

She was first up in the morning, before Marie even, and, though she got no thanks for it, would help the miserable

little scullion fill the coal buckets and water pails. She was
up long before Janey, who had to be dragged out of the
bed she shared with Miss Rundall. She was quick to master
the maze of the house, quicker still to master the complex
relationships below stairs.

She had Major Jerome spotted from the first. But it was
not until she had been in residence for almost a week that
she first saw the major, the minister and the stable lad at
play with bat and ball and realised why Cassie Montague
needed a personal servant of her own to guard against this
awful display of maleness. Nancy settled quickly after she
had made it clear just where she stood and that, unlike the
others, she was unwilling to be a counter in a game,
leastwise not *that* game.

'How are you faring, Nancy?' Miss Cassie asked.

'I'm farin' very well, ma'am, thanks.'

'How do you get along with Miss Rundall?'

'Oh, I think we know where we stand,' Nancy replied.

On Wednesday night, after she had returned from the
mission and had helped her mistress out of her day-dress
and into her night attire, she had come downstairs for a
late supper to find them waiting for her.

Simmonds had been there too but once fed he was
packed off to the hayloft and Nancy was left alone at the
table with the women.

At that hour the kitchen seemed unnaturally clean and
tidy. Every dish had been washed and racked, every pan
scrubbed and polished and shelved. The fire in the grate
by the big oven had been banked down for the night and
on the table, scrubbed almost white, a cold collation stood
in state upon a folded napkin, like a still-life painting.

All three servants were clad in cotton shifts and woollen
dressing-gowns. The cook's shift had a lace collar and an
embroidering of little yellow anemones. The willowy
servant, Janey, wore a fancy night-cap over her hair. They
did not seem to Nancy like servants at all, more like three
female goblins who came out at night to feast on leftovers.
She could easily imagine the broad-shouldered, big-

bosomed cook down on all fours on the flagstones, lapping at a bowl of cream like a gigantic tabby.

Miss Rundall – head of the table – dismembered a soused herring with an ivory-handled fork. She consumed the fish in slavering mouthfuls, drank ale from a jug, wiped her mouth on a napkin and studied the girls with tolerant amusement, though her eyes, Nancy thought, seemed to have been marinated in the same silvery-grey gravy as the herring.

'Did she have a nice time tonight, your lady?'

The words – *naice – ternit – yawr leddy* – came out distorted by innuendo.

'She always finds the mission service – nice,' Nancy answered.

'You been there before, ain't you?' Janey ate brown bread and butter and strips of boiled ham, slipped them down her long throat like a cormorant.

'Often,' Nancy said.

'Know the Hunter feller well then?' Janey said.

'If you mean Mr Allan Hunter, aye, I know him well enough.'

'He brought her ladyship home once.'

'So I heard,' Nancy said.

'He'd a-stayed too . . .' Janey said.

'If he'd a-been askit,' said Marie, and giggled.

Nancy, still clad in her plain brown dress, drank tea in silence.

It was like a court: three of them at one end of the table, she at the other.

Mutely, she watched Miss Rundall consume more herring, more ale and do her bit with the napkin.

'He'd a-have her if he could, is my guess,' Janey said.

Marie giggled.

'Have her?' said Nancy, though she knew fine what Janey meant.

'Given the chance,' said Janey. 'Given a suitable hop-hortunity.'

Marie giggled again.

'Have you ever met Mr Hunter?' Nancy said.

'Not us,' said Janey.

'Then you don't know what you're talkin' about.'

'All the same, men are,' Janey said, 'an' him no different.'

Miss Rundall said, 'Unless he ain't to 'er ladyship's likin'.'

'Oh, she likes him,' Nancy said, before she could stop herself. 'But only as a friend.'

'Is he your friend too, honey?' Janey said.

'Aye – honey – he's my friend too.'

'Likes the ladies then,' Miss Rundall said.

'Same as you do,' Nancy said.

Marie did not giggle. She glanced furtively at Janey who glanced at Miss Rundall as if communication came down from the cook in relay.

Miss Rundall said, slowly, 'Same as we do – what?'

Nancy folded a slice of brown bread and butter and ate it in two mouthfuls. She was not afraid of these women. She had her ally in Miss Cassie. She had been invited here. She gave a wry twist to her lips, swallowed the bread and butter and drank more tea.

The women and the girl, Marie, watched cautiously.

Nancy said, 'Mr Hunter's a gentleman.'

'That don't mean he ain't a-got a whatnot,' said Miss Rundall, 'an' we never knew a whatnot yet that was a gentleman.'

'I don't know what you're talkin' about,' said Nancy.

'The major says Mr Hunter fancies her,' said Marie.

'Then why hasn't the major told Mr Montague?' said Nancy.

'Maybe he has,' said Janey.

'Then why does Mr Montague let her go there?' said Nancy.

'Because he don't care,' said Janey.

'Nah, nah.' Nancy knew how to deal with gossip, even gossip as malicious as this. 'Mr Montague's sure of her loyalty. He knows, even if you don't, that the Seaforth

243

Street mission isn't a hot-bed of – of anythin'.'

'Anyhow' – Janey shrugged – 'I reckon her ladyship gets enough at home.'

'Oh, look, Janey, you've made Nancy blush,' Miss Rundall said.

'I'm no' blushin',' Nancy declared. 'I just don't like this sort o' talk.'

'What sort o' talk do you like then, honey?' Janey said. 'Sweet talk?'

'She's blushin' now, so she is,' Marie said. 'Big red cheeks, eh.'

'Maybe Nancy doesn't know what sweet talk is?' Miss Rundall suggested.

'Maybe Nancy's never had a man,' said Janey.

Nancy opened her mouth to blurt out a denial, then got control of herself. She had heard conversations far worse than this. But there was something in the confined nature of the kitchen, in the dressed-for-bed informality of the servants that made her turn hot with annoyance.

'Oh, she's had a man, I'm sure,' said Miss Rundall.

'If she came tae bed wi' me,' said Janey, 'I could tell if she'd had a man.'

Nancy turned the fork between finger and thumb, a little feat of legerdemain so deft that it was nothing but a blur of light. Before any of them could move the fork was hovering over Janey's hand.

They might know about beds and bedrooms and which man wanted which woman. They might titillate themselves with gossip and do what they wished to each other by way of appeasement, but Nancy was willing to wager that they had never felt a knife at the throat or had never seen a man gouged or a woman scarred. They did not know what violence was or understand how it could cut through everything.

'I sleep wi' no one,' Nancy said. 'No man, no woman.'

Janey's hand twitched and crept an inch across the table.

Nancy pressed the fork down, indenting the girl's flesh.

'Is that clear?' she said.

'Oh, yes, dear,' Miss Rundall said. 'I think you've made that clear.'

'Janey – *honey* – is that clear?' Nancy said.

'I – I – never meant nothin' by it. It was just – just a joke.'

'Sure it was,' Nancy said. 'That's why I'm laughin'.'

It was the middle of the morning when Nancy brought up the bundle of freshly laundered underclothing from the drying lawns.

Outside the air was clean and clear and the smells of spring had changed at last to those of summer. She could hear peewits crying and the chatter of sparrows and the smell of new-washed linen was like a breath of summer itself. She hummed with satisfaction at what had taken place in the kitchen last night for it had made her feel strong to stand up to the cook.

It was not until she reached the upper floor and entered the parlour that Mr Montague called the Turkish room that she experienced a sudden cloudy fear of repercussions over her rash act.

Mr Montague was alone in the small back room.

He was seated at the table, books pillared on each side of him, a pen in his hand. He was writing when Nancy breezed into the parlour with the bundle of petticoats and demi-skirts. He wore his ministerial suit of black serge but he had not put on his collar, nor had he shaved or combed his hair.

In the light from the window Nancy could see the dark stubble glistening on his long chin and a wisp of smoke from the cheroot that was balanced on the rim of a brass ashtray. She thought that he looked more like a soldier than a minister and only the severity of his features saved him from being too handsome. She had spoken hardly a dozen words to him since her first day when he had welcomed her to his household with a prayer and a blessing.

She wondered if Miss Cassie had gone to the water-closet along the corridor or perhaps to the little sewing-room

245

which protruded like a half-open drawer from the gable of the building.

She tried to slip unnoticed into the white bedroom.

'Nancy?'

She froze, and turned.

She was surprised that he had addressed her by her Christian name, though she had heard him call Janey by her Christian name too. She peeped apprehensively into the study.

He had his hands up by his chin and he was staring at her.

'A word with you, if you please,' Robert Montague said.

She put the laundry down on the ottoman and went forward to the doorway. She bobbed a curtsey, sure now that Miss Rundall had complained about her behaviour and that she was in for a reprimand if not dismissal.

A week ago she would not have cared. She would have gone off with her bundle, back to the sheds, back to Todd in Bengal Street, and put the whole episode behind her. But now she had established who she was and what her place might be, and had begun to get to know her mistress and to take pride in being her companion, neat-dressed and groomed, out there on the streets.

She stood dumbly before the minister and she felt her strength diminish.

'Are you happy with your position?'

'Aye, sir, I am.'

'I am aware that you have no relatives, Nancy, but that you do have certain friends and acquaintances in Ravenshill.'

'That's true, Mr Montague.'

'If you wish to visit them then you may have all of Sunday afternoon off.'

'I thought that was arranged already, Mr Montague?'

'I am granting you a little additional time. I have observed how you devote yourself to prayer and worship at Mr Lassiter's. For that reason there is no need for you to attend Sunday School. I insist, however, that you are back here by nine o'clock sharp.'

246

'Aye, Mr Montague, that's verra kind o' you.'

'I will tell Mr Jerome. He will see to it that there's no grumbling from the other servants. I suppose one might expect that sort of thing in the kitchens, hmmm?'

'Aye, sir, I suppose you might.'

'Nancy.'

'Aye, Mr Montague.'

'Do not rub Miss Rundall entirely the wrong way.'

'No, Mr Montague. I'll try not to.'

She was perspiring. She could feel a gripe in her stomach. She wondered what he knew of her, what scraps of gossip, true and false, Major Jerome had carried up to the master; what else the master might have had from Mr Armitage, and why he had brought her here at all. For a split second she suspected that he might know about Madame Daltry's, about Daisy. But nobody knew about Daisy, nobody except Mr Hunter, and she trusted him.

'That will be all, Nancy.'

She bobbed once more and, weakened by the interview, hurried out into the parlour to carry the laundry into the white bedroom, away from the Reverend Montague who, for all his apparent kindness, or perhaps because of it, frightened her more than ever.

Sometimes it alarmed Cubby Armitage to realise that he was approaching his forty-fifth birthday. He would look up from supper and pass remarks that a person less disinterested than his wife would have interpreted not only as regret but bewilderment, the wistful amazement that comes with the discovery that one is not in the least important in the scheme of things and that all too soon one will not be able to make any difference to anything.

'Do you know, dear,' Cubby would say, committing himself to another non sequitur. 'It's only thirty years since Glasgow had its first stockbroker.'

Norah nodded obediently.

'James Watson was his name.'

'Yes.'

247

'My father knew him slightly.'

'Yes.'

'Hardly a joint-stock company worth the name in those days.'

'Uh-mmm.'

'Nobody had ever heard of railway debentures or preference stock.'

'Mmm-uh.'

'Now . . .' Cubby would chew slowly on the delicacy that Mrs McFarlane had shipped up for him that evening. 'Now it's all so – different.'

'Cuthbert.'

'What?'

'You're dribbling.'

Cubby had supposed that his son-in-law would provide a more receptive ear for his wistful tales of how wonderful Glasgow had been 'in the old days', but Robert, it transpired, had no time at all for Cubby's reminiscences and, like almost everyone else Cubby knew, was impatient with self-questioning. He was not such an old buffer yet, however, that he tried it on with everyone. He did not, for instance, ever attempt to bend Pippa's ear or impress upon her how things had changed for the worse. Cubby knew that Pippa would simply put on a silly, pompous voice and, defying her moral upbringing, would mock him shamelessly. In any case his younger daughter spent most of her time at church or at the manse these days, drawn away from paternal influence by the gravitational pull of her brother-in-law's reputation.

Consequently he turned to Cassie for the reassurance that he needed at this difficult and confusing stage in his life.

To his chagrin, however, Cassie too suddenly turned against him by employing the very female whom he had dismissed from service.

'Why was I not informed?' he demanded.

'I did not think it was any of your concern.'

'My concern? My concern? She was sacked from our

employment. I mean, I dismissed her.'

'For what?' said Cassie. 'You never did explain the reason.'

They were alone in the front garden of the manse.

His daughter had a little pair of gardening scissors in one hand and a shallow wicker basket attached to her arm. He knew that Cassie was indulging him, for it was not her habit to play the rural wife, to snip the early summer blooms and fill up the basket with flowers and sprays of leaves. He wondered what the gardener would have to say about it tomorrow and just how much havoc his daughter might wreak before they went indoors again.

He followed her down the line of the beds, his city shoes imprinting the moist grass behind him.

Cassie wore slippers, fine, pearl-pink kidskin things that she had brought with her from Normandy Road. The rest of her clothing was new, at least he could not recall having seen her wear it before. A day-dress in plaid tartan with a half-hoop skirt that bobbed and nodded and, when she stooped, spread out about her appealingly. She looked, Cubby thought, alarmingly like her mother before the years had taken their toll.

Mortality breathed upon Cubby once more, damp and dark as the earth beneath the laurel leaves. He tried to take Cassie's arm, but his daughter drifted on, snip-snipping at the blooms that took her fancy.

'Cassandra, was it not – em – enough that I dismissed her?'

'No, Papa, it was not.'

'You were too young to understand.'

'Nonsense.'

'The girl was unsuitable. She had no respect for anyone.'

'Pippa and I liked her.'

Cubby's anger had diminished. He was aware that he had lost authority over Cassie and that there was no residue of affection to take its place. He could not say that he regretted his impetuosity in dismissing the Winfield girl for that whisper, the merest, faintest whisper of the scandal that lay at the back of her existence had troubled him more than anyone could imagine.

The Winfield girl had come at him like an echo from a period in his life when he had been too young and foolish to know what he was doing.

He had been in love with Norah Clavering. The fact that Norah had proved to be with child had only increased her desirability. He had been blinded not by romance but by lust. The tacit agreement of the Flails to his wedding, the haste and show of it, had confirmed his belief that Norah was an innocent party and that he must put prejudice aside.

When, sixteen years later, the Winfield girl had turned up in Normandy Road, when he had brought her into his home, it had not taken him long to realise that there *might* be a connection, however tenuous and improbable, between the workhouse girl and the baby he had abandoned on the shore. Even now, he could not be sure that Nancy Winfield and Norah's child were not one and the same. When he had tackled the bold little waif about it she had immediately jumped to the conclusion that he knew that she was carrying a baby of her own.

The irony of the error had not been lost on him.

She had provided him with the perfect excuse to be shot of her, to exorcise the ghost of possibility, the spectre of guilt, from his household.

'She was with child, Cassandra,' he said, at length.

'Yes,' said Cassie. 'Pippa and I thought that might be the case.'

'Did she – I mean, has she told you where her child is now?'

'Lodged with a nurse, I imagine.'

Cubby swallowed. 'And who the father is?'

'I didn't ask her that question.'

'But the child was born?'

'I expect so.'

'Cassie, for heaven's sake, what sort of person have you taken in?'

Cassie swung round, the rim of the basket brushing against his belly.

'Nancy has done nothing wrong, Papa,' Cassie snapped. 'Nancy Winfield has had none of the advantages in life that I've had. There are far worse things than bearing a child out of wedlock. My God, are you blind to what goes on about you?'

Cubby was nonplussed by his daughter's anger and dismayed by his inability to deal with it.

'I – I did not realise – I mean, that you felt so strongly.'

'You have no right to interfere,' she said.

'No, no, perhaps – perhaps I'll have a word with Robert.'

'About what?'

'To see – I mean, if there's anything I can do.'

'For Nancy, do you mean?' Cassie asked in a voice that indicated that she was close to tears. 'Or for me?'

Evening shadows were lengthening on the hills above the Clyde. The manse cast long planes of shadow upon the lawns. The night wind rustled in the shrubbery and, summer or not, Cubby felt a little chill steal over him. He wanted to be away, to be home again, to be seated at his own table in his own house where he was sure of his place, to be with Norah. At least he knew where he stood with Norah. He dug his pocket watch from his vest.

'Yes,' Cassie said. 'I think it's time you left.'

'Dinner,' Cubby said, apologetically.

'You may dine here, if you wish,' Cassie said, relenting a little.

'No, thank you, Cassie. I promised your mother I'd be home.'

'I'd send for Simmonds to drive you home but Robert has gone out for the evening and has taken the gig.'

'The walk will do me good,' Cubby said.

He loitered, watching her, unsure how to make his farewells.

'Let me accompany you to the gate, Papa,' Cassie said and, putting down the basket, firmly took his hand as if he and not she were the child.

* * *

Allan had worked the week on night shift and had slept so soundly through daylight hours that Mrs McGuire had sent up her girl to make sure that he had not passed away.

Longer hours of daylight meant that shift changes were conducted smoothly and the furnaces cooled and de-coked in record time. Summer air heightened the reek of the molten iron, and fumes and gases whirled in the soft dry atmosphere and when the sun westered in late evening the haze above the ironworks changed hue, took on the colours of summer itself, shaded and tinted like the petals of a rose. Beneath the pretty canopy, though, the heat in the rows was searing, the men laboured in lathers of sweat and the boy who filled the drinking pails was almost run off his feet.

Tea was Allan's tipple. He had no head for spirits, no taste for beer. On those evenings when he found Jerome prowling the works he did his best to avoid the man or, if trapped, would take the engineer up to the weigh-house for a mid-shift sandwich and to answer the major's questions and put some questions of his own.

On Saturday afternoon he visited Tom at Madame Daltry's.

On Sunday afternoon he was back in the parkway to wait for Nancy.

Grief had at last given way to serene patience, and he had even spruced himself up. He looked more polished and felt younger, as if being in love had rejuvenated him.

'How is she, Nancy? Is she enjoying the summer weather?'

'Aye. We go walkin' in the afternoons.'

'Where do you walk?'

'Round the garden an' out a bit on to the moor road.'

'Does Mr Montague permit her to walk out alone?'

'She's not alone. She's with me.'

'That's true,' Allan said. 'Do you take outings into Ravenshill?'

'We were in the town on Friday last, at the haberdasher's.'

'What did she buy?'

'Two pairs o' summer gloves. Ivory, with lace bracelets.'

Allan sighed.

They were on the stone quay at the top of the steps awaiting the ferryboat that would carry them across the river. The other passengers, six or eight of them, were seated on the bench by the ticket-taker's stall, all done up in their Sunday best.

'She bought me gloves too,' Nancy said. 'See.'

Allan glanced at the girl's hands, tiny as mouse paws, and at the pale peach, fine cotton gloves that covered them. 'They're very pretty, Nancy.' He paused diplomatically. 'What else have you been doing?'

'This an' that,' Nancy said. 'Bein' a lady's maid's not like bein' a real servant at all. It's easy work. I sew an' iron her petticoats an' dresses an' I help arrange her hair.'

'She must enjoy your company.'

'Aye, she does.'

'Does she not see her sister?'

'Miss Pippa? Now an' then.' Nancy hesitated. 'Pippa only comes when Mr Montague's at home. She's fair entranced wi' Mr Montague.'

'Are you entranced with Mr Montague?' Allan asked.

'Not me. I've no fondness for the man.'

'Is Cassie fond of him, do you think?'

Nancy gazed across the river to the little ferryboat with its cargo of Sabbath-day travellers. No spray today, no jagged waves, only the sun on the water and the boatful of passengers growing more distinct each minute.

Allan touched her shoulder. 'Is she, Nancy? Fond of him, I mean?'

Nancy shrugged. 'She's his wife, Mr Hunter. She's his wife.'

'She'll be even more o' his wife,' Todd said, 'when he plants a bairn inside her.'

'Aye,' Nancy said. 'It was in my mind to tell Mr Hunter that but I thought I'd better not be too forward.'

253

'What does he want wi' her, this Hunter mannie?'

'He's in love wi' her.'

'Is she in love wi' him?'

'I don't know.'

'But you're the go-between?' Todd said.

'I'm no go-between. I'm her – her companion.'

'Aye, that'll be right.'

'It's true. You mustn't think bad o' her just because she took me in.'

'Are you settled there?'

'Aye.'

'Is this it, then? Is this all I'm goin' to see o' you for the future?'

'Stop sulkin'. I don't know what the future holds.'

'I miss you, Nancy.'

'Miss me in your bed, eh?'

'I admit it.'

'Is there not plenty more where I came from?'

'I'm no' wantin' plenty more,' Todd Brownlee said. 'I just want you.'

'Ach, stop it. You'll be havin' me in tears next. Anyway, are you no' the man who couldna remember my name from one time to the next?'

'Do ye still hold that against me?'

She smiled and shook her head.

'Nah, nah.' She stroked his coarse grey hair with the flat of her hand. 'All that's forgotten.'

'It doesna seem like it.'

'Do you want your supper?'

'I do.'

'An' then what?'

He reached out and caught her wrist with a tenderness that made her guilt all the more extreme.

She could not abandon him. She could not put Todd Brownlee behind her. Perhaps his daddy *had* been from Africa and hanged for a horrible murder. It made no difference. If she made a baby with Todd Brownlee now, whether its little face was white or black, she would lose all that she had gained. Even so, she wanted to please him. She took his hand and placed it upon her breast.

It lay upon the material of her Sunday dress, big, paw-like fingers pressing lightly upon the ribbing of her bodice. She worked the buttons while he watched. When she had done she took his hand again as if it were a thing inanimate, guided it through the cloth folds until she could feel the weight of it brushing against her nipple and the tingle of desire spread through her.

She arched her spine, thrusting against him and felt him draw her to him and the huge, scarred hand rubbing gently against her breast.

'Let the supper wait, Todd,' Nancy whispered and drew him, without reluctance, towards the sunlit bed.

Sixteen

On the evening of 19th June, Robert Montague convened
the first meeting of the Ravenshill Church Extension Fund.
It was not composed of venerable gentlemen of the cloth,
of senior elders and spokesmen for the various missionary
societies that existed in and around Glasgow, for Robert's
purpose was to bring together men who would 'get things
done', and the less the world at large knew about his
scheme the better for all concerned.

They were admitted into the drawing-room on the
ground floor of the minister's residence by the minister's
wife and his pretty little sister-in-law.

Supper was laid out in buffet fashion. There were light
wines to drink, but no spirits, jugs of fruit cordial and for
those for whom no meal was complete without tea, a
great, fluted silver pot of best Indian. The long-necked
maid did her bit behind the table aided by Mr Montague's
ex-army friend, Major Jerome. Any apprehension that the
six guests felt as to the 'soundness' of Robert Montague's
proposal was dispelled by the informality of the evening's
proceedings.

It was after eight o'clock before the last plate had been
cleared, the last cup emptied and the heavy linen
tablecloth carefully removed. The maid departed. Mrs

Montague and Miss Armitage smiled their last smiles and went off to entertain themselves in the small parlour across the hall and the minister closed the drawing-room doors and brought the meeting to order.

'Do you know these people?' Pippa said. 'What does Robert want with them?'

'I know some of them,' Cassie said.

'Oh, I know some of them too,' Pippa said. 'It would be silly to say that I do not know Papa, for instance, or Mr Jerome. But what sort of business can Robert possibly have with an innkeeper?'

Cassie closed the door but not quite to the lock. From her seat in the back parlour she could look out into the hall. It was very quiet within the drawing-room, though. She thought she could hear Robert's voice sonorously leading the group in prayer, but that was all. She was disconcerted by Allan's presence in the house; less so by Mr Lassiter and Mr Hounslow. Unlike Pippa she knew all of the men whom Robert had assembled, all, that is, except the lawyer, Rendell Wilks.

Pippa said, 'I must say, I *am* impressed by your missionary friend.'

'Mr Lassiter, do you mean?'

'No, silly. Mr Hunter.'

'He isn't a friend,' Cassie said, then, changing her mind, admitted, 'Well, yes, I suppose he is.'

Pippa said, 'If I were set on building iron churches I'd want a manager who knew what he was about, wouldn't you?'

'Probably.' Cassie had been careful to give Allan no more attention than courtesy required.

'By the way,' Pippa said, 'where's your new maid? Where's Nancy?'

'Downstairs.'

'In the kitchen? I thought she was a lady's maid.'

'Papa is not pleased that I employed her,' Cassie explained, 'so, for the sake of harmony, Robert considered

258

it advisable that she did not put in an appearance. She's helping out below – just for the evening.'

Pippa was seated on a brocaded chair, knees together, hands folded in her lap. In that position, Cassie thought, she rather resembled Mama, prim and stiff and watchful. Unlike Mama, though, Pippa could not remain silent for long.

'Mr Hunter is a widower, is he not?'

'Yes.'

'How long since his wife passed away?'

'Two or three years.'

'Does he have children?'

'A boy, who is boarded out for nursing.'

'How convenient,' Pippa said.

'Pardon?'

'That he has no relatives.' She paused. 'Is he a man of principle?'

'What on earth do you mean by that, Pippa?'

'Is he a man given to prayer and fasting?'

'Do not be ridiculous.'

'Mission house people often are.'

'You know nothing about it.'

'Oh, but I do, dearest. I know more about it than you imagine.'

'Stop being so dramatic, Pippa.'

'I think he rather likes me, your Mr Hunter.'

'He isn't *my* Mr Hunter,' Cassie said, 'and he hardly noticed you.'

'You always say that. You said that about Robert.'

'And wasn't it true?'

'Absolutely.'

'Allan isn't interested in . . .'

'Allan, do you say?'

'Mr Hunter – Mr Hunter has no time for frivolous little girls.'

'Did he tell you so? Did he clasp you to his bosom and assure you that he has no time for "frivolous little girls". I take it,' Pippa went on, 'that Mr Hunter does not consider

259

you a frivolous little girl? Perhaps if I went along to
Seaforth Street every Wednesday evening, knelt on bare
floorboards and pretended to ooze sympathy for the poor
and needy then I would be considered a serious enough
proposition for a man like your Allan.' Pippa spoke in a
high, rapid voice, manner and tone at odds with each
other. 'You cannot have them all, Cassie. You have Robert
for a husband and that's what you said you wanted. So, I
will have what I want now, whether you approve or not.'

'I merely suggested that Mr Hunter—'

'Mr Hunter, Mr Hunter,' Pippa jeered. 'I have no interest
in your Mr Hunter, dearest. I'm merely suggesting that *you*
had better be careful.'

'What's been said? Has Robert . . .'

'Robert has more to do with his time than fret about
your flirtations,' Pippa said. 'Robert is not in the least
concerned about you.'

'Did Robert tell . . .'

'Why do you not love him?'

'Who says that I do not?'

'Mama, for one.'

'Mama?'

'Not in so many words,' Pippa amended. 'But she does
not think you love Robert. And I *know* that you do not.'

'You know, do you?' Cassie said, trying to keep her
temper. 'How would you know *anything* about marriage?'

Pippa leaned back. She wore now a more familiar
expression, that smug, secretive little smile that had
tormented Cassie throughout girlhood.

'I am not a child now, Cassie.'

A sarcastic retort hung on Cassie's lips but as she studied
her sister she realised that what Pippa said was true. For
whatever reason, Pippa too had changed and matured.

For a long moment the sisters stared at each other then
Pippa gave a toss of the head, theatrical as always, bobbed
to her feet and fluttered across the parlour to peep out of
the door into the quiet hallway.

'I wonder how long they will be?' she said, sighing.

'Hours, I expect,' said Cassie.

A narrow compartment at the rear of the hut in Seaforth Street served the Lassiters as both bedroom and parlour. However cramped it may have appeared to an outsider it was the only true home that the couple had ever known.

It had the cosiness of a private berth in an ocean packet and on those nights when rain beat down and wind rattled the corrugated iron roof Mr and Mrs Lassiter would lie together beneath the patchwork quilt and imagine that they were pilgrims embarked upon a voyage to some unknown shore. They would whisper softly, brows touching, and speculate on what they might find when they arrived, what treasures of the spirit would enrich their souls and ensure their love for all eternity.

On that June night there was no rain and no wind and the air in the mission hall was still and musty, like old hay turned over in the sun.

It had been many months since Albert had been out so late. He let himself into the mission hall by the front door and walked down the darkened aisle between the benches. Under the door at the rear of the hall he could see the glow of the Cosmos lamp and knew that Agnes had waited up for him. He entered the back room quietly. There was nothing much in the room: a table with a tapestry cloth upon it, a few ornaments and knick-knacks on the shelf over the iron fireplace, a stout brown box that contained his books and that served double duty as a night-table.

The lamp stood on the box. Agnes was propped up in bed by a grainsack pillow. She was wide awake, hair loosened, a Bible open on the quilt by her hand, her eyes bright. She held out a hand to him, her arm white and thin in the light from the lamp.

'How are you, my dearest? I thought you would be asleep by now.'

'How could I sleep with you not beside me?' Agnes said. 'Come, sit here and tell me all about it. Did you have something nice to eat?'

261

He took her hand, lacing his fingers into her fingers.

Her hand was cold, though her cheeks burned scarlet. She turned on to her side. Albert knelt on the floor by the bed.

'I ate very well,' Albert said. 'Look.' He fished in the pocket of his jacket and brought out a clean, spotted-red handkerchief which he carefully unwrapped. 'I brought you something tasty from the minister's table.'

'Oh, Albert. I hope you did not steal it.'

'Would I do such a thing? I asked if I might take a little something home for you, and I was given permission by no less a person than Mr Montague.'

Albert silently asked forgiveness from the Lord for the wee white lie. He broke off a fragment of cold salmon and offered the titbit to his wife.

She took it obediently and nibbled it, slanting her eyes to express delight. Albert watched, then offered another piece. 'More?'

She shook her head and reached for his hand again.

'What did the Reverend Montague want with you?'

Albert put aside the handkerchief. Hiding his disappointment that he had been unable to tempt her appetite even with such a delicacy, he removed his hat and put it on the floor, then, resting his elbows on the quilt, spoke softly to her, eye to eye. 'He has offered us a church, Agnes, a church of our own.'

'But how can he? Has he forgotten that you have no licence, that you are not ordained?'

'Mr Montague has not forgotten. It will not be an ordinary church. It will be a new type of church, a mission church. It will be erected right here in the heart of Ravenshill where our sort of people live and where they will be able to worship. He will put me in as a lay preacher. He'll build us a little house behind the chapel. And he'll furnish us with an organ to make music, and it will be grand, so grand. I will even have a pulpit to preach from, a pulpit of my own.'

'Where will the church be erected, Albert?'

'Behind Mr Sinclair's hotel, on the stretch by the embankment.'

'Where the sheds are?'

'Yes, where the sheds are.'

'What will happen to the poor folk who sleep there?'

'They will come here instead.'

'There's no room here, Albert. I do not understand.'

'No need to frown, Agnes. Reverend Montague is a man after our own heart. He will see to everyone's needs.' Albert drew closer, his brow against her cheek. 'Think of it, a church of my own, a new organ for you to play upon. And a house, a real house. I do believe, dearest, that our prayers have been answered.'

'Can Mr Montague do all this?'

'He has faith enough to move mountains.' Albert's enthusiasm got the better of him. He pushed himself to his feet and looked down on her, beaming. 'He has gathered together about him his apostles. That's what he calls us, those who will help him bring his plans to fruition: "his seven apostles". Mr Hunter and Mr Jerome, both engineers, will oversee the work. Mr Hounslow will provide the facilities at his Hercules works. Mr Sinclair will sell the tract of ground that presently lies to waste and Mr Armitage and Mr Wilks will arrange all the documents and licences and make all the payments on behalf of the fund.' Albert raised his hands and spread them. 'The seven apostles. There ain't nothing we can't achieve with Mr Montague to lead us.'

'Where will the money come from?' Agnes asked.

'From subscription, then, when we are ready, by the selling of shares.'

'Oh, Albert, what do you know of the selling of shares?'

'Not a thing, my love, not a blessed thing. I do know a grand opportunity when I see one, however, a chance to bring the good news to folk in need.'

'That's what we have always done.'

'Aye, dearest, but not like this, not on this scale.'

Her smile wavered. 'What do Mr Hunter and Mr

263

Hounslow think of the minister's scheme?'

'Oh, they are all for it, all for it, my dear,' Albert said. 'They will willingly do their part as I will willingly do mine. I mean, as *we* will do ours.'

'Albert?'

Albert Lassiter knelt again. 'Yes, dearest?'

'Sir Andrew Flail, where's he in all this?'

The missionary's eyes widened. He stared at his wife with something less than admiration for a moment then brusquely shook his head.

'Flail has nothing to do with it,' he said. 'Flail is not involved.'

With a little sigh, Agnes murmured to herself, 'I wonder why,' then, smiling again, reached up to clasp her husband's all-too trusting hand.

Beech and oak, chestnut and lime were all in full leaf and the gravel walks that ringed the parklands of Flail House were dappled with shadow that brilliant June morning. Mansion and lawns, dairy fields dotted with cows and distant pastures speckled with fat sheep all seemed to share a single dimension, as if they had been painted as an artificial exercise in perspective.

The minister, in formal garb, rode with more assurance than the landowner. He held the sparky roan stallion that Sir Andrew had picked out for him on a light rein, checking the animal's exuberance with knees and heels. Sir Andrew, on the other hand, could not discover the rhythm of the trot and barked at the flighty beast beneath him, sawing away now and then when the horse slavered and pulled crossly.

'It went well then, Robert?'

'Indeed. Much as I expected it would.'

'Did they agree to your proposals?'

'With minor dissensions, yes.'

'Did Hounslow not give you trouble?'

'Hardly trouble, as such. He sees work – paid work – coming his way.'

'Did you show them the designs?'

'Of course.'

'It is a practical proposal, is it not?'

'Thoroughly practical. I would not have been able to convince a man like Hunter, let alone Hounslow, with anything other than the genuine article.'

'So a church will be built?'

'The parts will be cast and forged section by section then bolted together by four men in two days. Cost in labour? Approximately thirty shillings. The building will stand firm against any sort of weather and will look quite noble when it's finished.'

'How many will you build, Robert?'

'Oh, just one.'

'And then?'

'Andrew, Andrew' – Robert reined the roan a little to keep himself abreast of the landowner – 'do not be impatient. I promised you land and land you shall have. The long piece behind Sinclair's as well as Hounslow's smaller portion.'

'You'll soak me for it, of course.'

'No,' Robert laughed, 'I will not soak you. You may have it at the declared price per acre.'

'Twice what you paid for it.'

'Three times,' said Robert, unabashed.

'Without the ironmongery upon it?'

'The ironmongery, as you call it, will be dismantled and sold, along with all the stock in the company. If all goes well I expect that Hounslow might be persuaded to become a majority shareholder.'

'Without a single owned acre to his name?'

'Finding land will be his business. I will, of course, express regret at the failure of the scheme and offer whatever assistance I can,' Robert said. 'Do not feel sorry for Edward Hounslow.'

'Would it not be more profitable in the long run to retain the company?'

'No.'

'Is this why you came to Ravenshill, Robert?' Flail asked. 'To make fast money?'

'I took the pulpit because it was offered to me,' Robert said. 'The rest – well, that came later.' He twisted a little at the waist and looked down upon his companion. 'I do not wish you to think that I will bring the Kirk into disrepute. I would not embark on any venture that would damage the parish's reputation. You will have noticed that, with the exception of my father-in-law, none of our congregation is involved.'

'The fact had not escaped me.'

'It's a commercial enterprise and the Presbytery, while informed of my intentions, have no governance over the matter. My money, not the church's, will prime the pump. Any failure will be my failure and no stigma will attach itself to you or to the parish.'

'I'm broad enough of shoulder to withstand a modicum of criticism, Robert,' Sir Andrew told him. 'But I would not wish to see your position here compromised to the point where you were obliged to resign.'

'It will not come to that.'

'Yet there is risk. Surely you must acknowledge that there is risk?'

'I acknowledge nothing of the kind.'

Sir Andrew laughed. 'I knew there was something different about you when I took you on. By God, I see what it is now. Nothing is going to stop you.'

'Nothing,' Robert said and, leaning across the saddle, patted his sponsor upon the shoulder. 'What could possibly stop me now? What, I ask you, could possibly go wrong?'

Then he laughed too and without awaiting an answer, dug his heels into the stallion's flanks, swung the beast out of the trees and galloped away across the parkland towards the stables, leaving Sir Andrew trailing, breathless, in his wake.

An understanding, to put it politely, had been reached

between Miss Rundall, her cohorts and Miss Nancy Winfield, but it could not be said that there was any love lost between them. In the case of Major Jerome there was a neutrality of feeling which indicated if not respect for, at least a degree of tolerance of the new lady's maid. He was not above passing the time of day with her when no other servants were within earshot.

Jealousy, back-biting and spite were never far beneath the surface, however, and the only person who seemed immune to the poisoned atmosphere was Simmonds, the stable lad who, by intuition rather than intellect, recognised Nancy as one of his own. He wasn't daft enough to confess his fondness for Major Jerome, his dislike of Reverend Montague or to slander the cook and her minions by telling what sort of things he had seen and heard. When Nancy sought him out in the yard of a morning or brought him a mug of ale on a warm afternoon, he spoke only of the time before he came to Bramwell, of his struggle to conform to what was expected of him, and how lonely it had been for him both in the Edinburgh orphanage and out of it.

Nancy would sit on a saddle or on the boot bench, out of sight of the kitchen windows, and would listen and nod and make sympathetic comments. She was so considerate of his tender feelings that Simmonds would always do what she asked of him, provided it didn't put him in bad with the cook, the minister or the major. So, in his innocence, poor Lukey saw nothing wrong in allowing Mr Hunter to drive the gig – with Mistress Montague in it, of course – part of the way home from Seaforth Street while Nancy and he walked some distance behind.

Often the gig would trundle out of sight and it would be a quarter-hour or twenty minutes before it would come into view again at the corner of the old Ravenshill Cross where the lane came up from the riverside. Mr Hunter would be standing by the horse's head, holding the rein, and Mistress Montague would be seated on the padded leather seat. Mr Hunter would nod when Luke and Nancy

267

appeared and would help Nancy up to join her mistress in the gig and would give Luke a sixpence for his trouble and then he, Luke, would drive the ladies the rest of the way back home.

Nancy would say to him, 'Now we don't need to tell the major that Mr Hunter drove the gig, do we, Luke?'

Luke would think about it and, finding no obvious harm in the deception, would say, 'Not if you say so, Nancy.' He would think about it some more and ask, 'Does Mr Hunter like drivin' the gig then?'

'Aye, he does.'

'An' he ha'n't got one of his own?'

'No, he hasn't.'

'Why don't he have one of his own?'

'No place to keep it, Luke.'

'Wouldn't Mr Montague like Mr Hunter drivin' our gig then?'

'I don't suppose he'd mind,' Nancy would answer, then add, 'But he might, Luke, he might. So we'll not say nothin' about it, you an' me, just to be on the safe side.'

Nancy had no conscience about persuading the boy to lie. It was hardly a lie, anyway, more of an omission. Luke Simmonds probably wouldn't be interrogated as to what went on after the mission services. Whatever took place between the couple when they were sheltered by the hedgerows of the lane would be, by Nancy's lights, quite innocent. She knew Mr Hunter well enough to be sure that he wouldn't take advantage of any woman, married or not, and it gave her pleasure to be party to such a romantic escapade.

In fact, there were times when she wished that it was she who was there in the gig with Allan Hunter, riding by his side through the soft summer dusk. But that would be too much to expect. Besides, she had a man of her own, of sorts, waiting in Bengal Street, her Sunday husband. If Miss Cassie chose to think of herself as Allan Hunter's Wednesday wife then who was she to say that Cassie was wrong.

Sometimes she would even think: *If only it was me. If only it was me.*

But it wasn't and never would be, for Allan Hunter could never fall in love with a workhouse girl, not when he was already so mad in love with the minister's fair-haired wife.

Cassie sat up close, skirts spread across the space behind the driver's bench, hand on her knee. Allan's right hand rested on hers, his fingers curled so that his thumb lay in the hollow of her palm. It was warm and unobtrusive at first then, as week succeeded week, he began to stroke the ball of his thumb gently against her palm, the only intimacy he seemed willing to ask for; yielding by degrees, drifting towards that moment when he would rein in the horse, brake the gig, turn towards her, and she would see his face lit by the flickering light of the lamp, his quiet, passionate eyes and his mouth, unsmiling, and the lips that she longed for with a longing almost unendurable.

They said little, only a murmured word now and then. It was as if he could not believe that he was alone with her, she could not believe that she had allowed it to come so far; neither of them sure where it would end. To talk of it would be to break the spell. That tiny, stroking motion of Allan's thumb within her palm was all there was; a gesture more loving than anything that Robert had ever done to her, or ever would.

On the last night in the month of June, when the sky was tinted pink and rose, the river running fast with a strong blue ebb, Allan halted the gig in the lee of the hawthorns that screened the track.

Cassie could see cargo boats and barges and the sails of clipper ships filled with the last of the sunlight and the city lights spread out thick as stars in the afterglow. She could hear the slithering of the river, the soft little wind that curled from the ebb and hawthorns stirring, grasses whispering, and her heart beating, beating in her breast. Allan turned. He slipped forward until his knees brushed her skirts. She felt none of the revulsion that Robert's touch brought, only a longing for this moment to endure, for clock and calendar to cease their accounting and leave her here with Allan. He kissed her mouth, drew closer and kissed her once more.

'I love you, Cassie.'

'You should not say it.'

'I can't help but say it. I love you. I love you more than I have ever loved anyone.'

'Including your wife?'

'Elizabeth is dead. You – we are alive.'

He kissed her for a third time then pulled himself back on to the bench and took up the reins. Just before the gig moved off, though, he turned to her and asked the question. 'Do you not love me?'

She sought his hand, found it and held it.

'Yes,' she said, 'Yes, I do,' and knew at that moment that her marriage was over in all but name.

There were eyes everywhere, eyes and ears and tongues ready to wag. It was the same in every corner, not just in Bramwell. If he carried her off to Glasgow or Paisley or one of the sullen little hamlets that straggled across the ridges towards the sunset, if he took lodging in a Highland inn or a hotel in Border country someone would be there who would recognise him and spread the word like wildfire back to the Presbytery, and he would be ruined just by the accusation.

It would probably please her to ruin him. Scandal would add drama to her limpid history. Once it had happened, though, she would turn clinging and would expect him to protect her from the outcome of her own silliness, and he would be obliged to be rid of her, as he had been rid of others before her.

Meanwhile he was safe within the church. The church was his refuge and his strength. No one would dream of accusing him of abusing the sanctuary of the church. The good folk of his parish assumed that they had discovered in him a clergyman so devout that he could collect all their miserable little doubts and misgivings and make something glorious of them, lead them, like lambs to the slaughter, into green pastures. The church then was his protection. Amid its stout pillars, under its roof beams, behind locked doors, he was free to do anything he wished to do, safe from prying eyes, from judgements earthly or divine.

After Wednesday class was over and he had bid goodnight to all the ladies and gentlemen who had turned out to hear his dissertation on the prophets of the Apocrypha, he returned to the steps of the pulpit and knelt there, a hand over his eyes, pretending to pray while Mr Grimmond shuffled through his duties and extinguished the last of the lamps.

There was still much light in the church. A strong ruby light from the west windows spilled across the aisles and pews and etched the rails of the gallery out of black shadow.

A clearing of the throat behind him: 'Ah'll be awa' now, Minister, if you're no' needin' me further,' Mr Grimmond said.

Robert raised his hand and rotated his wrist by way of reply. He heard the old man shuffle away. A moment or two later the side door that led to the vestry opened and closed.

He waited, less patiently than he would have liked. Then he rose from his knees into a crouch, crouched on the steps under the prow of the pulpit. He wore no formal robes, for this had been no service of exhortation but a teaching, a sharing of his intellectual gifts. He could feel the quality of the light behind him, the tension of the black coat across his shoulders, the taut fabric of his trousers strained at knees and thighs. He put his hand to his collar and wrenched at it as if the warm June evening had suddenly become stifling. He heard the side door open again, creaking, the sound sifting through the empty church, heard the seductive little voice saying, *'Robert, Robert, he's gone.'*

271

'Wait,' he said, thickly. 'Wait where I told you to.'

She giggled, and her silliness roused him. Unlike her sister, Pippa had no character, no substance, nothing to offer except ardour and devotion. He remained where he was for a moment then turned and looked into the interior of the church, frowning as if he suspected that perhaps she had become manifold and was arrayed all around him.

'*Are you com-ing, Raw-bert?*'

He could not deny that her carnality appealed to him. He stole down the corridor to the outer door and twisted the key in the lock. He turned on his heel and, unbuttoning himself as he went, stepped to the door of the vestry and thrust it open. She had not lighted the lamp. There was no need to light the lamp. The light from the tiny, slitted window fell like stained radiance upon the table. She had propped herself against the table, shoe heels digging into the floorboards. She had tossed up her skirts in readiness. The light tinted the froth of her petticoats and made her thin thighs pink.

She was as slender and agile as a child, he thought, but without a child's innocence. She had never been innocent, this one. She had been spoiled long before he had appeared on the scene. He felt a strange, terrifying affinity with her as if she might match him yet in will and dominance and had been born with a knowledge of the world that it had taken him half a lifetime to acquire.

She leaned back, elbows upon the table, her bonnet – for she still wore her bonnet – askew. She was grinning at him, giggling and grinning. When she saw his readiness she laughed as if this were a joke which they both might share.

'Take me, Robert. Take me, take me, take me.'

Immediately he pressed against her he found her ready. He felt her flex and withdraw, flex again, pressing her stomach upward and tilting her hips so that she absorbed him completely.

'Hold still, you little devil,' he hissed.

But she would not. She locked her knees about his waist

and her arms about his neck and rocked with him, crying out and giggling, while he, the Reverend Robert Montague, enjoyed at last a sense that what he was doing might be wrong.

BOOK THREE

The Affair

Seventeen

There was, of course, no honeymoon, no summer trip to Italy or France. Robert was too busy to contemplate leaving Ravenshill and, having no need now to placate his wife, simply ignored the subject.

Cassie was no more keen than her husband to be away from home. The pattern of her week was given substance by Allan Hunter. The long summer evenings went by like a flash. August came and went and the first breath of autumn stole in on the wind before, it seemed, she had recovered her poise from that first June kiss and the stolen kisses that succeeded it.

It strengthened Cassie to realise that her husband would not understand the value of a kiss; how it could represent a passion more celestial than anything to be found in the heavens, more satisfyingly than the effort of coupling that took place in the Turkish room two or three nights in the week. Even there Robert's ardour had diminished. There were nights when he would summon her to him and do nothing, would contemplate her, frowning, for three or four minutes then, with something bordering disgust, would dismiss her with a wave of his hand. Perhaps it was not disgust but merely boredom that affected him and he would mate with her now not for pleasure but only to have her conceive.

Robert had gathered about him everything that a man of standing might desire. There was nothing left to embrace but fatherhood. When he spoke of his own father, of Dada Montague, his conversation was neither bitter nor affectionate but somehow accusatory as if he, Robert, blamed Cassie for letting down the name of Montague, for reneging on the promise of fertility that he had made to the fat, dying, old minister in exchange for financial blessing.

How could she explain that her body was ignorant of his motives and was not a cask, a vessel that could be emptied of one fluid and filled with another. Not even Robert, for all his guile, could pull off that trick.

What gave Cassie power over her husband, more than she could ever have imagined possible, was the fact that she was loved by another man. What was there now but Allan, the weekly ride with Allan, the happy, not-quite-accidental meetings with Allan outside the haberdasher's or linen draper's or, once or twice, on the road that bordered the moor when she walked out with Nancy? There was no kissing on those occasions, of course, no touching of hands. But those stolen meetings meant more to Cassie than naked intimacy and assured her that she was still alive.

In her bedroom too were gathered tokens of Allan's love; nothing that would rouse Robert's suspicions: a seagull's feather, a posy of wild flowers, a smooth stone picked from the shingle and a tiny, silver comb that Cassie wore only on Wednesday evenings. In return she had given Allan a Psalter bound in red morocco, a large silk handkerchief and, at his request, one of her hair ribbons which he kept folded in his pocket like a talisman.

By agreement no letters passed between them, for the game, at root, was dangerous, a fact of which they were both only too well aware.

Their relationship was rendered more complicated by the fact that Allan was now overseer of work at Mr

Hounslow's Hercules Forge and owed a debt of gratitude to Robert for having arranged his temporary release from Flail's.

The so-called 'seven apostles' did not meet again, however.

One mid-summer assembly in the manse was all that Robert had deemed necessary. For the rest, each man laboured on a single part of the project, with Robert as linchpin. He had, of course, announced his intention to his congregation and begged their forbearance if he seemed slightly less attentive to pastoral matters for a month or two. Surprisingly, he did not invite his parishioners to contribute to the fund and rejected several offers of financial assistance which he referred to in private as 'widows' mites'.

His approaches to Session and Presbytery were direct. He did not go cap in hand to ask for permission to float the fund but rather presented it as a *fait accompli*, a scheme so obviously beneficial to the community, so obviously Christian in intent that he was astonished that no one had thought of it before. By all accounts, Reverend Montaguc's oratory was so inspiring that both Session and Presbytery gave him the nod without delay and, in so doing, opened the door to deceptions so complex that no mere clergyman could possibly have foreseen what Robert had in mind or how destructive his prodigious energy and zeal would prove to be in the end.

Cubby Armitage was Robert's first victim. He had been caught before the shooting season started, so to speak, brought to ground before he realised what was happening to him. He knew only that he was involved in something that he did not like and that his son-in-law was less deserving of respect than folk supposed. Money, Cubby decided, was Robert's god. The God of Abraham and of Isaac, the God of Moses and Aaron, the God of honest Scotsmen, that God, that living God had no claim on Robert's heart. Mammon was his idol, gain his objective, the rest of it merely empty promises.

Cubby did not deal directly with Robert. He dealt with that piece of thistledown, Rendell Wilks.

Wilks came and went from the office in Kennoway Square on an increasingly regular basis; so much so that Spratt and the other clerks no longer bothered to look up from their ledgers when the solicitor wafted through the bull-gate but simply held their palms down on the pages and waited, frowning, until the lawyer wafted out again.

"Zat him again, Mr Spratt?'

'That's him.'

The clerks looked towards the office door, poised and waiting, Spratt's hand already on the chair arm, his buttocks tense.

'*Spratt?*'

'Aye, Mr Armitage.'

'*Bring in the church account.*'

'Aye, Mr Armitage, right away.'

If Rendell Wilks had hesitated for a fraction of a second then Cubby would have been able to blurt out at least one of the one hundred and one questions that troubled him. Even if an opportunity for interrogation had presented itself, however, Cubby doubted if Wilks would give anything away. So Cubby would sit at his desk, mouth open, and stare at the grey-brown envelope that Wilks had deposited before him and wonder what outrageous instruction it contained this time, what astronomical sum Robert wished him to gamble with and from what source the money had been derived.

Rendell Wilks had the answers, of that Cubby had no doubt. Robert had answers too but poor Cubby was still in awe of his son-in-law, even if he was no longer dazzled by him. Fear had replaced respect. Caution had taken the place of obsequiousness and as summer cooled into autumn Cubby's admiration for the minister changed its hue and, like an oak leaf, withered and fell from the bough.

Cubby's suspicions that Robert was robbing the Church

280

Extension Fund had little or no basis. The scheme appeared to be bounding along merrily. Initial investments and purchases had all been made and paid for. Mr Hounslow had taken on the work of precision casting of the parts. Mr Hunter had been contracted from Sir Andrew to supervise the processes and Major Jerome – well, quite what Major Jerome did still remained a mystery. Mr Sinclair had agreed to a land deal for the wasted acres behind the Arms and Mr Lassiter, so Cubby was informed, was preparing himself to take over the management of the new church as soon as it was erected. There was talk of a dedication by Christmas. Robert was confident that nothing would go wrong.

If Norah had been less moody that autumn Cubby might have discussed his fears with her. If Pippa had been less enthralled by her brother-in-law then he might have mentioned his apprehension to his younger in the hope that she would offer him comfort, if not advice. If Cassie had not been Robert's wife – the same. He even wished that Charlie Smalls would return from America so that he might benefit from his partner's experience of the world, for if anyone understood deviousness in human nature and could spot a crook at a thousand paces then it was Charlie.

Finally, in desperation, he toyed with the idea of bringing the matter to Sir Andrew's attention for, when it came to business, Andrew Flail was without peer in the community. But something stayed Cubby's hand, some instinct warned him that the Flails were more involved than they appeared to be.

There was no one to whom Cubby could turn, nobody in whom he could confide. He would open the latest envelope that Wilks had brought him with trembling fingers and extract from it a sheaf of banknotes and a note signed, not by Robert – never by Robert – only by Major John James Jerome.

The note would instruct him to buy shares in this or stock in that or, now and then, to purchase certain securities that had been advertised in the *Glasgow Herald*.

Cubby would count the banknotes, put a ribbon round them, would call for Spratt to bring in the ledger so that he might remind himself, as if he needed reminding, just what stock the Ravenshill Church Extension Fund already owned and what sort of splits and divisions he would be obliged to make to reap the harvest that Robert expected. He would scrutinise the deed of ownership and think to himself that the fund was nothing but a nominal holding and that every penny within it, washed clean on the floor of the Exchange, belonged not to trustees, not to a board or partnership or committee but to one man, one signature – Major John James Jerome.

'A word, Major Jerome, if I may.'

'By all means, old boy.'

'In – em – I mean, in confidence.'

'Certainly, Mr Armitage. Step this way.'

The walls of the manse seemed to bristle with ears. Cubby suffered from the belief that his enquiring whispers would be heard by his son-in-law and that Robert would somehow punish him for his loss of faith. Sheer desperation had driven Cubby to tackle Johnny Jerome at home.

'In here, Mr Armitage. We'll not be disturbed in the small parlour.'

The door closed. Sounds in hall and drawing-room were cut off.

Neat and natty in a new dinner suit, Johnny struck a match with his thumbnail and applied the flame to the tip of a fresh Havana.

Cubby said, 'I would not want this to get back to my – em – to Robert.'

'No need to whisper. We can't be overheard.' Johnny released a cloud of cigar smoke. He wafted at it with a hand, picked a fleck of tobacco from his tongue, then said, 'It's about the money, ain't it, old boy? You think it's dirty money, don't you?'

'It's such a lot, such a fortune.'

'How much do you consider a fortune?' Johnny said.

'Don't you know?'

''Course I don't know.'

'But it's your – I mean, on paper it's all yours.'

'On paper ain't the same as in pocket, alas,' Johnny said. 'I'll have my share of it when all's said and done, same as you will, but how much is there just ain't my concern, leastwise not yet.'

'Whose money is it?'

'The fund's money.'

'I don't believe you, Major Jerome.'

'Oh-ho! Mutiny in the ranks, what?'

'I don't even know what I'm doing.'

'You're doing very well from what Robbie tells me. He's exceedingly grateful.'

'I don't want his gratitude,' Cubby blurted out. 'I do not appreciate being kept at arm's length by Mr Wilks.'

'Is it Wilks you object to?'

'Wilks, I suppose, is only obeying Robert's instructions.'

'Have you spoken to Robbie about your reluctance to help the cause?'

'The cause? What cause? In so far as I can make out,' Cubby said, 'there is no cause but acquisition.'

Johnny hesitated. 'As a matter of interest, Cuthbert, just how much does the fund currently contain?'

'Six thousand, seven hundred and thirty-six pounds.'

Johnny whistled. 'Do you say?'

'That does not take into account sums transferred to the Highland Bank, to *your* personal account in the Highland Bank, I might add.'

'I knew about those,' Johnny Jerome said. 'My signature was required on the transfer requests and deposit forms.'

'I can't go on with it,' Cubby said. 'I don't *want* to go on with it.'

'You think it's a bubble, is that it?' Johnny said.

'I know it's a bubble,' Cubby said.

'Do you want me to have a word with Robert, to clear the air?'

'*No,*' said Cubby loudly, then again, '*No.*'

Another hesitation: 'Have you spoken to anyone else about this matter?'

'Who would listen? Who would believe me?'

'So you haven't mentioned it to Norah, say, or to Cassie?'

'My daughter knows nothing of the market.'

'No, but she may know more than you do about Robert Montague.'

'What do you mean by that remark, sir?'

'Nothing, nothing impertinent, I assure you,' said Johnny, hastily. 'You're perfectly right, old boy. The less one involves women in this sort of thing the better for all concerned.'

'It's fraud, isn't it?' said Cubby.

Johnny balanced the cigar carefully on the edge of a small cherrywood sewing table. Smoke wavered, found the vertical and rose straight up in a thin, blue column. Cubby and Jerome studied it for a moment in silence.

'Cuthbert,' Johnny said at length, 'be careful. There's too much at stake and too many people involved for Robert to . . . Look, just do as he says, do what you're doing now. Leave the rest to fate.'

'Fate?'

'I mean, to Robert.'

'Are you warning me not to interfere?'

'I am, yes. You don't know him as I do,' Johnny said. 'There's nothing Robert wouldn't do to get his own way. There have been times in the past when Robert behaved almost as if he were possessed.'

'Possessed?' said Cubby. 'Possessed by what?'

'I don't mean that he's insane, really, not all the time. It's just that . . .' Johnny paused. 'Look, Cuthbert, just don't cross him, that's all.'

'You're in it too, aren't you?'

''Course I am. We're all in it.'

'No, I cannot be a party to fraud. If it comes to light it'll cost me my membership of the Exchange. My good name. Everything.'

'Robert doesn't care. Robert cares about nothing.'

'But he's supposed to be a man of God.'

Johnny gave a little snort of derision. 'God? What god? He lost faith in God years ago. Lost faith in everything. He has nothing to sustain him, Cuthbert, except what he can acquire.'

'And yet you remain his friend?'

'Yes.'

'Oh, God!' said Cubby. 'What sort of men are you?'

Johnny shrugged. 'The sort of man that you would like to be, Cuthbert, if only you had . . .'

Red-faced and perspiring, Cubby squared up to the major. Anger erased his politeness, eliminated his desire to be liked. He was swollen up like a little fighting cock. His fists, like talons, raked the air.

'If only, if only – what, sir?' Cubby shouted.

'If only you were willing to pay the price.'

'Oh, I know what the price is, sir. I know what wages sin pays out.'

'Death?' said Johnny Jerome. 'No, death is the ultimate banality.'

'At least I will not burn in hell,' Cubby shouted. 'Or do you consider hell to be banal too, too banal to be taken into account?'

'Ah, no,' Johnny said quietly. 'I believe in hell all right. I've been there, Cuthbert. So has Robert.'

'And where is this hell you talk of, tell me that?'

'Here,' Johnny pressed a forefinger to the centre of his brow. 'Right here.' Then, embarrassed by his own intensity, he stuck the cigar into his mouth once more and cocked it at a defiant angle. 'All of this, however, is a far cry from milking a little money from folk who can well afford it.'

'Is that how you see it?' Cubby said. 'Is that how you justify it?'

'I justify nothing,' Johnny said. 'I've said all I have to say on the matter, Cuthbert. If you wish reassurance – or the truth – then you must tackle Robbie by yourself. But I doubt if you will.'

'Will I not?' Cubby shouted. 'Why will I not?'

'Because you're afraid of him,' Johnny said.

At that moment the door of the small parlour opened. The men started and turned guiltily towards it.

'Ah, there you are, Papa,' Cassie said. 'We thought you were lost.'

'Not lost,' Cubby stammered. 'Just, just . . .'

Johnny Jerome glanced at him, brows raised a little, then, all smiles and affability, took Cubby by the arm and led him towards the door.

'Just chattin',' Johnny said.

'About what?' said Cassie.

'Nothing of any consequence,' Johnny said. 'Right, old boy?'

And Cuthbert, to his shame, agreed.

It seemed appropriate to Pippa that she should be taken on the Eve of All Hallows, that the man who did the taking was her sister's husband and the place where the deed was done was the Turkish room, upstairs in the manse. At last she understood why Cassie, her stubborn, upright sister, had paled under matrimonial onslaught and why she, a superior object in every way, thrived on the self-same treatment. It was because she did not in any sense belong to him, as Cassie did, and remained an equal partner in the division of pleasure.

From the first time she had clapped eyes on Robert Montague towering above her in the pulpit of Ravenshill church Pippa had sensed that he did not belong there and that Cassie would never be able to provide him with what he really wanted. That events had proved her right gave Pippa a great deal of satisfaction. She had exercised patience only because she was confident that Robert would not be able to resist the wicked appeal of making love to her where he had first deflowered her sister. The Turkish room, Robert told her, was the place for that.

As she lay in bed in Normandy Road Pippa would try to imagine her sister squealing on the ottoman or writhing across the sofa and, holding her hands to her breasts or belly, would envisage the pleasures that Cassie had denied herself that she, Pippa, would claim.

She loved Robert's vulpine smile, his hairiness, the dusty odour of his skin, that hard snatching fever which came upon him when she taunted him. It was greed of a kind that only she could share and which would surely reach its zenith when they lay naked together in the Turkish room.

'Tomorrow,' he told her. 'Tomorrow night.'

'All Hallows Eve?'

'Come to the manse at half past seven o'clock.'

'Cassie . . .'

'Will be gone for the evening.'

'Nancy too?'

'They will be at the mission.'

'And Johnny?'

'Leave Johnny to me.'

She could hardly contain herself. She longed for the moment when she would walk out into the blustery October night, walk alone under the lamps with the wind shaping her skirts against her thighs, knowing that Robert would be waiting for her. She was afraid that she would jump about and make a fool of herself and that Mama would forbid her to walk alone to Robert's house on a night when the dead were reputed to rise from their graves and witches rode their broomsticks over the sleeping townships, and even those who did not believe in such pagan nonsense were inclined to glance over their shoulders.

Robert was waiting for her in the hallway of the manse. The long-necked servant girl relieved her of her hat and cape. Robert took her arm and led her directly upstairs. He said nothing, gave no instruction, offered no explanation to the servants. When Pippa looked back from the turn of the stairs she saw Johnny Jerome standing below, arms folded.

She whispered, 'Do you think they know what we're going to do?'

'If they do,' Robert told her, 'does it matter?'

287

'Not one bit,' said Pippa, and laughed.

There was a subdued atmosphere in the mission that Wednesday evening that had nothing to do with the fact that it was Hallowe'en.

When Cassie and Nancy entered the hall they found many of the worshippers standing at the rear engaged in muted conversations. Even the children were fidgety.

'What is it?' Cassie said. 'What's wrong?'

'Dunno,' said Nancy, frowning.

'Where's Allan? Can you see Mr Hunter?'

'There he is,' said Nancy, pointing.

Allan was on the platform along with Mr Hounslow and Mr Lassiter. All three were gathered at the harmonium.

Cassie craned her neck and reported, 'I do believe he's crying.'

'Who? Mr Hunter?' said Nancy.

'Mr Lassiter. Yes, he is, he's weeping.'

The young women moved down the side aisle while shawled women and fusty men muttered explanations that Cassie hoped were speculation.

'Aye, it's the wife, she's dyin' at last.'

'No' her. She'll be out here any minute, you'll see.'

'What for's he bubblin' then?'

'Bad news. He's had bad news.'

'Must be Aggie, right enough. She never lookit well tae me.'

'Can you no' play the harmonicum, Edna?'

'Aye, go on, Edna. Gi'es a blast o' "Blessed Are Men".'

'Ah'll gi'e ye a slap 'roon the ear, Wullie McNish, if you're no' more respectfu' o' ma musical talents.'

'Allan?' Cassie said.

He looked round, smiled fleetingly then frowned, shook his head and gestured towards the stool upon which Mr Lassiter was seated. The preacher's shoulders were hunched, his hands clasped between his knees, his usually cheerful face crumpled with grief. He sobbed visibly and audibly. Banter between the old women and men ceased. They watched sympathetically, aware that something had undermined Albert Lassiter's optimism and that there was no humour in that situation.

When Allan shifted away from Mr Lassiter his place was taken by Edward Hounslow who knelt by the side of the harmonium and, without embarrassment, put a comforting arm about the preacher's shoulders.

'What is it, Allan?' Cassie whispered.

'It is his wife. She's been taken ill, seriously ill.'

'Where is she?'

'In the apartment at the back. A doctor is with her.' Allan glanced behind him, shook his head again and whispered, 'I don't think Albert can go on. Perhaps we might say a prayer for Agnes's speedy recovery, and then' – he shrugged – 'send everyone home.'

'Unfed?' said Nancy.

'I'm sure they'll understand,' said Cassie. 'What can we do, Allan? In what way can we help?'

'Feed them,' Nancy said. 'Feed them afore they go.'

'But what if Agnes dies?'

'At least she'll die knowin' that her flock's been fed,' said Nancy.

'Is the doctor still with her?' Cassie asked.

'He is,' Allan answered. 'It's grave news, I'm afraid.'

'I'll go to her,' Cassie said.

Allan put a hand upon her arm. 'I do not think that would be wise.'

'Why not? Should there not be a woman with her?'

'She's very distressed. She only wants Albert.'

'The meeting should have been cancelled,' Cassie said. 'Send them home, Allan. Tell them the reason and send them away.'

'Albert won't hear of it.'

'Even with his wife . . .'

'He loves his wife – but he loves God more.'

'Look at them,' Cassie said. 'It won't matter to them.'

'Aye,' Nancy said, 'it will, Miss Cassie. Believe me, it will. He's their man. They're his people. They expect him to be there when they need him.'

'That's ridiculous. All they want is a handout of bread.'

'Is it?' Nancy said. 'Is that all they want?'

'All right,' Allan said. 'I'll tell Albert that you will sit with her and that if her condition becomes worse . . .'

'I'll fetch him immediately,' Cassie promised. 'Nancy, will you be good enough to assist the young ladies with the tea urn?'

The young women watched anxiously while Allan relayed the information to Mr Lassiter who, mopping his face with a handkerchief, looked up at them with a brave smile and nodded his assent. He heaved himself to his feet, took a deep breath and raised his eyes towards the roof in search of divine aid.

Behind him Mr Hounslow peeled the cover from the harmonium and lifted up the lid. He seated himself on the stool and pumped awkwardly at the pedals, then, after sweeping a hand across his shock of white hair, put his fingers upon the keys and sought out a chord. The note vibrated loudly through the silent hall. Cassie fancied she could hear it singing in the beams and trembling through the metal roof, rising away and away into the blustery air overhead.

Mr Lassiter wiped his nose with the back of his wrist.

'Welcome,' he said, then, finding his voice, cried out, 'Good news, good news, an' welcome to each an' every one of you.'

With Allan to guide her, Cassie slipped from the hall into the room at the rear and closed the door quietly behind her.

Cassie had never seen anyone die before. She did not know what to expect, what might be revealed that would touch a nerve of terror within her and leave her tainted for ever more by fear of her own mortality.

She had visited the aged in company with her mother but had never been moved by their plight. They were old ladies, grey and passive, grateful for the attention that age brought them and it had seemed to Cassie that they were, if not eager, at least willing to slip off the burden and pass away as undemonstratively as possible. She had resented their meekness. With all the wisdom of youth she had felt that they had somehow courted their own demise.

Until she entered the cramped room in the rear of the Seaforth Street mission, Cassie had no idea what dying meant.

The globe of the lamp had been covered by a piece of green baize which smoked slightly around the edges and cast faint shadows across the unvarnished wall beyond the bed. Doctor Ross, an elderly gentleman, stood in a corner, thumbs in his waistcoat pockets, head bowed. He did not look up when Cassie entered the room. It was as if he wished to absolve himself from all connection with the woman in the bed and, demonstrating the paradoxical attitude of many burned-out physicians, preferred to treat her only from a safe distance.

The room was tiny, table and bed, chair and box all jammed together. Even in dim light Cassie could take in all the Lassiters' possessions at a glance, read there, as on a single page, the story of their years together.

She moved to the bedside, a half step beyond the door. Her skirts pressed outwards, shrinking the room still further. It came home to her then how snug a place this was, how she and her kind had expanded into wasteful luxury in which all intimacy was lost. Robert could not have endured such confinement, nor could she have survived a single day here in her husband's company. When she thought of Allan and her together in this slender box, however, she experienced a strange yearning for all that the Lassiters had that she did not.

'He – he's – preachin'?'

Doctor Ross glanced up with a frown, as if he expected the patient too to maintain a respectful silence.

'Mrs Lassiter,' he murmured, 'you shouldn't exert yourself.'

'Is Albert – preachin'?'

Cassie leaned forward and rested one hand upon the

quilt. She was no longer afraid. This was no touching picture; Agnes Lassiter was fierce and flighty and still fighting for her husband, still with him in spirit while her body, enfeebled and inflamed, writhed upon the bed.

'Yes,' Cassie said. 'He has commenced the service.'

'I told him – we – could not let them – down.'

The sweetish smell of medicines and of the woman's sweat rose from the bedding. Her hair was tangled like a mane, her eyes huge and luminous in the gaunt, white face. She propped herself up on one elbow. Vomit, freckled with blood, ornamented the lace of the night-gown that twisted across her breast.

Cassie unclipped her scarf and, while Ross watched impassively, wiped sickness from the woman's chin. She felt no revulsion in nursing a last-stage patient. She pinched the fingers of her glove in her teeth and drew it off and then, seating herself carefully upon the side of the bed, took Agnes Lassiter's hand in hers.

'He's giving them the good news, Mrs Lassister,' Cassie said.

'It – it is good too. I'll be there afore him to – to prepare a place fit for him at – at our Father's table. Our Lord will – welcome him wi' open arms, when – when his time comes,' Agnes gasped. 'I'll see to that. Aye, I'll – see to that.'

Her hand was all bone, the knuckles rough and swollen, but the nails were perfectly white, almond-shaped, like those of a lady. She leaned her cheek against Cassie's wrist and let the weight of her head fall forward.

From the hall came the sound of singing, an anthem Cassie had not heard before. With Mr Hounslow at the keyboard the old harmonium rang out resoundingly. Cassie could feel the music in the walls, the voice of the preacher louder than ever, and full of good cheer and optimism.

Ross said, 'Has she gone?'

Cassie shook her head. She did not ask if there was anything that medicine could do for the woman, for she knew that there was not. There was nothing to be done except hold Agnes Lassiter's hand and wait for the blessing.

'Will they – be fed?' Agnes whispered.

'Yes,' Cassie promised her. 'Yes, they will be fed.'

She heard the rattle in the woman's chest, the in-suck of breath and, leaning closer, felt the woman's lips brush her ear as if to impart a secret that could no longer be concealed.

'I want my Albert,' Agnes Lassiter whispered.

They waited at the mission as long as possible. They assisted the young women in dispensing tea and bread and, with Mr Hounslow's help, cleared the hall as soon as seemed decent. But Agnes Lassiter did not die immediately. There was no convenient time to pass away, it seemed.

There was a little whispered meeting in the empty hall. Allan promised to return mid-shift and Mr Hounslow, who seemed much affected by the sorrowful affair, indicated that he would personally call in at the mission first thing in the morning and assist Albert in making 'arrangements', if necessary.

Allan stood with Cassie in the deserted hall and held her hand tightly. She was not inclined to shed tears, however. She was moved, she was touched, but she was also quizzical. It was not her witness to the act of dying that had touched her but the notion that she, when her time came, might die unmourned. Gaslight dimmed, floor swept clean, urns glinting, the clean, hard sheen of teacups in their wooden trays; beyond that, to the right of the little platform upon which the shrouded harmonium loomed, was the door to the cabin where Albert prayed for a private peace and relief of all pain for Agnes.

Cassie said, softly, 'Did you grieve like that, Allan, when your wife died?'

'Yes,' he answered. 'I did not think that I could go on without her.'

'What saved you?'

'Tom saved me. I was not, as Albert is, alone.'

'Is he alone?' Cassie said. 'Will she not always be with him?'

'Always,' Allan said. 'But it is not the same.'

'What do you mean?'

'There, and not there,' Allan said. 'Albert Lassiter will have Agnes and only Agnes for as long as he lives – there, and not there.'

'And you?'

'I was saved. I fell in love again.'

Cassie could hear no sound from the room at the rear of the hall, neither prayer nor weeping. She had never been so close to anyone before as she was to Allan Hunter at that moment.

'Saved,' she said. 'Yes.'

Then she hurried out into the street to find Nancy and return to her husband on Bramwell hill.

It was late, very late when the gig drew up at the door of the manse. No lights were to be seen to the front of the building, except the lamp in its big wrought-iron holder above the front door. Within the house the darkness was accentuated by a subterranean glow from the basement stairs and a faint glimmer on the first-floor landing.

Even as Cassie and Nancy entered the hallway, the grandfather clock that nestled under the staircase struck the half hour past eleven and All Hallows Day was almost upon them. It did not seem like a Wednesday. It was as if the melancholy events of the evening had warped both clock and calendar.

'Will I come up wi' you, Miss Cassie?'

'No, Nancy. You may go straight to bed.'

'Are you sure?'

'Yes. I'm all right, really I am.'

'What about' – Nancy glanced up the darkened staircase – 'him?'

'Mr Montague is probably asleep.'

'Aye,' Nancy said, then, for no reason at all, added, 'Be careful, miss.'

When she reached the first floor Cassie knew that Robert was not asleep. He would surely be lying in wait for her, hard-featured, cold and demanding. When he learned what had delayed her in Seaforth Street he would be harder still. She knew him now. She could predict how he would react to her news of Agnes Lassiter's passing, how he would absorb her, Cassie's, sorrow into his malign need for novelty.

She heard laughter in Johnny's room, saw light under the door.

She paused, skirts held up, bonnet and scarf in hand, paused and listened to the laughter and then, straightening, she stole along the corridor to the door. She listened, heard boyish sniggering and harsh little cries, the sound of men's voices barking at each other like small cannon.

'Hoh, you devil. You have me now.'

'Do you submit?'

'I do not submit. Damned if I'll submit.'

'Queen and Jack not enough for you?'

'One Jack at a time, old boy, one Jack at a time.'

'Give in.'

'Shan't.'

Cassie knocked and, without awaiting permission to enter, pushed open the door of Johnny's room and stepped over the threshold.

They looked up at her, neither startled nor embarrassed.

They were seated cross-legged on the rug before the fire, clad in bathrobes, both of them, bare-legged and bare-chested. They were playing bezique. Cards and silver coin, some banknotes too, strewed the patterned rug and round about them, like toys, were ashtrays and a humidor, glasses and wine bottles and plates greasy with chicken scraps.

'Well, well,' said Johnny Jerome, cockily drunk, 'it's her ladyship wandered home at last. What say, old boy, shall we give her a hand?'

'I doubt if she will take a hand, Johnny.'

'Right you are, Robbie. Look at her mug, b'God. What's

wrong, *Mittress* Montague, meet a ghostie on the stairs, did you?'

Johnny sniggered and, letting his cards slide to the rug, leaned back and plucked a half-smoked cigar from an ashtray on the fender. Leaning on his elbow, he stuck the cigar in his mouth and puffed. His robe fell open, exposing wiry thighs downed with fair hair. He looked up at her then down and, pulling a face, flicked at the skirts of the robe with a gesture that was almost feminine.

'That ain't no ghostie, madam,' he said.

Far from being offended at the insult to his wife, Robert guffawed.

'I'll say it's not,' he said, then added, 'Now, Cassie, do tell us where you've been to this ungodly hour?'

She knew that they were drunk, at least partly so. But she was not shocked by their behaviour as she would have been a year ago.

'I was delayed at Seaforth Street because Mrs Lassiter is dying,' Cassie said. 'In fact, she may already be dead.'

A pause: Robert said, 'Not before time, what? Not before time.'

Nine days later, a week after Agnes Lassiter had been laid to rest and Albert had moved into McGuire's boarding-house, a gang of workmen arrived at the mission in Seaforth Street with hammers, spikes and pick-axes and razed the little building to the ground.

Eighteen

The first snow of the winter scored the skies over Glasgow and absorbed, piece by piece, Cuthbert's view of Kennoway Square. It was not much of a fall and nobody expected it to lie, nor did the granular flakes in any way diminish the bone-biting cold that had descended over the city. It was a foretaste, a forerunner of harsh weather to come, though, and the citizenry shivered and complained and trudged laboriously over the light, squeaking carpet as if they were already wading through drifts ten feet deep and wolves were running down Argyle Street and polar bears hunting the pack-ice below Jamaica Bridge.

The floor of the Stock Exchange was littered with paper scraps and pencil shavings and the big iron pipes that carried heat into the bargaining hall had not yet got up a head of steam. In addition a keen little wind had found its way through the antechambers and stirred the scraps and shavings and nipped at the heels of the clerks and brokers who clipped across the marble and dived up and down the broad slate staircase to the desks.

Cubby had spent the morning in the Exchange along with Spratt and a manic young clerk named McIlwham, one of a voluble new breed whose enthusiasm for making

297

money on behalf of clients seemed, to Cubby at least, to border on the indecent.

Cubby had been chilled since the moment he had risen from bed, a condition he gloomily ascribed to advancing years. The cold snap had increased his oppression. Even lunch with his peers, and a tumbler of hot toddy, brought no glow of comfort. Soon thereafter he assigned the dregs of the day's dealing to Spratt and McIlwham and returned through the snow to his chambers where, to his utter dismay, he found Robert lying in wait.

Not for Reverend Montague the discomforts of the stiff leather couch in the clients' waiting room with nothing to occupy him but back issues of *Scottish Pulpit* and *The Baillie*. Robert was installed before the fire in Cuthbert's office, heels propped on the brass fender, a ledger open on his knee. He looked, Cubby thought, like an undertaker taking his ease, except that Robert, in spite of his casual pose, was never at ease.

Cubby nodded glumly, took off his hat and overcoat, hung them on hooks by the door.

'You've had tea, I take it?' he said.

'Absolutely.'

'And toast, I see.'

'I am, thank you, replete.'

Cubby had been looking forward to planting himself at the hearth and warming his chilly buttocks at the fire. But he was unable to bring himself to approach his son-in-law and sidled away round the globe and the letter rack into the half bay window behind his desk. He wanted to shout out, *Get away from my fire, you fraud*, but a habit of respect for the cloth, plus fear of Robert's sinuous authority, dissuaded him.

Robert tapped the pages of the ledger with his forefinger.

'Interesting reading,' he said.

'Who gave you that?'

'One of your clerks.'

'Ledgers are supposed to be confidential.'

'Good Lord, man, it's *my* account.'

'No, it's not,' Cubby shot out before he could check himself.

Robert frowned. 'Well, technically – literally – no, I suppose it isn't.' He closed the ledger and rose. 'On the other hand, it is my capital that has been invested and if the speculations have paid off, as they obviously have, then the proceeds are mine.'

'Your capital?' said Cubby. 'It isn't your capital at all. It's fund money, other people's money.'

'Oh, is that what you think?' Robert said. 'Is that why you've been slandering me?'

'What's Jerome been saying?'

'Whatever Johnny says is of no importance. The fact is, Cuthbert, that you have no understanding of what's going on.'

'Fraud's going on. Deception's going on,' Cubby said. 'And I want no part in it.'

'Part in what?'

'This – em – this misappropriation of a public fund.'

'Ah, Cuthbert, it's just as well for you that I'm not litigious-minded or, relative or no, I would have you in court for impugning my good name.' Robert advanced to the desk and leaned his hands upon it, pressing Cubby back into the window bay. 'In the first place it is not a public fund. In the second place I have taken not one penny from anyone.'

'The subscription list,' Cubby interrupted. 'What about the subscribers? Have you not elicited money from them?'

'There are no subscribers,' Robert said.

'Oh, now you are lying.'

'Am I? Can you name one person who has donated money to the fund? Can you, Cuthbert? Are you, for instance, a subscriber?'

'Well, no, I . . .'

'Is Hounslow?'

'I assumed . . .'

'Hunter? Lassiter?' Robert went on. 'Mr Grimmond, our

church officer? Mrs Calderon? Do you think I'd rob the widow of her mite to feather my own nest? Is that what you think of me, Cuthbert?'

'No, Robert, I . . .'

Robert contemplated his father-in-law with an expression of indulgence, as if he, Cubby, was nothing but a misguided schoolboy in need of instruction.

'The money is mine,' Robert said. 'Every farthing so far invested has come out of my pocket. I have taken nothing from anyone. How can that be fraud, Cuthbert? Tell me, how is that fraud?'

'But you said – you promised . . .'

'To build an iron church. Which is precisely what I am doing.' He pointed to the chair behind the desk. 'Stop cowering in your corner, Cuthbert. Sit down. I'm not finished with you yet.'

Cubby, thoroughly abashed, obeyed his son-in-law. He seated himself on the chair, lowered his head and looked up at Robert from the tops of his eyes.

'I didn't realise – I mean – I thought . . .'

'That I was speculating with money that did not belong to me?'

'Yes,' Cubby admitted. 'Something of that nature.'

'Am I correct in supposing that you do not like investing in high-risk ventures, even on my behalf?'

A pause: 'Yes.'

'Do you wish to be released from your obligation, Cuthbert?'

No pause: 'Yes.'

'Well,' Robert said, 'I am not prepared to allow you to resign. You've done well for me so far and you will continue to do well for me. If you decide that you do not wish to represent me or if you dare to slander me again then' – he tossed a scrap of yellowing paper down upon the desk top – 'I will ask you to explain what *this* means. And if you will not, or cannot, then I will ask the same question of your wife.'

Cubby hardly appeared to glance at the paper scrap. He

certainly did not reach out to examine it.

'Oh!' he said. 'Oh, my Lord!'

'Twenty years does not change a man's character much and his hand not at all,' Robert said. 'I'm sure that a handwriting expert will confirm that the note was written by you.'

'Oh, Lord! Oh, Lord Jesus!' Cubby put his thumb to his mouth and sucked on it in search of comfort or, perhaps, wisdom. 'Why are you doing this to me, Robert? What harm have I ever done you?'

'What harm did you do to the child, Cuthbert? That's what you should ask yourself.'

'It was dead. I know it was dead.'

'Then why did you write the note?'

'I could not – in case – just because it . . .'

'Did you go back to the whinfield?'

'Yes.'

'To finish it off?'

'No, no.'

'You told Norah that it was dead, didn't you?'

Cubby nodded, head like a great lead weight. 'It was gone when I got back there. I thought . . .'

'Surely you must have known that it had been taken to the foundlings' ward. Wasn't that your intention when you scribbled this note?' Robert said. 'Or was it merely an afterthought, a sop to conscience?'

'Where did you – I mean, where did you find it?'

Robert threw up his hands. 'Did it not occur to you to check the ward entries for that day, Cuthbert?'

'After I sent the note to Beatty I was afraid to show my face there.'

'So you knew that it was alive?'

'I didn't know what to think.' He looked up. 'I was in no position then to enquire at the workhouse. I had no reason to.'

'Some years later, though, you hired children from the workhouse to be servants in your house,' Robert said. 'Why?'

'It was – em – in my position, expected of me.'

'Oh, Cuthbert, how badly you lie.'

'In case, in case,' Cuthbert blurted out. 'Damn you, can't you understand? I was so young when it happened. I did it for Norah.'

'I am sure that you did,' said Robert. 'What was the infant's name?'

'No name. It never had a name.'

'But she was given a name. You know what that name is, don't you?'

'No.'

'Cuthbert, you really should not endeavour to lie to me.'

'Not for sure. I do not know for sure.'

'Why did you take her into your house, Cuthbert?'

'To see if she . . .'

'If Norah would recognise her?' Robert suggested.

'No, rather to make sure that Norah did not,' Cubby stated.

'Ah! I see,' said Robert. 'Why did you dismiss her?'

'Because she wasn't suitable.'

'Because your daughters developed an affinity with her?'

'She was foolish and immature. She already had a lover; more than one, perhaps.'

'Like mother, like daughter.'

'How dare you say that about Norah!' Cubby cried.

'It is the truth, though, is it not?' Robert persisted. 'Like mother, like daughter. Only the daughter – Nancy Winfield – was not so fortunate as her mother. Poor Nancy Winfield had to pay the price of Mama's folly.'

Cubby got to his feet. He was hardly aware of the movement of his legs beneath him or of the threatening posture that he adopted.

His head was spinning and his brain was out of control. He had never known why he'd done what he did, except that he had desired Norah Clavering more than was decent. And the only way he could assuage that desire was through marriage. And the only way he could take her on was as damaged goods. He had never asked her about her lover. He had continued to sustain the belief that it was Ewan Flail and that he was performing a service to a noble family. He also remembered the slithering infant, prematurely born. The pink and bloody, skinned-rabbit thing lying mute upon the sheet on the bed between Norah's thighs. How loath he had been to touch it. And he had known that this thing, this curled-up creature could not be a Flail, that this little female beast was not alive at all.

And he remembered, or thought he did: *It's dead. It's dead. I must take it away.*

Yes, dearest, yes, take it away, take it away.

'Did you know her identity when you employed her as Cassie's lady's maid?' Cubby asked.

'Of course I did.'

Cubby said, 'If you tell Norah about this I'll – I'll kill you.'

'Hah!' Robert said. 'If you haven't the guile to lie properly, Cuthbert, how could you ever bring yourself to do murder?'

'I would. I will.'

'But only if I tell Mama?' said Robert.

'Or Cassandra. Or Pippa. Or anyone.'

Cubby glanced at the scrap of yellow paper.

As if reading his in-law's mind, Robert reached out and plucked it away. He folded it carefully and slipped it back into his pocket.

'I have no intention of telling anyone, Cuthbert,' he said. 'What would I gain from ruining your marriage or your reputation? On the other hand, I might be tempted to risk it if you do not do what I ask of you.'

'And what is that?' said Cubby.

'Co-operate,' said Robert.

In works as small and antiquated as the Hercules Foundry the importation of an overseer for specific jobs was not at all uncommon. Entering the Hercules was like being transported back in time and Allan revelled in the processes whereby each portion of the church was fashioned. He had to confess that he also enjoyed the deference shown to him by Mr Augustine, the general works' manager.

Mr Augustine was no less expert than Mr Hunter but he had been so long employed in the old-fashioned establishment on the banks of the Clyde that he had all but forgotten that progress elsewhere had revolutionised the industry. He did not resent Allan Hunter's meticulousness in overseeing the 'piling' of cut bars and the operation of the reheating furnace. Mr Augustine was flattered when Mr Hunter, who was after all, a trained engineer, deferred to him throughout the rolling, for the mill was old and under-powered, its single stoke engine slow and temperamental.

Transport to and from the Hercules was still effected entirely by horse-drawn wagon and the stables were almost as large as the forge itself. The smell of horse which pervaded the forge and the carbonated atmosphere of the casting shed brought back to Allan memories of his apprentice years, before steam-driven machines and deafening locomotives were commonplace.

Pleasure in his work, concentration on intricate designs and delicate castings did not relieve him of the strain of being in love with a woman who was wedded to another man, however. He was more in love with her than ever and had particularly admired her treatment of poor Albert Lassiter in his bereavement.

Agnes Lassiter had been interred in rural surroundings in the new cemetery to the south-east of Bramwell, a fine, fresh, unsullied place. The lair had been purchased by Mr Hounslow who had also put up a certain sum to lodge Albert at McGuire's boarding-house until such time as he felt well enough to return to his work. There had been little evidence of Reverend Montague throughout the sad proceedings. He had not attended Agnes Lassiter's committal or the mission hall service that followed it and had pled unavoidable Presbytery business as an excuse.

Albert did not care who conducted the service. Albert

was too stricken with grief to care about anything.

Although Cassie had not been with him at the graveside Allan felt as if she had been. She seemed to be present with him everywhere these days, even in the fires and fumes of the Hercules. It was as if she had become a memory of his youth, not a person of present and future but someone out of his past. He had no plan to wrest her from Montague. He was not the sort of man to lure her away with sweet talk and rash promises. When they were together they spoke of other things, never of what might come to pass between them.

Oddly enough, it was Johnny Jerome who brought Allan news of the clearing of the site of the mission hall and Jerome who introduced him to the notion that perhaps all was not static, that while he might be patient and content to adhere to the *status quo*, others most certainly were not.

Soon the last girder would be trimmed, safe load tested on an old but reliable cog-toothed spring balance. The last zed-piece would be brought from the forge for final measuring, the last ornamental corner drawn by its packthreads from a liquid plaster mould and sent for finishing. Then all the pieces, chalked and checked, would be boxed in straw-packed crates and transported out for assembly. And the job would be done. And he would return to his dull managerial duties at the Blazes.

They were casting the column of the wrought-iron font late that evening. Allan and Johnny Jerome were both in attendance. The manager had selected the base iron carefully. He had tested a lump for blistering and had no reason to suppose that the men who did the work would encounter difficulty with the intricate design.

Jerome and he stood back to watch the mould being filled. For all his slyness, Johnny Jerome was a true engineer. Allan was comfortable with the man when he played that practical role. A touch on the sleeve, however, a hand on the shoulder and similar gestures of intimacy discomfited Allan. He invented excuses not to be alone with Jerome and no longer made discreet enquiries about Mrs Montague's welfare.

'She's a very personable young woman, is she not?' Johnny would say. 'I certainly think so. Shame that she's tied. Otherwise, she'd definitely be worth the wooing.'

'I'm not sure I know what you mean.'

'Oh, come now, old boy, surely you find her attractive?' Johnny would say. 'I'm not much given to the worship of women but even I find Cassie Montague easy on the eye. Face and figure, if you know what I mean. I can tell you that she finds you attractive. If she was a lady of a different stamp and you were a man less principled – well, there might even be sparks, if you know what I mean. Wouldn't that give the stuffy folk of Robbie's congregation something to blather about?'

'If you suppose, Mr Jerome, that I would steal another man's wife . . .'

'The thought never crossed my mind.'

'Why does Montague allow her so much latitude?'

'Robbie is a very strange fellow,' Johnny Jerome said. 'I don't mind admitting that there are times when I think he's not quite right in the head. He doesn't care about Cassandra because Cassandra is already in his possession.'

'Have you been instructed to warn me off?'

'Good Lord, no.'

'There's nothing to warn me off *from*, I assure you.'

''Course there ain't. Not yet anyway.'

Allan did not respond. Behind him in the workshop the hammermen were licking the long beams of the new kirk into shape. He took refuge in the ear-splitting sounds and, just as Johnny made to touch his arm, moved away towards the open door.

Horses, massive, broad-shouldered Clydesdale stallions, chaffered in the wagon yard outside and horse-boys, thin as poles, groomed their charges in the fiery glow of the furnaces. Allan knew that Jerome *had* just issued him a warning but what it implied he could not be sure.

'Damn it all,' Johnny said, 'I don't care what you do to

Cassie Montague. All I'm saying, old boy, is that it would be very unwise to cross Robert at this time. I like you, Allan. As far as it goes, I like the woman too. I wouldn't want to see either of you hurt.'

'Hurt?'

'Look,' he said, 'Robbie – well, he *isn't* like you an' me. You don't know him. What he's done. What he can do.'

'What *can* he do?' Allan said. 'He's a clergyman. The Presbytery will keep him up to the mark.'

The clang of hammers had become louder and more persistent. Allan could feel metallic vibrations in the soles of his feet and the top of his head. Jerome too seemed suddenly aware of the deafening sound. He screwed his eyes shut for a moment then opened them again, very wide.

'Nobody can keep Robert up to the mark, not when the devil's in him.'

'Leave Cassie alone,' Allan said, frowning. 'Is that what you mean?'

'Cassie! Cassie! Is that all you can think about?' Johnny shouted angrily. 'I don't care what you do to Cassie Montague. Just don't, I beg you, *don't* stand between Robert and what he wants.'

'And what is that? What does he want?'

'Everything he can lay his hands on,' Johnny said.

'But that's madness,' Allan said.

'Yes,' Johnny said, grimly. 'That's just what I've been trying to tell you, old boy.'

Nancy was confident that Mr Lassiter would not remain idle for long. 'Idle' did not seem an appropriate word for the condition in which the missionary found himself but Cassie could think of none more suitable, unless it was 'languish' and she did not think that word quite fitted either. She missed the Wednesday evening services. She had not seen Allan for more than a week and, at Nancy's urging, wrapped herself up and left the manse at the usual hour of seven for the drive to Seaforth Street, more in hope than expectation.

Seated in the gig behind Luke Simmonds, she watched misty November rain pearling the lamps and coating the horse's flanks like white moss. The hood was up but, even so, sifting rain wetted the young women and they snuggled together under a blanket and protected their bonnets with broad cotton scarves. In spite of the dismal weather it was good to be out and about. Apart from Sabbath duties Cassie had hardly left the manse since the day of Agnes's funeral. She had seen nothing of her parents or Pippa, or of Allan in that time.

As the gig neared the mouth of Seaforth Street Cassie's spirits rose. She hugged Nancy's arm under the blanket.

'Will he be here, do you think?' she asked.

Nancy laughed. 'How would I know that?'

'He's your friend too, isn't he?'

'Aye, but . . .' Nancy laughed again. 'Hold your water, like Todd would say, an' we'll see in a minute if he's there or not.'

'Todd? Who's Todd?'

'Just a chap I used to know.'

'A sweetheart?' Cassie asked, lightly.

'Hardly,' Nancy answered. 'Nah, nah, I'd hardly call him a sweetheart.'

Luke Simmonds swung round. 'Is this the place, Mittress Montague?'

'Of course, this is the place.'

'Where is it then?' Luke said. 'Where's the mission?'

He halted the gig by the pavement's edge and all three of its occupants stared at the long bare strip of wasteland. A vista had opened between tenement walls and the wall of the warehouse that flanked the site. Of the tin hut nothing remained but a pattern upon the earth, an oblong outlined by brown puddles and two small fires of timber debris that hissed and smoked in the darkness.

'What's happened?' Cassie cried. 'Nancy, what's happened?'

'They've knocked it down,' Nancy exclaimed. 'My God, they've knocked down the mission an' never told nobody.'

Huddled in the doorway of a corn merchant's store were six or eight members of Albert Lassiter's congregation. The old ones, the shabby ones, widows with shawls and stooped old men with walking sticks and bedraggled beards, they hovered without purpose and did not even seem to know how to disperse. They seemed frightened of Cassie now, those folk with whom she had shared the joyful songs, the optimism of Mr Lassiter's preaching. They shrank away as the gig approached, cowered into the shadow of the corn store and some, those who were spry enough, hobbled around the corner out of sight.

'When did this happen?' Cassie called out. 'When was this done?'

No answer. Mute suspicion. It was as if with the mission gone they were no longer obliged to hide their dislike of Cassie Montague's bourgeois manners and fine, warm clothes. Nancy scrambled out of the gate at the rear of the gig and bustled across the pavement.

'You, Mrs Motherwell, you ken who I am. Now, tell me, who done this?'

'Cam' this mornin, so they did. Cam' early afore it was daylight.'

'Who were they?'

'They never telt me who they were.'

'What did they do?'

'Took it awa'. Five men an' a laddie, an' two big carts. Broke it down wi' picks an' hammers an' carted the remains off, load b' load.'

'The carts,' Nancy said, 'was nothin' painted on the carts?'

An old man shuffled out of the shadows, lifted his stick and pointed down Seaforth Street in the direction of the Blazes.

'Ah'll tell ye where the carts cam' from,' the old man declared. 'They cam' from Flail's Blazes. The name was painted on the side.'

Cassie leaned over the rail of the gig.

'And Mr Lassiter, sir? Where was Mr Lassiter when this was going on?'

'He wept,' the old man said. 'He saw it all, an' wept.'

'Where is he now?' said Nancy.

'McGuire's.'

Mrs McGuire, a clean-aproned, round-bodied woman admitted the lady and her servant without argument. Mr Lassiter's room was on the attic floor. The landlady directed them up a staircase so creaking and steep that it might have been redeemed from a keep, save that it had a carpeted runner upon it and, at the landings, a variety of potted plant with leaves so broad and black that they appeared to have been cut from tar paper.

Nancy led the way. Nimble as she was, even she puffed a bit on the upper slopes and, when the tiny platform landing of the attic floor was reached, slumped against the wall to catch her breath.

There were no potted plants at this altitude. Light came from a skylight, a patch of grey against the slope of the roof. A solitary door opened off the landing. Nancy knocked upon it then, with uncharacteristic nervousness, stepped back and hid herself behind Cassie.

After a lengthy pause, Mr Lassiter opened the door. He peered around it, his usually jovial features twisted by grief and suspicion.

'Who is it?'

'Do you not remember me, Mr Lassiter? I am Cassie Montague.'

'What do you want wi' me?'

'To see if there is anything we can do for you, anything you require.'

'They took it away,' Albert Lassiter said. 'They tore it down.'

'What happened to your furniture, your possessions?'

'Taken away. Sold, the ground sold. My mission sold for scrap. They won't give me a church. It was all just talk.

310

Vanity led me into the fowler's snare. I was taken in 'cause I thought the Lord would give me a kirk o' my own.' He covered his face with a shaking hand. 'There will be no good news for Albert Lassiter now his guidin' light has gone.'

'I'm sure it's only a matter of time until the iron church is built,' said Cassie, 'then you will be put in charge of it.'

'No, it's too late.'

'Mr Lassiter, may we come in?'

His suspicion turned to anger. 'Nah, you may not come in. You're one of his and he done this to me. He sold the land from under the feet of the Lord.'

'Who did? Was it Mr Hounslow?'

'It's Flail's land now. It's all Flail's land. There will be no church built on Flail's land. He'll see to that.'

'If we could come in for just a moment . . .' Cassie said.

'I've nothin' more for you to take,' Albert Lassiter said. 'Leave me be. For God's sake, leave me be,' and, stepping backward into the gloom, he slammed the door in Cassie's face.

Left alone on the attic landing, the young women stared at each other in dismay. 'I have never seen a man so changed,' Cassie said.

'Mr Lassiter's no' the only thing that's changed,' Nancy said. 'I think we should pay another call, Miss Cassie, if you're willin' to bear wi' me.'

'Of course,' Cassie said. 'Another call – on whom?'

'Archie Sinclair,' said Nancy.

Archie Sinclair was not playing host to his resident gentlemen that evening. Business in the dining-room was slack. Only four or five 'commercials' were propped at the tables, and the hall itself was deserted. It did not take the young women long to track the hotelier down. Leading her mistress by the arm, Nancy navigated her way down a back staircase and along a passageway that ran adjacent to the kitchens and, in no time at all, had Cassie outside again in the waste ground behind the building.

The drizzling rain had not abated but Cassie and Nancy hardly noticed it, for beyond the little wall that separated the hotel from the wasteland were lights and clamouring activity.

To the left, some two hundred yards away, the doors of the public house were wide open and workers from the Blazes stood about with pint mugs in their hands, watching their brethren labour by the light of flares and tar-buckets. Fine threads of rain held the light like muslin and Cassie's first impression was that the shrubs and stunted trees themselves were aflame. Beyond the old orchard, outlined against the railway embankment, she could make out figures and objects.

Nancy, with a little cry, dragged her on down the straggling dirt path that skirted the cottages, down through the bushes towards the embankment.

With a heavy tweed greatcoat draped across his shoulders and a beaver hat stuck square on his head, Archie Sinclair was huddled under the last of the stunted fruit trees, observing the demolition of the sheds that had stood since his grandfather's day. He did not seem pleased by what he saw, by the eagerness of the crew that attacked the rackety structures with hammers and pick-axes. The only cart in evidence was backed up by the lane that ran along the base of the embankment, for there was little of value to be hauled away for scrap.

Daft old tramps, inarticulate drunkards and half-starved women and children who had long taken Archie's charity for granted cowered behind the tar-buckets along the foot of the embankment. In the flickering light they looked, Cassie thought, barely human and they moaned and ranted at the labourers and shook their fists pathetically while the workmen jeered and roped another wall for felling like a tree.

Dust coagulated in the wet air; Cassie could taste it on her tongue. Her head told her that she was witnessing progress but her heart went out to the outcasts, ignorant and ugly though they might be, to whom the damp sheds had provided refuge.

When Nancy and she came up behind Mr Sinclair, he started and spun round. His face was pale and the wetness on his cheeks suggested tears. He had not been weeping, though. He, too, rode the balance between relief and regret but it was only curiosity that had finally brought him out to witness the end of an embarrassing history.

'Oh, it's you, Mistress Montague,' Archie said. 'What are you doin' here in this weather? Did Mr Montague send you?'

Cassie was taken aback. 'Why would my husband send me?'

'To be sure it was done,' said Archie Sinclair. 'Is that yourself, Nancy?'

'It is, Mr Sinclair.'

'It'll be a sore sight for you, this,' Archie said.

'What are y' doin' it for?' Nancy said. 'Where will they go now?'

'To the casual ward, I expect. It's where they should have been in the first place. I left it too long, so I did.' Archie sighed. 'Tell Mr Montague it'll be cleared by tomorrow. Then – well, it's up to him.'

'Are you saying that my husband ordered this done?'

'Did he not tell you?' Archie said. 'He's in charge o' the fund, and the fund bought the ground.'

'Bought the ground?' Nancy said. 'You sold the sheds?'

'Not the sheds, lass. I sold the acreage on which the sheds stand. Nobody wants the sheds. They're hardly worth cartin' away.'

'If,' Cassie said quietly, 'if there is a profit on the sale of the timber to whom will that profit go, Mr Sinclair?'

'To the fund, I expect.'

'Who negotiated the transaction? My husband or Mr Jerome?'

'Neither. It was arranged by an agent, Mr Wilks.' Archie glanced down at Nancy and plucked at the collar of his new greatcoat. 'I had to sell, lass. I should have sold years

313

ago. To tell the honest truth, the bank demanded an immediate repayment of the loan it made me.'

'The bank?' said Cassie. 'The Highland Bank, by any chance?'

'Aye. So you have heard what's happenin'?'

Cassie's reply was lost in the crash of a falling wall. It fell flat, like a playing-card. A moment later the unsupported gable of the shed swayed and toppled inwards and the shed was reduced to a pile of lumber and old straw.

'Well, there it goes,' said Archie. 'Good riddance to bad rubbish, I suppose.'

'How much land did my husband – did the fund purchase?'

'All of it,' said Archie. 'All of it except the public house.'

They were already moving on. Old men, travellers, drunkards and luckless women scuttled along the bottom of the embankment with their bundles tucked under their arms or hugged to their chests. Where they would find shelter now was no longer Archie's concern. The workhouse, the casual ward, the quays, a close or doorway in the city across the river? It no longer mattered to Mr Sinclair. Like Edward Hounslow, he had received his share of conscience-money and saw no harm in what he had done.

One scrawny wretch with an infant tucked into the bosom of her dress lagged behind. She shrieked and shook her fist at the wrecking crew and, failing to understand the nature of progress let alone commerce, danced with rage at what she perceived to be injustice. The labourers cheered and egged her on. Even when she stooped and picked up stones and hurled them at the men, they only laughed and, being young and agile, kicked the stones back at her.

'*Stop it,*' Nancy screamed. '*Stop it. In the name of God, stop tormentin' her.*' She ran forward out of the shelter of the bushes then, remembering who she was and how her position had changed, controlled herself. She looked back at Archie Sinclair and cried, 'Tell them to stop. Tell them to leave her alone.'

314

However power was measured, the servant of a lady had more than the wretch who crouched, weeping, with a half-dead child hanging from her breast. More too, it seemed, than the hot-blooded young labourers who stopped their game and stiffened as if they sensed in the servant girl an authority greater than theirs. 'Tell them, Mr Sinclair. Tell them,' Nancy implored.

Archie hung his head. He plucked at the collar of his new greatcoat and shrugged his shoulders as if he were not responsible for what the lads did. The challenge, however, was sufficient; the wrecking crew dispersed and shuffled off towards their ropes and hammers to resume work. But Nancy had been recognised. It had not occurred to her that she had lost the anonymity that poverty had provided.

The woman held on to the baby with one crooked arm. Its bald little head bobbed as she crabbed around the tar-buckets. Her hair was spiky in spite of the rain. Her face was daubed with blood from a withered wound on her scalp that the rain had opened up again. She showed her teeth like a jackal and moved with a wary, stiff-legged gait, feeling for the ground with her feet. Her eyes, yellow with hatred, were fixed on Nancy Winfield.

'You done this, y' bitch. You brung them here,' the woman shouted. 'You done it, Nancy Winfield, you an' yer fancy friends.'

Nancy gave a little cry. Stepping back, she groped for Cassie's hand as if Cassie would protect her against the enmity of her own kind.

Cassie's fingers closed on her wrist.

The workmen, obeying a chivalrous instinct, surrounded the screeching woman and allowed Nancy to be drawn away until, struggling frantically, she plunged into the stunted boughs and ran for the safety of the road.

Cassie burst in through the door of the back parlour, bonnet hanging loose and shoes trailing mud across the carpet.

She was not unduly surprised to find her sister seated

315

demurely on the other side of the hearth from her husband. She had already calculated that Robert would be ready for her indignant outburst and would have some plausible excuse to offer. Instead, he had defended himself by entertaining a guest; if Pippa could be called a guest. They were drinking tea from the best china and the small silver service stood upon the tray where Janey had placed it.

Pippa seemed startled by Cassie's sudden intrusion but Robert, saucer balanced on his palm, looked up and said mildly, 'Do you see? I told you so.'

'Told her what? That I would be back early?' Cassie snapped. 'That there would be no preaching at the mission tonight, or any other night for that matter? Why was I not informed, Robert? Why did you not tell me?'

'I assumed your friend Allan Hunter would let the cat out of the bag.'

Pippa put down her teacup and made as if to rise. 'I really must be on my way now. I did not realise that it was so late.'

'Sit,' Cassie snapped.

'Come now, Cassie,' Robert said. 'I would prefer you not to squabble with me in front of a visitor.'

'What's she doing here, anyway?'

'I came to see you,' said Pippa.

'On a Wednesday?'

'Now, Cassie, contain yourself. If you wish Pippa to remain then kindly be good enough to put our private affairs aside.' He placed his forefinger on the knob of the teapot. 'Will you take tea?'

'No, I will not take tea.'

'Go upstairs then.'

His manner was not stern, his authority modified by Pippa's presence.

Cassie flung off her bonnet and cape, stripped off her gloves and, still standing, continued to confront her husband. 'And if I do not?'

Robert shook his head. 'I am sorry about this, Pippa.'

'Why do you apologise to *her*?' Cassie said. 'Why do you not ride down to Seaforth Street or to Sinclair's land and apologise to the men and women whom you have turned out into the street?'

'Oh, so that's it,' Robert said.

'Did you expect me *not* to find out?'

'Calm yourself, Cassandra. You're not making sense.'

'Did you neglect to inform me what was happening in Ravenshill because you knew I would demand an explanation?'

'Explanation? I owe you no explanations, Cassie,' Robert said, then to Pippa, 'Come, my dear. I'll have Simmonds pull out the gig and, if you will allow me, I will drive you home.'

'Running away, Robert?' Cassie said.

His lips tightened. His flinty little smile printed a curlicue of flesh, like a scar, at the corner of his mouth. Cassie felt a sudden stab of fear at the thought of what he might do to her; then anger swept away fear. Why, she thought, *should* she fear him?

Robert ignored her question. 'Pippa?' he said.

But Pippa was transfixed. Still seated on the low chair by the table at the hearth she stared up at Cassie.

'Did you know about Robert's plans, Pippa?' Cassie said. 'Did he tell you that he had ordered Mr Lassiter's mission demolished and the ground behind Sinclair's hotel levelled, that he doesn't care if he deprives poor folk of–'

'Poor folk,' said Pippa, evenly, 'deserve what they get.'

'I see that Robert did tell you,' Cassie said, 'and apparently he judged you well.'

'What do you mean?' Pippa said, colouring slightly.

'I mean,' said Cassie, 'that Robert is a fraud and a liar.'

'That's enough, Cassie.'

'He has sold both parcels of land to Flail.'

'At a fat profit, I hope,' Pippa said.

'Huh!' Cassie snorted. 'You *are* a well-matched pair. You should have married her instead of me, Robert.'

'Do not talk nonsense,' Robert said.

317

'It isn't nonsense,' Cassie said. 'I am not going to stand by and watch you defraud innocent people out of all that they have. Tell me, how much did you have to pay Sinclair?'

Robert sat back. 'Oh, enough to tempt him.'

'And Hounslow?'

'He got the work. He is not established yet and does not have much capital to draw upon.'

'I had thought better of him,' Cassie said.

'You simply fail to understand the essence of business, Cassie,' Robert told her. 'There *will* be a church, you know. Your good friend Allan Hunter is intent upon that.'

'I expect Mr Hunter was more difficult to buy off.'

'He is not "bought off", as you put it.'

'I am glad to hear it.'

'He will still be your shining knight,' Robert said. 'But he will do what I ask him to, none the less.'

'What will that be?'

'He will construct a church and, after that, he will be employed by Hounslow when that gentleman takes over the patent for the construction of other churches. When I sell the company to Hounslow, you see, Hunter will be part of the arrangement.'

'Does Allan know how you plan to use the fund?'

'Of course not, not yet. He'll not refuse Hounslow's offer, though. He has too much at stake to turn it down.'

'So you've tricked him too, have you?'

'I have tricked no one, Cassandra. If you had been a little less hot-headed and had paused to make enquiry you would have learned that I will fulfil my end of the bargain to the letter. It isn't my fault that these gentlemen expected more than I ever promised them.'

'The fund . . .'

'The fund is mine. Every penny put into it is mine,' said Robert.

'The investors . . .'

'There are no investors.'

Lying back in the chair with his legs extended, Robert

contemplated her with amusement. Following his lead, Pippa too leaned back as if she were well enough versed in financial matters to endorse everything that Robert had said.

'Now,' Robert said, 'may I escort your sister home?'

'Does Papa know what's going on?' Cassie asked.

'Of course.'

'And does he approve?'

'He makes money out of it,' Robert said.

'Has Papa spoken to you about it, Pippa?'

'Don't be silly,' Pippa said. 'I'm only a little girl.'

'Well, I am not a little girl,' Cassie said. 'I'm not satisfied, Robert. I want to know more about this scheme of yours.'

'By all means,' Robert said. 'I have nothing to hide.'

'We'll see,' Cassie said. 'We'll see just what you have to hide.'

And Pippa, touching a finger to her lips, giggled like a knowing child.

Nineteen

When Norah entered the bedroom at half past nine o'clock she was astonished to find her husband still in bed. Nothing showed of him except his nose and eyes, for he had turned on his side and had cowled the sheets around his head in the manner of an Arabian traveller.

'Are you sick, Cuthbert?' Norah enquired from a safe distance.

It was Cubby's turn to be uncommunicative. She moved around the bed, stooped down and addressed the five square inches of Cuthbert that peered out at her.

'Sick?' she said again.

No answer.

Norah had breakfasted in the company of her daughter and had then begun to prepare herself for the weekly parade to church, to assemble hairpins and ribbons and the quantity of outer garments needed to keep her long body warm within the parish church. She had been troubled by vague anxiety when Cuthbert had not appeared at table, for normally he tackled Sunday breakfast with appetite and a hearty anticipation of a day spent to-ing and fro-ing between the house and the kirk.

'Doctor required?' she asked.

Cuthbert's face, the little she could see of it, was flushed

321

and his expression reminded her, rather, of a small, unplayful pug dog. His eyes were wide open and staring, mouth set in a pouchy line. He seemed to stare not at but through her as if whatever ailed him had rendered her invisible.

Norah moved closer to the bed and placed her face close to his.

'Church,' she warned. 'Late.'

He did not stir, did not move a muscle. Even his lips seemed paralysed so that the words came out in a whisper. 'Have I not been good to you, Norah?'

'Pardon?'

'Have I not been good to you?'

Fearing that he had lost his mind entirely, she stepped back a pace. His eyes rolled upward, following her anxiously, pleading for an answer.

'What *is* wrong with you, Cuthbert?'

'Have I treated you badly?'

'Doctor definitely required,' Norah said.

He sat up with alarming suddenness, the sheet still cowled about his head. He reached out for her. She only just evaded his grasp.

'I did it for you. I did it for you,' Cubby declared, tears on his cheeks. 'I would not have done it if it had not been for you.'

'What are you blathering about, Cuthbert? Have you lost your mind?'

'I cannot go to church.'

'Eh?'

'I cannot enter the door of God's house again, not after what I've done.'

Brooding had finally affected his brain, Norah decided. She was not surprised. He had been taken by this fit of mental constriction a week ago, had been withdrawn and silent ever since.

'Tell me that you forgive me, Norah. I cannot ask forgiveness of God but I can ask forgiveness of you. I've done a terrible, terrible thing and he knows it, he knows it.'

'Who knows it?'

'*He* knows.'

'God?'

'Robert.'

Humour him. Yes, Norah told herself, that's what one does with lunatics.

She assumed an expression of interest, eyebrows raised, lips peeled back in a rictus of sympathetic indulgence.

'Robert? Why, yes, of course, I should have guessed that you meant Robert. Tell me what Robert knows and what terrible thing you've done.'

How little she thought of her husband, sitting upright from the waist, all wrapped in sheets like Lazarus. She did not consider him man enough to have done anything worthy of guilt. *She* was the one with the secrets, that one sinful episode in the past which, as the years rolled on, became more and more consuming until there were times when she thought that her one achievement was to have preserved that love intact for more than half a lifetime.

Now Cuthbert wanted to take that from her too, to claim guilt for himself.

Cuthbert said, whispering, 'He knows about the child.'

'Child?'

'Your child, the dead child.'

And it was gone. In an instant it was all gone. She felt as if the organs of her body had suddenly been sucked dry, as if the blood in her veins had been drawn off and there was nothing left of her but arid flesh.

She groped behind her for the chair and tottered into it.

Cuthbert whipped the sheet from about his head and, with his voice strengthening, said, 'He knows what I did, Norah.'

'Took it away. Buried it.'

'No, I didn't bury it. Oh, God! It wasn't dead.'

'And Robert knows?'

'Yes. Yes.'

'How does he know? Does he know my Samuel? Did Samuel tell him?'

323

'What? I mean,' Cubby said, 'who?'

She clenched her fists to her breasts. 'Has Samuel come back for us?'

Cubby scrambled out of bed. 'Didn't you hear what I said, Norah? Robert knows what I did with the baby. He's threatening me and I can't do anything about it. He has my letter, you see.'

'My letters to Sam Taylor?'

'Who the devil is Sam Taylor? What are you raving about, woman?'

The brooding silence was gone. Cubby had shed his guilt. He had untangled himself from responsibility as easily as he had untangled himself from the bedsheets. He stood squarely before her, nightshirt taut over his belly, white knees braced like those of a recalcitrant horse.

'*My* letter, *my* note, damn it. The letter I sent to Beatty at the workhouse. He has it. Robert has it. That's what I mean, Norah. Robert Montague knows.'

Norah blinked. She thrust her hands into her hair and stammered out her question. 'Is – is she alive?'

'Apparently,' Cubby answered.

'Where is she? Is she here?'

'Nobody knows what became of her,' Cubby lied. 'That's beside the point, Norah. The point is that Robert Montague knows what you did all those years ago and what I did too. He has us under his thumb because of it.'

'He's Cassie's husband.'

'And a minister of the Church,' Cubby said. 'Look, my dearest, I wouldn't have burdened you with this distressing news except that I do not know – I mean, I am at a loss to – I need advice, Norah. I need sensible advice.'

'She's still alive, Cuthbert.'

'Probably, probably. Look, my love, Montague is rooking a church fund to build himself a fortune. He's using me to invest the money. No, not even to invest, to gamble with. He's speculating on the market. He's insatiable. He'll stop at nothing, not even at blackmail – for that's what it is – to get what he wants.'

'What *does* he want?'

'I do not know. I honestly do not know.'

Norah groped for that rational portion of her mind that seemed to have slipped out of her grasp like a piece of soap.

'Has he told Cassie about us?' she said.

'If you mean the child – no, I don't expect he has.'

'We must find out if she's alive, Cuthbert.'

'If she is – what about Robert? What do we do about Robert Montague? He has it in his power to ruin me, you know.'

She was very still now, fingers cupped about the buns of hair as if she were listening to faint voices from the spheres.

Cubby stared at her, saying nothing. He was relieved to have told her, to have got off with half the truth. He trusted her to come up with a solution that would save him, that would restore everything to what it had been before, to that proud, comfortable, petty little existence when all he had to worry about was the state of the market and what would appear for supper.

After a minute or more Norah lowered her hands from her head to her knees and pushed herself stiffly to her feet.

'What?' Cubby said.

'Dress.'

'Dress? Is that all you have to say?'

'Church.'

'I cannot face him.'

'Face him you will, Cuthbert,' Norah said. 'We will face him together.'

'Together? But what . . .'

She turned her head stiffly and fixed her eyes upon him. If he had anticipated tears, there were none. But instead of the translucent vacancy that had troubled him for years, there was in Norah's gaze now a basilisk quality, so stern, so determined that Cubby quailed before it.

'We must show him,' Norah said, 'that he has more to fear from you than you have to fear from him.'

'But I *am* afraid of him.'

'No, Cuthbert,' Norah said. 'If Robert was not afraid of you he wouldn't have attempted blackmail.'

'Why should *he* be afraid of *me*?'

'That,' said Norah, 'is what we will have to find out.'

'How, but how?'

'One step at a time, Cuthbert. Now dress.'

'For church?'

'For church,' said Norah Armitage and, for no apparent reason, kissed him coldly on the brow.

Lunch on Sunday was never leisurely. It was served at the double and consumed on the run, for the servants, including Luke, were obligated to attend morning service and it was left to Johnny Jerome to ensure that the stove remained fired and that the pots and pans did not scald.

Johnny did not object to performing such menial tasks now and then. The least he could do to make amends for being 'a heathen' was to pitch in behind the lines. In any case, the chores were hardly arduous. Miss Rundall left everything ready and Janey, up early, set the big table in the dining-room before she left. All the major had to do was baste the meat, put on the potato pot and, shortly before one o'clock, prepare the gravy.

Sunday morning then was Johnny's time alone in the house. He used it to poke about the place and nose into matters which did not concern him. He was expert at prying. He could move through the rooms and apartments without disturbing so much as a mote of dust and would slide open drawers and cupboards and pick about among the contents in a manner so deft that no one would ever guess that the small, inconsequential secrets that every household held had been uncovered.

Initially Johnny had found the exercise only mildly stimulating, but of late it had acquired more point. He no longer squandered precious minutes in scanning the female servants' *billets doux* or on pondering the exotic nature of the items that he unearthed from the back of

Miss Rundall's closet. As soon as the front door closed on the church-goers Johnny headed upstairs to the Turkish room and through it to Robert's study and the squat, steel-lined, green-painted safety box that was hidden in the base of the big bookcase there.

The safety box was easy meat for Johnny Jerome. It would in fact have been easy meat for anyone who knew where Robert hid the keys.

Three small keys, one for each visible lock, were tucked in the spine of the fourth volume of Hossack's *Old Testament Concordance*. What might have fooled a burglar, though, was the lever at the rear of the box, a tidy little mechanism secreted beneath a metal plate, which released the bar lock and gave access to the safe's deep compartments. It did not fool Johnny. He had watched Robert open the safe many a time back in their army days when security was a matter of necessity, not of honour.

Once the safe was open Johnny would squat on the rug before it and count the banded wads of banknotes that Robert had accumulated during the preceding week. He would read the private correspondence that had passed between the minister and his sponsor, between the minister and Rendell Wilks, and he would admire again the deviousness of the man.

As November deepened and winter gripped, however, Major Jerome received a sign that the demon had again taken possession of Robert Montague's reason and that madness was again on his mind.

The appearance of laudanum among the papers was the turning point. The discovery of a jade-green bottle of tincture of opium marked the moment when Johnny acknowledged that he might soon have to quit Ravenshill and abandon his boon companion to his fate.

What the laudanum signified and how Robert intended to use it were questions that Johnny could not yet answer. He had seen the substance used too often in the past to be blind to its dangers. Laudanum: a drug, a medication, a pacifier and, in the hands of the unscrupulous, both a toy and a weapon. In the Barrack Hospital in the Crimea there had not been enough of it to relieve the pain of the sick and dying; yet just across the Bosphorus they were sipping it from wine glasses and sucking it from wads of gun cotton. And many an English officer, let alone the Embassy ambassadors, had vials of the stuff in their dunnage to send themselves off to bye-byes on the breast of a rosy dream.

Once, when he, Johnny, had come down with 'famine fever' Robert had purchased a quantity of laudanum from a Turkish Customs official; had nursed him through the near-fatal illness with clean water, lime juice and the stuff from the jade-green bottle. But there was no cholera in Ravenshill. When he unstoppered the bottle and sniffed the heady fumes, Johnny thought of the men who had died screaming for its lack rather than those who lived for love of it.

The inexplicable appearance of the substance in Robert's private safe brought Johnny up short. He did not, of course, remove the bottle; nor could he raise the subject with Robert. He was stuck with the knowledge that an opiate had been purchased and stored for a purpose and with the dire imaginings that came with the memory of how it had been applied in the Crimea, how Robert had used laudanum not only to save life but to take it.

He had suspected then that Robert had lost his reason. But acts of madness during the course of that filthy war were legion; the sinful neglect that allowed brave men to die in hospital dormitories with only a demented chaplain and his jade-green bottle to carry them beyond all suffering and bring them to meet their Maker.

'*How many, Robbie? My God, how many have you put away?*'

'*More than my dada could possibly count.*'

'*Your dada?*'

'*How else do you enter a soul into heaven?*'

Laudanum and a pillow painlessly parted the soul from the body. There were no angels to guide you to eternal rest. Only Chaplain Montague, no angel of mercy but a demon in disguise, a man enraptured by his ability to murder without compunction, to choose for others death over suffering.

Carefully Johnny put the bottle back where he had found it and, wiping his fingers on his flanks, backed out into the Turkish room and seated himself weakly on the ottoman. He shivered at the realisation that Robert had not left his demon behind in the Crimea, had not burned it out of him in desert places or found any power strong enough to exorcise it.

Robert had brought it with him, dormant but not destroyed, brought it here to Ravenshill.

Johnny stared, dismayed, into the white bedroom, while below in the empty manse the hall clock struck eleven.

When she stepped out of the kirk into the November afternoon Nancy heaved a sigh of relief. There had been times that morning when she had felt like joining the gulls' chorus and shrieking out that the clergyman was no better than a hypocrite and that the congregation would be better off praying *for* him rather than with him.

She was glad when the service ended, and she hurried down the narrow stair and made her way to the front door to join her mistress for the short ride back to the manse. Today was a special day, difficult and, in its way, dangerous. She had invited Cassie to go with her to Greenfield and she was afraid that something would happen to spoil the plan or that Robert Montague would somehow be one step ahead of her.

It was not the minister who barred her way, however, but Mr Armitage. Penned in by the exodus from the church, she found herself pressed against Mr Cuthbert Armitage's bow-windowed waistcoat and unable to retreat. To her surprise, Mr Armitage raised his hat and forced a red-faced smile.

'Winfield?' he said. 'Nancy?'

'Good day t' you, Mr Armitage.'

'Are you – I mean, how are you? Are you well?'

329

'I'm fine, Mr Armitage.'

His hand loitered uncertainly in the region of her shoulder. His face was only inches from her own and, as she watched, he leaned even closer and peered intently into her eyes. She felt a flicker of anger at his rudeness but she did not attempt to draw away and endured his scrutiny for several long seconds before she whispered, 'What's wrong wi' you, Mr Armitage?'

He shook his head in bewilderment. 'Nothing.'

Then, from the vicinity of the gate, Mrs Armitage called out, 'Cuthbert, come along,' and, much to Nancy's relief, Cuthbert turned on his heel and scurried obediently away.

It was not uncommon for Cassie to cry off from the Sunday afternoon preaching. Precedent had been set by Mrs Calderon who had often been heard to declare that she had no more to learn about Holy Writ and heard enough of her husband's nonsense at home, thank you. Consequently, the parishioners of Ravenshill did not expect the minister's wife to subject herself to the blast of her husband's scriptural authority every time he stepped into the pulpit.

With his teaching notes tucked under his arm, Robert hurried off in the gig again at a quarter to the hour of two and, only minutes later, Cassie and Nancy set off to catch the ferry that would carry them across to Greenfield where Allan was waiting to greet them.

Cassie had no clear idea why the meeting had been arranged but she suspected that Allan wished to introduce her to his son, a gesture which she regarded as a natural progression in their relationship.

It was a grey day but not unpleasant, not as cold as it had been of late. She walked by Allan's side, arm in arm. Here in Greenfield, separated by the river from Robert and Robert's parish, she felt secure. Nancy walked just ahead of them, turning now and then with a little skip step to join in the conversation.

'Do you know what he is doing?' Cassie began. 'My husband, I mean.'

'I think,' Allan said, 'that he has sold two packages of land to Flail. He is obligated to erect a church upon one of them, probably on the site behind Sinclair's, since it is the larger. There will be plenty of ground left, though, and Flail has long coveted both sites.'

'The church, does it exist?'

'Aye,' Allan Hunter said. 'It will be ready for assembly in about three weeks' time, as soon as the foundations are made ready. That won't take long.'

'An' will this church – what? – work?' Nancy asked.

'It is a perfect building,' Allan told her. 'The design is very clever. Everything that your husband claimed for it is true. It can be put up intact and be ready for occupation in a matter of days. Jerome and I will oversee the bolting together.'

'It won't fall down then?' said Nancy.

'Certainly not,' Allan said.

'So, in a sense, my husband will have kept his promise,' Cassie said.

'In a sense,' Allan said. 'Except that I don't think he will build another. It's my guess he'll sell the patent outright to Mr Hounslow who will be quite prepared to buy it. It wouldn't surprise me if a price had already been settled between them.'

'I would not have thought it of Mr Hounslow,' Cassie said.

'He's a businessman. There's nothing wrong in the transaction.'

'Except that Ravenshill has been left without a mission and the destitute have been flung out on to the streets,' Cassie said. 'That was not the purpose of the so-called fund. Although I'm beginning to think that all you so-called "apostles" knew that all along.'

'Except Mr Lassiter,' Nancy put in.

'Yes,' said Cassie, 'except poor Mr Lassister.'

She was puzzled by the mechanics of the deception that

Robert had conceived and disgusted by the manner in which he had hidden himself behind charity when there was no drop of charity in him. She sensed, however, that Allan was reluctant to commit himself to criticism of a man, Hounslow, who might soon become his employer and she did not press him further.

They had reached the corner of the parkway and she was led down a lane that separated the smelly little village of Greenfield from the heights of the Daltry residence. Nancy seemed anxious and would glance back at Allan now and then as if she doubted the wisdom of bringing Cassie here at all.

Madame Daltry's academy was still and quiet, not grim though, for its trim lawns and handsome trees gave it an air of solidity which was enhanced by the appearance on the driveway of a pompous gentleman in the cutaway overcoat of a steward or butler. As he emerged from the gate he let his eyes slide over the women and tweaked the ends of his waxed moustache. He said nothing, ignored them as if they did not exist.

'The kitchen gate, Mr Hunter?' Nancy asked.

'Not today, lass.' Allan ushered Cassie ahead of him. 'Today we go in by the front.'

In his present mood it seemed to Robert that Pippa's disregard for the bustle about them was not just selfish but malicious.

There were elders conversing in the aisles, Sabbath School teachers chatting in the church and Mr Grimmond was pottering about, gathering psalm books from the rented pews. Two young women from the Christian Fellowship were scouring the floor beneath the benches for a lost glove and, as usual, three or four mature female parishioners were loitering by the side door in the hope that the minister would spare them a glance.

Pippa had insinuated herself into the vestry where he was towelling himself down after the exertions of delivering his teaching sermon. He told her not to close the door, for he was not foolish enough to take her there on a Sunday afternoon with the kirk still humming like a beehive. Besides, he was no more tempted by Pippa today than he was tempted by the doe-eyed wives of corn merchants or the daughters of haberdashers who lingered outside.

He worked the towel around his jaw and across the back of his neck.

'What is it, Pippa?' he said. 'What do you want?'

'I want to tell you something.'

'This is hardly the time or place for confidences.'

'I believe I'm expecting.'

His heart skipped a beat. 'Expecting what?'

'A child, a baby.' She smiled at him broadly, and raised one eyebrow. 'I have all nature's signs.'

He experienced a sudden desire to strike her down, to wipe the fatuous smile from her sweet little face but he continued to ply the towel until the violent urge passed away.

'Are you surprised?' Pippa said. 'After all we've done together.'

He had lain with a hundred women and had never yet spawned a child. He did not suspect Pippa of lying *per se*, rather of a kind of hysteria so apparently rational that an inexperienced man might easily be taken in by it.

The Fellowship girls passed along the corridor, one with the lost glove in her mouth like a retriever. He heard their chatter diminish and other, distant voices echo in from the church. He gave a wry little grunt and tossed the towel down upon the table.

Pippa said, 'What shall we do, Robert?'

She was still smiling. He was amazed at the trust that she put in him. Did she imagine that he could rewrite the law? Surely even someone as intrinsically stupid as Pippa Armitage must realise that any form of marriage between them would be impossible – even supposing that his wife, her sister, could be conveniently removed from the scene. What was the point of Pippa's question? What shall *we* do,

Robert? She paired them in the predicament and probably thought that it would be as simple to bind him to her in reality as it was grammatically.

'Shall I tell my papa?' she said.

'No, Pippa, not yet.' Robert took his watch from his vest pocket and consulted it as if to decide what hour *would* be appropriate to break the news of his infidelity, her pregnancy. 'Look, I must be on my way. I have the evening—'

'How can you be so calm?'

She expected him to panic and in his panic to become her slave and the slave of the phantom child. He was tempted to tell her that he did not believe her, that he knew that there was no live embryo within her. He was generous enough to allow her to cherish her illusions, at least for a while longer, however. If she wanted drama then he would give her drama. He would teach her that the line between farce and tragedy was wafer thin.

'When will it begin to show?' he asked.

'What?'

'The child, Pippa, when it will show upon you?

'I – I do not know.'

'You cannot be far gone.' He reached for his overcoat. 'By which I mean that we do not have to rush into decisions.' He took her by the arm. 'Now, if you will allow me a little time to consider our position I will discuss it with you at greater length.'

'We must run away together.'

'No,' he said. 'No, I do not think that is feasible.'

'There is no other solution.'

'Oh, I think there is,' Robert said.

She tried to force tears but managed no more than a moist film that simply made her look more innocent. Her conceit far outstripped her cunning. He felt almost sorry for her. After all, she had given him a brief wicked thrill the like of which he hadn't experienced in several years. But the prospect of 'running away' with spoiled, dark-haired Pippa and living with her in embarrassed exile was quite laughable.

She clung to him like a flower to a wall. He looked over her head at the open door and disentangled himself as swiftly as possible.

'I knew I could depend upon you, dearest,' she whispered, still trying for a catch in the voice, a tear in the eye. 'I knew you would not let me down.'

That much was true, Robert thought, as he steered her towards the outside door. If by any remote chance Pippa *was* carrying his seed then he knew of a hundred and one ways to be rid of it.

Neither Allan nor Cassie had the heart to press the workhouse girl to reveal more of her secrets. They watched her hurry off towards the bridge with a feeling if not of relief certainly of anticipation, for they were eager now to be alone.

Dusk was stealing along the surface of the river. In the trees behind the Daltry house the rooks were settling noisily for the night. The ferryboat, with lighted lamps, looked fairy-like in fading light, its canvas sail, mist-filled, as pale and weightless as a thistledown skimming the still grey waters of the Clyde.

The influence of the children had softened Cassie. She could not bring herself to fret over the glimpses of the past that Nancy had revealed. She knew that she had been taken on trust and that Nancy's gesture was both practical and sentimental. She had taken the little girl, Daisy, on to her knee and had been permitted to feed her candy that Allan had brought along. She sensed that she was being invited to make a commitment, for while she might pull herself back from the rags and tatters of Ravenshill's street urchins and the ugliness of its anonymous poor, she could not deny the attraction of Nancy Winfield's child; so clean and pretty, so polite and well bred that she might have been a sister and not the product of some joyless coupling on the paving of the quays.

Even the visitors' parlour in which they met the children had seemed cosy and secure. A bright fire had burned in the grate and the carpet had been brushed and the brasswork polished. Madame Daltry had been full of smiles, as charming and attentive as any salon hostess. There had been nothing but pleasure in the events of the afternoon. Pleasure too in meeting Allan's son, in observing how, after an initial period of surliness, young Tom Hunter had romped with Nancy's daughter and how the two of them, like sister and brother, had shared the sweetmeats that Tom's papa had brought.

Nancy had asked for nothing. No vow had been extracted, no promise made. None the less, Cassie knew why she had been taken to the Daltry residence, why she had been introduced to Nancy's daughter and why the workhouse girl had chosen to share her secret. It was a plea for understanding and a desperate grasping at security on behalf of the child.

On the ferryboat in the dusk Cassie was no longer confused. She had been foolish to doubt Allan's loyalty. Nancy had taught her that much if nothing else. Now that she was alone with him the warm feelings of the afternoon increased. She sat contentedly in the seat by the stern, Allan's arm about her waist, his hand in her hand. Behind them the trim green lawns and stately trees of Madame Daltry's residence faded into the gloaming.

'Do you know where Nancy goes on Sunday evenings?' Allan said.

'No,' Cassie answered. 'I believe that she may have a friend.'

'A gentleman friend?' said Allan.

'Would it be wrong of her, do you think?'

'Not at all, not if she cares for him.'

'And if he cares for her,' Cassie said.

'Daisy's father?'

'Somehow I do not think that is the case,' Cassie said.

Allan was quiet for a moment. He watched the wavelets spread back from the hull and ribbon away across the oily water behind the boat, then he said, 'Why don't you have children, Cassie?'

'I have not been married long enough.'

'You have been married now for the best part of a year.'

'The best part?' Cassie murmured. 'No, not the best part of anything.'

'Are you unhappy?'

'Not when I am with you.'

'I had hoped you might say that,' Allan told her. 'What of the rest of it?'

In the bow were two old men in shepherds' plaids, each with a dog at his side. On the seat behind them were four women, not young, clad in respectable bonnets. The ferrymen, father and son, worked oar and rudder and the little sail filled with the mist of the river which, now that the sun was going down, had become cold. But coldness could not touch Cassie, not that afternoon.

In a half-hour she would be in the manse. An hour after that she would be seated in a pew to the left of the pulpit listening to her husband preach the truth about a God in whom he did not believe. He, Robert, was his own god, as demanding and jealous, as proud, remote and indifferent as the mysterious God of the Pentateuch.

She could not bring herself to answer Allan's question unequivocally. He had asked about love of a sort that had no meaning in the context of her marriage to Robert Montague. If she told the truth then he, being a different sort of man entirely, would not understand.

'Provided I have your friendship, Allan, the rest is of no consequence.'

The ferry swung in with the current and the shore loomed large. The wooden walls of the yards, the pillars of the old quay and the stone ramp that led up into the streets of Ravenshill crowded upon her but, not caring who saw, she clung to Allan for comfort, for the assurance that whatever happened he would look out for her just as she would look out for Nancy's child from now on.

Robert threw his hat and overcoat to the floor for Janey to pick up and, beckoning to Johnny, stalked directly into the back parlour. He went to the corner cabinet, poured brandy from a decanter into a glass, drank it in a swallow and immediately poured himself another. He seated himself by the smoking fire and looked up at Johnny with a strange, pained grimace.

'Trouble, old boy?' Johnny asked.

'A complication,' Robert answered. 'Nothing that cannot be dealt with.'

'From what quarter? Is Armitage balking, or is it Hunter?'

'Neither,' Robert said. 'It's the small sister. She believes that she is carrying my child.'

'Ah!' Johnny exclaimed. 'That's a complication I hadn't expected.'

'It isn't true, of course. It's all in her imagination.'

'Are you sure? I mean, accidents do happen.'

Robert looked past the major towards the door. 'Where is my wife?'

'Gone out.'

'Gone where?'

'With Winfield.'

'To meet Hunter, I expect,' Robert said. 'She's in league with him, you know. They arrange secret meetings.'

'Hardly secret,' Johnny said. 'I mean to say, you do rather encourage them; the mission and all that.'

'Between the Winfield girl and Hunter, I mean.'

'Really? Have you evidence of such meetings?'

'I need no evidence,' Robert said. 'I was wrong to bring her here. I should be rid of her soon, I suppose.'

Johnny cleared his throat. 'Well, at least you can't lay the blame for young Miss Armitage's delicate condition at Hunter's door.'

'I can lay the blame where I like,' Robert said. 'She's trying to trap me, Johnny, that's all there is to it. Pippa Armitage is no more pregnant than you are.'

'Then why are you fretting?'

'In case she blabs.'

'That was always a risk.'

'Damn it, Johnny, do you not know me well enough to realise that I enjoyed the risk more than I enjoyed – never mind. The point is that the stupid little fool could not have picked a worse time to threaten me with her lies.'

'If they are lies.'

'Oh, they are. They are. Don't you see, she thinks I love her.'

'You can't possibly marry her.'

'Of course I can't marry her.'

'What does she hope to gain from feigning a pregnancy then?'

'She wants to ruin me.'

'Come now, old boy. How can a sixteen-year-old girl possibly ruin a man in your position?'

'With ease,' Robert said. 'If she opens her mouth, if she tells anyone that we have lain together then everything I've worked for will collapse around my ears. No, Johnny, I must be rid of her.'

'She's Cassie's sister,' Johnny said. 'You can't just buy her off.'

Robert put the glass down on the marble hearth. He seemed calm again, almost pleased with himself, as if the situation had teased his ingenuity. Observing the change of mood, Johnny felt a little ripple of fear in the pit of his stomach.

'No,' Robert said, 'but I *can* marry her off.'

'But if, as you say, she's not expecting at all . . .'

'Marry her off regardless. It's enough that she believes she's pregnant.'

'Who'll take her on?' Johnny said. 'I mean to say who's going to step up to the altar with a giggling little creature who is already carrying somebody else's bairn?'

Robert answered with a wide, slow smile.

'Christ Jesus!' Johnny exclaimed.

'Ten thousand pounds and a safe passage to any corner of the world that takes your fancy within three months of the deed being done. How's that?'

'Not for fifty, not for a hundred thousand . . .'

'As a friend, Johnny?'

'God, Robbie, do you know what you're asking me to do?' Johnny said. 'In any case, it's impossible.'

'Why is it impossible?'

'Because she does not love me. She does not even like me. In fact, she hardly knows I exist. She has eyes only for you, Robert. You said so yourself. She wants you, not me, not some substitute.'

'Marry her, Johnny, then abandon her. I can make Pippa agree to it, you know.'

'Oh, and how will you do that?'

'Keep her here in the manse as part of the family. It would be perceived as an act of fraternal generosity if I shoulder the burden of responsibility – after you disappear, of course.'

'And the child?'

'There *is* no child, I tell you.'

'Would you have both sisters under you together? How would you talk them into that manoeuvre when one detests you and the other adores you?' Johnny shook his head. 'In any case, Pippa is bound to blab. Whether you marry her to me or to the King of Anatolia, she'll not be able to keep her mouth shut.'

'Then I must shake her off by other means.'

'What other means?'

'Be rid of her.'

'Same as you got rid of the boy?' Johnny said. 'Billy.'

'Billy died of cholera,'

'This is Ravenshill, Robbie, not Scutari. Cholera is not conveniently available to carry off Miss Pippa Armitage.'

'No saying what might carry her off if you don't.'

'Christ Jesus!' said Johnny. 'Surely, you're not putting this on to me.'

'It is only a suggestion, Johnny. Food for thought. Ten thousand pounds, cash in hand, for acting the part of loving husband for a month or two.'

'And the girl, Pippa?'

'I'll take care of Pippa.' Robert said. 'Now, Johnny, dwell

on what I've said, give my proposal careful consideration.'
   'When do you need an answer?'
   'As soon as I get back from the north.'
   'The north? What are you doing in the north?'
   'Visiting my dada,' Robert said.
   'What? What for?'
   'To say goodbye,' said Robert.

Twenty

It came as no surprise to Nancy to find Todd drunk. He was sprawled across the table with his head on his arms when she let herself into the room and he did not raise himself to greet her.

She left him where he was while she tackled the greasy plates and pots that littered the table and picked up the soiled shirts that were strewn upon the floor. She cleaned and filled the kerosene oven, raked clinker from the grate and coaxed the smouldering fire into life again. With the sleeves of her Sunday-best dress rolled up, she filled the water pail and coal bucket and remade the bed. She worked around Todd's insensible form. She worked quickly and grimly, for she was disappointed in Todd Brownlee and resented his lack of character.

She had arrived in Bengal Street in high spirits. The meeting between Miss Cassie and Daisy had gone better than she had anticipated. She had been proud of her wee girl and it warmed her to see how well they got on together. She had carried that good feeling with her to Bengal Street to share with Todd, but had found him incapable of sharing anything except the dregs of whisky in the bottle he hugged in the crook of his elbow.

It was after seven o'clock before Nancy completed her

chores. She sat by the fire sipping tea from a chipped cup, and thought of how fortunate she'd been to escape the tenement, how prudent not to trust this man with her secret and with Daisy's future.

Daisy and Miss Cassie had met now. They would meet again, if not next Sunday, then the Sunday after that. She would make sure that there would be no more bleak kitchen yards or gloomy halls for Daisy. Her friendship with Mr Hunter had not been enough to impress Madame Daltry but the appearance of a nice, genteel young lady was more than enough to secure Madame Daltry's respect and, most important of all, to ensure that Daisy had a guardian ready-made just in case anything untoward should happen.

She washed the teacup and put it on its hook, rinsed the teapot and sluiced out the leaves.

In Bramwell manse the dinner table would be set in readiness for the family's return from evening service. In the kitchen below stairs too the table would be set for late-night supper. However much she despised Miss Rundall, Nancy appreciated her cooking and the affected gentility of her manners which – she looked round – were surely better than this.

She leaned down and stared along the level of the table at Todd's heavy, bearded features, all slack and torpid and weak. If he was booked for night-shift tonight then he would not be fit for it. How long had he been drinking, she wondered, how much of his wage had he squandered?

'Todd, Todd, can you hear me?' She shook his shoulder, felt him rumble and stir. 'Todd, do you have work to go to?'

'Uh? Naw.' He opened one bleary eye and, still without raising his head, gave her a twisted smile. 'Nancy, it's yoursel', is it?'

'Aye, an' I have to leave soon.'

He propped his huge shaggy head on a scarred hand and stared at her, red-eyed. 'Leave?'

'To go back to Bramwell. You know that's where I live.'

'Time is it?'

344

'Late. You've been asleep.'

'God, I'm so tired.'

'Lie down then. I'll help you.'

'Lie wi' me, lass.'

'I canna. It's too late.'

'Nancy, Nancy, lie wi' me a wee while.'

She hauled at his arm and forced him to his feet. He was still dressed in his coarse canvas work jacket and, by the smell of him, had slept in it yesterday as well as today. She wrestled with him, took his weight, got him out of the jacket. In spite of her annoyance she felt sorry for him, and concerned. How long since he had eaten? How long since he had washed? How long since he had had a proper fire to warm his big, old bones?

She sighed and helped him to the bed. He sat down upon the mattress, hands by his sides, fingers smoothing the neat, flat surface of the bedclothes. His expression was still stupid and dazed. She could easily have robbed him tonight, taken every penny he possessed. He would be none the wiser, would assume that all the money had gone to O'Toole, in drink. She would not rob him of his hard-earned wage, of course. She had taken enough from Todd Brownlee and, when she thought of it, had given him precious little in exchange.

'Come on, old soul,' she said. 'Get in below the clothes. I'll sit wi' you as long as I can.'

He nodded obediently, raised one leg and then the other while Nancy tugged off his stockings and his breeks and folded back the clean sheets and let him tumble into bed. He straightened gradually as if every sinew ached. He groaned, twisted on to his hip and stared at her, not blinking now.

'Are you no' stayin', Nancy?'

'You know I can't.'

'A wee while?'

'A wee while, then.'

He stuck one hand from under the sheet and she took it. She sat by him but would not lie down. She did not want

345

to tempt him to make love to her. She did not feel like making love tonight. Did not, in truth, wish to run the risk of conceiving another child. To bear a child to Todd Brownlee now would be disastrous.

As if he'd read her mind, Todd said, 'Is it because o' my daddy?'

'Shut your eyes, Todd Brownlee. Awa' t' bye-byes.'

'Him bein' a black man, an' all?'

'Daddy, Daddy, finnan haddy,' Nancy whispered.

She reached over, brushed a wisp of hair from his brow and crooned the daft little nonsense rhyme over and over until, soothed at last, poor old Todd Brownlee drifted back off to sleep.

Madame Euphemia Daltry was no less appealing out of context than she was within it. She travelled up from Greenfield in a hackney and arrived in Mr Rendell Wilks's chambers completely unruffled by the arctic winds that whipped through the city streets.

She was clad in a short plum-coloured pelisse, fur-lined, and a day-dress of a hue that Mr Wilks could only define as cherry red. She wore a hat with a peacock's feather and cross-laced mittens that made her hands seem even more dainty than they were. The effect of all this finery on a bitterly cold Monday morning was to create a little glow about Madame Daltry to which gentlemen, even down-at-heel legal gentlemen, would be drawn and, like waxen dolls, softened to the point of melt.

First words: 'I do hope you remember me, Mr Wilks?'

First response: 'Madame, who could ever forget?'

He had stoked the fire high enough to power a fair-sized steamship. He had a kettle singing on the hob and a saucepan with a couple of duck eggs chuckling near to the boil. A none-too-clean bib was tucked about his neck. He had also just completed a session of toast-making and piles of bread smoked appetisingly somewhere in the midst of the paperwork that littered his desk.

Holding the pan at arm's length, Mr Wilks took

Madame's dainty little paw, raised it to his lips and lightly kissed the back of her mitten.

By Mr Wilks's lights the greeting was prolonged. It was followed by a rush of actions so brisk, however, that Madame Daltry was quite dazed by them. The pan vanished, the bib disappeared, a chair materialised behind her knees and, in no time at all, Mr Wilks was ensconced behind his desk, arms folded and head cocked attentively.

'Now, Madame Daltry,' he said, 'what may I do you for?'

'I beg your pardon?'

'A little joke,' said Rendell Wilks. 'Not amusing?'

'The humour of lawyers is so refined that a lady from the suburbs must be excused for not understanding it, sir.' Madame Daltry favoured him with a dimple and a glimpse of tooth. 'It is not a laughing matter which brings me to Glasgow upon such a chill morning.'

'I'm sure it's not. Would you care for tea?'

'Later, *peut-être*.'

'To business then?' Mr Wilks suggested. 'Business, perhaps, concerning my visit to your establishment at Greenfield and my enquiries at that time?'

'Not unconnected, sir,' said Madame Daltry.

'The Winfield girl?'

'The same.'

Mr Wilks unfolded his arms and stared at Madame Daltry as if she were the star from the east. 'How interesting!'

The lady picked at the back of her mitten. 'I do not wish you to suppose, Mr Wilks, that I am endeavouring to profit from the misfortune of others. Nor that I am given to exploiting the confidences of the majority of my clients.'

'Certainly not, tut-tut.'

'I would not breathe words to anyone regarding the transactions of my less ordinary charges. On this occasion, however, and having regard to your interest in the welfare of Nancy Winfield's daughter, I feel that the rules of prudence which I have set for myself are not to be regarded as sacred.'

'No one would blame you for that, Madame,' murmured Mr Wilks. 'I am, as you know, the soul of discretion.'

'Are you?' said Madame Daltry. 'Really, I know nothin' of the sort.'

'Try me then,' said Mr Wilks. 'Try me with the name of Daisy Winfield's father, for instance, and let us take it onward from there.'

'Do not be so hasty with me, Mr Wilks,' said Madame Daltry. 'It is not the identity of the child's father that is important but the identity of the mother.'

'The mother? I thought Winfield was . . .'

A flutter of the mitten silenced him. 'It seems we have been mistaken,' Madame Daltry went on. 'Naturally I cannot divulge this information to you, Mr Wilks, unless I have your promise that you will act upon it only with the utmost caution. If, that is, you feel compelled to act upon it at all.'

The movement from behind the desk to the front of the desk was so swift as to be almost invisible. Suddenly Mr Wilks was there before her, hand laid across his waistcoat in the approximate area of his heart.

'My word, Madame, is my bond.'

'Now,' the lady continued, 'it is not for me to profit from . . .'

Mr Wilks plunged ahead of her: 'From the misfortune of others? No, certainly not. However, if *my* client proves himself sufficiently appreciative of any information which I am obligated to pass on to him then I take it that a gift to show gratitude would not be refused?'

'A gift to me, Mr Wilks?'

'To no other.'

'Why, that would be the sort of gentlemanly gesture that one could not politely turn down.'

'Indeed, it would,' said Mr Wilks. 'Who's the mother?'

'Cassandra Montague.'

'Uh-huh! And the father?'

'Probably – I say only probably – Mr Allan Hunter.'

'May I ask how you arrived at this conclusion?'

'By observation. Cassandra Montague came to see her child.'

'That's all?'

'Is it not enough?'

'Not for me, it's not,' said Mr Wilks. 'Nor for my client.'

'It is enough for me,' said Madame Daltry, without the trace of a dimple. 'I have been in the child-raising business for fifteen years, sir, and I've seen some strange things in my time. I do know a lady when I see one, however, and, by Harry, I know a lady's child. Daisy Winfield never came off workhouse stock.'

'We know that already, do we not?'

'*Mais oui!*'

'Never mind the Frog talk, Madame Daltry,' said Mr Wilks. 'It's tricky enough to unfurl this tangle in English without you confusin' me with some foreign tongue. Listen carefully. Winfield's the half-sister, bred off the mother and raised in the workhouse?'

Madame Daltry gave a curt nod.

'Winfield wasn't disemployed by Cuthbert Armitage then, wasn't sent a-packin'? She was paid to take the honourable daughter's bastard off on the q.t. and pretend it was her own? Is that what you're sayin'?'

'It is.'

'So my client married damaged goods, just like old Cuthbert before him?'

'It is not so tangled after all, you see.'

'But how can the Reverend Montague not know what a mess he married into?' Rendell Wilks said. 'Surely he thought he was gettin' a virgin maid.'

'There are ways to disguise such things.'

'Armitage's wife might know what to do. In fact, it wouldn't surprise me if she was behind the whole thing. She'd hardly want her precious daughter to go marryin' a works manager, would she?'

'It is not what has been done but what might be done that's important, Mr Wilks. I am sure of my ground.'

'If what you say is true why did Montague hire me to

349

enquire about the Winfield girl and the father of her child?'

'Because he only knew a little of the truth?'

'A truth which emerged . . .'

'In the marriage bed,' said Madame Daltry.

'Right you are, Madame, right you are.'

'I do not say that Hunter *is* the father of the Armitage child but he has been friendly with the Winfield girl from the very first. He even offered to pay Daisy's keep-fee.'

'And he showed on Sunday in company with Cassandra Armitage?'

'Who is now Mrs Montague. Yes.'

'Oh, there's money here,' said Rendell Wilks, gleefully. 'There are fees for me and donations a-plenty comin' your way, Madame Daltry, if we play the cards right.'

'By informing Mr Montague?'

'Oh, no, no,' said Rendell Wilks. 'By takin' on another client altogether.'

'And who might that be?'

'Cuthbert Armitage,' Mr Wilks said.

'Will Cuthbert agree to become your client?'

'He'd better,' said Rendell Wilks and, whipping round, produced a saucepan out of mid-air and tempted Madame Daltry with the offer of a duck egg; very hard boiled, of course.

Nancy and Cassie lingered in the sewing-room at the corridor's end and the longer they remained there the more reluctant they became to go off to bed. It was a form of intimacy that Cassie had not enjoyed since Pippa and she were girls and on that November night the weather conspired to increase the sense of daring that the young women shared.

The first great winter storm roared down from the north and broke like a gigantic wave upon the prow of the manse. It shook the lead-paned windows of the sewing-room and howled in its narrow chimney. The last of the coals had been put upon the fire long since but a fierce draught in the flues kept the embers hot and the atmosphere within the corner room was warm enough for the young women to shed their upper garments and go about bare-armed.

Kneeling on the settle beneath the diamond window, they peered out at the storm and watched the sleety rain congeal into snow. Now and then it seemed that the flying droplets were thickening and a thin coating of mush-ice would form on the glass and slide down to the sill, but then it would turn wet and furious again and a big, brawling gust would snatch the mush-ice away and peel it off the ledges and hurl it into the trees. Cassie and Nancy were stimulated by the wild air and could not tear themselves away from the window and the warm hearth and sensibly retire to bed.

They had carried a chocolate pot and china cups into the sewing-room, had lighted a lamp, built up the fire, pushed the dainty chairs back from the hearth and had spread themselves like picnickers on the rug. They had nibbled soft candy and had drunk hot chocolate, chattered and laughed like silly sisters while the wind snarled and shook the building with increasing ferocity.

Robert was far away. They were safe from his disapproval. He had packed his bags and left that morning. He had given Cassie no prior warning that he intended to visit his father who, it seemed, was ailing again and might not last the winter. It was not a sudden emergency that had summoned Robert north, however, for he had arranged for a young assistant, Mr Onslow, to be sent from the Presbytery to conduct the parish services in his absence, and that sort of thing, Cassie knew, took time.

Whatever Robert's reasons for undertaking an arduous railway journey at that season of the year, Cassie had been relieved to see the back of him.

Now, long after supper, she had Nancy all to herself. Safe and secure in the little sewing-room they talked freely about the children and about Allan Hunter and, when those subjects were at last exhausted, fell to making fun of Cookie Rundall, Janey and even Major Johnny Jerome, while the force of the gale increased and sleet slapped against the diamond panes.

It was well after midnight before common sense edged them out of the sewing-room. They stole down the darkened corridor, the lamp held out ahead of them. The wind filled the whole house with hollow boomings and phantom creakings, and Nancy and Cassie clung to each other in mock terror as they approached the door of the Turkish room and the pit-like darkness of the main staircase.

'I'll come down with you, Nancy, as far as the hall.'

'No, miss, no. I'll be fine.'

'Take the lamp then.'

They paused, close to the stairhead. Nancy looked down into the hallway. It was filled with stirrings as well as sounds. Even in the faint light of the lamp she could see the carpets rippling on the polished floor far below.

'Aye, I will then, Miss Cassie, if you can manage wi'out it.'

'Go on, Nancy. I'll wait here until you're safely down.'

Nancy, on tiptoe, kissed Cassie's cheek.

'You're awful good t' me, Miss Cassie,' she said. 'You've a good heart. You'll look after me an' mine, won't you, miss?'

'Of course I will, Nancy.'

The girl kissed her again, then scurried down the staircase, the lamp bobbing ahead of her. Cassie waited by the rail until Nancy and the lamp were gone. She was cold now and just a little apprehensive as she felt her way along the corridor and to the door of the Turkish room and let herself in.

Firelight flickered wanly, giving the room shape but no definition. She moved, groping, towards her bedroom and then, without knowing why, turned and looked towards the study. He was standing in the doorway, almost invisible against the blackness of the room.

Fear clutched at her heart. She covered her breast with her arm, her stomach with her hand and, hardly daring to breathe, waited for her husband to speak. There was no attempt at communication. The figure in the doorway remained as mute and motionless as an apparition.

Cassie swallowed her terror.

'Robert?' she said. 'Robert?'

'No.' A pause. 'No, it's me.'

'Johnny? Major Jerome?'

'I'm sorry.' He stepped forward: Cassie stepped back. 'I didn't mean to startle you. I thought you were in bed. I thought you were asleep.'

'Well, you *did* startle me. You gave me a dreadful fright. What are you doing here, Mr Jerome? Why are you prowling about my private suite at this hour of the night when my husband is not at home?'

'Oh, no,' Johnny Jerome said. 'Don't start on that tack again.' He stepped forward another couple of paces. 'I came up for this, if you must know.'

'What is it? I cannot see properly.'

A match scratched. Flame bloomed up around his face. An instant later the wick of a lamp streamed out smoke and light. He lifted the lamp up so that she could see the decanter in his hand.

'Brandy,' he said. 'I'm stealin' Robbie's brandy.'

Cassie let out her breath.

She tried to hide her fear, though the sight of Johnny Jerome in a robe, bare-legged and barefoot was less than reassuring. He was still male, still like Robert in manner if not in appearance; she trusted him no more than she trusted her husband.

'I'm out of drink,' Johnny Jerome told her. 'Clean out. Who can sleep without a skinful on a night like this?' Another pause. 'I really did think you were asleep, sorry.'

'Take your brandy,' Cassie said, angrily. 'Take it and leave. I'm very tired and I wish to go to bed.'

He made no further apology, offered no further excuse. He gave her a little bow and slipped out of the room swiftly and silently and padded barefoot down the corridor.

Cassie, thoroughly rattled, hoisted up the lamp and steered her way unsteadily to bed.

Age must be catching up with me, Johnny thought, as he rested, trembling, against the guard rail at the stairhead. I just cannot take this any more.

He was so shaken by his confrontation with Cassie Montague that he doubted his ability to make it down the stairs without tipping head over tail and breaking something more precious than Robert's best decanter in the process.

It was not the unexpected appearance of the young woman that had frizzled his nerves. It was what he had discovered – or, rather, had not discovered – in the safety box in Robert's study that had reduced him to a tattered wreck.

Johnny leaned on the rail at the top of the stairs and looked down into the dark hallway. He tried to be calm, to assure himself that he was jumping to the wrong conclusions. But he could not. At length, he pulled the stopper from the decanter and drank a couple of mouthfuls. He let the liquor trickle down his throat in the hope that it might melt the incapacitating lump of fear that threatened to choke him entirely.

But he could not ignore the fact that the laudanum bottle was missing from the safe, and the obvious conclusion that Robert and the bottle had travelled north together.

The coachman was reluctant to undertake the long drive from Inverness to Cleavers in darkness and in snow. Only the offer of five guineas roused the Highlander's fighting spirit and, with an extra horse harnessed into the shafts and a full bottle of whisky tucked under the seat, he set off along the road with his tall, black-garbed passenger wrapped in a rug inside.

It would have been more sensible, and less expensive, to spend the night in one of the town's comfortable hotels, to make his way to Cleavers in the morning. But Robert did not grudge the Highlander his blood money. The weather was closing in and the railway journey had been sluggish to say the least of it, with the locomotive pressing through small soft shelves of snow that, by midnight, would be drifts too deep to pass.

The mountains were already thick with the first winter fall and the leaden sky that layered the horizon promised worse to come. He had to reach Cleavers before the road closed – after which bad weather and impenetrable drifts would suit his purpose admirably. He would have Dada all to himself, all except for the housekeeper whose name he could not recall, a woman so old that she had been deaf and half blind last time he had visited his father the best part of fifteen years ago. He had nothing to fear from the old woman. She would do exactly what he told her to do, say exactly what he told her to say and no awkward questions would be put to someone whose faculties were so obviously spent.

The snow thinned out as the road lifted on to the shoulder of the moor of Overton. Gnarled pines sheltered the track and green moss and dark brown hag absorbed the flakes and consumed them. The coach pressed on, the horses heaving themselves into a trot when the summit was reached and the road ran down past Four Farms and the wan lights of the scattered parish came into view.

Robert sat with the black leather bag upon his knee. He hugged it with one arm as if it were a dog that needed reassurance. He had not eaten in ten hours but he had drunk a little whisky and warm water at the halt at the May Ferry. He would eat again in a little while, break bread with Dada in the gloomy dining-room of the gloomy stone manse that clung to the edge of the kirkyard a mile out of the village of Cleavers.

He had told the coachman that his father was dying. He had not begged for sympathy. He would not degrade himself by seeking sympathy when hard cash would get him what he wanted.

'Is it the manse you would be after?' the coach driver called down to him.

'Yes.'

'Aye, well now, there it is.'

Robert leaned his brow against the glass and looked out as the coach rolled downward towards the house.

Light from the coach lamps and light from the lantern that burned over the door of the manse itself illuminated the stone-built building and the path that slanted up to it from the gate.

On the slope above crouched the darkened church and the wall of the kirkyard and the crescent arch that was all that remained of a priory that had stood here a thousand years ago; all of it so old, so bleak, so uncharitable that Robert involuntarily hugged his leather bag for comfort and to assure himself that all would be well.

Cleavers manse was a place not of peace but of agitated slumber, troubled by bitter grievances and the hurt of old unsettled scores. It seemed a fine irony that the slave-trade money had wound up here, that old Bob Montague's fortune had found repose not in the pockets of whores and innkeepers or in the pineapple plantations of the southern seas but here in the Highlands of Scotland where the faces were white and the souls as black as coal.

Robert climbed down unaided from the coach and heaved his luggage after him. He said nothing to the driver who, with a snap of the reins and a shout to the horses, had already begun to swing the coach around for the cold haul back to Inverness.

He stood quite still, staring at the little manse.

He could hear the wind curling over the tops of the pines that surrounded the kirkyard where, in a day or two, his father would be buried.

The path was lit by the flickering lantern that his father insisted on hanging above the doorway. There was only one light within the manse, a parsimonious candle held close to the window of a ground-floor room, his father's face floating behind it as he peered out to see who had

356

arrived at his gate at this late hour.

'It's me, Dada,' Robert murmured. 'It's only me,' and, lifting his baggage, walked carefully down the slippery path towards the opening door.

Luke Simmonds had been dead to the world for several hours. He was young enough to put all thought of the dangers of high winds out of mind and within minutes of his head hitting the shuck pillow he was fast asleep.

He slept on a straw mattress in a wooden cubicle built into the hay-loft. He had a box for his clothes and another for his boots and a little stool to sit upon, which was all he needed to be comfortable. The hay kept the room warm even on the coldest of nights and he had received from Major Jerome a plentiful supply of coarse woollen blankets.

He was rolled up snug in three of them, nothing showing but a tuft of fair hair, when Johnny put his head over the top of the ladder and shone the lantern into the cubicle.

Below, the horses were restless but not in panic, for the walls of the stable were thick and the wind drove down and around the building, broken by the bulk of the manse. Two unsociable cats stared sulkily at the major, their eyes yellow in the lantern light.

Johnny hoisted himself to the top of the ladder and, with the lantern held out before him, ducked into the narrow space by the stable lad's bed. He was dressed in boots and breeches, a flannel shirt and a floppy knitted garment that he had hardly worn since the war. It was only the brandy circulating in his bloodstream that kept him from fainting with cold.

He looked down at the boy for a moment and then gave him a little shake.

'Lukey, Lukey, waken up. I have to talk to you.'

Luke blinked and sat up, wide-eyed, immediately wide awake.

'What is it, Mr Jerome? Have ye come t' see about the horses?'

'No, lad,' said Johnny. 'I've come to see about you.'

357

Twenty-One

It was eight days before Cassie next heard from Robert, five days after that before he returned to Bramwell.

Blizzards had closed the railway line and post roads and the Highlands were cut off from the south. Even in Ravenshill the snowfalls were heavy enough to disrupt all but the river traffic and, for two long days, the town was isolated by drifts and high winds. Work ceased at the Hercules, slowed almost to a standstill at Flail's Blazes and the occupants of the manse on Bramwell hill were forced to confine themselves indoors during the worst of the weather.

The thaw and the letter arrived together. Snow melted in great dribbling wedges and shot from the sloping roof of the manse as the wind swung to the west and brought warmth with it. In the drawing-room, Cassie read the letter that had been delivered with the noon post.

She looked up, frowned, and said, 'My father-in-law is dead.'

'Yes,' Johnny Jerome stated. 'I expect he is. How long ago?'

'Last week,' Cassie said. 'He passed away peacefully in his sleep. Robert was with him at the end.'

'What a fortunate coincidence,' Johnny said.

'There's been delay about the burial. Because of the blizzards. Robert will stay until such time as all his obligations have been fulfilled.'

'He'll be buried in Cleavers, of course? The old boy, I mean.'

'In the kirkyard by the church. Robert will participate in the service and, if the weather relents sufficiently, will address words of consolation to his father's congregation on Sunday before he leaves. He will lodge in Inverness until such time as his father's will is made known and executed. In view of the climatic conditions he does not require us to join him in the north but he suggests that we should prepare ourselves for a suitable period of mourning.' Cassie glanced up again. 'He has written separately to the Presbytery and to young Mr Onslow who will continue to minister to the parish here until such times as Robert can return to his duties.'

'Mourning,' Johnny said. 'Black serge and crepe armbands. I suppose the decencies will have to be observed.'

'Did you not care for Angus Montague?' Cassie asked.

'He did not care for me,' Johnny said. 'In fact, we only met once, ages ago, in Edinburgh. But, no, I think you might safely say that there was no love lost between us.'

'Are you not sorry that he is dead?' said Cassie.

'He was an old man. Sick, too. I reckon his time had come.'

'Robert will be upset.'

'The reading of the will might console him.'

'Will Robert inherit?'

'Surely he will. Oh, the odd bit of this and that will go elsewhere,' Johnny said. 'A legacy for the housekeeper, a modest endowment to parish funds to put up a window or install a pew. Shelf of old books to Matthew Salmond. That sort of thing.'

'There won't be much left, I expect,' Cassie said. 'Not out of a Highland minister's stipend.'

'What!' Johnny exclaimed. 'Has Robert told you nothing?'

'What do you mean?'

'Angus Montague was rich, wildly rich. Now all of it will fall on Robert.'

'Rich? How could that be?' said Cassie.

'Old money. Family money.' Johnny opened his mouth, then thought better of it. 'Not up to me. I'm sure Robert will tell you just what he's worth when he gets back.'

Snow trundled off the roof and fell in a slushy heap outside the drawing-room window. Cassie sat quite still, Robert's letter in her hand.

'How long will I have to wear mourning?' she asked.

'For an in-law? Three months should do it,' Johnny said.

'In that case I will need a full wardrobe.'

'I reckon you will,' said Johnny.

Robert sat to the left of the pulpit in the awkwardly angled chair where visiting preachers were stationed. He kept his hand over his face for much of Onslow's harangue as if grief had exhausted him.

Through his fingers he could see the congregation observing him with sympathy and admiration. They had seen him in full flow often enough, had seen his features dark with anger but they had never seen him quite so majestically moved before. He knew how to convey suffering, especially in profile. Long-fingered hand bridged across his brow, the occasional suppressed sigh would seem manly and admirable to all the flock and, if he did not overdo it, might even wring tears from the more susceptible ladies, those who longed to succour and comfort him in his hour of need or, for that matter, out of it.

If only they had known what he was worth how much greater their admiration would be, how much more ardent his female disciples would become, for experience had taught him that nothing excited the bourgeoisie quite so much as contact with wealth.

In the pulpit in Cleavers he had been coolly received. He had not been revered as his father had been, simply because he was not like his father. Many in the tight little Highland community resented him for his English manners and Lowland voice and did not give a jot about his performance of the eulogy. He had ridden out through the white drifts with relief, knowing that he would never again clap eyes on the place where his father lay or on the miserable little parish over which his father had presided.

Now he was home in Ravenshill. So rich that he might do anything he wished. So rich, in fact, that he wanted to laugh aloud, to leap to his feet and shout that he was no longer bound to them and would stay with them only on condition that they let him have his way.

He had acquired in a stroke one hundred and thirty-eight thousand pounds in realisable assets and had bought off the guilt that had plucked at his sleeve like a beggar and scratched on his door like a thief. He had bought off the memory of war and the horrors of the Barrack Hospital. He would buy off Johnny too when it suited him. In future he would concentrate on increasing old Bob Montague's fortune by squeezing from this pathetic little society every penny that he possibly could and creating an empire of his own from his dada's loveless legacy.

The congregation rose.

Robert rose with them.

They sang 'When I Survey the Wondrous Cross' to the tune of 'Rockingham'.

Robert sang with them.

Suffering and death? Communion? He recalled the verse that they would not sing, the last in Watts's original hymn, *Praise from all the ransom'd race, For ever and for evermore.* That's what they were, yes: a ransomed race. Only *he* was free of guilt, alone and free at last.

When Mr Onslow deferentially vacated the pulpit the Reverend Montague climbed into it and, hidden by the post, crouched for a moment and pretended to pray. Then he stood up and put his hands on either side of the Bible on the lectern and looked down on his people.

'I have lost my father,' he said. 'My father has gone to a better place.'

And all the fools below him sighed.

Johnny knelt on the Indian rug. He applied the keys to the locks of the safety box. He found the catch at the rear, slipped it, heard the bar slide upward and pulled open the door.

He put his hand into the safe and discovered that the bottle had been returned to its hiding place.

The laudanum bottle: half empty.

Head bowed, Robert sat on the ottoman clad only in a dressing-robe. He clasped his knees with his hands and contemplated Cassie as if unsure whether or not he wanted her. In fact, he had not requested that she attend him in the Turkish room. She had emerged from the white bedroom of her own free will.

She was dressed in a plain longcloth nightdress. He could see the shape of her body through the garment and the purity of the image inclined him to indulge himself.

He opened his hands like a supplicant.

'Cassie,' he said. 'Come here.'

'Wait,' she said.

'Why must I wait?'

'Are you not in mourning?'

'Mourning is for public rooms, not here.'

'I want you to tell me how he died.'

'Of congestive heart disorder. Insufficient oxygen to his lungs.'

'He smothered, in other words.'

'What do you say?'

'Is that not how it is when the lungs thicken and the blood cannot carry the fluids away?'

'I had not realised that you were so well versed in medical matters.'

'Johnny told me,' Cassie said. 'He saw many such deaths in the Crimea.'

'What else did Johnny tell you?'

'Nothing. He said that I should put my other questions to you.'

Robert flicked the folds of the robe modestly over his knees and thighs and braced himself for interrogation.

'Ask then,' he said.

'Were you with him when he died?'

'I was.'

'At the moment of death, I mean?'

'No, I was not with him at the final moment.'

'Where were you?'

'Below, with the housekeeper.'

'Where was the physician?'

'The physician had not been sent for,' Robert said. 'My father was subject to frequent night-time attacks. For that reason I refrained from sending for the doctor immediately. I would have done so first thing in the morning, of course, if Dada's condition had worsened.'

'Are you saying that his condition improved?'

'The doctor would not have been able to reach Cleavers even if he had been sent for.'

'Because of the snow?'

'Yes.'

She moved towards him then veered to one side and seated herself on an upright chair to his left. He adjusted position, squaring himself to face her.

'How much did your father leave you?' Cassie asked.

'Did Johnny suggest that you ask me that too?'

'It is for my own information, Robert. I am, after all, your wife.'

'Dada left me a very great deal of money.'

'Ten thousand pounds, twenty thousand?'

'More, much more. The exact figure, including all assets, has not been finally calculated.'

'How did this fortune originate?

'Handed down from my grandfather and from his father before him. And, as large sums of money tend to do, it gathered momentum from generation to generation. To answer your question, Cassie, I am a very wealthy man.'

'That was not my question. I asked where the money came from.'

'All right. From slaves. My forebears were slave traders. My grandfather, Bob, owned a fleet of ships built to transport human cargo.'

'Where did the slaves come from?'

'Africa, the Caribbean.' Robert spread his hands. 'I'm really not familiar with the sordid details.'

'Sordid? Do you think that trading in slaves is sordid?'

'Of course I do. It's un-Christian and uncivilised.'

'So you did not inherit a fleet of ships or a warehouse full of black men and women?'

'Do not pretend to be simple-minded, Cassie. It does not become you,' Robert said. 'My father was ashamed of his father's profession. That was why he, Dada, dedicated his life to the Church. He did not, however, pour the money away or burn it in a bonfire. He lived frugally and invested the stained inheritance in things that would be of benefit.'

'To whom?'

'To the commonweal,' said Robert.

'That's a pretty word for it,' Cassie said, sarcastically.

'Look, Cassandra, I cannot take responsibility for my grandfather's morals. The money is mine now. I will see to it that it is used wisely. I can do no more. I cannot erase the past.'

'So you will build for the future?'

'That is my intention.'

'Churches?' Cassie said.

At that instant it struck Robert just how little conversation he had had with his wife in the year since their marriage. Their time had been divided into public appearances and intimate engagements. He had sought for conversation and companionship elsewhere. He had assumed that she would remain passive, like the girl he had taken to the altar, that she would not flourish in the cloistered atmosphere of the manse. He had been wrong. He had erred in allowing her the companionship of a lady's maid, in fostering her friendship with Hunter, in granting her any sort of separate existence.

Now, even in the Turkish room, she was showing spark and character and unsuspected perspicacity, qualities he had always despised in women.

'Yes, churches,' Robert said.

She put her hands to the side of the chair and shifted it as a child might move a hobby-horse. Robert found himself leaning away from her as if he were afraid that she might ride him down.

'With your money?' Cassie said. 'A little of your vast wealth?'

'It is not that sort of wealth, Cassandra. It is not hard cash,' Robert explained. 'I have inherited investments. Shares in companies. Securities. Do you know what securities are?'

'I know what churches are,' Cassie said. 'I know what land is and what it is worth to the right person.'

'Has your friend Mr Hunter not told you that we will be erecting our first church in a week's time?'

'Yes – and he has told me where.'

'The site is ideal.'

'What Mr Hunter has not told me is who will have the pulpit.'

'That still has to be settled.'

'Is it not to be settled on your say-so, Robert?'

'Oh, certainly, I will have a say but it is a Presbytery decision in the end.'

'So, it will not be Albert Lassiter after all?'

'I doubt if he will be acceptable.'

'Mr Onslow?'

'A more likely candidate.'

'Why did you lie to Albert Lassiter?' Cassie asked.

'I did not lie to him.'

'You promised him the pulpit.'

'I promised him nothing of the sort,' Robert said.

'Did you promise him the pulpit to get him to abandon his mission?'

'The mission was nothing but a tin hut on a valuable site.'

'Ah!' Cassie said. 'If only you'd known that Agnes Lassiter would pass away when she did then you need have promised him nothing. What will he do now? Albert Lassiter, I mean.'

'I do not care what he does now,' Robert said. 'I am not responsible for Lassiter. Hounslow will take care of him.'

'And the company, *your* company?' Cassie said. 'And Allan Hunter? Will Edward Hounslow take them off your hands too?'

'What have you heard?'

'Enough,' Cassie said.

She was neither angry nor afraid. Her coolness irked him more than her sharpness.

'Is it your friend Hunter's job that concerns you?' Robert said.

'No, it's your mendacity, Robert, your hypocrisy.'

'There's nothing hypocritical about doing business.'

'Is it not hypocritical to lie to harmless men and to deceive people for your own profit?'

'I do not have to listen to this. This is not the voice of reason.'

'It is the voice of truth, though, is it not?'

'Truth?' Robert said. 'Do you want truth, Cassie? The truth is that you have not been a good wife to me. I married you for companionship but you prefer to spend your time giggling behind my back with your maidservant or sneaking off to meet Hunter. And you have not borne me children.'

'That is not my fault, Robert,' Cassie said. 'If willing has any effect on nature, however, then I will never bear you a child.'

'Will you not?' Robert said. 'Well, we will have to see about that. Take off your nightgown and we will begin the remedy at once.'

'I will not.'

'Aye, lady, but you will.'

367

She rose from the chair and walked towards the door of the white bedroom. There was no haste or panic in her retreat. It was done with a patient indifference that maddened him almost beyond endurance. He was inflamed by her uprightness, her priggish refusal to acknowledge him for what he was and to accept his superiority, as her sister did: yet he did not want Pippa. He was bored with Pippa's childish corruption. He wanted his wife's devotion and he would wring it from her if necessary.

Even so, he might have let her go, might have been generous enough to permit her one small triumph over him if she had not stopped at the door of the bedroom and confronted him with that smoothness which he could never acquire or emulate.

'I do not think you can give me a child, Robert,' she said. 'Perhaps you should persuade another man to do that for you, too.'

He ran at her. Came at her so rapidly that she could not escape.

She stepped back. She reached out a hand to close the door.

He was already upon her. He carried her before him, flung her across the side of her bed. For a split second she lay passive beneath him, her blue eyes, wide open, staring up into his face.

And then she resisted him.

And then she fought.

She fought with a fury that matched his own. She was young and strong and determined in her hatred of him. He had failed to possess her, to claim that part of her for himself. He rocked hard against her belly, thrust her into the soft mound of bedding. She kicked out, tore at him, flailed and slapped. When he ripped at the longcloth nightgown she caught his hair in her fists and tugged and thrashed his head this way and that.

She was so young, so strong that he could not find her, could not enter her. She seemed to have grown six limbs with which to fight him off. He tried to smother her struggles with his body and only when that failed did he grope for a pillow. He found one against the bed-head, dragged it across her eyes, nose and mouth, pressed his elbows into it until, subdued at last, she quietened and fell still. He took her easily then. Staring into the blank fabric of the pillow he counted to the rhythm of his breathing, each exhalation marked by a thrust of the loins so that his ejaculation came before her lungs were empty of air.

Sitting back, he plucked the pillow away. He heard her gasp, gasp and suck breath, gasp and cry out as if, at last, he had roused passion in her where there had been none before.

Pillow held lengthways in both hands, he straddled her.

Smiling, he said, 'More, Cassie, more? You may have it all if you wish.'

Rather to his regret, she managed to shake her head. He laughed, lobbed away the pillow and unsaddled himself.

Then, still laughing, went out into the Turkish room to find himself a brandy and perhaps a good cigar.

In his scuffed brown oilcloth smock he was almost invisible in the shadow of the laurels. He might have moved closer, might have prowled under windows and listened undetected at doors if he had had a mind to. But he had not used up all his common sense just yet. He knew that he had come far enough, that being close to the manse was all the satisfaction he could expect for one night.

He had no hope of seeing Nancy, of course. It was near midnight and the servants in a decent house like this would be long ago in bed. The lamp in the hallway had gone out a half-hour since and the only light visible lay behind the curtains of a third-floor window.

Nancy would not be up at this hour. He watched the window more out of curiosity than expectation. He saw nothing of interest, only faint shapes and a stirring of the curtains and grey sleet turning white against the thin ribbons of lamplight that escaped into the darkness.

369

Sleet did not bother him. He was a man for all weathers, patient and hardy. He had learned to move like a slow-worm through the darkness of the town, to do his work and receive his pay. And if this was Bramwell, where Mr Dunlop had no contracts, what did that matter? If a passer-by noticed him he would hoist up the empty basket he'd brought from Bengal Street and stagger under it as if it were full and they would avert their eyes and hurry on home to their warm beds and their wives.

He could afford an hour out of the night time, his own time, to be near Nancy, looking out for Nancy. It was better to be here, near her, than back in the room with just the kerosene stove and a bottle for company.

It was better too, he knew, for her to be snug inside the walls of the minister's house than in the tenement. He did not grudge her the security she had found for herself. Nor did he envy it. He was a nightman born and bred and she was a lady's maid. If he continued to love her that was his failing not hers, something he would just have to endure as he had endured so many other things throughout the years. But surely she would not grudge him his cold station in the garden, not bothering her at all, just watching, watching until some part of him was satisfied and he could bring himself to leave and trudge back to the tenement and curl up and fall asleep.

He stood in the shadow of the laurels until the lamp in the upstairs room went out and the minister's house became dark.

And soon after that he went home.

It was an iron-grey day in the iron-grey town when Robert Montague's first church rose up out of the bare earth. The snow had gone and the air was still and hazy and bitterly cold. Even Hounslow's hardy gangers wore mittens and leather gloves to keep their flesh from freezing to the metal plates and bars during the process of construction.

Cold or not, many came to watch and marvel at the small miracle as between dawn and nightfall on a winter's day a building went up where no proper building had stood before. Owners and managers of ironworks, forge foremen, manufacturers of bolts and rivets, and several members of the Vulcan Club all appeared on the site to observe the stages of construction and to talk with Allan Hunter and Mr Augustine who were both on hand to supervise.

By nightfall the shell of the new kirk was in place. It stood out solidly against the line of the embankment. It did not soar to heaven like a monument of stone but had otherwise all the appurtenances of a 'real' kirk, including a stout little steeple to accommodate the bell.

Cast-iron pipes lay under grillework beneath the aisles; a furnace would supply heat in winter and an ingenious steam-driven fan would pump cool air through the vents in the hot summer months. The interior would be equipped with a gallery rail and black iron stairs, font and pulpit would be erected and the narrow windows glazed. For warmth the pews would be made of wood bolted to iron tee angles and in due course the aisles would be laid with deck oak to deaden sound and a small pipe organ would be installed in a niche in the west wall. Woodwork and organ would come later, of course.

What mattered to the ironmen on that December day was that the church was up, a creation of beams and plates and girders that had come, boxed like Christmas gifts, from the Hercules foundry at a cost that even a struggling parish could afford. All those gentlemen who had a stake in it, and many who hadn't, were sufficiently impressed to mingle with members of the parish board and Presbytery at the 'topping-out' reception which Robert gave, at his own expense, in the dining-room of the Ravenshill Arms.

Everyone who was anyone showed up. The Flails were present, Ewan as well as Andrew, and all the so-called 'apostles', save only Mr Lassiter who was still in mourning for his dear wife and had not, in any case, been invited.

The affair was graced by the presence of wives and daughters which saved it from degenerating into a

371

drunken spree; members of the parish board and Presbytery were not so far removed from ironmen in manner and habit when the wine flowed like water and the spirits came out of a bottle.

The dining-room was crowded. Buffet tables groaned with red meats and cooked chickens and the clatter of cutlery and glassware all but drowned out the conversations, not all of them commercial, that took place between the guests as soon as prayers and speechifying had been put out of the way.

'Edward.' Robert buttonholed the owner of the Hercules. 'Edward, I would like you to meet the Reverend Oliver Stacey of the Scottish Foreign Missionary Society.'

'Impressed, sir, very impressed,' said Reverend Stacey, over a handshake. 'Now, if we wanted two of these things, how long would it take to fill the order and just what, round terms, would it cost us?'

'I will leave you to it, gentlemen,' Robert said and, tapping each man's shoulder by way of *adieu*, drifted off into the crowd again.

'Robert, Robert.' Pippa found her brother-in-law's arm. She drew herself close and whispered, 'Darling, where on earth have you been?'

'My dada died. Did you not hear?'

'Yes, and you inherited his money.'

Robert patted her hand. 'Who told you the sad news? Cassie?'

'Papa, silly. Papa knows everything.'

'Not absolutely everything, I trust?' Robert said.

'No, not about – about that. We must tell him soon, though.'

'Why?'

'Because of the child.'

'Oh, yes, of course.'

'Oh, Robert, you haven't forgotten about the little one, have you?'

'I think of it – and you, dearest – every day.'

'Well, now you are rich you won't need to be a minister

and we can go away together. To Italy, or perhaps to America. Would America not be nice?'

'Ideal,' Robert said, still smiling. 'However, Pippa, this is not the proper time to discuss our future together. I have important people to talk to.'

'Am I not important?' Pippa pouted. 'Are you abandoning me?'

'Only temporarily,' Robert said. 'See, I will find you a beau.'

'I do not want a beau. I want you.'

'A beau for the evening, Pippa, that's all.' Still patting her hand to calm her he swung round and snapped his fingers soundlessly, a gesture that brought Major Jerome sliding smartly out of the throng. 'Now, Pippa, Johnny will look after you. Won't you, John?'

'Delighted, old boy, positively delighted. Now Miss Armitage – Pippa, may I call you Pippa? – shall I fetch you a little glass of something, or perhaps a plate of cold cuts to satisfy your appetite?'

'Robert?' Pippa said, querulously.

But Robert had already moved away.

Cubby was doing his best to avoid Robert Montague. He had only seen the iron church from a distance but even a glimpse of it had raised in his breast a strange choking sensation, as if the building were giving off fumes like one of Flail's coke ovens. He had come to the reception only because Norah insisted on it and he had suffered that same choking sensation when Montague had risen to make a speech and accept the plaudits of the sycophants who had assembled to praise his ingenuity.

It had taken three glasses of mulled claret to restore Cubby's ability to breathe freely. Nevertheless, he spent the best part of the evening sidling around the buffet tables in an effort to evade his son-in-law and steer clear of his daughter, Pippa, who did nothing these days but smirk as if she knew something that he, Cubby, did not.

Cubby had other things to fret about too. When he saw

his wife in close conversation with the workhouse girl, for instance, he gagged on a slice of roast beef and had to be clapped on the back before asphyxia laid him out cold.

In his present nervous state he could not help but imagine that what he was witnessing was a *confession* between mother and daughter, that at any moment his undemonstrative wife might let out a shriek of accusation, might turn and point a bony finger and condemn him before the multitude.

Cubby was still coughing when Cassie reached his side and Hunter pushed a chair under his buttocks.

'Are you ill, Papa?'

'Nah-ah, Nah-ah,' Cubby gasped, dabbing a napkin to his lips. 'Wrong way. Went down the – ah – wrong way.'

Hunter offered him a glass of claret. 'Take a sip of this, Mr Armitage.'

'I think he's had enough of that, Allan,' Cassie said.

Cubby caught the chap's hand, relieved him of the glass, drank from it, coughed again, then cautiously raised his head. 'Are they still together?'

'Who?' said Cassie.

'Your mama and – em – the girl.'

'She is talking with Nancy, I believe.'

'What are they – em – saying?'

Cubby caught the glance that Cassie exchanged with the manager. In spite of his condition, he noticed how pale Cassie was, how drawn, and felt selfish for his lack of interest in her welfare. After all, he was only Montague's unwilling servant; Cassie was Montague's slave. He steeled himself and, supported by Allan Hunter's arm, got to his feet again. The lights from the chandeliers danced before him like fireflies and the din of many voices buzzed in his head like a swarm of bees. He was sweating slightly and did not resist when Cassie mopped his brow with her handkerchief.

'Are they talkin' about *me*?' Cubby asked.

'I doubt it,' Cassie said. 'What could they possibly have to say about you, Papa?' She touched Hunter's arm.

'Perhaps you would be good enough to take my father out to the doorway, Allan. I think a breath of fresh air might do him the world of good.'

'Of course,' Hunter said and, supporting Cuthbert as if he were senile, prepared to steer a course for the hotel foyer. 'Where will I find you, Cassie? Where will you be?'

'Here. I will wait for you here.'

Tipsy with anxiety and fuddled by claret though he was, Cubby thought he recognised affection in the look that Hunter bestowed upon his daughter, and in the smile that she bestowed upon Hunter in return.

'What's going on here?' Cubby mumbled.

'Nothing, Papa. You've had a drop too much to drink, that's all.'

'Hmmm, prob'ly right. Prob'ly right.'

He shot one quick nervous glance in Norah's direction and then, leaning against the manager, let himself be led away to cool his heels in the hallway beyond the door.

'Drunk again, by the look of it. Never could hold his liquor,' Norah said. 'Who's he with? Do you know that man, Nancy?'

'Aye, Mistress Armitage. That's Allan Hunter. He'll be fine wi' Mr Hunter. Mr Hunter'll take good care o' him.'

'Hunter – of the ironworks?'

'That's the chap.'

'On good terms with my daughter?'

'They're friends.'

'Is Mr Hunter a mission man?'

'He is, Mistress Armitage.'

'Is that where you met him?'

'In a manner o' speakin',' Nancy said.

Nancy knew that she should not have been here at all, really, but the Flails' lady's maids had been granted permission to enter the dining-room and both Mr Hunter and Cassie had insisted that she accompany them.

She had been given beef to eat and a glass of cordial to drink.

At first it had seemed strange to be in Archie Sinclair's dining-room as a guest and not a scuttling servant but she had soon grown used to it and had been quite the thing when her former mistress had invited her to sit with her and engage in conversation. She had never been intimidated by Mrs Armitage the way she'd been by Mr Armitage.

'He seems fond of you,' Norah Armitage said.

'Mr Hunter? Nah, he's more fond o' . . .' Nancy checked her tongue just in time. 'He's a friendly chap, Mistress Armitage, that's all he is.'

'My daughter obviously enjoys his company.'

'Aye, I suppose she does,' said Nancy.

Together they watched Allan Hunter lead Mr Armitage out of the dining-room door. Then Mrs Armitage was staring at her, not strict in her expression but with a faint little smile upon her lips, almost wistful, as if something in the room or in the situation had stirred a happy memory.

'Lovers?' Norah Armitage asked.

The question would have seemed shocking if it had been asked by anyone but Mrs Armitage. She had always been uncommonly direct. Even so Nancy was flustered and did not know how to reply.

'You would know, would you not?' Norah said.

'Aye, I think I'd know,' Nancy admitted.

'Would you tell?' Norah said. 'Would you tell me?'

'I wouldn't tell anybody else,' Nancy said.

'Are they?'

'No.'

'Does she care for him?'

'Aye, as much as she can, since she's married.'

'Does Mr Montague know of it?'

'I canna say, not for certain.'

'I have to know, Nancy. I have a reason.'

Nancy held the conical-shaped cordial cup in both hands and rubbed the smooth glass with her thumbs.

Norah Armitage's shrewdness had caught her off guard. She did not feel that either her loyalty or Cassie's reputation were threatened by the woman, however. There was an undertow of sympathy in Mrs Armitage's manner and not, as might have been expected, outrage.

'She reminds him of his wife,' Nancy said.

'Married?'

'No, his wife died a while back.'

'Did he confess as much to you?'

'Aye.' Nancy put down the glass on the vacant chair by her side and raised her eyes to the gallery that clung like a swallow's nest high in the corner above the dining-room. 'Up there.'

'Up there? When?'

'On the day o' the weddin',' Nancy said. 'We were both up there. That's when he first saw Miss Cassie.'

'And?'

'Fell in love wi' her, I think,' Nancy said.

'Think?'

'I shouldna be sayin' these things.'

'I have a reason,' Norah Armitage said again. 'I need to be sure.'

'Aye, Mr Hunter loves her.'

'Does she love him?'

'I think – aye, she does.'

'How much?'

'She wouldn't do anythin' wicked, Mistress Armitage. She'd never do anythin' to shame you or Mr Armitage.'

Without haste, Norah Armitage raised her arms and placed her hands on the pads of hair that protruded from beneath the brim of her hat. She held the position for ten or fifteen seconds then said, 'You are very loyal, Nancy. Too loyal, perhaps.'

'I don't know what you mean, Mistress Armitage.'

'To Cassie, to your mistress.'

'She's good to me.'

'What would you do for her?'

'In what way?'

'Would you help her?' Norah Armitage said. 'Would you help me to help her, if it comes to it?'

'Comes to what, Mistress Armitage?'

'I don't know yet,' Norah said.

'Is it – is it t' do wi' Mr Montague?'

'What do you think of him, Nancy? The truth now.'

'He scares me.'

'He scares me too.' Norah Armitage leaned over and patted Nancy's hand, not patronisingly. 'It isn't right, Nancy, is it?'

'No, Mistress Armitage,' Nancy agreed.

'And if we could put it right?'

'I'll help you if I can,' said Nancy.

The opportunity to keep her promise arrived sooner than Nancy anticipated. She had said nothing to Cassie about her conversation with Norah Armitage, for she was unsure what was required of her or how she, a servant, could possibly assist her mistress in escaping from a loveless marriage.

Indeed, Nancy was not even sure that it was right and proper to come between a man and his wife. Marriage was marriage, after all. If she had taken Todd Brownlee at his word and had become his wife she would have regarded herself as bound to him for life. If Todd had gone on the bottle again, if he had beat her, if he had starved her she would still have been his wife. She would have swallowed her hurt and would have slipped into that state of acceptance which was the lot of many women whom she had met in the soda factory. If you were rich, though, it was different. Rich women could pick and choose, reject and dismiss; all that would come down to them would be a bad reputation, and that never lasted long.

When they had left the reception at the Ravenshill Arms and had ridden home all together in the little gig, Nancy had studied Mr Montague closely. She had stared at him so intently, in fact, that he had become aware of it and had scowled at her so that she had been obliged to look away.

She had realised then that what she had told Mrs Armitage had been the truth. Robert Montague *did* scare her. He frightened her in a way that Todd Brownlee had never done, that no man, not even Mr Ferris, had ever done. He frightened her because he looked at her as if she existed only because he tolerated her existence and that if he chose to do so he might snuff her out.

It was her fear of Robert Montague that led her to eavesdrop. She did not set out for the stables to eavesdrop. She set out for the stables to find Luke Simmonds and give him a glass of strong ale that she had saved from the new barrel that Miss Rundall had tapped just before luncheon.

Cassie was with Pippa in the drawing-room. Nancy did not know where Mr Montague was. He had taken himself off soon after Pippa had turned up and the sisters had been thrown reluctantly together. There had been a strange, flat atmosphere in the house all morning as if the erection of the iron church and the reception that had followed it had marked an end, not a beginning. Cassie had remarked on it but Robert Montague had just smiled his thin smile and had gone off to dress for the day.

Nancy carried the mug of ale carefully out of the back door of the kitchen and across the cobbled yard. The sky was leaden and the air, even at noon, was numbingly cold. It would be one of those afternoons when day would filter swiftly into dusk and the lamps would be lit early and the fires built up.

She called out Luke's name but received no response. She placed the pint mug on one of the posts and climbed the ladder to the loft, still calling out to him. It was not unknown for Luke to fall asleep after he had eaten his midday meal, for he was by habit an early riser and had half his day's work done before the other servants dragged themselves out of bed.

Nancy was close to the top of the ladder. She held on to the rungs with both hands for she was uncertain of heights and called out again to Luke, to waken him. There was no reason for what she did next. She could not be sure, later, whether she had heard a sound and if so why that sound should have alarmed her. But something moved her to pull

379

herself up into the loft and, tucking her knees to her chest and drawing in her skirts, to sit there with her back to the hay ramp as still as a mouse. Below her she could see the ale pot on the top of the post in the slant of grey daylight through the open door. There was no sound at all from the horses.

She held her breath when Robert Montague came into the long stable and, looking up past the stalls, called out, 'Johnny, are you there?'

The minister was clad in the long black topcoat and shiny half-calf boots that he wore when he went walking. His familiar half-topper was tipped back on his head and a scarf of soft grey wool was wrapped around his throat and mouth as if to hide his face. His manner seemed not so much angry as impatient. He fumbled inside his coat, drew out his watch and consulted it, then he stepped to the doorway again and looked out. He rocked on his heels for a moment or two and then, to Nancy's alarm, returned to the bottom of the ladder and barked Johnny's name up at her. The ale pot was inches from his head. He did not seem to notice it, however, or if he did, did not consider it worthy of attention.

Nancy sank back into the hay ramp and drew her knees to her chest.

Robert Montague turned away. He walked the length of the stalls and back again and then, with his back to her, unbuttoned his overcoat and made water into the runnel that ran beneath the outer wall. Nancy closed her eyes.

'Ah, there you are, old boy.'

'Damn it, Johnny, what's all this about? I'm cold.'

Nancy opened her eyes, inched cautiously forward and squinted down into the stable. They were together, Major Jerome and Reverend Montague, but not at ease with each other. The major wore tweeds and a beaver hat and brown leather shoes that clumped and clacked on the flagstones whenever he changed position.

'Sent the lad to the Bramwell smithy.'

'Is the horse lame, or is it the pony?'

'Neither. Just a shoeing. Just getting Luke out of the way, really.'

'Does this "urgent matter" concern Simmonds?'

'No, I wanted a private word with you, Robbie, that's all.'

'Why all the damned secrecy? Surely you could have had a private word with me indoors?'

'Walls have ears, old boy.' Johnny Jerome leaned against the doorpost and, twisting, glanced out into the yard. 'Where are the women?'

'Oh, so that's it,' Robert said. 'You're avoiding Pippa too, are you?'

'Sort of,' Johnny said. 'I'd thought we might take a toddle on the moor for half an hour, if you're game.'

'Well, I am not game,' Robert said tartly. 'If you have something to say to me, Johnny, say it and be done.'

'Very well. I cannot marry Pippa.'

'I thought that would be it.'

'It's not that I won't marry her,' Johnny said. 'It's just that she would not have me, not if I was the last man on earth. It's you she's after, Robbie, and nobody else will do as a substitute. Even if she is carrying a child . . .'

'Which she is not.'

'Which *may* not be the case,' Johnny Jerome went on. 'Still, it's abundantly clear that she wants nothing to do with me.'

'One conversation hardly constitutes a wooing,' Robert said. 'The girl isn't going to drop into your arms like one of your street urchins. You will have to try harder, that's all.'

'Trying harder is not the answer.'

'What is the answer?' Robert asked.

'I think you know that already.'

'Do I?'

'Please, Robert, do not press me.'

Nancy shifted her weight to ease the cramp that had started in her shins. A few fine crumbs of dust dithered down into the stable below. She could see the dry haze clearly against the gelid daylight and waited for the men to notice it, for the anguish of discovery. But Montague and Jerome were locked in discussion, each intent upon the other, and neither man seemed to see the little drift of dust fall and settle.

'Tell me, Johnny, what is the answer?'

'Do what you did to your dada.'

'And what, pray, did I do to my dada?'

Johnny shook his head, then, with a throaty sound, shook it more vigorously. 'What you did to those lads in Scutari.'

Robert Montague seemed to relax. He laughed. 'I eased their pain, Johnny. All I did was ease their pain. Is it not my Christian duty . . .'

'Damn your Christian duty. You put them away.'

'Are you suggesting that I put away my own father?'

'I don't know – I don't *care* what you did or why you did it,' said Johnny Jerome. 'I just do not want to be a party to *any* of it.'

'It would not be so easy to "put away", as you have it, a healthy young girl. I mean, that would hardly be construed as an act of mercy, would it?'

'Even if you put down the other one, you couldn't marry her sister.'

'I am being given a choice now, am I?' Robert Montague said. 'How kind of you, Johnny, how terribly kind and tolerant.'

'Och, man, man.' The major covered the side of his face with one hand. 'What makes you behave like this? You have everything here in Ravenshill, everything you said you ever wanted. You've nurtured a deal with Flail which will net you ten or twelve thousand pounds. You'll sell your share in the fund to Hounslow for another eight or ten. You still have your pulpit and the respect of half the folk who live in Ravenshill.' He paused, shaking his head. 'And all that money, that fortune from your dada's will. Good God, Robbie, *why* did you have to seduce little Pippa Armitage?'

382

'Because I wanted to.'

'God, God! What *do* you want? What *more*?'

'Everything.'

'What *is* that? What does "everything" mean?'

'The opposite of nothing, I suppose,' Robert said.

Johnny shook his head. 'Where will it end, Robbie? Where can it possibly end? Will it end with Pippa Armitage?'

'Oh, no, no. That it will not.'

'Where then?'

Robert shrugged. 'With the grave, Johnny, perhaps only with the grave.'

'You allow that girl far too much licence,' Pippa said. 'If she was my servant I would not let her prance about so. Nor would I allow her to talk to me in such a familiar manner.'

'It is perhaps as well, then, that Nancy is not your servant.'

'When I have a lady's maid she will do as I say and she will respect me.'

'Has Papa promised you a maid?' Cassie asked.

'Papa? No, why would Papa promise me anything?'

'Because he will be paying the poor lass, will he not?'

'Why do you say "poor lass" in that awful tone of voice?'

'Because I would not like to be your maidservant,' Cassie said.

She had grown so weary of Pippa's preening manner that she felt no need to be polite. Robert's indulgent attitude had encouraged in Pippa a sense of superiority which was quite out of keeping with her position in the household.

'I will have more than one maid, of course,' said Pippa. 'I will have several, I expect. They will not be common workhouse girls either.'

'If that is your ambition,' Cassie said, 'then you must find yourself a wealthy husband. And that is not something that you are going to do sitting in our parlour every evening.'

'Are you telling me I'm not wanted?' Pippa said.

Cassie had not been herself since Robert's return from Cleavers. Although he had not used the pillow upon her again, his assaults had become more frequent. Ritual had gone by the board. He took her without preliminary once or even twice each day. His love-making was mechanical and sullen, even laborious at times and Cassie knew that his intention was to have her conceive.

When he had put the pillow over her face she had sensed the element of madness in him that Johnny had hinted at, a lust to dominate and possess. Fear had made her wary and stayed her attempt to stand against him, to be her own person. None of this was Pippa's fault, though.

Cassie relented.

'Of course you're wanted,' she said. 'You will always be welcome here.'

For several seconds the sisters sat in silence. Neither had bothered to find occupation, to take up a piece of embroidery or a book and there was no pianoforte for Pippa to play upon. They had never been much given to card games; the game that they had played since childhood had been diverting enough. Now, however, the rivalry between them seemed to have lost its point.

'What would you say if I came to live here?' Pippa asked. 'Would you still make me welcome?'

'Live here? Papa would never allow it.'

'Oh, he might be persuaded. I mean, what if he sent me away?'

'Sent you away? Why on earth would he do that?'

'If he did, Cass, would you take me in?'

'It would not be up to me. It would be up to Robert.'

'Oh, I think Robert would take me,' Pippa said. 'He is such a charitable man, he would not refuse me a bed.'

'Is there a point to this, Pippa?' Cassie said, wondering if she had misjudged her sister's acumen. 'Have you been squabbling with Mama?'

'Mama never squabbles,' Pippa said. 'No, my dear, I am merely speculating. I mean, it is not unusual for spinsters to reside with a sister and be protected by a brother-in-law.'

'Come now, Pippa, at the age of sixteen, you can hardly be classed as a spinster in need of protection.'

'Do you find the prospect objectionable?'

'Well,' said Cassie, trying to make light of it, 'I simply do not see any reason for it. You are perfectly comfortable at home and Papa is not going to pack you off without reason or just cause.'

'Cause,' said Pippa, smiling to herself. 'Just cause, yes.'

'Besides,' Cassie said, quickly, 'you will never find a husband if you become part of this household. There are no eligible bachelors lounging in our drawing-room. Unless' – Cassie hesitated, amused by the thought that had just struck her – 'unless you have designs on Major Jerome?'

'Johnny Jerome? Lord, no!' Pippa declared.

'I saw him paying you court last night, did I not?'

'He was only being polite, because Robert was too . . .'

'What?'

'Because Robert told him to.'

'Johnny is very obedient, very obliging,' Cassie said. 'He can be very charming too when he puts his mind to it.'

'But he does not like women,' Pippa said.

'Perhaps that is a pretence.'

'It is no pretence. He will never marry. Robert told me so.'

'Did he? When?'

'Oh, some time ago.'

'I do not recall such a conversation,' Cassie said.

'Perhaps you were absent when it took place.'

'Robert has never discussed Johnny Jerome with me.'

'I expect there are lots of things that Robert has not discussed with you, things that a man does not impart to his wife simply because she shares his bed.'

'What do you mean by that, Pippa? Are you implying that Robert confides in you rather than in me?'

'I'm implying nothing of the sort,' Pippa retorted and

might have gone on in the same taunting vein if at that moment the door had not burst open and Nancy Winfield stumbled into the parlour.

Pippa stiffened. She drew her shoulders back like a little adjutant and snapped, 'What's the meaning of this? Have you no manners? Have you not been taught to knock and await permission before you throw yourself into a room?'

Cassie scrambled to her feet and crossed quickly to the servant girl who, white-faced and trembling, seemed almost on the verge of a swoon. 'Nancy, what's wrong? What's happened to you?' she said and, to Pippa's consternation, led the workhouse girl by the hand to the armchair by the fireside and, kneeling, continued to hold her ice-cold hands.

Nancy stared first at her mistress and then, raising her eyes, at Pippa. Her mouth opened and closed. She seemed to be gasping for air like a fish flung out of water. She clung tightly to Cassie's hands and, after a moment, colour returned to her cheeks and she appeared to gain control of herself. 'It's – it's nothing, Miss Cassie. I didna mean to butt in.'

'Is it the cold?'

'Aye, it's the cold, just the cold.'

'Are you sure? If you are indisposed you may go to bed, you know.'

'No, I – I'll be fine in a minute.'

'Tea,' Cassie said. 'That's what you need. Tea and toast for all of us.' She turned from the waist. 'Pippa, be good enough to ring the bell and inform Janey that we will take tea here as soon as it's convenient.'

'Three cups, I suppose?' said Pippa, sourly.

'Yes,' Cassie answered. 'Three cups,' then, to her sister's disgust, put both arms around the servant girl and hugged her to make her warm.

If the woman, Mrs McGuire, had not seen her before, and in good company at that, she would not have admitted Nancy to Allan Hunter's rooms.

As it was, Mrs McGuire could not deny that the girl was exceedingly agitated and that she undoubtedly had something more urgent than hanky-panky on her mind. Even so, the lodging-house keeper accompanied the girl upstairs and waited with her until Mr Hunter, recently risen from bed, answered the knock upon his door. Frowning, he assured her that he would take responsibility for the girl's moral welfare. Still muttering under her breath, Mrs McGuire left them to it – whatever 'it' might be.

Allan's room in the lodging-house was not as squalid as Nancy had imagined it would be. He had brought from his former home a number of items that added colour to the drab surroundings: a patchwork quilt covered the narrow bed, for instance, and rows of books and prints ornamented the mantelshelf and the top of a small mahogany tallboy. A single upholstered chair was neatly positioned beneath a standard lamp and upon a miniature dressing-table were Allan's shaving bowl, a hot-water jug and a razor.

He still had a towel about his throat when Nancy intruded upon his toilet and in his surprise at seeing her he did not think to remove it until her account of the conversation between Jerome and Robert Montague was concluded.

'What did you do then, Nancy? How did you get away?'

'I waited 'til they left, Mr Hunter, then I sneaked back to the house.'

'Did they see you, do you think?'

'I'm not sure. No.'

Her fear was palpable. Allan felt it too as a tightening of stomach muscles and a sudden little rash of perspiration around his throat and neck where the razor had recently passed. Like Nancy, though, he tried to appear calm.

He had seated her in the armchair. She perched on the edge of the leather cushion, hands twisting in her lap, face as pale as parchment in the light from the window. Allan removed the towel from his collar and wiped his cheeks with it then seated himself on the bed and continued his questioning.

'Did you tell Cassie what you overheard?'

'I intended to, aye,' Nancy said. 'But she had Pippa wi' her an' then I thought I should tell you first.'

'Pippa is expecting a child, you say?'

'That's what I heard, Mr Hunter.'

'Whose child?'

'Reverend Montague's. He's for Major Jerome marryin' her but Major Jerome won't do it.'

'That's bad enough, Lord knows,' Allan said. 'But the rest of it . . .'

'Aye, it doesna bear thinkin' about.'

'Nancy, are you sure that you heard correctly?'

'He done for his father, Mr Hunter. He said he'd "put him away". What else could that mean?'

'It could mean he'd buried him.' Allan suggested.

'Nah, nah, Mr Hunter. It means he murdered him.'

'I cannot understand it. Why would Montague do such a thing?'

'For the money he'll inherit.'

'But surely he would have had his inheritance soon enough without taking such an appalling risk? From what I've heard, Angus Montague was an elderly man in poor health.'

'Mr Montague couldna wait. Anyway, he's done it before.'

'*What?*'

'He murdered men in the Crimea.'

'Oh, yes, but that was warfare, surely.'

'In the hospital there. He – he "put them away" too.' Nancy looked at Allan Hunter out of clear, blue eyes. 'Do you think he *couldna* do it? Do you think a man like Reverend Montague wouldna do it if it suited him? I heard him say how he had done it before an' how he would do it again.'

'Do what again, Nancy?'

'Murder.'

'Cassie?'

'Aye, maybe,' Nancy said. 'Or maybe Pippa.'

'If she's carrying his child, yes,' Allan Hunter said. 'I've always thought that Montague was ruthless – but murder?' He shook his head. 'We'll have to get her away, Nancy.'

'I know it,' Nancy said. 'We'll have to warn Miss Pippa too.'

'No, not until Cassie is out of his reach.'

'Will I tell her what I've told you?'

'No,' Allan said again, sharply this time. 'I beg you to say nothing to Cassie in the meantime. We must move cautiously. If, as you say, Montague is wicked enough to murder his father out of greed there's no saying what he might do if he feels threatened.' He rose and crossed from the bed to the window, hardly more than a single step. He stared through the glass into the side street, brooding for half a minute or more, then he swung round again. 'We must make him show himself, Nancy.'

'What d' you mean, Mr Hunter?'

'We must force him to expose his true nature.'

'How can we do that? Reverend Montague's a powerful man in Ravenshill an' as clever as the devil himself.'

'Leave it to me, Nancy,' Allan said. 'I have a notion how we might topple Montague from his pinnacle before he does more harm.'

'What do you want me to do, Mr Hunter?'

'One thing only: bring Cassie to Madame Daltry's tomorrow afternoon.' He reached down, brushed Nancy's cheek and gave her a smile of reassurance which was not wholly convincing. 'Will that be difficult?'

'Nah, Mr Hunter, not difficult at all.'

'Once I have seen her and spoken with her,' Allan said, 'then we will decide how and when to act. First, though, I must talk with Cassie.'

'Tomorrow afternoon?'

'At two o'clock.'

'I'll have her there,' said Nancy.

Twenty-Two

It seemed strange to be alone with Allan Hunter in another woman's house. The fact that the house was filled with children made it stranger still.

Cassie had needed no persuasion to accompany Nancy to Madame Daltry's on Sunday afternoon, however, for she was eager to talk with Allan and seek out his opinion on the changes that were in the air.

The dread that had marked the months of Robert's courtship, the shocking humiliations of marriage were as nothing compared to the anxiety that troubled Cassie now. She knew that Robert's couplings were no longer intended to provide him with pleasure or break her to his will but to possess her by laying a child upon her. Giving birth to a child would surely weaken her position in the household and give him an inescapable hold on her future. There were too many things going on that Cassie did not understand, things that she hoped Allan might be able to explain.

Madame Daltry was no longer stand-offish. If anything, her obsequiousness was almost jarring. She made no complaint when Mr Hunter sent Nancy out on to the front lawn with the children 'to take a breath of air', and saw to it that tea was delivered to the couple in the visitors'

391

parlour, together with a plate of little yellow seed cakes decorated in the French style with pink icing and green angelica. Madame Daltry would have lingered with 'her guests' and engaged them in conversation if Allan had not pointedly requested a moment or two alone with Mrs Montague. Madame Daltry's simpering smile suggested knowingness and collusion.

The woman departed and Allan and Cassie were left alone in the trim parlour. Allan wasted no time on small talk.

'Cassie, I must put discretion aside and ask you this,' he began. 'Does Robert Montague treat you well or badly?'

Cassie answered without hesitation. 'He provides for my comfort but, no, he does not treat me well.'

'Would you leave him?'

'Leave him? I do not understand?'

'Would you quit his house?'

'How can I? I'm his wife.'

'I've heard that Montague is not what he seems to be.'

'And what is that?' Cassie asked.

'Decent and upright.'

Cassie said nothing.

She wore half mourning, a grey dress with a black cape and black kidskin gloves. She remembered her silly experiment with magenta drawers and wondered if Allan, too, recalled that night and how he had behaved towards her.

'I have reason to believe that you may be in danger,' Allan went on. 'In danger from your husband.'

'Do you wish me to quit my marriage so that I may be with you?'

'It's true that I do want you for myself,' Allan told her. 'But I'm not like Robert Montague. I won't lie and cheat to get my own way.'

She should have risen at once to Robert's defence. But she could not bring herself to do so. She thought not of the Turkish room but of Albert Lassiter, of Johnny Jerome's casual insults. Thought of Miss Rundall, Janey and the ogling child, Marie. Towering above them all like some great swart shadow stood the minister of Ravenshill, Robert Montague, her husband.

'Why should I quit Robert's house at this time?' Cassie said. 'What danger is there to me that was not there before?'

'Nancy overheard something.'

'Why did Nancy not tell me of it?'

'She did not know what to do. She came to me.'

Cassie recalled the afternoon, two days since, when Nancy had burst into the back parlour; how Pippa had been preening; how upset Nancy had been. It had happened then, for sure.

'Why do you say that I am in danger?' Cassie asked.

'There are things about Montague that you do not know.'

'Are you sure of that?'

'Things that it is better for you not to know.'

The pillow over her face blotting out the light, robbing her of air, reducing her to an object, reducing Robert to a violent force that might enter and destroy her as the whim took him. What could Allan Hunter have found out about Robert Montague that was worse than that? She was not only receptive but trusting, eager to swallow anything that Allan might say that would excuse a betrayal of her marriage vows.

'No,' Cassie said, 'you must tell me, Allan.'

'Oh, Lord. I would give anything not to be the one.'

'What did Nancy hear?'

'That your sister – your sister and Montague are . . .'

Cassie sat very still.

Steam rose from the pretty china teapot on the tray. From the passageway came the singing of children, a childish rhyme that skipped along and marched away before Cassie could make out the words.

'Pippa,' she heard herself say. 'Yes.'

'I'm sorry, Cassie. I'm sorry to be the one to have to tell you.'

'Is it true? Is there no doubt?'

'Little, I think,' said Allan. 'There's more: worse.'

'Is she carrying his child?'

'That may also be the case.'

'How did you learn of it?'

'Nancy overheard Jerome and Montague. They were discussing what to do about it.'

'How to be rid of it?'

'Something of that nature,' Allan said. 'If it is the case, Cassie, then you will have grounds to inaugurate a divorce proceeding against him.'

'He would find a way to stop me,' Cassie stated. 'Robert would not allow himself to be publicly humiliated.'

'That's what I mean, Cassie. That's why I believe you're in danger.'

'If I brought proceedings against him it would ruin my sister and my parents too. More than Robert's career would be destroyed by the scandal.'

'Cassie,' Allan told her firmly, 'you must think of yourself first of all.'

She felt tears rim her eyes.

She thought of Pippa, how Pippa had been taken by the man, how eagerly her sister had flung herself into corruption, held by the power of a man whose egotism knew no bounds. She had been betrayed, betrayed on all sides; yet she felt no anger, only sorrow.

'If it's true,' she said.

'Do you think Nancy would lie about such a thing?'

'If it's true,' Cassie repeated. She looked up, held Allan's gaze and felt the tears dry on her lashes. 'If it's true – will you have me?'

'If you mean do I love you and will I stand by you,' Allan said, 'I think you know the answer without asking.'

'Will you take me away from Ravenshill?'

'Yes.'

'And your work?'

'I've a little money put by,' Allan said. 'Not much but enough to see us safe out of here.'

394

'And Tom?'

'He will come with us, of course.'

'And I'll take the blame, all of the blame.'

'To protect Robert, to save his reputation?'

'To save myself,' said Cassie.

'Why do you do this, Pippa?' Robert Montague demanded. 'Why do you persist in badgering me on the Sabbath when you know how occupied I am?'

He let the girl flounce past him into the drawing-room and closed the door behind her. He advanced into the room, threw his overcoat upon the sofa and his hat after it. He stripped off his gloves and crushed them in his fist.

'Have I not told you a dozen times that you will be taken care of?'

'I do not want to be "taken care of", Robert.' Pippa's anger was palpable and frantic. She rounded on him in a whirl of skirts. 'As to why I "badger" you upon a Sunday, when else do I see you nowadays? You will not allow me into the vestry. You will not meet me in the garden. You avoid me as if I were a leper. We haven't been alone in weeks.'

'Please, do keep your voice down.'

'Do not tell me, *please*, that you are in mourning. I have seen no evidence of mourning from you. Do you spurn my sister because you're "in mourning"? I'll wager that you do not. What is *wrong*, Robert? Do you think it's *not* your child, that you are too high and mighty a man to put a child into me?' She pattered up to him, caught him by the sleeve. 'Do *something*, Robert. I *must* know where I stand.'

He endeavoured to put his arms about her, but she would not be placated. She flounced away, hot with temper.

If he had had more time and there had been less risk of discovery he might have spread her upon the rug and consoled her with something better than false promises.

As it was, all he desired was tea and a buttered scone. He was hungry and thirsty after his afternoon labours and dinner tonight would be served late. He could not allow Pippa to remain in such a state, however, in case Cassie walked in upon them.

'If you calm yourself, Pippa,' Robert said, 'I will tell you what conclusion I have reached and what I propose to do about the circumstances in which you find yourself.'

'In which *I* find myself' she shrilled. 'Does it not concern you too?'

'Certainly, it does,' said Robert, smoothly. 'It concerns me very greatly. The stumbling-block – I mean, the difficulty – is that I have commitments in Ravenshill which I cannot readily abandon.'

'My sister,' Pippa snorted.

'Cassandra is the least of it.'

He caught her and brought her on to the sofa by his side. He put an arm about her shoulder and held her hand in his, a position he had rehearsed a hundred times with grieving widows and the mothers of ailing children. One dose of laudanum adroitly administered would put Pippa out of her misery and bring instant peace, but the risk was too great for the gain.

He spoke in a low voice, vibrant with sincerity. 'Listen to me, listen to me, Pippa. I cannot abandon Cassandra for the simple reason that it would bring scandal down upon us both and—'

'I do not *care* about sca—'

A finger pressed to her lips, a hand pressed lightly against her throat: his touch silenced her. 'Listen, listen. Bear with me for five or six weeks longer, that is all I ask of you. I have certain financial transactions to bring to a conclusion which require my presence here. Then . . .'

'Then will we run away?'

'That may not be necessary.'

'What may not be necessary?'

'To leave Ravenshill.'

'But . . .'

'What do you want, Pippa? To be with me? To live with me?'

'Yes, that and . . .'

'You cannot be my wife.'

'In America . . .'

'Not in America, not in Peru, not anywhere. Even if Cassie was divorced from me, I cannot marry you.'

Pippa nodded. 'I know, I know, I know.'

'So,' he said, in a soft purring tone, 'what's to be gained by running off?'

'We would be together.'

'We can be together here, my dearest.'

His forefinger brushed her lips, which were dry, he noticed, and beginning to crack from the influence of winter weather. Hand upon her throat, he felt the quick, hot little pulse at the side of her neck beating against the ball of his thumb.

'No,' Pippa said.

'Listen, listen to me. If you were to marry Johnny, my friend Johnny Jerome . . .'

'No, Robert.'

' . . . then you would have a husband and a father for your child and . . .'

'*No, no.*'

'Listen to me, Pippa – then Johnny would leave, never to be seen again, and I would keep you here and care for you as if you were my wife.'

'*No, no, no, no, no, n . . . n . . . n . . .*'

Incoherent with rage, she beat upon him with her fists. It was all he could do to restrain her. He glanced behind him at the drawing-room door and, for the only time since Pippa had brought him her news, felt terrifying panic. If Cassandra walked in now all his schemes, all his plans, all the pleasure he had stored up for himself would be wiped away in an instant. What he had done in Cleavers would be negated. He would have the money, of course, but he would also be saddled with this craving child. And he would lose his pulpit, his congregation, his wife and his

397

home. All the elements that he had carefully acquired to provide security and hide his demon from the world at large would be gone in a stroke, all because this foolish girl would not see reason.

He closed one hand upon her throat. Then reluctantly removed it.

He was not mad. He must not behave as if he were mad. He must not give in to the demon again. He must not discard reason entirely. He certainly did not want to swing for worthless little Pippa Armitage.

'Now that I know your mind on the matter, Pippa,' he said, 'I will, of course, make other arrangements.'

'What other – arrangements?'

'I will conclude my business here and book passage for us on an Atlantic crossing as soon as I possibly can.'

A little smile fluttered upon her cracked lips and her eyes became big and round. '*What?*'

The moods of women never failed to fascinate him. There was no thought in their heads, only response, only reaction. They heard what pleased them and nothing else. High colour still burned on her cheeks and her pupils were as large as moons but the anger had drained from her as soon as it seemed that she would get her own way.

'I had to put it to you, Pippa,' Robert said. 'I had to be sure.'

'Will we go . . .'

'Away?' Affectionately, indulgently, 'Yes, of course we will.'

'Why did you say – the other thing?'

'A passing thought, that's all. It might have been nice to stay here and deceive your sister. But no, no. You are right. It would be too much to ask of anyone. Besides,' he paused, 'I doubt if Johnny would take you on.'

She frowned. 'Why ever not?'

Robert did not reply to that puzzled question. He took her hands again and, with great seriousness, said, 'I really and truly do require five or six weeks, Pippa, to secure our future. I must liquidate my assets and ensure that our finances are in apple-pie order before we slip away. I must also make provision for Cassandra. You would not grudge her that, would you?'

Pippa pouted, making him wait.

'No,' she said, at length. 'No, dearest, I would not grudge Cass her provision, not when I have you to compensate.' She emitted a little giggle. 'Perhaps, after we're safe away, Johnny will take *her* on. What do you say, Robert? What do you say to that?'

Murderous impulses almost overwhelmed him again. He could feel the demon clamouring within his brain, shouting at him to be rid of this impediment as he had been rid of so many others. He wondered what name the demon had and what it would take to cast it from him. He wondered too what form the devil would take if it ever became visible. He stared at Pippa's sniggering countenance, felt his fists close, nails bite into his palms. Every muscle and sinew was rigid with loathing and disgust. Disgust at the image of Cassie with Johnny Jerome, his wife bedded with the hairy little engineer. He leaped from the sofa and, his back to the girl, fought to regain his composure.

When he turned again he was smiling.

'Hah!' he said. 'Yes, that would be a fine irony.'

'It will not matter to us, though, Robert. We will be far away.'

'Yes, Pippa,' Robert said. 'Far, far away,' just as the door opened and Cassie, smiling and sweet as a charm, breezed into the drawing-room.

'The weather's closing in again,' Johnny said. 'It'll be a night for the fireside tonight, Pippa, hmmm?'

She looked up, sniffing, as the major steered the gig down the driveway towards the gates. He had not put up the hood and she could feel the first granules of snow upon her cheek. Papa said that snow before Christmas meant a hard winter.

'Why are *you* taking me home?' she asked. 'Where's Simmonds?'

'Having his supper. He has to eat sometime, you know.'

More than snow stung Pippa's cheek. She had been rushed out of the manse only minutes after her sister's arrival, pointedly given what sailormen called the 'heave-ho'. Cassie's initial friendliness had concealed a steely mood. Only signals from Robert – a tiny frown, a shake of the head – had kept Pippa steady and stilled her protests as she was ushered out into the dusk. Robert had accompanied her as far as the hall and, with Cassie observing from the drawing-room, had pecked her on the cheek and whispered, 'Remember your promise, my dearest,' before he had handed her over to Jerome.

Did Robert really believe she was *that* gullible? That she could not see through his lies? The insult to her intelligence hurt her most of all. Her dream of finding happiness with Robert was, she realised, only childish fantasy. He had no intention of abandoning Cassie and quitting Ravenshill. Pretending that Robert loved her was pointless. She must be mature enough to admit it.

She hugged her cloak about her and leaned close to the major, as much for warmth as for support. Johnny glanced at her, detached one hand from the reins, placed his arm about her waist and drew her closer still. Even in the cold night air the major seemed to emanate a strange dry heat that for some reason reminded Pippa of straw.

'Are you still trying to court me?' Pippa enquired.

'Me, old gal? Not I.'

'He told you to court me, did he not?'

'Do you wish me to take my arm away?'

'I have no objection to your arm, Mr Jerome,' she said. 'I'm not made of porcelain. According to Robert, you do not wish to – to take me on?'

The major was not fazed by this turn in the conversation.

He shrugged. 'If I was a marrying sort of man – which I'm not – then I would not require to be prompted by Robert Montague.'

'So you do find me attractive?'

'Lively, shall we say. Lively.'

'Is that, in your book, a virtue in a woman?'

'Naturally.'

'But you won't take me on, will you?'

'No.'

The cottages that piled up behind Bramwell's main thoroughfare were pale in the swirling dusk. Snow flurries outlined the rooftops and billowed across the road that led to the highway.

Pippa said, 'Did you ever consider it?'

'What's that?'

'Marrying me?'

'Certainly, I considered it,' the major said.

'Why?'

'For the money that Robert offered me.'

'I see.' Pippa said. 'Was it a large sum?'

'Quite tidy,' Johnny Jerome said. 'But money wasn't the only factor.'

'What were the others?'

'I considered it because I love him too,' Johnny said. 'Because I would do anything to please him.'

'Except marry me?'

'Robert should never have asked me,' Johnny said sadly. 'He knows better than anyone what I am. He should never have offered me money either. I *might* have done it for love – but he couldn't understand that. He thought that he and I were cut from exactly the same cloth. And it turns out we're not.'

'He knows nothing about love, does he?' Pippa said.

'Nothing at all,' said Johnny. *'Are* you carrying his child?'

'I may be.'

'Are you?'

'No.'

'Then leave him, forget him, have no more to do with him.'

'I can't,' Pippa said. 'Can you?'

'Oh, yes,' the major said. 'Oh, yes. I have to.'

'After all these years? Why?'
'Because this time he's gone too far.'

For the first time in months Mr and Mrs Montague faced each other down the length of the dining-table without the presence of a sister-in-law, an ex-army major or even the long-necked servant girl, Janey, to distract them.

Johnny had eaten early and, professing fatigue, had taken himself off to his room. Janey, always prone to quinsy, had come down with a 'throat' and was tucked up in bed with a hot salt stocking tied beneath her chin while Nancy fed her camomile tea and lemon juice.

Robert picked at his food disconsolately and ate little. Cassie, on the other hand, consumed more than her share, as if to demonstrate that, come what may, nothing would impair her appetite. When he attempted conversation she answered him brightly.

It was all front, of course, a brave act. The sight of Robert in Pippa's company had riled her beyond measure; not the audacity of it so much as the duplicity, the realisation that they were in it together, a conniving pair. She had no sympathy for Pippa's predicament. She could not regard her sister as other than a willing partner in the affair. Youth and foolishness were no excuse. But Allan was right: she must look out for herself and acquire that same quality of unremitting selfishness if she were to survive a marriage that had been doomed from the start.

'You preached well tonight, Robert.'
'Thank you, my dear.'
'It's a pity that there were so few in church to hear you.'
'The weather . . .'
'Why did Pippa not wait to join us?'
'The weather . . .' Robert said again.

He twisted a piece of meat on the tines of his fork, contemplated it, then put it into his mouth. He chewed carefully, as if his teeth ached.

'You look weary, Robert. Are you not yourself?'
'Quite myself, thank you.'

'Perhaps you have "a throat" coming on too. Like poor Janey.'

'No, my throat is fine. I'm tired, that's all.'

Cassie helped herself to another slice of beef from the serving dish, added a potato, poured gravy, wordlessly offered the dish to Robert. He shook his head.

Cassie said, 'You have not thought to ask me what I did today.'

'Went walking with Winfield?'

'Yes. We met Mr Hunter. Allan.'

He met her gaze, held it for an instant then pushed away his plate and crossed his legs awkwardly beneath the table top.

'He enquired after your health,' Cassie said.

'How kind of him.'

'He has been offered a managerial position by Mr Hounslow.'

'Will he take it?'

'He might.'

'He would be a fool not to.'

'Oh, one thing Allan is not is foolish.'

'What is he then? To you, I mean?' Robert said.

'A friend, a very dear friend.'

'Do you admit it?'

'Why should I not admit it?' Cassie said. 'There's nothing shameful in having a friend. Allan is no more to me than, say, Pippa is to you.'

Robert sat back. She could hear the toe of his shoe tapping on the underside of the table. There was no other sign of temper and his expression, as always, was impassive.

'Pippa is a relative,' Robert said. 'A blood relative.'

'Under law, not in fact.'

'What do you say?'

Cassie speared another potato, transferred it to her plate, crushed it with her fork and ate it. She did not know why she did so for her hunger was already satisfied and the bands of her skirts pressed uncomfortably upon her ribs.

She ate defiantly for, like an actor upon a stage, she needed something upon which to focus her attention and disguise her true feelings.

'Oh, nothing,' Cassie said, airily. 'It's just one of the many things about which I know nothing.'

'What is?'

'The law.' She ate a last mouthful, put down her fork and knife. 'In any case it's hardly a suitable topic for the dinner-table – not when you're so tired.'

'Do you resent your sister spending time here?'

'Not if it suits you, Robert.'

A long pause: 'I think she may have a fancy for Johnny.'

'Indeed?'

'I cannot be sure, of course, but it wouldn't be a bad match, would it?'

'On the contrary. It would be a very suitable match. Very convenient,' Cassie said. 'Johnny had better be quick, though.'

'Quick? What do you mean?'

'In case she's snatched away by another.'

'Another? There is no other.'

'Then Johnny has nothing to worry about, does he?'

He stared at her expressionlessly for several seconds and then, unfolding his legs, pushed himself away from the table. He said, 'If you will excuse me, Cassandra, I have work to do upstairs.'

'So soon,' she said. 'And you so tired. Will it not wait?'

'No.'

'What about your pudding?'

'My apologies to Miss Rundall. Perhaps the pudding will keep.'

'Perhaps it will,' said Cassie. 'I do hope so.'

'May I go?'

'You may,' Cassie said and, with feelings of triumph and relief, watched her husband retreat from the room.

Allan was seated in the armchair in his room, stockinged

feet extended towards the hearth, a much-thumbed copy of Bunyan's *The Pilgrim's Progress* open upon his lap. The allegory had consoled him in the months after Elizabeth's death when he had imagined himself less a pilgrim in search of salvation than a fugitive from the cruelty of this earthly realm.

Tonight, however, the book lay neglected, for he dreamed not of reunion with the dead but of union with the living, with Cassie Montague, who no longer seemed unattainable. He stared not at the page but at the fire. Its fine blue flickers reminded him of her eyes and the warm red ruffles that curled about the coals were like the desire that licked at his heart. He was not tormented by the nature of his love for Cassie Montague, found no dichotomy between physical and spiritual need and carried with equanimity the whole untidy bundle of emotions that loving and being loved had laid upon him.

It was around eleven when a knocking sounded upon his door. For an instant he wondered if it might be Cassie. Or Nancy, perhaps, bearing an urgent message from the manse. He laid aside the book and got hastily to his feet.

'Mr Hunter, Mr Hunter, please open to me.'

He pulled open the door to admit Albert Lassiter. It surprised him to find the missionary there, for Albert had been closeted like a hermit for weeks now.

Only that forenoon Allan had spent an hour with him in the gloomy attic. They had prayed together, had talked of Agnes, her goodness, her suffering, and the great void that her departure had left in Albert's heart, a void that not even the Lord could fill. But the man who faced him now was not self-pitying and defeated. In his agitation there was anger and in his anger some signs of the righteous energy that had once made him the man he was.

'I've been out, Mr Hunter,' Albert declared. 'I've been out to see the mission.'

'But the mission's gone, Albert,' Allan said gently.

'No, but it ain't, Mr Hunter. Only the building is gone. They're still there, my flock, Agnes's flock, still out there.

405

They need us more than they ever done. You've got to come and help me.'

Snow peppered the collar of his threadbare overcoat. He was unshaven, as rumpled and untidy as one of the outcasts that Nancy had lived with in the sheds. But there was a light in his eye that had not been evident for weeks.

'Calm yourself, Albert,' he said. 'Where have you been?'

'I saw the church. It's locked and barred with iron. That ain't right, Mr Hunter.'

'Montague's church, do you mean?'

'Aye, Montague's church.'

'Is that where they are, your flock?'

'Shiverin' cold, pressed into its scant shelter like lost lambs.'

'Why, though? Why are they there?'

''Cause they ain't got no place else to go.'

'What about the casual ward?'

'Too late. They're locked out. Come along, Mr Hunter, I begs you.'

'But what can *we* do, Albert?'

'At worst,' said Albert Lassiter, 'be with them in their hour of need.'

No cigars for Charlie Bremner, Flail's weighman, this dark winter night. He had his fire and his kettle, though, and the new nightshift manager gave him no trouble. As he smoked his pipe peacefully and listened to the snow pattering against the shutter he remembered with a wistful smile Major Jerome's fine Havana cigars and cheerful company.

It was near midnight. The last of the coal wagons had gone through hours ago and no pig-iron trucks would be shunted out before daylight. Log and tally were laid out neat and Mr Patterson wouldn't appear until the shift's end, for Mr Patterson was not stern like Mr Hunter and not given to regular rounds, and he, Charlie Bremner, could doze undisturbed. He was only half awake, in fact, when a whack on the shutter on the embankment side of the cabin frightened him half to death.

He shot out of his chair, pressed himself against the desk, arms spread out as if it were his intention to defend log book and inkpot with his life.

He cried out in a quavering voice, 'Who's that? Who's there?'

The shutter yawned. Grains of snow whirled into the cabin and a blast of cold air caused Charlie to clench his teeth so hard that the stem of his clay broke and the pipe tumbled to the floorboards, scattering sparks and ash.

Mr Allan Hunter clambered over the sill into the cabin.

'Och, it's yoursel', Mr H–Hunter? G–gave me a fair fright, so y' did,' Charlie Bremner stammered. 'Are – are ye back? Are ye back wi' us?'

'No, Bremner, I am not,' Allan Hunter told him.

'What are ye doin' here then?'

'I came for these,' the manager said and, without further explanation, plucked a shovel and a fire-axe from the tool rack and the half-filled coal bucket from beside the grate. He stepped towards the window with them.

'Ye canna steal our tools, Mr Hunter.'

But the manager had already climbed over the sill and, ducking awkwardly under the shutter, was back between the rails, shovel and axe across his shoulder, bucket hanging from his fist. Bremner leaned from the window, craned his neck and peered along the lines towards the long curve that ran over the bridge behind Sinclair's hotel.

'Mr Hunter, Mr Hunter,' he cried out in confusion.

Allan Hunter paid not the slightest heed, however, and loped rapidly away into the darkness and the swirling snow.

He had given the woman his overcoat and the old man his scarf. He could feel cold closing about him like a fist, the wind cutting like a knife blade through his shirt. His shoulder was bruised with the bounce of the axe and the shovel, and his right arm felt as if it had been broken at the

407

elbow by the weight of Bremner's coal bucket. Physical discomfort served only to increase his determination, though, to fire him with a strength that he had not known he possessed. He trotted between the sleepers and the rails until he reached a point where the track curved towards the bridge. He stopped there, shouted a warning, and flung axe and shovel ahead of him. Cradling the bucket to his chest, he leaped down the slope that towered above the iron church and ran to the doorway where the remnants of Lassiter's flock cowered down out of the wind.

Albert had put his coat about one of the women. He lay by her, his arms about two small girl children. A baby was stuffed like a doll into the vee of his jacket and vest. Snow mounded against his thighs and back, marking him in outline, and the whimpers of the children melded with the hymn he sang and his soft little cries of 'Good news!'

Close about him the men shuffled and swayed like bears. Not many, to be sure, only five or six at most; they were old men and mad men and one at least was crippled by drink, but they waited for Mr Lassiter and his friend to see them right, to make sure that in the morning when the light came again they would still be alive to face another day. Six men, two women, four children and a baby: Albert Lassiter lay with them as if he too were an outcast, with only a voice left to soar in the darkness.

He called out to Allan Hunter, 'Thank God, thank God you're here.'

'We must get them inside, Albert.'

'Aye, and soon.'

'Can you stand up?'

'When I have to, aye.'

'Then stand. I need your help.'

Chain and padlock were more than symbols of ownership. They seemed to be the very mark of men like Montague.

Allan felt his lungs expand with freezing air and blood flow strongly throughout his body. What he had lacked before had been purpose, the quality that his wife and son had added to his existence and which Cassie Montague had restored. He struck out angrily. He rammed the blade of the shovel under the chain and levered down upon it, tightening the links against the arch of the padlock. He had no notion as to who really owned the church, where Montague's paperchase of documents, deeds and titles led. To Hounslow, perhaps? To some mysterious 'fund' that would be milked to appease the greed of men who had no need of it? All he knew was that he stood with the destitute now and that he did not care for the system that had brought them low and had left them locked out and neglected.

'Push, Albert,' he said. 'Push down on the spade.'

Albert Lassiter had given the baby back to its mother. He was on his feet, but not steady yet. He swayed, braced himself with a hand on the iron doorpost, then, straightening, gripped the handle of the shovel and pumped down upon it. Allan swung the axe above his head, found the point of balance and brought the back of the blade down upon the padlock. He heard the clang of metal ring within the building and felt the shock of contact in his sinews. He swung again and shattered the padlock's brazen seam. The chain slackened and dropped away. He stepped forward and swung once more, cracking the door lock. Then he pushed the door inwards and stepped into the black interior of the church that he had helped build.

He would need candles, blankets too if he could find them. He would rob coal from the wagons that stood a quarter-mile away along the track, and dry kindling to lay a fire in the furnace. He had come this far and he would not give in. He laid the axe aside and stepped outside again. He lifted two of the children, one under each arm, and carried them out of the biting wind while Albert helped the women to their feet.

It gave Allan a strange feeling to be inside the hollow shell of the church, to hear the wind moan and to smell new metal, with everything hard-edged in the faint pearly light from the newly glazed windows. The outcasts crowded behind him, still and silent at first, waiting for him to tell them what to do. Then he heard an old man's spluttering cough, the baby's cry, somebody stumbling and cursing. And he thought how apt it was that they should be first here, that they should make up Montague's first congregation.

'Whose house is this?' a woman asked.

'Your house,' Allan Hunter told her.

And somewhere in the half-dark Albert added, 'Amen.'

Norah Armitage was wide awake. She lay on the flat of her back with her arms folded across her breast and listened to her husband breathing and the quaint sounds that the old house made as the beams shrank and boards narrowed and the glass in the window frames contracted in the blast of a winter's night.

Norah had never experienced the balmy winds of the Caribbean, the torpid heat of the African coast, had never been lashed by icy gales off the Cape of Good Hope. She had never slept under a moon as large as a house. But when Cuthbert's house creaked on a cold winter's night she would still think of Sam Taylor riding the waves in a tall-masted clipper and would try to remember what he had looked like, what tales he had told and what songs he had sung there on the banks of the Clyde. But for the life of her, she could recall little about her sailorman now, except his broken promise and the worry and the pain of carrying his child to term.

'Mama?'

Norah sat bolt upright.

'Mama, I need you.'

She was framed in the door of the bedroom, a pale figure, shivering and barefoot in a flimsy nightgown. Norah slipped out of bed and padded swiftly across the cold floor, leaving Cuthbert to roll over and slide back into sleep.

'What is it, Pippa?' She knelt before the girl, just as she

410

had done when Pippa had been a child tormented by nightmares. 'Have you been dreaming?'

'Mama,' Pippa said in a whimpering whisper, 'Mama, I'm bleeding.'

Cuthbert cupped the beaker in both hands and drank deeply. There was more rum than hot chocolate in the mixture and he felt the fumes cut through his drowsiness and bring him to his senses. He huddled closer to the smoking fire and, tugging his dressing-gown about him, looked up at his wife bleakly.

'He did what?'

'Seduced her.'

'When did the – em – the act take place?'

'Not once, a dozen times.'

She stood above him, one elbow on the mantel that overhung the fire. She had a half glass of brandy in her hand and she gulped it down like an old salt. She was very upright, though, very courageous. He had always admired his wife, as well as loving her, for just the qualities that she evinced at this crashing moment of crisis. She was, he thought, more manly than he was.

'Where?' Cubby heard himself ask.

'In the vestry of the church. In the manse. What does it matter?' Norah said. 'He took her at every opportunity, apparently, as and when he liked.'

'Why did she not stop him?'

'She claims she loves him.'

'Dear God! Her sister's husband.' Cubby shook his head. He wondered why he was not more shocked. 'How is she now?'

'Settled and almost asleep.'

'But, I mean, was it – em – did she miscarry?'

'Of course not.'

'Thank God for that.'

'Is that all you can find to say?'

'Well, at least there isn't a child to contend with.'

'If she *had* miscarried it wouldn't have been a child. It

411

wouldn't have been anything at this stage.' Norah transferred the brandy glass from one hand to the other. 'As it happens, it was only a delayed period – which was only to be expected after what she's been through.'

'Yes, yes, yes.' Cubby held up a hand. 'Enough, Norah, please.'

'Do you suppose this is just woman's trouble?' Norah said. 'You cannot wriggle out of responsibility this time, Cuthbert.'

'I did not go to bed with him, did I?' He looked up, frowning and unsure. 'I mean, I'm not the one who – em – succumbed.'

'Are you blaming Pippa?'

'I suppose I am – partly.'

'He's a minister of the Gospel. He's married to Cassandra who, in case you had forgotten, is our daughter too. There's no sidestepping responsibility this time, Cuthbert Armitage. No hiding what's happened. No workhouse to take away the consequences.'

'Hold on,' Cuthbert said. 'I did what I thought was right.'

'No, you did what you thought was best for you.'

'Very well, very well,' Cuthbert said. 'Have it your way, Norah. The point at issue is, is Pippa all right?'

'She feels better now that she has told me everything.'

'How did he . . .'

'He promised to run off with her.'

'Never!'

'She believed in him. She believed in him so much that she imagined she was carrying his child.'

'Ridiculous!' Cuthbert said.

'She was in *love* with him, Cuthbert.'

'That's no excuse. Did she not spare a thought for her sister's situation – our situation too, for that matter?'

'*Our* situation? *Our* situation? What *is* our situation?'

'There's bound to be a scandal.'

'Of course there will be a scandal. There will also be a divorce.'

412

Cubby put down the beaker and held out his hand in the hope that Norah would take it. 'Well, I cannot say I'm surprised. I have long believed Montague to be capable of all sorts of wickedness. It is, however, not a matter for us. It's a matter for Cassandra.' He paused. 'If, that is, Cassie has to be told.'

'How can she not be told?'

'It's over now, is it not?' Cubby said. 'Pippa has surely seen the error of her ways. Best thing to do is make plain to Montague that we want no more to do with him and . . .'

'And how do we do that?' Norah snatched her hand away from his groping fingers. 'How do we abandon Cassie without giving her a reason. Do we continue to dine at the manse? Do we continue to attend kirk services as if nothing had happened? Do we smile and pretend that all is well, knowing that Montague has had *carnal* knowledge of Pippa and that he'll be laughing up his sleeve at us? That is hypocrisy, Cuthbert, and I for one have had enough hypocrisy to last me a lifetime.'

'But Pippa's all right, is she not?'

'Pippa is *not* all right, Cuthbert. Pippa is damaged beyond repair.'

'Norah, Norah, what do you want from me?'

'I'll tell you what I want, Cuthbert, I want revenge on Robert Montague for what he has done to my girls.'

'Now, Norah . . .'

'Now Norah, nothing,' she snapped. 'With your aid, or without it, this time I intend to bring him down.'

Twenty-Three

'How long did you think you could get away with it, sir?'
Robert Montague demanded. 'Did you suppose that I
would not be made aware of what was going on in my
property?'

'Your property, Mr Montague? I was under the
impression that this building belonged to the Presbytery,'
Allan Hunter said.

'No, sir,' Robert said. 'In that you are mistaken. The
church has not been completed, nor has it been con-
secrated. The fact that you helped cast a few of its parts
does not give you the right to take possession of it.'

'I did not take possession of it. I merely—'

'I know what you did, Mr Hunter, and you too, Lassiter,'
Robert said, 'and I am prepared to overlook the serious
nature of the offence on condition that it does not happen
again.'

'Aye, but it will happen again,' Albert Lassiter said. 'It'll
happen when it's needed again.'

'Do you wish me to have you arrested? You, and the
rabble who—'

'Rabble?' Albert said. 'They ain't rabble, Mr Montague.
They are the poor folk who our Lord puts into our charge.'

'I am obviously not so well acquainted with the wishes

of our Lord as you profess to be, Lassiter,' Robert said. 'I do know the law, however, and the law clearly states that the breaking into and entering of a privately owned property, for whatever reason, is an indictable offence.'

They were gathered outside the iron church in cold winter daylight. The sun had not long risen and it held no warmth and only served to make the scene seem more bleak and icy.

'Where are they, Hunter?' Robert said.

'Oh, they've gone, sir,' Allan answered.

'Sneaking away in case they were caught, I suppose,' Robert said.

'Gone to look for somethin' with which to fill their bellies,' Albert said.

'And you gallantly remained behind,' said Robert Montague.

'To pay for the locks,' said Allan.

'Hoh! Now there's a contrite gesture if ever I heard one,' Robert said. 'To pay for the locks? How will you pay for the locks, Hunter, if you are out of work?'

'I am not out of work.'

'After this affray, sir, you may very well be out of work.'

'Is that not a matter for Mr Hounslow to decide?'

'Hounslow will do as I say.'

'Does he own the building, by any chance?'

'For your information, he does not,' Robert answered.

'Who *does* the church belong to?' Albert enquired.

'At this moment, the building belongs to a fund of which I am the executive,' Robert said. 'What matters is not who owns the building but what has been done to it.'

'The Lord says, "Suffer the little children to come . . ." '

'Do not, sir, do *not* throw Scriptural quotations at me when you have no concept of their proper interpretation.'

'Oh, I know what they mean, Mr Montague. I can feel what they mean.'

'Do you know what imprisonment means?'

'Aye, Reverend, and I know what that feels like too.'

'There are places for these people of whom you think so

highly. Provision is made for their welfare under the statutes of the law. They may apply for Poor Relief or they may take refuge in the workhouse. There is no reason for them to suffer hardship; nor for you to take it upon yourselves to provide for them, particularly when it is at my expense.'

'You took away what they had and gave them nothing in return,' Albert Lassiter said. 'You made promises which you ha'n't kept.'

'Oh, so that's it? You are striking back at me because you weren't given charge of the pulpit?'

'That's enough, Mr Montague,' Allan warned.

'And you, sir.' Robert rounded on the manager. 'I will thank you to leave my wife alone.'

'Your wife? What does Cassie have to do with it?'

'Leave her alone, Hunter.'

'Will I give you my word, Mr Montague?' Allan said. 'If I do, how can you be sure I'll keep my promise?'

'Are you not a man of your word?'

'As much as you are, Mr Montague,' Allan Hunter said.

Cubby left Bramwell by the early morning train and arrived at his chambers in Kennoway Square long before his usual hour. He caught his clerks at breakfast, a leisurely event which occupied that pleasant period of the day before the post arrived and the Exchange opened its doors.

When Mr Cuthbert Armitage stalked into the outer room there was a tremendous upheaval around the long hearth and a general scramble in the direction of desks and tables. Work was supposed to begin at eight and by any definition 'work' did not include brewing tea, frying bacon and toasting umpteen rounds of bread. Cubby paid not the slightest attention to his greasy-fingered clerks, however. He stalked through the office as if in a trance, passed into the inner sanctum and closed the door behind him.

It was a good half-hour before the door opened and the

417

stockbroker reappeared. He uttered no command but, with a grim expression, beckoned to Spratt to join him.

Mr Spratt was gone for the best part of ten minutes. When he re-emerged he looked bewildered. He went to the storage room and gathered a file from this shelf, a folio from that, while the clerks watched him apprehensively. Arms laden, Mr Spratt crossed back through the bull-gate, headed towards the door of the stockbroker's office; then stopped.

He looked almost dazed as he turned and said, 'He wants a price from the floor and he wants it urgent.'

'On what, Mr Spratt?'

'The Oran, Algiers and Morocco Great Desert Railway Company.'

And, in unison, the clerks cried out, '*No!*'

Norah's letter was delivered by special messenger and brought to the dining-room by Johnny Jerome. He put it down by Cassie's plate, watched her slit open the envelope and read the note that it contained.

She glanced up. 'Where is my husband?'

'Gone to the church.'

'Please send Nancy to me,' Cassie said. 'I will be going out.'

'Will you be gone long?' Johnny asked.

'Not long. I am visiting my mama at Normandy Road.'

'No harm in that,' said Johnny.

'No, Major Jerome, no harm at all.'

It came as no surprise to Cassie to receive a letter from her mother. She had never underestimated Mama's powers of observation or her skill in detecting 'mischief' in her daughters. More than mere mischief was involved now, though, and Cassie felt her stomach knot with apprehension when, at about half past ten o'clock, Nancy and she were ushered into the front parlour in Normandy Road.

The east-facing room had always been pleasant on sunny mornings and sharp, clear winter light made everything seem vivid.

Norah was seated, stiff and upright, by the fire.

'I wish to speak with my daughter privately, Nancy,' Norah said. 'If you go downstairs Mrs McFarlane will give you refreshment.'

Nancy, saying nothing, dropped a curtsey and left.

Cassie seated herself carefully on a horse-hair couch. She had always disliked the old-fashioned, knobbly object with its back-breaking upholstery and cracked leather but somehow this morning it seemed appropriate to perch upon it, as upright as her mother.

She tried to contain her anxiety but she could not and, after a moment, blurted out, 'Where's Pippa?'

'Pippa will not be joining us.'

'Is she unwell?'

'Resting.'

Cassie said, 'Why have you asked me here this morning, Mama?'

Norah answered, 'To enquire about Mr Hunter.'

'Mr Hunter?' Cassie was taken aback. 'What about Mr Hunter?'

'Do you love him?'

'What kind of a question is that?'

'A perfectly sensible question,' Norah said.

'I do not know how to answer. Allan and I are not lovers, if that is what you mean.'

'That is not what I mean,' Norah said. 'He loves you. Do you love him?'

'I am a married woman.'

'I had a lover once,' Norah said. 'Before I married your papa.'

'Mama!'

'If he had kept his promises I would not have married Cuthbert.'

'Who was this – this man?'

'A sailor. His name is unimportant. I would have gone off with him if he had not let me down.'

'Does Papa know of it?' Cassie asked.

'He knew that I was with child, of course, and that it was not his child.'

419

'And yet he married you?'

'Yes.'

'He must have loved you very much.'

'I suppose he did,' Norah conceded, 'in his way.'

'It is not the same thing. I am married to Robert Montague and I am not carrying his child.' Silence: then Cassie said, 'Is it true, Mama? About Pippa?'

'Yes.'

'Did she admit it?'

'Yes.'

'So she is carrying Robert's child?'

'No.'

Cassie let out her breath. 'Did she miscarry?'

'Never was a child. She imagined it.'

'And you?'

'I did not imagine it,' Norah said. 'My baby was stillborn. Nobody knew of it. Nobody except your father.'

'Why are you telling me this now?' Cassie asked.

'To help you decide what to do.'

'Leave Robert, do you mean?'

'Divorce him,' Norah said.

'If I divorce him,' Cassie said, 'what will become of Pippa?'

'I will see to Pippa,' Norah promised. 'I do not want her to suffer unduly but she must bear part of the blame.'

'Are you saying that she betrayed me?'

'Of course she did.'

'I am not in love with Robert Montague, Mama.'

'I would have thought less of you if you were.'

'I cannot think what possessed me to marry him.'

'We were all taken in, dear,' Norah said. 'Even if there was no other man, if you had not learned what it is to love and be loved, then I would recommend that you take out a bill of divorcement against Robert Montague.'

'If I do it will bring shame on my sister.'

'Yes.'

'It will hurt Papa dreadfully.'

'Papa will stand by you whatever you choose to do.'

Cassie said, 'The man you loved, Mama, the sailor?'

'What about him?'

'What if he had come back for you after you were married to Papa?'

'Would I have run off with him?'

Cassie nodded.

'No,' Norah said. 'By that time I had children. I was no longer my own person.' She paused. 'There's one chance – and chance it is – for a woman to find what she wants. I missed that chance.'

'Are you telling me . . . ?'

'I am telling you, Cassie, that this is your opportunity and that you had better seize it while you can.' Norah paused. 'I notice, dearest, that you have shed not one tear over the fact that your husband deceived you.'

'He has deceived me before; not with other women, not that I know of,' Cassie said, 'but he has deceived me in so many other ways. I think Robert is a man without a heart.'

'And Mr Allan Hunter?'

'Quite the opposite.'

'Is that your answer?'

Cassie hesitated. 'If we leave Ravenshill where will we go?'

'Mr Hunter will know what to do,' Norah said.

'It will be a scandal in any event.'

'Your papa and I will stand by you,' Norah said. 'I have only one thing to ask, Cassie. If you do leave Ravenshill will you take the girl with you?'

'The girl?'

'The workhouse girl.'

'Nancy? Of course.'

'Does she have a child?'

Cassie hesitated, then nodded. 'A little girl.'

'Take them both with you. If it's a matter of money, Cuthbert will see you through.'

'Why do you ask this, Mother? Why does Nancy concern you?'

'She must not be left behind,' Norah stated.

'Because of Robert?'

'Yes.'

'Is that the only reason?'

'Yes.'

'I agree to that condition. And Allan won't balk at it. He's fond of Nancy too.' Cassie looked up. 'It seems that I have reached a decision in spite of myself.'

'In which case you must proceed with caution. Give Robert Montague no hint of your intention. You must make arrangements with Mr Hunter, make everything ready, then leave without a word.'

'But you will take the blame for it, Mama.'

'Blame? What blame?'

'Robert will blame you for my desertion.'

'Let him try,' said Norah Armitage. 'Oh, yes, just let him try.'

Of all the times for Mr Wilks to choose to pay a call on Mr Cuthbert Armitage none could have proved more disastrous. If Spratt or some other senior clerk had been present in the outer office, not skimming about the floor of the Exchange, perhaps the lawyer might have been waylaid and warned that Cuthbert was in no mood to be trifled with.

The sensation that Cubby had caused by asking for a quotation on the Oran-Algiers Railway stock had not entirely died away, however, and Rendell Wilks had been through the bull-gate and heading towards the inner sanctum before anyone noticed him. A mouth opened here, an inky hand was raised there but it was too late to prevent the lawyer's entry into what the young apprentices regarded as 'the lion's den'.

The lion, as it happened, had recently summoned up a teapot full of strong tea and, with his reading glasses perched on his nose and a cup steaming in his hand, was bent over a great pile of Charles Smalls's reports from the far-flung corners of the pig-iron empire. It had not been difficult to select the Oran-Algiers Railway Company as an investment that was bound to lose money. The desert railway project was a joke in every coffee house the length and breadth of Great Britain, a byword for folly in every exchange. It would provide the cornerstone of Cuthbert's revenge against Montague, a means of taking back that which he had given to his faithless son-in-law. Might have worked too, if time had been on Cubby's side.

With the appearance of the spectral Rendell Wilks, however, and seconds after hearing the lawyer's 'little proposition', Cubby Armitage's patience, like his temper, went up in flames and investing in dud stock on Robert's behalf was no longer a satisfactory option.

'Mr Armitage,' Wilks began, 'a moment of your time, if you please.'

'What is it now, Wilks? Can you not see I'm busy?'

'Busy as a bumble bee, yes. Good for you, Mr A., got to keep the wheels of commerce a-turnin', what?' Wilks seated himself before the desk and parted the stacks of paperwork before him so that he could see and be seen. 'Take but a moment, though, take but a trice to hear what I've got to say.'

'Is this another order from Montague?'

'Not eck-zactly, no.'

Cubby tipped up his glasses and cradled the teacup in both hands. He scowled. 'What then?'

'Something in which our client might very well be interested – concerning, sir, your daughter.'

Cubby put down the teacup. 'Which,' he said, 'daughter?'

'The one with the secret,' said Rendell Wilks.

'Pippa!' Cubby fought hard against an inclination to sink his head into his hands. Then he peered up, scowling. 'But surely Montague knows about Pippa's condition?'

For an instant Rendell Wilks looked blank. It was odd to see the lawyer stripped of his I've-got-your-measure assurance. He seemed suddenly smaller and grubbier. 'Pippa?' he said, puzzled.

'My daughter,' Cubby said.

'No, no. Your daughter Cassan-dera,' Wilks said. 'The one as has a bastard child boarded with Madame Daltry.'

'Beg pardon?' said Cubby.

'The one who passed herself off as unsullied to the Reverend gentleman. The one who had for a lover a certain Mr Hunter, late of management at Flail's Blazes. The one who bore him a daughter – Daisy.'

'But – but Cassie has no children.'

'Ah, but she has, sir. Can't keep a secret hidden, leastwise not from Rendell Wilks.'

'I see,' said Cubby. 'Who invented this preposterous story? Madame Daltry? Tell me, how much will it cost to buy your silence?'

'Shall we start at twenty guineas, on a monthly basis?'

'Why not?' Cubby said. 'Why not start at fifty? Before we get down to terms, however, I would like to know what I am actually paying for.'

'Our discretion, sir, our absolute discretion.'

'Am I paying for this child, Daisy, who is purportedly the product of intimacy between my daughter Cassandra and Mr Allan Hunter?'

'Sadly, that's the way of it.'

Cubby ascended. The paper stack tilted and toppled, spilled on to the floor by the side of his desk. 'Are you mad, Wilks?' he shouted.

'Now, now, Mr A., no need to be hasty.'

'One child,' Cubby ranted. 'One innocent child, born to a workhouse girl – oh, yes, Mr Wilks, I know whose child Daisy is, and whose child Nancy Winfield is – and suddenly I'm being soaked twice over. Once by Robert Montague, now by you and that French harlot, Daltry.'

'Madame Daltry ain't no . . .'

'It's madness, Wilks. Sheer madness. I will not be blackmailed, not by you, and not by Montague. Get out.'

'Well, if you feel so strongly . . . time to consider . . .'

'*Get out, damn you.*'

'Is that your last word, Mr Armitage?'

'*OUT*,' Cubby roared and, before Wilks could whisk

himself clear, flung open the office door and with a well-aimed kick to the hindquarters helped the lawyer on his way to the stairs.

He slammed the office door and, for three or four minutes, stood behind it, panting, then – being Cubby – he went behind his desk again and swallowed a draught of lukewarm tea. Then he sat down and, still quivering, thought about things, particularly things related to Robert Montague so that, before Spratt returned with a quotation on the price of stock on the Oran-Algiers Railway Company, Cubby had put that protracted mode of revenge behind him.

It was not enough to ruin Robert Montague financially.

He must destroy him, if he could.

'Spratt?'

'Aye, Mr Armitage.'

'Take down a letter, if you please; a confidential letter.'

'Aye, Mr Armitage; a letter to whom?'

'Major John James Jerome.'

Perhaps, Allan thought, this would be his last full day of employment in Ravenshill. He was under no illusions as to the power of the minister. He had defied a parochial authority and would surely be made to pay for it. If he was paid off he would find no door open to him in Ravenshill or Glasgow and, unless he missed his guess, in any ironworks this side of the Border.

While he attended to his duties about the Hercules and gave Mr Augustine last instructions about improvements in the casting of the parts, he watched the conveyances come and go about the small brick-built building on the south side of the yard; Montague's gig and Andrew Flail's carriage among them. Throughout the morning, he expected to be summoned into Edward Hounslow's presence, to be reprimanded for his gesture of defiance and be sacked on the spot for, in his experience, men of business would always band together. He did not regret his impetuosity, however, did not consider it rash. In fact,

Albert and he planned to make a stand again that very night.

By tonight, surely, it would make no difference what he did. He would have lost his job and would be free of obligations and constraints. Free to defy Robert Montague on all fronts.

It was mid-afternoon before a lad came out into the yard to summon Mr Hunter to the accounting office. Allan walked through the afternoon sunshine, through the reek of smoke from the furnace heads, past the casting sheds and across the patch of frosted ground that separated the works from the offices. He ran his hand over his hair, straightened his collar, tugged down his jacket and entered the corridor that led to the inner office.

It was not a place of grandeur or glory. There was no panelling on the wall, no boardroom table, no portraits glistening in the light from the window. It was, in fact, a plain room used mainly by draughtsmen and the arithmeticians who calculated the costing of each job of work. That afternoon the room was clear of drawers and calculators, though paper rolls and ledgers, inkpots and long rulers were still in evidence on the smooth oak tables.

Edward Hounslow was perched, most ungrandly, on a four-legged stool close to the stove at the room's end.

'Come along, Hunter. Don't dawdle.'

'I believe you sent for me, Mr Hounslow?'

'Of course I sent for you. Did you not expect to be sent for?'

'Aye, sir. I did.'

'What have you to say for yourself?'

'In mitigation, do you mean?'

'Mitigation,' Hounslow said. 'What sort of word is that for an ironworks' manager to use on a cold afternoon?'

Hounslow's expression was weary but not severe. He shifted on the stool and beckoned Allan to approach.

'Warm yourself,' he said.

'I'm not cold, Mr Hounslow.'

'Then you are fortunate. Was it not cold last night?'

426

'It was, sir. Bitterly cold.'

'Is that why you did it?'

'I take it,' Allan said, 'that Reverend Montague has made a complaint?'

'More than a complaint. Sir Andrew Flail has also been to see me.'

'If I might ask, sir, what does this matter have to do with Sir Andrew?'

'He is – or was – your principal employer.'

'I'm sacked then?'

'From Flail's, certainly. Robert Montague insisted upon it.'

'I presume that I am no longer employed here either?'

'I do not dance to Montague's tune,' Edward Hounslow said. 'In fact, you might say that Montague has learned a few steps from me this afternoon. I may do business with these men, Hunter, but unlike them I'm a man of my word. Is Albert Lassiter still installed at the lodging-house?'

'Aye, Mr Hounslow.'

'What escapade do you plan for this evening?'

'To open the church again, if necessary.'

'To take an axe to the door?' Edward Hounslow said. 'To pilfer coal from Flail's wagons? Tut, Hunter, this is the behaviour of common criminals.'

'We can't stand by and see the poor folk . . .'

'Suffer? No, no more can I,' Edward Hounslow said. 'However, Mr Hunter, I must warn you and your friend Lassiter that I'll not be as lenient as Robert Montague. I will not have my property damaged.'

'Your property?'

'The iron church belongs to me now.' Edward Hounslow said. 'It is mine to do with as I see fit.'

'The Presbytery?'

'Have no part in it. The deeds were all in Montague's name. He, apparently, has discovered that he has no use for an iron building, after all. He was very anxious to be rid of it and sold it on the spot – for more than it's worth, of course.'

427

'First he wants a new church and then he changes his mind. Strange behaviour, sir, if you ask me.'

'Not strange at all if you look at it from Montague's point of view,' Edward Hounslow said. 'The entire scheme was an elaborate ruse to acquire town land for the Flails. Montague dreamed it up, executed it, and claimed all the profit for himself.'

'Did you suspect that it was a ruse all along, Mr Hounslow?'

'It did occur to me, Mr Hunter, aye.'

'Why did you not say?'

'Because I too am a man of business. I got what I wanted out of the negotiation. I acquired the patent on the church design, and work for my men,' Edward Hounslow said. 'I also received a tidy sum of money for the old tin mission. More than I would have received if I had sold it straight and above board to Sir Andrew. I'm not as good a negotiator in financial matters as our man of the cloth, it appears.'

'Nor as greedy.'

'Be that as it may, the iron kirk is mine now.'

'May I ask what you intend to do with it, Mr Hounslow?'

'Show it off.'

'Empty?'

'No, I'll have it floored and pews put in. Nothing too expensive. And in due course I will install a harmonium because I have a fancy to polish up my musical skills again.' He slid from the stool and dug his fingers into his overcoat pocket. 'In the meantime I would be grateful if you would instruct Albert Lassiter to ensure that my property suffers no further damage. If he wishes to admit himself and any of his flock who wish to share worship with him, please tell him to use the conventional mode of entry.' He held out a big round key-ring and shook it until it jangled like a tambourine. 'Take it, Hunter. Give it to Lassiter. Tell him – well, you know what to tell him.'

'That he has a new place to preach in, a brand-new mission hall?'

428

'Yes. And he had better not thank me for it – not publicly, at any rate.'

Allan grinned. 'Just one thing, Mr Hounslow.'

'What's that.'

'We'll need coal.'

'I'll have two loads delivered this evening.'

'Aye, sir. Oh – and blankets.'

'Hunter' – Edward Hounslow shook his head ruefully – 'get out of here before I change my mind.'

'Yes, Mr Hounslow,' Allan said and, with the iron key-ring clinking in his fist, hurried off to tell Albert that good news had returned to Ravenshill.

The end came sooner than Johnny had anticipated. Events, it seemed, were rushing him towards a decision, albeit one that he would have preferred not to have to make at all. It was a little after four o'clock when he received Cuthbert Armitage's letter. He scanned it in the kitchen corridor by the flicker of a stableyard lantern. He looked up and around guiltily, although he knew that Robert had gone to dine at Flail House and would not return until late.

He stuffed the letter into his pocket, went on across the yard to hang the lantern on its hook and to look in on Luke Simmonds who, seated in the gloom of the tackroom, was polishing a riding saddle that Robert hardly ever used these days. Johnny said nothing to the young man. He stared at him for a moment or two then returned to the warmth of the kitchen and, with the letter hidden in his pocket, consumed a ham sandwich and two cups of black coffee in Miss Rundall's company before he went upstairs to his room.

Once there, his easy manner crumbled like chalk. He extracted Armitage's letter from his pocket with trembling hands and, kneeling on the rug before the fireplace, read it through carefully before he burned it and stirred the ashes into dust.

Johnny remained closeted in his room until half past seven when, washed, shaved and dressed for the evening, he took himself downstairs and joined Cassie Montague in the dining-room. He could not pretend to be his usual jovial self, however, and ate in brooding silence.

Towards the end of the meal, after Janey had removed the pudding plates, Cassie Montague asked, 'Will you be going with Robert to Dundee?'

Johnny glanced up. 'Dundee? When is he going to Dundee?'

'Tomorrow,' Cassie said. 'Did he not tell you?'

'No, he did not. How long will he be gone?'

'Two or three days, apparently,' Cassie answered. 'He is to deliver a midweek Christmas address at the Memorial kirk and, I believe, will also attend to business arising from his father's will. I'm surprised he didn't tell you.'

'Two or three days, do you say?'

'Until Thursday or Friday.'

'Not longer?' said Johnny.

'You must ask Robert that,' Cassie said. 'I do know, however, that he has not notified Mr Onslow to stand in for him. And I see from the parish day-book that he has a dozen christenings to perform after morning service, so he obviously intends to return before the Sabbath.'

'Two days,' Johnny murmured. 'Oh, God!'

'What is it? What's wrong?'

'Nothing.' Johnny opened his eyes again. 'No. Everything is wrong. Listen, Cassie, listen to me very carefully and heed what I have to say. Do not be here when Robert gets back.'

'What do you mean?'

'I mean leave here, leave the manse. Take the Winfield girl with you and clear out. Go home to your parents' house. Go off with your manager. *Just do not be here when Robert returns from Dundee.*'

'Did Robert put you up to this? Is this another of your games?'

'No, damn it. I wish it were,' Johnny said. 'Please, Cassie, do as I ask.'

'Why should I listen to you of all people?'

'Because if you don't,' Johnny said, 'something bad will happen.'

'To whom?' Cassie said.

'To you, to Nancy, to anyone who happens to be at hand.'

'But not to you, Major Jerome?'

'No,' Johnny answered. 'No, ma'am, not to old Johnny Jerome.'

Although it was very late, Johnny was not asleep, or even in bed, when Robert returned from Flail House.

Clad in nightshirt and dressing-gown the major lay sprawled in an armchair before the embers of the fire, sipping brandy and smoking a last cigar. He may have appeared to be in a state of hedonistic ease but his ears were pricked and his muscles taut and when he heard the sounds of Flail's coach on the drive outside he grew even more tense. He finished the brandy at a swallow, threw the cigar, half-smoked, into the grate and, before Robbie knocked on his door, was so reduced by fear and melancholy that he rocked back and forth in the chair, hugging himself like a little old woman.

Robert opened the door and looked around it.

'Ah, there you are,' he said. 'Still up, I see.'

'Still up,' said Johnny. 'Still guarding the fort, old boy.'

'Been with Flail, supping.'

'Supping claret, by the state of you,' Johnny said. 'Rather too much claret, what?'

'Andrew keeps a good cellar. Done – did – full justice to it.'

'Do you want to sit down?' Johnny said.

'No, better go up. Sleep.'

'Long day tomorrow?' Johnny said. 'Long journey ahead of you?'

'What? Yes, Dundee.' Robert swayed slightly. 'Should finish it by Friday. Dada's business. Odds and ends, that's all. Final settlement.'

'You didn't tell me you were going away.'

'Did I not? Forgot. Clean forgot.'

'Cassandra told me.'

'Good for Cassandra, my little missus.' Robert laughed. 'Got rid of the iron church today. Sold it to Hounslow. Got rid of Hunter too. No more of that scoundrel. After my wife. Need my wife to make babies.'

'That's what wives are for,' Johnny said, sadly.

'Better go up.'

'You'd better, yes.'

'Hold the fort?'

'Hold the fort,' Johnny repeated.

'Count on you?'

'Count on me.'

'Goo'night then, Johnny.'

'Goodnight, old boy.'

Johnny came forward, walking square and flat-footed. He laid a hand lightly on Robert's breast and, struggling to hide his tears, kissed him.

'Goodbye, Robbie,' he said.

'Goodbye?' said Robert Montague. 'Will I not see you in the morning?'

''Course you will,' said Johnny. 'Bright and early, before you go.'

'Like the old days?'

'Just like the old days,' Johnny said and closed the door behind his friend, knowing that he would never see him again.

The major's warnings carried little weight with Cassie. Even so, she needed no persuasion to pack essential belongings and, accompanied by Nancy, to escape from Bramwell manse as soon as Robert was safely out of the way. She thought that she would experience some sense of loss as the gig passed out of the gates and turned towards Normandy Road. But she did not. She felt only relief, overwhelming relief that her marriage to the minister was effectively at an end.

She was not naïve enough to believe that she had seen

the last of Robert Montague, however. He was too possessive to release her without a struggle. But once she was safely installed in Normandy Road at least Robert would not be able to do her physical harm. She had told the servants only that she intended to spend the mid-week at her father's house and had evaded Miss Rundall's pointed questions about the weight of luggage required for such a short stay. Of Johnny there had been no sign at the breakfast table and Luke, when questioned, had indicated that the major had gone off on foot about half past nine o'clock, heading towards the town.

Cassie was inclined to leave a letter for Robert but Norah advised against it. There would be time enough for confrontations, Norah said, when Robert returned from Dundee.

Allan would dine at Normandy Road that night and the precise timing of events would be discussed then.

Tomorrow the children would be brought out of Madame Daltry's and settled in Normandy Road. The last of Cassie's belongings would be fetched from Bramwell manse so that by the time Robert came home he would find all trace of her gone and his hold over her broken.

He might cry 'desertion' as loud as he liked, Norah said, but his threats would fall on deaf ears. If he wished to discuss the preliminaries of a divorce Cuthbert would be happy to accommodate him and would begin by showing him the deposition that Pippa had dictated concerning her seduction at the minister's hands. Then there would be no question of Cassie and Allan Hunter remaining in Ravenshill, of course. It would be up to Allan to decide whether they would flee to England or abroad. Norah favoured a fresh start for the couple in Boston where Cuthbert's partner, Charles Smalls, had excellent connections in the iron trade and suitable employment for Allan might be found. Once Cassie had departed Robert would be at liberty to play the martyred husband and perhaps continue with his ministry, or to take himself elsewhere.

It all seemed just too cut and dried. Robert would have tricks of his own to play yet, Cassie had no doubt. But even she could not have foreseen what the minister had in store before the week was out.

'Is this a bribe, old boy?' Johnny tapped the document that lay on Cuthbert Armitage's desk. 'If it is what makes you suppose that I will fall for it?'

'The fact that you are here,' Cubby said. 'The fact that you did not show my letter to Robert.'

'Robert is out of town.'

'Oh, I know that,' Cubby said. 'I know a very great deal more about your chum Montague than I did a year ago. He'll not be back in Bramwell until Thursday at the earliest – which gives you approximately one day and a half to make up your mind.'

'Is the figure accurate?'

'To the penny,' Cubby said.

'Are you telling me that if I sign three simple little pieces of paper then I might walk away with twenty-nine thousand pounds of Robert's money?'

'Ah, but it isn't Robert's money,' Cubby said. 'It is your money, Major Jerome. See, it's your name on all the documents. Montague's name does not appear anywhere. The so-called "fund" is yours to draw on. There's nothing illegal in converting the full sum into cash, if that is what you choose to do.'

'How did you manage it, Cubby?' Johnny said. 'I mean, how in the name of God did you manage to trick a wily old dog like Robbie into trusting you with his hard-earned?'

'I didn't trick him,' Cubby said. 'He tricked himself. He assumed that I was too cowardly to be other than honest.'

'How much of this sum comes from the sale of land?'

'Approximately sixty per cent.'

'And the rest?'

'From speculation on the market.'

'By God, I wish you were my stockbroker.'

'You should thank your stars I'm not,' Cubby said. 'If you

must know, Major Jerome, it was originally my intention to "bust" Montague by investing every penny in a venture which, I assure you, would have been sensationally unsuccessful and would have wiped out Robert's – I mean, your – profits at a stroke.'

'Why did you not do it, then?'

'Because it wasn't enough.'

'Enough for what?'

'To offend him,' Cubby said.

'Then you don't know Robbie Montague as well as you think you do,' Johnny said. 'He may seem to be sanguine about his capital but, believe me, if you had lost one farthing that Robert thought was his then he would certainly be "offended". What's his is his for ever. He's more than just grasping. Money is only a part of it. He is possessed by a force that ordinary folk cannot imagine.'

'That,' Cubby said, 'is precisely what my dear wife said of him.'

'Shrewd woman, your wife,' Johnny said. 'Was writing that letter to me her idea too?'

'No. I thought of that,' Cubby admitted.

'Why?'

'Because if you stake your claim to what is legally yours then you will be obliged to quit Ravenshill and never meet with Montague again.'

'I'm only too well aware of that,' Johnny Jerome said.

'I want him to realise that friendship has its price.'

'You want to hurt him?'

'Aye,' Cubby said, 'and relieving him of twenty-nine thousand pounds will not cause him enough pain. Losing your friendship will hurt him more, will it not?'

'Yes,' Johnny said. 'I think it will.'

'You see,' Cubby said, 'I'm not trying to deceive you, Major Jerome.'

'But you are tempting me to betray my oldest and dearest friend.'

'When the last deeds are signed would he not be coming to you, Major Johnny, sticking a document under your nose and telling you to sign it? After which all this money would be transferred to his own account. How much would you see of it then?'

'Precious little,' Johnny admitted.

'How much did he promise you to marry my daughter Pippa?'

'I might have known that would come up,' Johnny said.

'How much?'

'Ten thousand.'

'Was it not enough?'

'Not nearly enough.'

'Is twenty-nine thousand closer to the mark?'

'What?' said Johnny. 'To marry Pippa?'

'Certainly not,' Cubby said. 'Enough, I mean, to cause you to abandon a man who would have sold you like a slave, a man who breaks his promises as easily as others break straws. What do you suppose Montague would do if the shoe was upon the other foot? Do you suppose that he would hesitate?'

Johnny rubbed his chin thoughtfully. The melancholy that had wrung his heart last night had gone. The moment he had burned Armitage's letter he had known what he would do. In fact, he had already said his goodbyes.

He gave a rueful grunt. 'Robert underestimated you rather badly, Cubby. He thought you were a fool, and you are not.'

'My wife would not agree with you,' Cubby said. 'Be that as it may, Major, it's not what I've done but what you are about to do that concerns us.'

'If I sign those papers . . .'

'And I countersign them,' Cubby said.

'Quite! If I sign those papers then I can walk off with twenty-nine thousand pounds, free, clear and legal?'

'You can.'

'And Robert can do nothing?'

'Nothing,' said Cubby.

'Oh, damn it,' Johnny said, sighing. 'Give me the pen and the inkpot and let's get it over with, once and for all.'

* * *

Pippa was lurking in the bedroom upstairs. If Cassie had expected to be showered by tears of contrition then she was in for a disappointment. Pippa was seated in a basket chair by the window, a shawl drawn about her shoulders like an invalid. When Cassie came into the room she flicked the ends of the shawl theatrically and swung round to face her sister. She had, indeed, been weeping but they were tears of anger, not shame.

'Have you come here to gloat?'

Cassie, taken aback, shook her head. 'Of course not, dear. I've—'

'I know what you've done. You've deserted him. How could you?'

Cassie clenched her fists against her skirts and tried to control herself. It was strange to be in this room again: the pastel-shaded bedroom with the two little beds where Pippa and she had passed their childhood together. She did not feel at home here now, and she certainly did not wish to stay. Nostalgia did not appeal to her character. She remembered the bickering, the petty squabbles and the tedium of listening to her selfish little sister complain about everyone and everything.

'How dare you accuse me, Pippa,' Cassie said. 'Do you not think that I have every right to leave Robert Montague after what he has done to me?'

'He did nothing to harm you. If you hadn't found out . . .'

'Found out?' Cassie said, trying not to sound shrill. 'Found out that he had taken *you* for a lover? How could I not find out, since you were – so – so enthusiastic, so keen to tell the world how you had got the better of me.'

'Is that what you think?' Pippa tossed aside the shawl and leaped to her feet. 'Well, I will have you know that Robert did not choose me. I chose him. And I would have had him too, if you hadn't stood in my way.'

'Pippa, I was – I am his wife.'

'And a bad wife you were. Robert told me that you were never a proper wife to him.'

437

'I do not believe you.'

'He told me that I would have been a better wife to him than you were.'

'When did he tell you such a thing?'

'When we were . . .'

'Oh, you liar!' Cassie exploded. 'He took his pleasure with you, that's all. Robert would not deign to confide in someone like you.'

'You could not give him children.'

'And could you?'

'I tried. I tried,' Pippa cried. 'If it hadn't been for you . . .'

'Me? What did I have to do with it?'

'How can you bear to leave him for that ironworks' trash?'

'How dare you! How dare you, Pippa Armitage!' Cassie said. 'If you think that Mr Hunter and I were – that we did what you did with my husband then you have more than one sin to answer for.'

'I *loved* him. I *still* love him.'

'Then you may have him. If you can find a way, you may have him with my blessing. It's no more than you deserve.'

Neither recriminations nor forgiveness would make a bit of difference to Pippa. For the first time Cassie felt herself detached, not just from her wilful sister but from Robert Montague too. Her future lay with others now: with Nancy and the children and, of course, with Allan who loved her in a way that Pippa would never understand.

'I will never have him now,' Pippa said.

'No, I doubt that you ever will,' Cassie said, then, suddenly weary of her sister's histrionics, she turned and left the bedroom without another word.

'Why, Mr Armitage,' Madame Daltry said with her sweetest smile, 'this is an unexpected pleasure.'

'Is it?' Cubby said dryly. 'Did you expect your accomplice Wilks to turn up brandishing a twenty pound banknote?'

'Mr Wilks?' Madame Daltry's dimple faded into her

painted cheek. 'I don't believe I know Mr—'

'Rubbish!' Cubby said. 'You and he are as thick as thieves. You may count yourself fortunate that I do not have a sheriff's officer with me.'

'Instead, you have come with Mr Hunter and Miss Winfield. How nice!'

'I have come for my son, Madame Daltry,' Allan Hunter said. 'I wish you to have his clothes packed and ready in a quarter of an hour.'

'A visit, a holiday?'

'I am taking him home to live with me.'

'Oh, now, really, is that wise?'

'Wiser than leaving him in the care of a blackmailer,' Allan said.

'That, Mr Hunter, is a slander.'

'Then you may seek redress through law,' Allan said. 'Meanwhile, I will take my son to reside with me.'

'An' my daughter, too,' said Nancy.

They were all together in the parlour, none of them yet seated. The work of instilling good manners and respect for authority went on about them, a vague hum of little voices reciting numerical tables and simple rhymes. For a second or two Nancy's determination to take Daisy away from this secure and comfortable sanctuary wavered.

'You too, Nancy?' Madame Daltry said. 'What has come over you? Daisy is doing so well with us. So well.'

Nancy felt Allan's reassuring hand upon her arm. She did not entirely comprehend why Cuthbert Armitage was here with them, but she trusted Allan Hunter and lifted her chin defiantly to the woman who, in her ignorance, she had once worshipped as a saint.

'Daisy will do better wi' me, Madame Daltry,' Nancy said. 'If you will pack her things an' make her ready, I'll be takin' her home at once.'

'Home? What sort of home can you provide?' Madame Daltry said, putting pretence aside. 'Come now, it isn't you at all. It's her natural mother who wants her back, is it not?'

'Her mother? I'm Daisy's mother,' Nancy said.

'Nonsense!' Madame Daltry snapped. 'One thing I have learned over the years and that is how to recognise good breeding. It cannot be disguised. Daisy is too fine a little person to have sprung from *your* loins.'

Nancy did not know whether to be insulted or flattered on Daisy's behalf. Before she could respond, however, Mr Armitage suddenly put his arm about her shoulder in a gesture that was unexpectedly protective.

'There you are wrong, Madame,' he said. 'Quite wrong. The child in question *is* Nancy Winfield's. I will vouch for it. Aye, under oath in a court of law if it comes to it. As to breeding, I would not say too much about that if I were you. As it so happens my partner, Charles Smalls, has certain contacts among the demi-monde, certain acquaintances with long memories.'

'What do you mean?'

'You are no more French than I am, Madame Daltry. Your money did not come from an aristocratic source. It came from a house in Leith, I believe, a night-house which you and your former partner operated at considerable profit.'

'*Mon Dieu*! What is this you say?'

'That you are a deceiver, ma'am,' Cuthbert told her, his arm still about Nancy's shoulder. 'That you are a born deceiver who isn't fit to be in charge of the welfare of small children.'

Nancy was flanked by Allan on the one hand and by Cuthbert on the other and felt more secure than she had ever done. She understood perfectly what Mr Armitage was saying and could tell by the expression on Madame Daltry's face that he had come very near the truth. She had no idea who Charles Smalls was or how that gentleman had acquired his information about the woman's past but she recognised now in Madame Daltry's painted smile a certain pain and in the eyes a dreadful anxiety.

'I am an honest woman,' Madame Daltry said. 'I do nothing here that would harm my little charges.'

'Except blackmail,' Cuthbert said. 'You are, at best, an

honest hypocrite, Madame Daltry, I will say that for you; which is why I am here today with Miss Winfield and Mr Hunter, to make sure that you remain honest – and to give you an opportunity to make amends. Do you take my meaning?'

The woman pursed her lips. 'Wilks,' she said. 'You paid Wilks, didn't you? You bought him off at my expense. I *knew* I should not have listened to that man.'

'I did not pay Wilks and I will not pay you,' Cuthbert said. 'I would be obliged, however, if you would find another stockbroker with whom to do business in future. Perhaps Mr Wilks can suggest someone. In the meantime, I am acting on Miss Winfield's behalf and with her consent. The child, Daisy, will leave with us within the hour. And,' Cuthbert went on, 'if I hear one more word, one more threat of extortion, from you, Madame, or from any one of your disreputable associates, I will make certain that the Board of Inspectors are informed who you are and that your establishment is subjected to scrutiny.'

'But that would harm my babies,' Madame Daltry cried, shedding tears at last. 'Oh, Mr Armitage, if my school is closed where would they go? Who would look after my poor lost babies?'

'Who would look after you? Isn't that what you mean?' Cuthbert said.

'Would you ruin me, Mr Armitage?'

'No, Madame Daltry, that I will not do. But I ask you to remember that rumour is a two-edged sword and that it can cut you down just as easily as you tried to cut down my daughter.'

'He's behind this, is he not?'

'Wilks? No, I told you . . .'

'Not Wilks. Montague.'

'Montague?' Cuthbert said, alarmed. 'My son-in-law?'

'I should not have listened to him either,' Madame Daltry said, still leaking tears of self-pity. 'I should not have let him see the child.'

'The child? Whose child?'

'Her child,' said Madame Daltry, waving a plump hand in Nancy's direction. 'He came to look at *her* child.'

'Why? Why would Mr Montague do that?' Nancy cried.

'In case he ever needed her,' Madame Daltry said.

They had been prisoners too long to face the outside world without tears. The little bribes that Allan offered in the form of candy had no soothing effect at first. They clung to each other in the face of uncertainty, unsure what would become of them in the mysterious land across the river. Tom was less afraid than Daisy. He comforted her as best he could. He protected her by glaring at everyone on the ferryboat, his father included, and even raised his fist when Cuthbert stooped to offer a few reassuring words.

In spite of the relief that the adults felt to be safely away from the Daltry residence, it was not a happy journey. It had not occurred to Nancy that the minister might know of Daisy's existence and might use an innocent child to threaten and persuade Cassie to return to him. The 'rescue' of her daughter had come not a moment too soon. No matter how distressed the children might be, at least they were no longer pawns in Reverend Montague's game, were no longer at the minister's mercy.

If she had known what Madame Daltry really was, of course, she would have taken Daisy away from Greenfield months ago. She had been mistaken to suppose that a genteel upbringing would ensure Daisy's happiness. She understood now that being a lady did not necessarily confer happiness, that it would have been better for Daisy to have been raised in love in the dreary heights of Bengal Street than in the confinement of Madame Euphemia Daltry's establishment. She realised that she had served her daughter ill. She should have married Todd Brownlee and made a proper home for her child. She should have taken her chances with a future which for all its harshness and uncertainty would have been *her* future, and Daisy's too.

It was too late now to return to the tenement, to ask

Todd to forgive her. She had thrown in her lot with the Armitages and, for her own sake as well as Daisy's, must trust herself to them.

The children sat huddled together, prim and mannerly and anxious as the ferryboat slewed and bumped against the steps. They were too young to understand that everything was for the best and that they had nothing to fear.

The ride in the hackney carriage that Mr Armitage had hired to carry them in style to Normandy Road cheered Tom and Daisy. The novelty of riding in a big coach behind a pair of horses was exciting enough to smother apprehension, and they graciously allowed themselves to be propped up at the window and to have the sights of Ravenshill pointed out to them.

Good manners and brittle politeness were soon replaced by chatter and by the time the hack deposited them outside the Armitages' front door the questions were coming thick and fast. When the queer-looking woman with the frizzy hair, who was waiting on the steps to greet them, bent down and lifted Daisy into her arms Tom did not object. He glanced up at his father then tentatively reached out his arms to be lifted up too and, thus secure, was carried into the Armitage house.

For an instant Nancy was resentful. How could she be otherwise? The rapport between Norah Armitage and her little girl was apparent. They went off together into the front parlour as if nobody else existed and by the time Nancy had helped bring in the luggage and Mr Armitage had paid off the driver, the woman and Daisy were deep in conversation before the crackling fire. Nancy watched, almost enviously, while Norah Armitage took off Daisy's bonnet and loose coat and with a little silver brush that seemed to have appeared from nowhere brushed her fair curls. Tom, not to be outdone, was waited upon in similar manner by Miss Cassie.

Just behind her, Allan Hunter whispered, 'You mustn't mind, Nancy. She'll always be your wee girl, you know.'

'Aye, Mr Hunter,' Nancy said. 'I suppose she will,' and

then, not knowing quite what else to do, went downstairs into the kitchen to help Mrs McFarlane serve the afternoon tea.

Pippa, still pretending to be ill, did not appear at all, not for tea and not for dinner. She could not have been oblivious to the noise of children within the house but if curiosity moved her to quiz the mousey little maidservant who brought up her supper on a tray, she was not brazen enough to show her face to anyone. The room was her room now and whatever arrangements had been made to accommodate the sudden flood of guests, Pippa had no intention of being inconvenienced.

The fact that she was not consulted or approached, not by Mama and certainly not by Cassie, riled her and when, shortly before seven o'clock, she heard some infant hand rattling upon *her* piano she almost lost her temper and had to restrain herself from abandoning her exile.

Instead, she lay stomach down upon the bed, kicked her heels into the air and punched the pillows and cried into them. Wept for the baby she had never had, for the man who had been her lover but who had somehow managed to resist loving her. Wept until sobs changed into whimpers and then, exhausted, she rolled on to her back and lay there, thumb in mouth, mooning over what might have been and what had been and what would never be now, until with a last little snort and a sigh she finally fell asleep.

They lay together, side by side, in the old box-sided bed that had been brought down from the attic and assembled in the small back bedroom on the first floor.

The room had been fired early that day and was warm and well aired. Even so, the smell of Madame Daltry's 'school' clung faintly to the children; not an unclean workhouse smell but a soapiness that reminded Norah of her days as a governess. She was also reminded of Samuel Taylor, for Nancy's child bore a strange resemblance to the sailorman, a distinctive shape to mouth and chin and a way of glancing up at you, haughty and at the same time appealing, that brought tears to Norah's eyes.

Cassie and Nancy had put the children to bed and had stayed to give them reassurance. Norah had bided her time. She had come alone to the room only after the children were asleep. She wanted to stand, as she stood now, looking down on Daisy's tousled head, at the pretty little face relaxed in sleep. She had to be sure that the resemblance was not just wistful imagining but actual. And it was. It was.

She had not resisted when Cuthbert had discharged Nancy from service and had not enquired as to his reason for it. Even now when she studied the workhouse girl she could detect in her nothing of herself and nothing of Samuel Taylor. It was as if the affinities that should exist between mother and daughter had been severed with the birth-cord and dependence upon Cuthbert had robbed her of natural feeling. In Daisy, though, she saw traces of Samuel, and of herself, experienced them in her heart and nerve ends. And with that recognition came fear for the child's future and guilt at what had been done to Nancy.

She heard him behind her and turned. Cuthbert stood quietly in the doorway. He said nothing, did not smile. She looked at her husband and the question hung on her lips. If she asked him now she knew that he would tell her the truth. All she had to say was, 'Is Nancy my child?' and she would watch Cubby nod and would hear him reply, 'Yes,' and all pretence would be gone and with it all semblance of the gratitude that she had put into the marriage in place of love. Cuthbert waited in the doorway, ready to answer; but Norah could no more put the question into words than she could disguise her tears.

'They're so – so pretty,' she said. 'Makes me want to cry.'

'Yes. Very pretty.'

'And so peaceful. They look as if they belong here.'

'Yes,' Cuthbert said and, fishing in his pocket, brought

out a spotted handkerchief into which he loudly blew his nose.

'What's wrong with you?' said Norah, sharply.

'I wish I knew, dear. I wish I knew,' said Cuthbert and, taking her by the hand, led her out of the children's room and downstairs into the hall.

Twenty-Four

The circumstances that brought Nancy to Bramwell manse at half past eight o'clock on Wednesday evening were ordinary enough: a day-dress, a favourite pair of shoes, a box of trinkets, items that Cassie wished to retrieve before Robert returned and which she, Nancy, had volunteered to collect.

There seemed to be no harm in it. Mr Hunter had offered to accompany her. But Mrs Armitage had said that it might be better if Nancy went alone as there was less likelihood of the servants' suspicions being aroused.

Cassie had stated that the major would do nothing to prevent the retrieval of the items, however, as he was by no means ill-disposed to her 'escape' from the marriage and had indeed urged her to leave Bramwell on more than one occasion. Mr Armitage had agreed with his daughter. Jerome, he'd said, would not stand in Nancy's way, not if he knew what was good for him. Nancy did not understand what Mr Armitage meant. It hardly mattered. It would take her no more than a half-hour to walk to the manse; ten minutes or so would see the items packed into a valise, and Luke would drive her back to Normandy Road. When that was done there would be no need for any of them to return to the minister's house ever again.

There was discussion, to which Nancy was not party, as to the best course of action to follow in the days ahead. Norah favoured an immediate departure from Ravenshill, a flight to some safe haven down the coast; Robert Montague's veiled threat against Daisy Winfield was not to be taken lightly. Allan, however, declared that he felt a certain obligation to his new employer, Edward Hounslow, and that he did not wish to depart from Ravenshill immediately. He was also keen to see Mr Lassiter settled in the iron church and to ensure that Montague made no further trouble for the missionary.

'I thought that you were in love with my daughter?' Norah said.

'Oh, I am, ma'am. Indeed, I am,' Allan said. 'But it seems somehow dishonourable to scuttle off like a thief in the night.'

'No saying what Montague will do if he finds you here,' Norah said.

'What can he do?' Cassie said. 'We have the children safe with us and Robert would not be so foolish as to try to abduct them from Papa's house.'

'He'd better not try,' said Cubby.

'How long will it take to settle your affairs, Allan?' Cassie asked.

'Two or three weeks,' Allan said. 'That will give us ample time to book passage on a fast ship to America. We'll sail from Greenock, all of us, Nancy and the children included, soon after New Year. January's not the best time for an Atlantic crossing but there's no help for it.'

'Go tomorrow, first thing,' Norah persisted. 'Take lodgings in Greenock and sail on the first available vessel.'

'No,' Cassie said. 'Allan's right. It's too much like running away.'

'It is running away,' said Cubby.

Cassie glanced at Allan. 'Too cowardly?'

'Aye,' Allan said. 'I'd rather square up to Montague in person than leave it all to you, Mr Armitage.'

'I'm not afraid of that scoundrel,' said Cubby, stoutly. 'I

have his measure now. Besides, he'll not dare make *too* much fuss about Cassie's desertion or the Presbytery will have him out of the parish. Not even Flail will be able to protect him. If Montague wants to hang on to his pulpit then he had better behave like a gentleman or I'll report to the Kirk Session everything I know about him, which is – em – rather a lot.'

'Will he, in fact, survive the scandal?' Cassie asked.

'He'll survive anything, that one,' Cubby said. 'Yes, my dear, Montague will appear to be the injured party. For that reason, he'll not risk making more fuss than he has to. It will be announced as a separation, though everyone hereabouts will know that it's not. In due course Montague will petition for divorce which, as you want nothing from him, we will not contest.'

'Are you still concerned about him, Cassie?' Allan asked.

'Only as to what he might do,' Cassie answered.

'Nothing,' Cubby said. 'He can do nothing. His wings have been thoroughly clipped, believe me.'

'Then will we wait?' said Allan.

'Yes,' Cassie agreed. 'We'll wait.'

The kitchen was filled with smoke and brandy fumes. All across the board were the remains of the evening meal. Chicken bones, scraps of roast beef, pastries, half-eaten pies and the ruins of a cherry tart were strewn among beer jugs and bottles. The girl, Marie, was sprawled on the table, her stays undone and her small, conical breasts exposed. She was flushed red as a boiled lobster and held a cigar in finger and thumb before her pouting lips and sucked on it without enthusiasm while Janey, clad only in her shift, egged her on by waving a tankard above her head.

Miss Rundall was seated in a Jacobean chair that had been brought down from the hall. She too was half undressed. Stockinged feet propped on the table, her gargantuan calves and thighs exposed, she cradled a full brandy glass to her bosom and clenched the stump of one

449

of the major's cigars in her teeth. Her eyes, though, were livid and alert and when Nancy slipped in through the door from the yard, she noticed her at once.

'Well, now, girlies, who 'ave we 'ere?' she said.

Janey stiffened, then, seeing that it was only Winfield, struck an angular pose and extended the tankard mockingly.

'Come tae join us then, Nance?' she cried and then, sobering, said, 'Here, y' ain't brought the mistress with you, have yer?'

'Ain't no mistress with 'er.' The cook removed the cigar from her mouth. 'She's come for more o' the lady's things, ha'n't you now, sweetheart?'

'You sure, Cookie?' Janey asked.

''Course I'm sure. Ladies like their things same as we do. She's come for to collect more pretty stuff from upstairs.'

'Aye, I have,' Nancy said. 'So I'd best get on wi' it.'

She edged around the table in the direction of the stairs that led up into the house. Janey was too swift for her, however, and stepped out to bar the way.

'The mistress ain't never comin' back, ain't that right, honey?'

'She's – she's visitin' with her mama,' Nancy said.

'She's run off with a *maaan*,' Janey crowed. 'We heard. We heard.'

'Where's Major Jerome?' Nancy asked, dry-mouthed.

'Gone,' said Janey. 'Run off too.'

'I dinna believe you.'

'We . . . we's . . . ceb'ratin',' Marie muttered thickly.

'Took Lukey with 'im,' Miss Rundall said. 'Packed all his truck first thing this mornin' an' he was gone, with the lad, by 'alf past one.'

'Us next,' said Janey. 'Us, t'morra.'

'We'll see, we'll see,' said Miss Rundall.

'Let me past,' said Nancy.

'Stab me again, will yer?' Janey said.

'I might,' said Nancy. 'Let me through. I've work t' do upstairs.'

'Work? Ye ca' that work?' Janey stepped closer to the lady's maid, the tankard held up like a hammer. 'I've a score t' settle wi' you first.'

'Let 'er go, Janey,' Miss Rundall said.

'She'll tell the mistress.'

'Makes no matter now. Let 'er go.'

'Ah'll be damned if . . .'

At that moment Marie reared up and was violently sick. Janey leaped back in disgust. And Nancy, seizing her chance, tugged open the kitchen door and ran like the wind up into the darkened house.

He had been alone in the austere little study behind the Turkish room for a half-hour or more. He had lighted only one candle. He knelt in front of the rifled safe with the letter laid before him on the carpet. He might have been praying, except that his eyes were wide open. Brown leather bag and half-topper stood outside on the ottoman but he still wore his heavy alpaca overcoat and scarf. His breath hung before him in a pale grey cloud. He did not feel the cold in the unfired room. He had stopped trembling some ten minutes ago.

Whatever instinct had moved him to return early and had prompted him to enter the house unannounced kept him still, kept him silent. It was as if he were awaiting another sign, a signal from the demon within that he must move forward again, advance towards a meeting on the ground of being that would lift him at last out of his despair.

The rage that was in him did not consume him. It burned like cold fire. He wanted her now. He wanted her as he had never wanted anything. He had come back full of anticipation, obsessed with the thought that he might surprise them together, Hunter and Cassandra, observe at last her unleashed passion, her sweaty body tangled in sheets, hear the white bedroom ring with her ecstatic cries. Sense told him that it would not be so; yet he hoped against all logic that it might be so for the power it would give him over her and for what he might learn from it.

The house, though, had been dark and empty save for the shaft of light in the kitchen window at the root of the gable wall. On entering the hall, he had been greeted by laughter, by the shrieks of female servants entertaining themselves below. He had listened at the top of the kitchen stairs and had felt only envy, envy and disappointment because they had reverted so thoroughly and shamelessly to type. What did they know of authority, or of despair? They were weak, ignorant creatures and not worth punishing. He would deal with them leniently, but only after he had discovered why Johnny had left the house at their mercy, and where his wife had gone.

The rifled safety box and Johnny's letter explained everything. The safety box was empty. The laudanum bottle had vanished; bonds too, documents relating to the sale of land, even Cuthbert Armitage's anonymous note concerning the abandoned child. The money, the banknotes that he had carefully hoarded, had been swept away. There was nothing left within the safe except Johnny's letter to explain the mystery of the deserted house and reveal the crime behind the crimes. Old Johnny had cleaned him out.

He did not do what other men might have done; did not charge downstairs to Johnny's room to confront a man who had already vanished; did not rush out into the stableyard to shout in vain for Luke Simmonds. He respected Johnny far too much to suppose that he would allow himself to be caught. He knew that he would never see or hear from Johnny Jerome again and he knelt before the safe in the cold back room grieving for Johnny Jerome.

His father's legacy seemed immaterial now. He had lost that which he had struggled to find, that for which he had made so many sacrifices. All that was left was a tainted inheritance, a barren wife, a mistress whom he could not control and a cold, cold rage which grew and swelled within him moment by moment. He waited for the demon to stir and move him on, for the ground of his being to shake, for the devil to reveal himself at last.

He was still kneeling there when he heard a scuffling upon the stairs and footsteps in the corridor. The door of the Turkish room creaked open. Cassandra, he thought, Cassandra has come back. But there was no light, no light came with Cassandra. He turned his head and blew out the candle.

He heard rather than saw her cross the Turkish room and enter the white bedroom. He watched light bloom in the globe of the lamp. He got stiffly to his feet and walked across to the bedroom door.

She was crouched by the dressing-table. One drawer was open. Clutched in her fingers was the carved ivory box that contained a collection of the trinkets with which Cassandra adorned herself. Her face was pinched but her eyes, those large, clear-sighted eyes, stared back at him, startled but unafraid.

'Winfield,' he said, 'where is my wife?'

'She isnae here, Mr Montague.'

'Where is she?'

'At Normandy Road.'

'Visiting, I take it?'

'Nah, Mr Montague. She's not comin' back.'

'Why are you here?'

'To gather some o' her things.'

'To steal her things, hm?'

'She wants . . .'

'To steal from me, hm?'

'Mr Montague, I've been sent to collect . . .'

'Who sent you?'

'Miss Cassie.'

'Do you not mean Mrs Montague?'

'Aye, sir. Aye, I do. Mistress Montague.'

'Is she with Hunter?'

'She's wi' her daddy, at her daddy's house.'

'Do not lie, girl.'

'I'm not lyin', Mr Montague.'

'You are. You are lying to me, Winfield.'

'She's left you, Mr Montague,' Nancy said. 'That's the God's truth.'

'Liar!' he shouted, and struck her across the face with his fist.

He struck her again, violently. She fell to the floor. The trinket box flew from her hands and burst open, scattering earrings, brooches and necklaces across the dressing-table. He dragged her up by the arms and threw her across the bed. She bled from nostril and lip. He braced himself over her and peered into her face. Her eyelids fluttered. She struggled into consciousness. Her eyes opened. She looked up at him, still without fear, then sucked in her cheeks, gathered saliva into her mouth and spat blood into his face.

He wiped his hand slowly across his cheek. He did not stop to think whose daughter she was now, whose child she might be. She was everything he detested in nature, everything that stood against his will: a workhouse girl who had refused to learn her place. She deserved no mercy.

He reached blindly for a pillow, pressed it across Nancy's face, leaned his weight upon it and held it there, held it there until all her struggles ceased.

'Nancy should be back by now,' Allan said. 'Could Jerome have delayed her, do you think?'

Cassie clung to his arm and looked along Normandy Road in the direction of Bramwell. The wind, slight but wintry, had swung to the north-west and the sounds of night-shift work at the Blazes fluttered in and out of earshot. There was nothing to be seen but a sliver of moon-light among slow-moving clouds and the faint, faint shape of the hills across the river.

Cassie shivered a little, tugged her shawl about her shoulders and hugged Allan's arm. She was more anxious than she pretended to be for she did not want to alarm him unduly. She was well aware, though, that Nancy had been gone for almost an hour and a half.

'Johnny would not keep her,' Cassie murmured. 'If anything, he would want to be rid of her as quickly as possible.'

'She wouldn't . . .' Allan hesitated. 'I mean, she wouldn't run off.'

'Of course not,' Cassie said. 'She has no reason to run off. Where would she go? Daisy is here with us.'

'Aye,' Allan said. 'And Daisy is all Nancy cares about.'

'Could she have stopped off at the new church, by any chance?'

'It lies in the other direction,' Allan said.

'Will Mr Lassiter be there tonight?'

'He's there every night,' Allan said. 'Nancy is just – late.'

'I do not like it.'

'No more do I,' Allan said. 'We'll allow her another quarter-hour.'

'And then?'

'I'll go down there, shall I?'

'Yes,' Cassie said. 'I think that might be wise.'

Fortunately Miss Rundall had a head for strong drink and was still very much in control of her senses. Soon after Nancy had vanished upstairs she roused herself to clear the bottles from the table and instructed Janey to put the remains of the food away in the larder. Although she resented having to do a scullion's work, she took it upon herself to carry the dishes to the tub in the taproom at the corridor's end, for Marie, who had jettisoned her dinner, was flat out in bed.

Winfield's appearance had triggered a measure of caution in the cook. She had no sure knowledge of what was going on upstairs; why Major Jerome had gone off with Luke in a hired hackney or if the rumour that Janey had picked up about Cassie Montague having 'another man' was, in fact, true. Miss Rundall had no wish to abandon a ship that might not be sinking, however. The position in Bramwell was most comfortable and she still nurtured a fond hope that everything would be restored to normal as soon as the master returned.

She wrapped a shawl about her and carried the greasy dishes down to the old taproom where the fire under the copper boiler was still alight.

She filled the tub with hose and hand-pump, threw a handful of soda crystals into the water and transferred the dishes from the draining board, then, just as she turned to bring down the pans, glimpsed through the tiny window a flicker of light in the stable doorway outside.

She pushed aside the pans and peered out into the yard. Her first thought was that the major had returned. Her second thought was that Nancy Winfield had gone out in search of Luke. And then the cold truth dawned: the master had come home early.

Miss Rundall sucked in her breath. She must be quick, very quick. She must spruce herself up and urge Janey to appear sober in case the minister crashed in on them. She was on the point of pushing herself away from the window when something unusual struck her: Reverend Montague was not coming into the manse. He was leaving it. Puzzled, she watched him shroud the lantern with a sack and lead the horse into the yard.

By lantern light he backed the animal into the shafts of the gig and buckled the harness straps. He was not dressed for the road, though. He had no hat upon his head and his overcoat flapped, unbuttoned, about him. He walked with long jerky strides, darting his head this way and that as if an enemy might be lurking in the shadows. He paused, stared directly at the kitchen windows for a second, then blew out the lantern and guided the horse out of the yard, the empty gig trundling along behind.

Miss Rundall pushed herself away from the window and waddled down the corridor as fast as her legs would carry her.

She called out to Janey, 'He's back. He's back. The master's outside.'

'What?' Janey gathered her dress up to her throat as if that would somehow be enough to restore decorum

456

to the kitchen. 'What's he doin' back?'

'I don't know yet.' Miss Rundall busily buttoned her bodice and stepped into her shoes. 'I'm a-goin' upstairs to find out.'

'What! No, you ain't. You can't.'

'Hush, sweetheart. Hush,' the cook said. 'He won't see me, I'll make sure. Get Marie up. Wash 'er face. Change 'er petticoat.'

'Wha' for?'

'In case he comes down 'ere.'

Miss Rundall wasted no more time on Janey. She headed across the kitchen and mounted the stairs that led up to the hall. For a large woman she moved with remarkable speed and she was hidden in the deep recess under the main staircase several minutes before the minister reappeared.

The front door lay open. The gig was backed towards the steps, the horse tethered to a wrought-iron rail. The minister's urgency had communicated itself to the animal and it jerked its head and snickered restlessly. Beyond the conveyance Miss Rundall could make out the shrubs that flanked the driveway, their broad evergreen leaves tossing in the wintry little wind from the river. She wondered if Mr Montague had encountered Nancy or if the lady's maid had left before the minister arrived. She heard no conversation upstairs, no arguments or reprimands, only a queer thudding sound and a grunting that came closer and closer until it seemed to be directly overhead. She pressed herself back against the panelling and watched the minister drag the Winfield girl across the floor of the hall.

It did not immediately occur to Miss Rundall that Nancy might be dead. The girl's skirts were ruched up, her stockings wrinkled. Her bonnet, though tied tightly about her throat, had ridden across her face in a manner that seemed coy. Miss Rundall almost expected her to wink, as if this were nothing more than a piece of horseplay that had got thoroughly out of hand. But the Reverend Montague was too methodical to be playing a game. He dragged the girl away from the staircase by the arms then changed position, took her instead by the ankles, flopped her over on to her back and pulled her across the polished floor towards the front door. Nancy's limbs were limp and pliant. There was blood upon her face. At that moment Miss Rundall realised that the lady's maid was dead, that the minister, her master, had murdered her.

He left the body lying in the doorway. He stepped back to the staircase and vanished from sight.

Miss Rundall considered making a dash for the kitchen but Mr Montague reappeared almost at once. He carried one of Nancy's shoes and, while Miss Rundall watched, stuffed it into the pocket of his overcoat. He stood above the corpse for a moment, hands on hips, then squatted down, slipped his arms under the girl and lifted her in his arms. He staggered slightly, braced himself, slung the body across his shoulder and carried it out to the gig.

The horse reared and dragged against the rein, slewing the gig wheels across the gravel. Reverend Montague barked at the beast. He caught the rein with one hand and, like a coal-heaver unloading a sack, tumbled Nancy into the back of the vehicle. He straightened, wiped his hands on the breast of his overcoat and then, carefully and patiently, buttoned the coat up to the throat.

He ran a hand through his hair and returned to the hallway.

Miss Rundall, terrified, pressed herself into the recess. Mr Montague did not notice her. He inspected the staircase, glanced towards the door that led to the kitchen then, with the toe of his boot, carefully erased a little smear of blood from the floor and went outside again.

He closed the front door quietly behind him.

Miss Rundall broke from her hiding place and scuttled across the hall to the drawing-room. Pushing small furnishings over in her haste, she stumbled to the window just in time to see the gig roll away. Reverend Montague was seated upright on the board. The vehicle rounded the curve of the drive and headed downhill towards the gates. Her heart was thumping like a steam pump. She felt queasy with fear. She leaned her brow against the glass and continued to watch the driveway just in case the master should come back. And then she saw shrubs move and a great black hunched shape emerged from the evergreens.

Beast-like and lumbering, it too set off down the drive towards the gates.

Miss Rundall fled for the safety of the kitchen.

She burst in upon Janey and Marie and, striving to control herself, announced, 'Time to go, girls. Pack up, we're leavin'.'

'What, now?' said Janey.

'Now. Tonight. At once,' said Miss Rundall.

'Where are we goin'?'

'Anywhere,' Miss Rundall said. 'Somewhere where there ain't no men.'

They were gone, all three, in twenty minutes, scurrying away down the lane that led into Ravenshill.

A quarter of an hour later Allan Hunter arrived on Bramwell hill to find the manse deserted.

From the moment he had lifted the pillow from the girl's face Robert had been filled with a stupendous sense of elation. He felt no pity for the workhouse girl, no remorse at what he had done. Rationally he knew that she deserved it. She had stood between him and what he wanted. She had come between a man and his wife. She, a mere servant, had been more loved than he was. For an instant he had almost possessed her; not as he had tried to possess Cassie; not as he had tried to possess Johnny. He had taken the breath from the workhouse girl for different reasons altogether. Killing Cassie's half-sister had been an act of purgation, less satisfying, perhaps, than killing Johnny or Pippa, but an admirable substitute none the less. Now he knew what it felt like to kill in anger: infinitely more thrilling than taking a life in cold blood.

There was no excuse for what he had done, no saving grace or comprehensible motive. That, Robert thought, was the beauty of it. He had yielded entirely to impulse. He had challenged the demon within him. Had cried out aloud to show that he was not afraid, that he was not an empty vessel after all, that he would move to meet his Maker without fear and without humility. He had finally drawn a line under that night a half-dozen years ago when, moved by pity, he had smothered the young soldier in the Barrack Hospital at Scutari and, in so doing, had proved himself capable of anything. He had needed no god after that, only a place to hide from the devil within.

He rode through the streets of Bramwell without a trace of guilt, bowing to the men at the corner, to the women at the pump, smiling at children. His only regret was that he had forgotten to put on his hat. Somebody was bound to comment on that breach of social etiquette and he would be obliged to explain to the elders that he had been summoned from home to attend a burial – if not a burial at least a committal – and that the business of disposing of the dead was something that did not always require the wearing of a hat.

On the floor of the gig behind him Nancy's body flopped and rolled.

He would return the little fish to the river and the river would take her to the sea, that great heaving sea of sinfulness which was the province of the God of Abraham and of Isaac and out of which, in the End days, each soul would be plucked anew. He would gladly return the little fish to the river. Nobody would find her there.

If, by chance, they did he would declare that he had no knowledge of her. No one would challenge him. If the servants claimed that they had seen her in the manse he would denounce them as liars. If Cassandra reported that she had been sent, he would deny that she had ever arrived. Was he not Robert Montague, revered in the parish? Was his voice not the voice of authority? Was his word not law? His grandfather would understand what he had done, what he had made of himself. Old Bob Montague would be proud of him. One slave was much like another, after all, and old Bob had buried a few in his time.

Beneath the layer of elation, though, grief and anger bubbled like hidden springs: grief at a suffering he could not comprehend; anger that he still had found no reason to exist. Johnny gone, Dada gone, Pippa gone. Cassie never there at all. He tried to smother his sorrow by thinking of his grandfather, ridden with disease and mad as a hatter, buried among the poor on a hillside in Wallasey; of the treasure his grandfather had left behind, the accumulated sorrows of a slave-race converted into cash. He felt the ground shift downwards, the demon stir within him.

No. No. No. No: he would get off with it. He always got off with it. He was Robert Montague, far too clever to be caught.

He drove the gig at no great pace through the village to the ferry road.

Hawthorn and bramble closed about him. The horse clopped forward obediently, well under his control. He sang beneath his breath the 2nd Psalm of David, in its original form. He had learned it when he was four years old but to this day did not entirely understand its meaning. *Why rage the heathen? and vain things why do the people mind?* He remembered his grandfather singing the psalm so lustily that he had known even then that old Bob Montague had needed no meaning to be happy.

When he had done what he had to do with the workhouse girl he would ponder the verses anew. He might preach to them on Sunday. He had preached to the Metrical Psalms many times before. He could always wring some relevance from them, even if he did not understand what it was or what it meant.

He raised his voice and sang: *Thou shalt, as with a weighty rod of iron, break them all; And, as a potter's sherd, thou shalt them dash in pieces small.*

Behind him, moving like a shadow, Todd Brownlee blundered down the river road, trailing the voice in the darkness.

* * *

461

Three or four hundred yards above the ferry steps the gig stood empty. The horse cropped at withered grasses by the verge and the gate in the bramble hedge hung open. Todd had not been this way in many years but he remembered the place from the days of his youth when Mr Beatty would lead the lads out from the foundlings' ward and they would fish from the sandbanks that were no longer there and hunt rabbits and hares in the whins.

He remembered the place well enough to pick his way along the track that led to the water's edge. The whins stirred in the wind. He could hear the hiss of their stiff brown spikes and the water lapping on the pilings that had replaced the sandbanks and, as he got closer, the suck of the tide on the flood.

He wept as he plunged through the bushes, wept at the memory of what he had lost, in the knowledge that Nancy was gone for good.

Across the river the lights of the town pricked the blackness. Against the necklace of light Todd could just make out the man who had carried Nancy away. He carried her across his shoulders like the carcass of a lamb. He was tall and walked with long strides and bore the burden effortlessly. He came out of the bushes on to open ground along the top of the wall.

The wind was stronger here and the fires of the Blazes a mile to the east threw a flickering glow against the underbelly of the cloud. The man was plainly visible. Todd watched him toss Nancy to the ground, move forward, crouch on top of the pilings and look down into the river below.

Todd wiped the tears from his face with his sleeve and waited among the whins. Only when the man returned from the river's edge and lifted Nancy up again did he show himself.

He stepped forward and said, 'What are you goin' to do wi' her?'

The minister held Nancy high against his chest, heaved up so that she was offered in his arms like a sacrifice. He did not seem surprised that he had been interrupted at his work and he answered without truculence.

'I am putting her away,' he said.

'She's mine,' Todd said. 'Give her tae me.'

'That I will not,' the minister said. 'Go on about your business.'

'*Give her tae me.*'

'Can you not see that she's no longer living?' Robert Montague said. 'It is my business to put her away. That is all there is to it.'

'You're not puttin' her in the river,' Todd said.

'I'll do with her as I see fit,' the minister said and, swinging round, trotted towards the wall.

Todd struck him in the small of the back. He fell forward on to his knees. Todd struck him again. Nancy's body slid from the minister's grasp and lolled into the weeds that fringed the pilings.

Iron beams, oak staves and the broken stones of the facing wall loomed up. Robert writhed among them. Todd caught him by the leg and drew him back from the edge. There was no blood upon him but his long face had turned pure white with the pain of the blows to his spine. He seemed incapable of movement now, only of speech.

He raved, and shouted like a madman. 'Do you not know who I am?'

'Aye, Mr Montague, I know who you are. But what about me?' Todd said. 'Tell me what my name is?'

Robert lay propped on his elbows, head and shoulders raised. He was mad now and there was no hiding it. Even Todd could see the madness in him, pared down out of nothingness. The wind animated his dark hair but his expression was suddenly calm and only mildly bewildered as he considered the stranger's question.

'Satan,' he said, at length. 'I think your name is Satan.'

'Aye,' said Todd, 'maybe you're right.'

Then he put a knee into the minister's chest, clasped his head in both hands and with a swift, clean, snapping motion broke Robert Montague's neck.

Twenty-Five

In the days immediately following her husband's death and the murder of her maidservant Cassie Montague was plagued less by grief and guilt than by policemen and examining magistrates. Officials ruled the roost and her several appearances before the procurator-fiscal suggested that there were those in authority who suspected that either she or Allan Hunter had negotiated Robert's death and that the lady's maid, Nancy Winfield, had unfortunately turned up in just the wrong place at the wrong time.

The discovery of the gig by an early morning ferryman had led to a search of the whinfield and the finding of Nancy's body. It had been neatly laid out under a whin bush, skirts modestly tucked in, bonnet tied under her chin, her hands folded across her breast.

Someone, possibly the murderer, had even taken the trouble to bathe her face with water and to wash away blood from her nose and lips. For all his experience in the finding of corpses Mr McIver, Bramwell's constable, was moved by the sight of the Winfield girl. He knew at once who she was and where she came from. There was something too respectful, too tender in her laying-out to suggest that she had died from natural causes but he did not, at that very early stage, entirely rule out suicide.

It was not until the bruised and battered body of Mr Robert Montague, the respected parish minister and Biblical scholar, was hauled from the river near Renfrew in the latter part of the afternoon, however, that the little local tragedy blossomed into a notorious cause célèbre.

Even in Scotland there were some things that money could not buy, the pace of the law being one of them. So confused and demanding were Robert's affairs that it seemed to Cassie that she was still her husband's prisoner throughout that winter and spring, still in thrall to the minister of Ravenshill and that the bonds of her marriage to Robert Montague would never be broken.

The problem of deciding precisely what crimes had been committed and if some party or parties unknown had been involved in the murders consumed a great deal of time and the house in Normandy Road was perpetually besieged by fiscal agents and sheriff's officers as well as the lawyers that Cubby employed to ensure that his daughter received justice and that the orphan, Daisy Winfield, became under law his ward.

In the latter instance the absence of any other person willing to lay claim to the welfare of the child eventually swung the decision in Cuthbert Armitage's favour without his having to submit to the humiliation of confessing before the court that the little girl was his grandchild or having to prove that her mother had been a victim not only of the ultimate crime but also of abandonment and neglect.

Nancy was buried up on the hill, head to toe with Agnes Lassiter. Her coffin was carried from the hearse by four of the five men who had cared for her. Proceedings were conducted by young Mr Onslow, Ravenshill's minister depute, in spite of some grumbling from Session and Presbytery whose members were anxious to disassociate themselves from the scandalous events that had taken place in the parish. Albert Lassiter suffered no such

466

inhibitions, of course. He flung open the iron church to all who wished to attend a service of thanksgiving for the workhouse girl, that poor little servant of the Lord, whose life had been cut short by the hand of wickedness but who had brought light and joy to all who had known her during her few brief years on earth.

They were all there, that windy, wintry January evening, all the regulars, old and young, seeking the warmth of the unfinished iron building and the free bread and butter that would be dispensed afterwards, along with the sustenance that Albert Lassiter poured forth from a temporary platform erected below the stalk of the pulpit. It mattered not to them that the mission had changed location or that it was crowded with strangers; the old harmonium was firmly in place and the tea urn too and Mr Albert Lassiter was his old self again, giving them the Good News hot and strong.

Only those who came to seek sensation or find fuel for further scandal were disappointed. All the rest were satisfied, one way or another, though Mr Lassiter's eulogy had too much force and not quite enough sentiment for some, and for others, Norah, Cassie and Cuthbert among them, carried so many memories that they wept unabashed throughout.

Archie Sinclair also shed a tear or two. So, oddly, did Mr Beatty, down from the superintendent's villa on the Toll Road. But the big man, a stranger, hunched on an iron bench in the servants' gallery, remained dry-eyed, his scarred hands clasped between his knees, the bottle in his pocket clinking dully whenever he rose to sing.

There was no sign of Major Johnny Jerome or the stable lad, Luke Simmonds – prime suspects in the act of murder – for they, it seemed, had vanished into thin air and were never seen or heard from again.

No tears were shed, not one, at the interment of the Reverend Robert Montague. He was in death that which he had never been in life – a serious source of embarrassment. What was he in the end, the minister of

Ravenshill: a suicide, a murderer or a victim too? Fiscal indecisiveness and the enigmatic language of the enquiry's published findings left far too many questions unanswered and it was generally agreed that an 'open' verdict was no more than a sop to Kirk authorities and an exercise in saving face.

When at last Robert's body was released for burial it was transported by rail north to the Highlands and put under ground by his father's side in the bleak little graveyard that hung above the kirk of Cleavers. Only three men were there to see it done, Professor Matthew Salmond, Mr Allan Hunter and little Cubby Armitage; no women at all, not even Pippa who had been sent to London to lodge with relatives of Charlie Smalls, to lick her wounds and weep and, in due course, to mend her broken heart.

It was a strange bitter-sweet summer for Cassie Montague. She grieved for Nancy Winfield and suffered nightmares of guilt over the thought that she had somehow been responsible for the poor girl's death. Not even Allan could console her or assure her that Nancy had not been intentionally sacrificed to make them free, that what had happened to her in the Bramwell manse could not have been foreseen. None of them had known how seriously disturbed Robert Montague had been, for the cleverness of the man had disguised his derangement and violent disposition and Nancy, alas, was only a random factor in Robert's inevitable downfall.

Not all the Armitages' friends and acquaintances were of that opinion, however. Many thought that somehow or another the minister's wife had been responsible for what had happened to the pastor of Ravenshill. Tongues wagged and fingers pointed every time Cassie or her mama showed themselves in town. They were cut by the Coulter sisters and pointedly ignored by the Flails. Only old Mrs Calderon was kind enough, or curious enough, to invite them, and the children too, to call upon her for tea.

Swiftly, very swiftly, Cassie Montague and the Armitages found themselves excluded from the community, ostracised and isolated. Found too that it did not matter, for with two lively young children clattering about the house and galloping around the garden there was more than enough activity at home to keep the women occupied while the guardians of the law wrangled interminably about the legality of Robert's last will and testament.

Cassie had little interest in the fortune that would fall to her and no interest at all in the claims and counter-claims that poured into the lawyers' offices from Robert's distant relatives. Papa would handle all that; Papa aided and abetted by Mr Charles Smalls who had conveniently returned from America and was wryly amused by the 'fix' that stuffy Cubby Armitage had got himself into while he had been away. It was fortunate that Charlie Smalls was not a vindictive type of person, for the scandal cost the stockbrokers a great deal of money in lost business; the Flails' accounts for a start and many others besides.

'Damn them,' Charlie said. 'For two pins I'd sell up here and move the whole caboodle off to New York.'

'New York?' Cubby said in alarm.

'Boston, if you prefer it.'

'But our trade is here, Charlie.'

'The heck it is,' Charlie said. 'New World, Cubby, new money. America, that's where real fortunes are to be made, believe me.'

'Oh, I do, I do,' Cubby said. 'It's just that . . .'

'That travel's not for you, old chap?'

'No, not for me,' Cubby answered; then added, 'Not yet, at any rate.'

For Cassie, though, the future lay with Allan and the children. As spring warmed into summer and settlement of the Montague inheritance seemed imminent, Allan took a decision on her behalf. He booked passage for all of them on the iron clipper ship *Oberon*, due to sail from Greenock in July on a return voyage to Boston. He knew only too well what he was taking on, not only Cassie, not only Nancy's child, but responsibility for the Montague fortune, slave-money, tainted and tarnished, which frightened him much more than the prospect of penury had ever done.

Norah and the children, attended by Eileen, a little mouse-brown workhouse girl who had been hired as a nurserymaid, walked ahead of them along the path that followed the river line.

The grasses were tall now and the old pastureland west of the whinfield was lush and cows from the Bramwell farm grazed inland from the shore. Across the breast of the Clyde, through the spars and masts and moon-sails of the river traffic, was a glimpse of the tip of Madame Daltry's residence and the elegant trees that sheltered it. It was afternoon, a long, hazy afternoon, with the wind from the south and no sounds but the slapping of the water on the shore and the hiss of the grasses and, now and then, a drift of hammering from the Blazes so faint as to be hardly heard at all.

Allan held her hand. There was no longer any need for secrecy and pretence. Cassie had already promised to marry him as soon as it was proper to do so, to step up before a justice in the city of Boston and declare that she was free-willed and in her right mind and that she would take the man, Allan Hunter, to be her lawful husband with all that that entailed; that she would be a new woman, a new wife, in a new land. They would have married in Ravenshill before departure if Cassie had had her way. But Allan was too set in traditional ways and wanted no more scandal if it could be avoided. He wanted, he said, to leave her widowhood behind along with all the rest of it.

They walked along the footpath, hand in hand, watching the children.

Tom was obstreperous now, the discipline of Madame Daltry's school forgotten. He ran and flung his arms out, kicked at stones and vanished, much to Norah's concern, into the tall grasses only to a leap out a moment later in a pirate pose, his summer cap turned front to back and his collar undone.

Daisy, in contrast, had become more of a lady than ever. She was no longer stiff and stand-offish and she would accept any hand that was offered to her, but the haughty little mannerisms that she had copied from Madame Daltry's staff had been smoothed away by natural affection. She trotted along by Norah's side, looking up now and then at the gaunt middle-aged woman as if her curiosity had been tweaked; then, with a smile, she would rub herself against Norah's skirts and show her the posy of wild flowers that she had gathered from the verge.

The man was seated by the side of the path. From a distance he seemed not unlike the characters who had begun to frequent Mr Lassiter's new meeting house, iron-church men who were neither outcasts nor drifters but had a foothold in a niche of society that was too opaque to classify, solitary men who lived not on but close to the knuckle and kept themselves very much to themselves.

His appearance was disreputable, his canvas jacket dirty, his hair and beard matted, yet something in his manner, an air of sadness, robbed him of menace. Even when he pushed himself to his feet and slipped the black bottle back into his pocket he did not cause alarm. He was huge, though, broad-shouldered and deep-chested and his hands, though they trembled a little, were as brown and scarred as bear paws.

He looked not at Norah, not at the nurserymaid but at the children who stopped some yards short of him and stared up at him in wonderment.

Cassie and Allan quickened their steps and caught up.

'Good-day to you,' Allan said. 'It's a fine afternoon, is it not?'

'Aye, sir, it's all that,' the man answered in a soft mystified voice that came low out of his chest.

He looked at no one, not Allan or Cassie or Norah, only at the children.

'Do we know you, by any chance?' Cassie said. 'Have we met before?'

He shook his head. The mane of hair, grey as slate,

471

JESSICA STIRLING

tossed this way and that and he raised one hand up as if to
keep it respectable.

'Can I ask . . .' he began. 'Can I ask the names o' your
babbies, sir?'

'Why, man, what interest . . .' Allan began.

Cassie touched his sleeve, frowned and said, 'Tell the
gentleman who you are, children.'

Tom puffed out his chest and pouted his underlip. 'Tom
Hunter.'

'An' you, wee lass?'

'I'm Daisy Winfield, sir,' she said and, just before the
man turned and lumbered away into the grasses, offered
him a wild flower from the pretty little bunch in her hand.